P9-EKY-214

CHRISTMAS COVER-UP

LYNETTE EASON

Recycling programs for this product may not exist in your area.

ISBN-13: 978-1-335-40655-2

Christmas Cover-Up
First published in 2013. This edition published in 2021.
Copyright © 2013 by Lynette Eason

Her Mistletoe Protector
First published in 2013. This edition published in 2021.
Copyright © 2013 by Laura Iding

This edition published by arrangement with Harlequin Books S.A.

For questions and comments about the quality of this book, please contact us at CustomerService@Harlequin.com.

Harlequin Enterprises ULC
22 Adelaide St. West, 41st Floor
Toronto, Ontario M5H 4E3, Canada
www.Harlequin.com

Printed in U.S.A.

CONTENTS

Lynette Eason is a bestselling, award-winning author who makes her home in South Carolina with her husband and two teenage children. She enjoys traveling, spending time with her family and teaching at various writing conferences around the country. She is a member of Romance Writers of America and American Christian Fiction Writers. Lynette can often be found online interacting with her readers. You can find her at Facebook.com/lynette.eason and on Twitter, @lynetteeason.

Books by Lynette Eason

Love Inspired Suspense

Holiday Homecoming Secrets

True Blue K-9 Unit

Justice Mission

Wrangler's Corner

The Lawman Returns
Rodeo Rescuer
Protecting Her Daughter
Classified Christmas Mission
Christmas Ranch Rescue
Vanished in the Night
Holiday Amnesia

Visit the Author Profile page at Harlequin.com for more titles.

CHRISTMAS COVER-UP

Lynette Eason

For it is by grace you have been saved,
through faith—and this is not from yourselves,
it is the gift of God.

—*Ephesians* 2:8

To my Lord and Savior, who loves me unconditionally and died so I could live.

Thanks to my ACFW Suspense Loop friends for your brainstorming help on this series. So many great ideas and suggestions went into this story. Couldn't have done it without you!

ONE

Keys clutched in her left hand, Detective Katie Randall stared at her vandalized front door. She hadn't noticed it when she'd pulled into the drive; she'd been too busy thinking about her sister's cold case and the man who'd been assigned to help her work on it. Lucy had disappeared fourteen years ago from her front yard and it was time Katie and her family found closure.

Now she'd come home to this.

She'd parked in the drive and grabbed her stuff from the car, still thinking about canceling the meeting she had coming up in about five minutes.

It was only when she'd gotten closer to the house that she'd seen the splintered wood around the doorknob. And the Christmas wreath lying on the porch.

The hair on the nape of her neck spiked, and she stepped back. She set her briefcase and keys on the porch. The chilly December wind found its way under her collar, and she shivered as she mentally flipped through her options at lightening speed.

Her nerves tightened, muscles bunched. She pulled her weapon from her shoulder holster as she backed down the steps of the porch. With her left hand, she snagged her cell phone from the back pocket of her khaki slacks and pressed the speed dial number for Jordan Gray, the man she was supposed to meet in less than five minutes. She couldn't let him walk into a potentially dangerous situation without some warning.

He answered on the third ring. "Almost there."

"Don't pull in the drive. Someone's either been in my house or is still there."

"Give me thirty seconds."

"I'm calling for backup. I'll be inside. Mariah might be here and need help."

Mariah Sims, Katie's friend and roommate. Mariah usually got home before Katie.

She hung up on his protests and orders to wait for him. Hesitating, she debated whether or not to call her partner, Gregory Lee, but decided Jordan, a former FBI agent, would be able to handle this just as well as Gregory.

And he was closer. She dialed 911 and within seconds had backup on the way. Once the address went out, every officer within a ten-mile radius would be on her doorstep.

She made her way up the porch steps again. Christmas lights lined the railing. Katie stood to the side of the broken door and nudged it open. "Mariah? Are you here?"

Silence greeted her call.

Katie whispered up a silent prayer for Mariah's safety.

She glanced over her shoulder as Jordan's car edged to the curb in front of her neighbor's home. He climbed out, weapon in his hand as he jogged over to stand beside her. She'd hired him through Finding the Lost to locate her missing sister. The Finding the Lost organization, founded by skip-tracer Erica James, specialized in locating missing people. From private investigators to contracted FBI agents to police detectives, a plethora of talented men and woman worked tirelessly to help others reunite with lost loved ones.

Katie had hired the organization and then had second thoughts about doing so when she discovered who would handle her case. Jordan Gray. She knew him slightly because of her connection to Erica, his boss, but hadn't realized Neil Gray was his brother. The brother who'd been killed in a jail cell after Katie arrested him for drunk driving.

Before she had a chance to tell Jordan she'd decided she couldn't work with him, he'd called fifteen minutes ago to let her know he was on the way to her house.

He was ambushing her and she hadn't been able to put him off. Now she was glad for his presence. She gestured to the open door. "Will you cover me?"

He didn't waste time chastising her for not waiting on him. "What's the layout?"

"Foyer leads straight into the great room. Two bedrooms and a bath to the right, kitchen and dining to the left. My bedroom is also to the left behind the garage."

"I'll go right, you go left."

Katie stepped into her house and caught her breath. Chaos greeted her. Cushions pulled off her couch and slashed. Bookcase overturned and coffee table shoved on its side. The Christmas tree she and Mariah had decorated lay on its side, ornaments crushed from one end of the room to the other.

A thud from the back of the house caused her to stiffen and shoot a glance at Jordan. "You hear that?" she whispered.

"Yeah. Where'd it come from?" He kept his voice low.

"I don't know."

"Is your roommate here?"

"She usually parks in the garage, but I don't know if her car's in there or not." She would have checked before entering the house, but the windows for the garage had blinds on them. And they were closed.

Katie moved farther inside, sidestepping the mess. Jordan went right, weapon in front of him.

Katie passed the open-area kitchen on her left, rounded the breakfast bar and stepped into the hallway. To her left was the utility room, to the right the half bath and the exit to the back porch that ran the length of the house.

The half bath sat empty. All that was left was her room and bath. Her room looked like the great room area: destroyed.

She ignored the anger at the invasion and headed back to join Jordan.

"Freeze! FBI!"

Katie did for a brief second before she realized the yell wasn't aimed at her.

A crash. Running footsteps.

A dark-clothed figure raced past the doorway where she stood and into Mariah's bedroom, with Jordan on his heels. Katie bolted after them.

The intruder leaped over the bed and wrenched the French doors open. Jordan followed and Katie turned to race from the bedroom, back into the great room and out onto the back porch.

The French doors swung open and the figure halted when he realized Katie had him cut off. She pointed her weapon. "Freeze! Police!"

He obeyed for a millisecond, then vaulted over the railing. Again Jordan followed while Katie spun and took the steps two at a time to the yard, where Jordan tackled the man. Sirens screaming, three cruisers pulled up to the curb.

* * *

Jordan ducked as a fist swung around toward his face. As the intruder's punch met air, Jordan pulled back his right arm and let his knuckles crunch against the guy's jaw. Dazed, the fight drained from the man, and he lay on his back panting, glaring as the sting of the hit faded.

With her gun in her right hand, Katie used her left to toss a pair of handcuffs to Jordan.

"Let us know if you need help."

Jordan looked up to see three officers, guns drawn, ready to jump in. He sucked in a lungful of air. "I think we got it."

Katie walked over and continued to cover the man until Jordan had him on his stomach, hands cuffed behind his back. "You have the right to remain silent…" Katie read him his rights as Jordan patted the man down. Finding no weapon, he rose to his feet.

When she was finished, she looked at the officers. "This will just take a minute, then he's all yours. She shoved her intruder over to the steps of the porch. "Sit."

Jordan watched the man obey. Reluctantly and with narrowed green eyes that glinted with anger.

Katie looked at Jordan. "You're not FBI. Why'd you identify yourself as such?"

He felt a flush start at the base of his neck. Then gave a small shrug even as the shadows danced across his mind. He pushed them away. "I am again as of last month. Simply doing some consulting work with them."

"Oh."

He spread his hands, palms up. "They asked."

"Right. Well, that should make my lieutenant happier." Jordan knew her lieutenant hadn't been too keen on Katie having access to her sister's files, but he had finally caved, especially when she'd explained that she was hiring an outside organization to help. He'd been intrigued by the idea and finally agreed as long as she kept him updated. And worked the case on her own time. As far as Jordan could tell, she'd kept to that promise.

She stared at him a moment longer, then turned her frown at her intruder. "Who are you, and what were you doing in my house?"

His gaze lowered to the badge on her belt. "You're a cop?"

"I am."

"And you're FBI?" He directed his question to Jordan, who gave a sharp nod.

"Figures." He clamped his lips and looked away. Jordan decided the guy was younger than he'd originally thought. Maybe in his mid-twenties.

"Your name?" Katie demanded.

"Wesley Wray."

"What were you looking for, Mr. Wray?" Jordan asked.

Wesley shrugged. "Whatever I could find. Jewelry, cash, whatever."

Katie snapped his picture with her iPhone and emailed it directly to her office with instructions to find out everything possible about this man. "So this was just a random thing? You picked my house out of all the ones in this subdivision?"

"Yeah, I guess. It looked like an easy hit." He shook his head and muttered, "Didn't know you were a cop."

Jordan saw skepticism skitter across Katie's face and knew she wasn't buying the guy's story. Jordan hauled the man to his feet. "Come on, you can tell the rest of this sad tale downtown."

As he stood, Wesley's gaze landed on Katie's brief-case sitting on the front porch. "Your laptop in there?"

She frowned. "It is. Why?"

"Nothing."

Jordan led Wesley to a waiting police cruiser. Jordan recognized Chris Jiles as one of the officers. Chris locked his hand around Wray's upper arm and looked at Katie. "You all right?"

"Never better."

"Right." He helped Jordan get Mr. Wray secured in the back of the cruiser. She walked over and shook hands with Chris. "I'll be down to the station shortly to fill out a report. Stick him in one of the interrogation rooms and let him sit for a bit."

"Will do. You need a crime scene unit?"

"Why? We caught him red-handed and he confessed. Let's not waste lab dollars on a simple B & E."

He shrugged. "Your call."

Chris drove off with his prisoner, followed by the other officers who'd shown up. Katie turned to Jordan.

Dressed in pressed khaki pants and a blue button-up shirt, she had her straight blond hair pulled back in a ponytail with a plain band. Her light brown eyes still glinted steel. A faint dusting of freckles and no makeup would make a lot of women look plain. Katie, however, was a natural beauty.

He ignored the zing of attraction he always seemed to get around her and followed her up the front porch steps.

Romance, attraction, whatever it was he felt when he spent time with her was not an option. Katie Randall had killed his brother—at least in his parents' eyes—and while he'd work with her on this case, getting personal was out of the question. And besides, she'd gone out her way to avoid him ever since she'd learned he would be the one handling the case.

They stepped back inside and the destruction greeted them.

Even though she'd already seen it, he heard her suck in a deep breath and let it out slowly. "Looks like you're going to have your hands full cleaning this up."

She sighed. "Looks like. Fifteen days until Christmas and this. Lovely. Just what I wanted to come home to." She grimaced. "Okay, I'll stop whining now. Sorry."

He gave a short laugh. "I'll help."

Really? And why was he offering to spend more time with her than necessary? She lifted a brow. "I'll probably call a cleaning crew, but thanks."

Relieved—yet strangely disappointed—he nodded and looked around. "Mariah's not here, obviously."

"No." She walked into the kitchen and looked out the window into the garage. "Her car's not here. She either stayed late at work or stopped somewhere on her way home."

Jordan tilted his head toward the back of the house. "Your office is trashed, too."

Katie spun on her heel and walked to her office. *Trashed* was a kind word. "He asked about my laptop. Do you find that strange?"

"Yes. A bit."

Katie walked to Mariah's room. Mariah had gone crazy with Christmas decorations. Decorations that were still in their place, none broken, none touched. Jordan followed. She said, "But he didn't touch anything in here."

"Maybe he just didn't have time to get to it."

"Maybe."

"Or he was just interested in your stuff and not hers."

"But why? And why ask about my laptop?"

"I think we'll have to get Mr. Wray to answer those questions."

Katie rubbed her head, hoping the action would push away the building headache. "I guess this means our meeting is on hold."

"Again."

Katie felt a flush of guilt stain her cheeks. It was true. She'd been putting him off, delaying their getting together. Every time she was around him, she expected him to bring up his brother. And her part in the man's death. Her avoidance of Jordan was unusual. Normally if she needed to address something unpleasant, she did it and got it over with. Not so with this man. "It's not like I planned this."

"No, but you've been avoiding meeting with me. You're the one who came to us, remember? I've been working this case for the past two weeks. I need you to be available to answer questions when they come up. By putting me off, you're making it exceedingly difficult for me to do my job." He studied her. "And after you went to all that trouble to convince your lieutenant to grant us access to files and everything related to Lucy's case."

Katie grimaced at the memory of going to her lieutenant and unashamedly begging him to allow them to do this. "I know. I know," she groaned. "He really didn't want to, but he likes me. Although he did warn me that if this came back to bite him, I'd be checking parking meters until I retired." She rubbed her eyes. "It'll help that you're back with the FBI. He's not like some who get defensive about territory. He welcomes any help he can get."

A faint smile crossed his face, then faded. "Is your reluctance because of Neil?"

Katie stared at him, taken aback by his bluntness. Then a small kernel of anger formed in her belly. She curled her fingers into fists then had to make a concentrated effort to relax. It wasn't his fault she didn't want to talk to him. Not totally, anyway. "Yes, it's partly because of Neil. I didn't really expect Erica to give this case to you." Erica James, the director of Finding the Lost, was one of Katie's closest friends. "She knows what happened with Neil and—and I just—" She broke off and swallowed hard. "Although I suppose it makes the most sense with your FBI connections." She frowned. "I can drive."

"That's all right, I don't mind. Where will you and Mariah stay until you get this cleaned up?"

"Good question." Relieved not to talk about his brother just yet, Katie pulled her phone out and started to dial Mariah's number when she heard a car pull into the drive. She walked out onto the front porch to see her roommate climb from her vehicle.

Mariah spotted Jordan and waved. "Hey, you two, what's going on?" Jordan and Mariah had met once when Jordan had come by to pick up information regarding her sister's kidnapping.

"We had a break-in," Katie said.

Mariah's pretty green eyes went wide. "A break-in? Are you all right?"

"Yes," Katie assured her, then explained what had happened. "But it's pretty bad inside. I think we need to find another place to stay until a cleaning crew can come out here." She paused. "Although your room looks fine. He didn't get that far."

Jordan said, "He just raced out the French doors. But your stuff didn't look touched."

Mariah bit her lip and tucked a stray hunk of chocolate-brown hair behind her ear. "You think he'll come back?"

"No, we caught him. But the kitchen and den area aren't livable right now. He slashed the cushions and—"

Mariah rushed past her and into the house. Her outraged cry made Katie grimace. Her roommate raced to Katie's bedroom, then the office and finally her own bedroom. Tears stood in her friend's eyes. "I don't want to stay here. And you can't. He slashed up your mattress."

"I know."

Mariah took a deep breath. "We'll stay with Grandma Jean. She has that big ol' house with plenty of room. She'd love it if we crashed there for a few days."

Katie smiled as she thought of the spry eighty-year-old woman who still lived life to the fullest. "All right, you ask her. I've got to get down to the station and question our intruder."

Mariah shuddered. "I can't believe someone would break into a cop's house."

Katie shrugged. "I don't think he knew I was a cop." She frowned. "I can't help thinking this isn't a random break-in."

Mariah fished in her large shoulder bag and produced her phone. "I'll throw some things in a bag and call Grandma Jean and tell her we're coming."

Katie looked at Jordan. "Guess I'll do the same, then we can go. I'll take my car and you can ride with me if you want. Mariah's grandmother only lives about a mile from here, so I can bring you back here to get your car before I go over there for the night."

"That sounds good."

Katie smiled then walked into her destroyed bedroom. The smile slipped away and anger swept over her, hot and swift even as she gave thanks that Mariah hadn't been here when the intruder broke in. She grabbed an overnight bag and threw some items in it, including work clothes for the next day. She then examined every inch of her bedroom even though she knew Wray hadn't taken anything. Her jewelry box lay open, but nothing was missing.

A shudder of revulsion went through her. She dealt with criminals every day. But she'd never had one in her house. Her bedroom. It made her skin crawl.

Katie spun toward the door, anxious to get out of the room, and ran into Mariah coming from her bedroom. Her friend said, "We're all set. Grandma Jean's excited to have company tonight."

"I'll call someone to come clean this up, and we'll put better locks on the doors." She paused. "And maybe an alarm system."

"All right. I'll see you later tonight, then."

Katie nodded and joined Jordan, who waited patiently in the den. "I'm ready."

He followed her outside and stopped at her vehicle. She opened her door and looked at him. He placed a hand over hers. The heat of his palm seeped through the back of her hand, warming her. "What is it?" When he hesitated, she took a deep breath. His spicy cologne filled the air. Katie told herself she had to ignore the fact that she found him attractive and focus on doing what they needed to do so they could part company. "Jordan?"

He said, "I know my parents blame you for Neil's death, but I didn't realize—"

She tensed. "What?"

"You blame yourself for my brother's death, too, don't you?"

TWO

She climbed into the car and shut the door. Jordan walked around and did the same, wondering if she was going to answer him. Then she bit her lip and nodded. "Yes. He was just a kid." She cranked the car and backed out of the drive.

"You were doing your job."

"I know that," she snapped. Then took a deep breath. "Sorry."

"It's okay. Neil was at a party and he'd been drinking. He decided to drive home rather than be smart and call someone to pick him up."

"What male is smart at the age of twenty?"

A short, humorless laugh barked from him. "None. Not a single one."

"But he shouldn't have died because he was just stupid."

"No, he shouldn't have."

She drew in a deep breath. "I didn't know what would happen. I let him make a phone call and put him in the holding cell. Then I went to do the paperwork and about an hour later—"

"I know."

"There were so many arrests that night," she whispered. "It was crazy."

"It was New Year's Eve. It's always like that."

"There was no choice but to fill the holding cells up."

"Katie, you don't have to justify that night to me. I've worked law enforcement. I know what it's like." He swallowed hard and sighed. "You had no idea a meth head would kill two people with his bare hands before someone could get in there. You can't predict what's going to happen in those cells. Most of the time nothing does." His jaw tightened, and his eyes narrowed. "The fact is, if my brother hadn't chosen to be stupid, he'd still be alive."

His anger vibrated between them. He was still furious with Neil. But not with her. Not anymore. He looked at her and felt frustration swamp him when he couldn't read her expression. "So do you want me to quit looking into your sister's kidnapping or not?"

Katie bit her lip and glanced at him. "I don't know, but knowing you don't hold me responsible for Neil's death helps."

"I don't, but I'll be honest, my parents do and I'm afraid I'll never convince them otherwise."

She flinched and nodded.

He pinched the bridge of his nose. "You came to us."

"I know that."

He thought about all the work he'd already done, the people he'd questioned, the answers that produced more questions. "I can't do my job without your cooperation. Your sister's been missing for fourteen years. Do you want me to keep working on trying to find out what happened to her or not?" Trying to find a person missing for the past fourteen years was hard enough, but trying to find one without the cooperation of the one who'd hired him would be impossible.

"Yes. No." She hissed out a breath and tightened her fingers around the wheel. After she made a left turn, she said, "It's harder than I thought it would be."

"Why?"

"Because every time I look at you, I think of Neil. I think of your father in the morgue and his—" She bit her lip and looked away.

His phone rang and he snagged it, deciding to take the call and give her a bit of breathing room. "Hello?"

"Jordan. This is Erica."

"What can I do for you?"

"Have you had a chance to talk to Katie?" He and Erica had discussed Katie's reluctance to have him lead the investigation into her sister's disappearance.

"In the process now."

"Sorry, didn't mean to rush you. I'm just concerned."

"I know. I'll give you an update soon." He hung up and turned back to Katie. "That was Erica."

"Why did she assign my case to you?" Katie asked.

"Because I had just finished up with one and had the time to take it." He paused. "Did you tell her anything about our background?"

Katie shook her head.

"So she didn't know." He sighed. "Look. If you don't want me working it, I'll tell Erica. But you should know everyone is slammed right now. When Erica finally found Molly after three years and brought her home, those front-page headlines had people coming out of the woodwork. There are so many cold-case disappearances with desperate family members thinking Finding the Lost is their only hope. If you back off of Lucy's case now, it might be a while before someone else can pick it back up."

She drove without speaking until they were almost to the station. "I don't know if I can work with you. You're a constant reminder that I caused someone's death. How can you work with me day in and day out and not think about him? Not remember? Not feel some kind of anger toward me?" Her low voice reverberated with pain that echoed his own.

His heart hurt when he thought of his twenty-year-old brother. He'd been dead for a little over a year and the pain still cut sometimes.

Neil, the black sheep. The wild young man just sowing his oats. Neil, lying in the coffin because he'd chosen to drink and drive and then get stuck in a cell with the wrong person. Neil, whose dark secrets, known only to Jordan and the medical examiner, went to the grave with him, leaving Jordan with the burden of what to do with them. Especially the question of whether or not to tell his parents the truth about what really had been going on with Neil. Like his drug problem. "Neil doesn't have anything to do with me doing my job."

She pulled into the parking lot of the station and turned off the vehicle. She looked at him. "How can you be objective? Your brother is dead because I arrested him and stuck him in a cell with a crazy person. How can you not blame me, too?"

"For starters, you didn't know the guy was crazy. And second, my brother is dead because he made some really bad choices. I don't blame you, I blame Neil and the guy who killed him. Period. Those are the only two who deserve the blame."

"Like you said, your parents don't feel that way."

Jordan closed his eyes, remembering his father's confrontation of Katie at the morgue. Paul Gray had stared daggers at Katie. "You killed my son!"

Katie had winced and held out a hand. "I'm so sorry this happened. Neil ran a stop sign right in front of me. I pulled him over and he was—"

"You did this. You!" He'd jabbed a finger, stopping millimeters from her chest, cutting off her sorrowful words. "Neil called me. Said he didn't know why he'd been arrested, that it was a case of mistaken identity. You made a mistake, and an innocent boy died because of it. I hope you can sleep tonight knowing how well you did your duty." The thick sarcasm cut.

"Sir—"

His father had turned on his heel and marched away, never looking back. And Jordan had just stood there and let the man blast Katie. Then again, he'd wanted to do the same thing. Before he'd learned the truth about everything. That Neil was into drugs, buying, selling and using. And he was in deep.

The pain of that day swept over him once again.

The agony on Katie's face shook him. "He wasn't innocent like your parents believe, but Neil shouldn't have died because of that choice," she reiterated with a whisper.

"No, he shouldn't have." Jordan rubbed a hand down his face. "This is why you've been avoiding me?"

"Mostly."

He nodded. "All right. We've gotten this far in talking about it, but we'll have to finish this conversation later. Let's go see what our prisoner has to say."

Katie nodded and climbed from the car.

* * *

Katie stepped into the police station. Jordan nodded to an officer and said, "I want to speak to Kurt over there. His father and mine are friends. I'll be there in just a minute."

She nodded and took a right down a long hallway. She stopped in front of a room labeled Interrogation Room #2 and took a deep breath.

Questioning a suspect always gave her an adrenaline rush. Mr. Wesley Wray was no different. She knew Jordan would be watching from the observation window. Katie stepped into the interrogation room and dropped a file on the table in front of Wray. She sat across from him and settled one hand on top of the file. His eyes followed her movement. She asked, "You've got quite a history of breaking into places, don't you?"

His gaze snapped up to meet hers. He narrowed his eyes, leaned back and crossed his arms. "So?"

She shrugged and kept her voice conversationally light. "What do you do when you're not in jail, Mr. Wray? Do you have a family?"

His brow furrowed. She'd confused him. "Yeah. I got a wife and a kid that live over behind the Beacon."

The Beacon. One of Spartanburg's most well-known landmarks. Anyone who came through the city as a tourist stopped to eat there. But one didn't want to live behind it. It was one of the toughest areas in town, where residents kept their doors locked and their weapons nearby.

"So I want to know, out of all the houses in Spartanburg, what made you pick mine?"

"I told you, Detective, it was empty and looked like an easy hit. I thought I'd be in and out before anyone got home. End of story."

She leaned in. "Oh, no. I think there's a lot more to that story than you're telling, and we're not going anywhere until I'm satisfied you've given me quite a few more details. Why did you ask about my laptop? Is there something on there you're interested in?"

For a brief second, Wray looked startled, a deer caught in the headlights, then he sneered and leaned forward, the tic alongside his mouth betraying his emotion. "Look, lady—"

"That's 'detective.'"

"Detective," Wray sneered. His face cleared, the tic stopped. "There's nothing else to tell. I needed some cash for a hit. Your house looked ripe."

Katie studied him. "You're not a junkie."

He lifted a brow and shrugged. "I didn't say the hit was for me."

She slammed a hand on the table and he jumped. "Quit playing me! What were you doing in my house?"

Jordan shoved his hands in the pockets of his jeans. If he didn't, the temptation to burst into the investigation room and wrap his fingers around Wray's throat might just be too much for him.

He slid a glance at Gregory Lee, Katie's partner. The man had come when he'd heard the call over his radio. Jordan said, "She holds her own, doesn't she?"

"She's sharp. Can spot a lie a mile away. Only you know as well as I do she shouldn't be in there questioning him."

"I know. You going to get in there and tell her to get out?"

"In a minute or two."

Jordan smothered a smile. Gregory was a good partner. He stood about two inches over six feet, and Jordan knew he'd just celebrated his thirty-third birthday, because one of Katie's excuses for not meeting with him last week was because she had a birthday party to attend for her partner.

"You have any thoughts on why Wray would have been in Katie's house?"

Lee shook his head. "No."

"Any cases y'all are working bring anything to mind?"

Gregory finally looked at him. "Nothing in particular. Why? You don't think this was a random thing?"

"Do you?"

Gregory shrugged. "Cops don't have any special protection when it comes to a breaking and entering."

"I know. It just seems…odd. He breaks into her house at five-thirty on a Tuesday afternoon. That's about the time a lot of people are coming home from work. Why risk being spotted by a neighbor or the homeowner walking in on him…like Katie did."

"Good questions." Gregory eyed him. "Why don't you pass those on to Katie?"

"She'll think of them."

Katie looked up and scratched her nose.

Gregory said, "That's my cue." He breathed a sigh of relief. "She's not pushing. She's going to let me push the guy." He shot Jordan a look. "Guess I'll get to ask those questions." He slipped from the observation room and soon was in the interrogation room. Katie pressed the file into his hands and within seconds joined Jordan. "You look tired," he said.

"Tired and frustrated."

Jordan nodded. "I understand. But just one question."

"What's that?"

"If Wray didn't pick your home by accident, then what was the reason behind the break-in?"

"Exactly what I've been trying to figure out."

Unfortunately, Gregory didn't get anything else out of Mr. Wray, either, and they left with more questions than answers.

On the way to the car, she asked, "What are your plans tonight?"

"I'm going to stop at my parents' house, then head home. I need to go over some notes."

She cocked her head. "Do you work all the time?"

Jordan flashed her a tight smile. "Of course. Don't you?"

She blew out a short laugh. "Yeah. Pretty much." She paused and bit her lip.

"What is it?"

Katie sighed. "Are you going to tell your parents we're working together?"

Jordan pressed his lips together as he pondered that question. "I don't know."

She nodded, her eyes troubled. Jordan found himself wanting to soothe the agitation there. He wanted to take her in his arms and reassure her that it would be all right. He swallowed hard and resisted the desire to act on those feelings.

He pictured that day in the morgue. Looking down at his brother's face. Surrounded by his parents' grief and Katie's guilt-ridden eyes.

He shuddered. Yeah. Better to turn those feelings off now before they developed into something that would break both of their hearts.

THREE

Wednesday morning Katie woke to the sun streaming through the blinds and a headache she wouldn't wish on her worst enemy. Except maybe her uncooperative intruder from yesterday. Yeah. He could have it.

She squinted against the light and held a hand to her throbbing head, wondering who'd stabbed her just above her right eye. She glanced at the clock. Eight-fifteen. Where was she?

Oh, right, Grandma Jean's. And today was Wednesday. Grandma Jean would be at her weekly Bible study and Mariah, a crime-lab technician, would have left for work about thirty minutes ago.

Katie moved and the room tilted. She groaned and decided the pain felt like little men with ice picks were assaulting her head.

Medicine first.

Call in sick second.

Once she'd ticked both items off her list, she closed the curtains over the blinds and crawled back under the covers. Bracing her head against the headboard, she kept her eyes shut and let her mind spin.

Time passed in a blur. It seemed like mere minutes

when her cell phone rang, jarring her from her twilight sleep. A quick glance at the clock told her it was lunchtime. Her stomach growled in agreement.

She answered on the third ring. "Hello?"

"Katie? You all right?" Jordan asked.

She supposed her froglike voice might have clued him in that something might be wrong. "Yeah. Had a bad headache."

"Had? As in it's gone now?"

She considered the question. "Not entirely, but it's better. Manageable."

"Manageable enough to meet me for lunch?"

Did she want to? Not really, because she had a feeling what the topic of conversation would be. But she'd made this decision to pursue her sister's case. A case that wouldn't even exist if Katie hadn't turned her back on Lucy for just a little too long. Lucy had been seven years old when fourteen-year-old Katie had helped a neighbor with her groceries. When she'd returned to the yard, Lucy had been gone. And Katie had been blamed by her parents ever since. Especially her mother.

It wasn't too late to back out, but she knew deep down she didn't want to do that. She needed to know what had happened to Lucy, needed somehow to absolve herself of this raging guilt she'd carried for the last fourteen years. "Sure. What'd you have in mind?"

"I think I remember you like pizza?"

"Of course."

"How about Gino's?"

The little pizza place about three minutes from Grandma Jean's house. She swiped a hand through her hair. "Give me about thirty minutes."

"Deal."

"And I'm paying for mine, okay? I mean, this isn't like a date, right?" she blurted. Silence from the other end. She fought the mortification at her silly assumption that he had even thought about paying for her lunch.

She opened her mouth to apologize only to hear him say on a choked laugh, "Well, if I'd been thinking along those lines, I'm not now."

"Sorry, sorry. I didn't mean to make things awkward. Was actually trying to avoid that by clearing that up before we met."

He gave another low chuckle and she knew if she looked in the mirror, she'd be beet red. "You can pay for yours. See you soon, Katie." His silky goodbye sent shivers dancing up her spine. Oh, no. She had *not* just done that, had she? Why, oh why couldn't she just keep her mouth shut?

And yet she couldn't extinguish the spark of excitement that flared at the thought of being with him again. "It's not a date," she reminded herself as she flew through her routine, her headache all but gone.

Twenty-six minutes later, she walked through the door of the popular pizza café and spotted Jordan seated at a back table with a large pizza at the center. Christmas music played in the background, and a toasty fire added to the warmth of the atmosphere.

Katie slid into the chair opposite him. A glass of iced tea sat in front of her and she took a swig. He handed her a plate and a napkin. "Pepperoni all right?"

"More than all right. It's my favorite."

"That's what I've heard."

He had, huh? Erica?

She waited for him to mention her embarrassing moment on the phone, but he seemed to have let it go. She relaxed and for the next few minutes they ate while Katie wondered about the man across from her.

"What's your story, Jordan?"

He stilled, glanced up at her then back to his pizza. "What do you mean?"

"You used to be with the FBI full time. Why did you leave to come work for Erica?"

"Partly because Brandon asked me to." Brandon Hayes was Erica's brother and partner with Finding the Lost. And Jordan's roommate. He chewed his food and swallowed. "It's a long story."

He obviously didn't want to talk about it, but she decided not to let him off the hook that easily. "I've got time." He knew her entire sordid mess of a story. Would he trust her enough to share his background?

He stared at her then looked down at his food. "I was working with the Crimes Against Children division. Fighting online predators. I messed up and a kid died. End of story."

Katie gasped. "Jordan, I'm so sorry."

He continued to eat in silence, but Katie knew there was more. She decided to go for broke. "How did you mess up?"

He paused, set the uneaten piece of pizza on his plate and sighed. "I was outsmarted."

She stared at him, skeptical. "I can't see that happening."

For a moment his eyes thawed and the grief that had been there faded a fraction. "Thanks for that." He shook his head. "The guy on the other end of the computer had routed his IP address through so many different places, I was having a hard time tracking him. When I finally got a lock on him, it was too late. He'd killed the young girl and taken off."

"Was he ever found?"

"Yes. The next day, when he tried to snatch another kid."

She considered his story. "Is that why you only work cold cases at Finding the Lost? Like my sister's case? Like Molly's?" Jordan had been a key player in finding little Molly James, Erica's daughter, who'd been kidnapped three years ago. Molly had been reunited with her mother six months before and was adjusting well thanks to a team effort. That was one case Katie would never forget. She'd worked countless hours looking for Molly and had forged a deep friendship with Erica as a result.

Jordan's nostrils flared, her insight seeming to surprise him. "It's that obvious, huh?"

She shrugged. "Maybe not to the ordinary person, but I just put two and two together."

"Right." Jordan tossed his napkin onto the table like he'd lost his appetite. "Can we get into the details about your sister's case?"

She'd pushed enough. "I suppose it's time."

Jordan steepled his fingers and said, "Two weeks ago, you asked us to look into your sister's disappearance."

"Right."

She shook her head. "I can't believe it's already been fourteen years. In some ways it seems like she's been gone forever. In others, it seems like it was yesterday."

"I took the information you gave me and the information from the file and tried to piece together the events of that day. I wanted to bounce everything off of you, see if you had anything else to add." He paused. "And would have already done so if you had taken my calls."

She grimaced. He stayed silent, but kept his gaze on her face. "I'm sorry. It's not your fault." Katie paused and considered what she wanted to tell him. She finally said, "You know, I became a detective because of Lucy."

He nodded. "Erica mentioned something along those lines."

"In the beginning, I did what I could on my own time to find her. But I kept running into brick walls. I got frustrated and angry that I wasn't making any progress. It became an…obsession. Once again, the case was taking over my life." She licked her lips and took a swig of her iced tea. "The first time was when she was taken. My parents worked so hard to find her—flyers, press conferences, interviews, everything. And of course I did what I could to be involved and help, but I was fourteen. I was powerless." She swallowed hard.

"I hated that feeling. But now *I* was doing something." She sighed. "My lieutenant had been very understanding, but I'd reached the limit on his patience. He was ready to put me on suspension because I was letting it affect my performance on my other cases. I had to stop if I wanted to save my career, my sanity. So I did."

And she felt guilty for that. "I told myself I would take a break and get back to it. And I came to Finding the Lost because I thought it would be good to have some outside help to keep me from becoming obsessed."

"How long has your break been?"

"A year."

"So after a year, you decide to start searching again. Why the hesitation now?"

She rubbed her eyes. "Part of me is scared that I'll do it again. Let it become an obsession. And as much as I want to know what happened to her, that can't happen.

And—" she picked at imaginary lint on the sleeve of her fleece "—I'm afraid of what I'm—we're—going to find."

"You're scared we're going to find out she's dead."

Katie looked up. "It's been fourteen years, Jordan. You know the odds as well as I do." She took a deep breath. "Don't get me wrong. I want to know what happened to her. And yet… I don't."

"You can't have it both ways." He gentled his tone.

"I know that." She rubbed a hand down her weary face and closed her eyes. "I just… What if she's dead?" she whispered. "How will I tell my parents that? How will I live with it?"

Jordan leaned over and took her hand. The warmth of his fingers on hers made her shiver. "Won't it give you some closure? One way or the other? All these years you've held out hope. Even if she's dead, wouldn't you finally be able to put it behind you?"

Katie shrugged and bit her lip then said, "I don't know. That's the problem. I simply don't know."

Jordan sighed. "Well, I've got information. I need to know what you want me to do with it."

She shook her head. "Finding Lucy is why I'm here. I've been kidding myself thinking I could just let it go permanently." She took a deep breath and met his gaze. "I've got to know one way or another—and I think my parents do, too." After shredding her napkin into tiny pieces, she firmed her lips and looked him in the eye. "So tell me."

Jordan pulled at his lower lip. Then he said, "I called a friend at the bureau and asked him about the case, got the file emailed to me and did some research. Your lieutenant was nice enough to let me have the local law enforcement file so I could compare the two." He set that on the table in front of her.

She glanced at it. "Who have you talked to so far?"

"A lot of people. Particularly those who still live in your old neighborhood."

"Go on."

He pulled out a notebook and flipped through a few pages. "I tried to get in touch with your neighbor Elaine Johnson."

"She's still alive?" Katie asked.

It surprised him she didn't know. "Yes. She's old, but she's definitely alive. The only problem is, she wasn't home. I've been by her house three times and she's not there. I asked some of your neighbors where she is and one of them thought she was visiting her son in Georgia. Another said she was in the hospital. And yet another said she thought she was in a nursing home. I'm tracking her down."

"How about that. Elaine Johnson's still alive." She gave a breathy laugh. "Wow. I mean, I knew she was a year ago, but she was in the hospital with congestive heart failure the last I heard. I ended up deciding to take my break before I was able to talk to her, but I would scan the obituaries in the paper thinking I'd see her name. When I never did, I figured I just missed it." She bit her lip and shook her head. "She didn't see anything anyway that day. She was with me in the house when it all happened."

Jordan nodded. Elaine Johnson. The next-door neighbor who'd needed help with her groceries. Katie had carried several bags into the house and then returned to her front yard to find Lucy missing.

She swallowed hard. "Who else have you had a chance to talk to?"

"Some of the other neighbors, but no one seemed to notice anything odd that day—until you called the cops and they swarmed the neighborhood. I'm still trying to track down a few people I haven't gotten in touch with, people who've moved out of the neighborhood, but there aren't many. I want to question every neighbor who was within sight of your old front yard."

"I already did that, but maybe a new person asking even the same questions will spark something that'll produce different answers." One could hope. "A couple of hours after Lucy disappeared, I remember the detective, Frank Miller, coming out and questioning everyone even though the uniformed officers had already done it." She finished off her last slice of pizza. "I watched him go house to house. I even followed him to see if I could listen in and learn anything."

"Did you?"

"No. In fact, he was mad when he caught me. Told me to go on home and let him do his job. I remember smarting off to him and telling him he must not be much of a detective since my sister was still missing." Jordan winced and she nodded. "Yeah, he wasn't too happy with that."

"I guess not."

"I still see him around the precinct every once in a while. He goes out of his way to avoid me."

"Detective Frank Miller. I spoke to him, too. He feels bad about not finding Lucy. It's obvious that talking about the case brings back unpleasant memories, a sense of failure." Jordan flipped the page in his notebook. "He's forty-five years old now. Your sister's case was one of his first, but his partner, Danny Jackson, was a veteran."

"I talked to him last year, too. He retired a few years ago."

"He was close to retirement fourteen years ago. He said your sister's is one of the cases that still haunts him."

"So did talking to them help? Because it didn't do much for me. He's very gruff, but I don't think I should take it personally. I think it's just how he is."

"He was gruff with me, too. And I'm not sure if talking to him helped. He basically told me to mind my own business. I'm still going through the file and all their notes." He tapped the notebook against his palm and studied the woman across from him.

She intrigued him and while he didn't want it to be so, it was. For the first time in a long time, he was attracted to someone. Interested in getting to know her on a deeper level than just a working relationship.

And it had to be someone he couldn't pursue. He pictured his parents' reaction if he were to announce that he was seeing the woman they blamed for their younger son's death.

And winced.

No, unfortunately, Katie Randall was off-limits.

Her phone rang and she snagged it. "Hello?"

"Ms. Randall, this is Deep Clean Services. I just wanted to let you know we arrived at your house about seven-thirty this morning and will be done in about an hour."

"Thanks for letting me know."

She made payment arrangements, hung up and told Jordan the news. "Guess that means Mariah and I can go home." She frowned. "Strangely enough, I'm mourning the Christmas tree the most." Katie sent a text to her roommate to let her know, then turned back to the file. "All right. What else is in here?"

Katie moved over to sit beside Jordan in the booth so they could see the file without one of them having to try and read upside down.

Sitting beside him, she noticed his cologne once again, the strength that emanated from him. His warmth. She shivered at being so near him and swallowed hard. An attraction to this man was just not an option. And yet no matter how much her mind protested, her heart had decided to take matters into its own hands.

Focus. *Focus.* "You know I got this file from the department and copied everything in it. I used to study it at night when I couldn't sleep." Which had been often.

They scanned the notes, turning the pages one by one. A small slip of paper, stuck to the back of the sheet she'd just been reading, caught the edge of her fingernail and fell off. Katie picked it up. "What's this?"

Jordan took it from her. "Looks like an address."

"It was stuck to the back of this. Looks like there's food or something on it." She scraped the mess off with her fingernail. "How did I miss this?" she muttered. She knew how. She'd been in a hurry to get the file copied before her boss caught her once again working her sister's case and had returned the original file without seeing the small slip of paper. "Let's see where the address is." She grabbed her phone and punched it in the GPS app. She looked up at him. "It's a place called Jake's Diner. About thirty miles away, in Anderson." Katie bit her lip. "Why would this be in here?"

"It's a sticky note. Probably Frank or Danny answered

the phone and wrote it down. Is there anything else with that information on it?" he asked.

They flipped through the file again. Twice. Katie shook her head. "Nothing."

Jordan rubbed his chin. "Feel like a road trip?"

She stood. "Definitely. Let's go." Katie headed for the cash register and Jordan followed.

At the door, he said, "I'll get the car. You pay."

She gaped at him. He widened his eyes, the picture of innocence. "What? I wouldn't want you to think I was trying to turn this into a date or anything."

Katie felt the flush start at the base of her throat. "Cute, Gray. Real cute."

He winked. "I'll get the next one."

FOUR

Jordan gave himself a mental smack upside the head as he pulled his car around. Mere minutes ago, he'd reminded himself that an attraction to Katie was not a good thing, and then he'd turned around and deliberately flirted with her. What was he thinking? He sure didn't want to give her the wrong idea.

Or the right idea. That he was interested in her. Because that interest could go nowhere as long as his parents blamed her for Neil's death. He groaned and rubbed his eyes. *Lord, I'm going to need Your guidance on this one.*

He could see Katie inside paying. His phone rang and when he saw his father's number on the screen, guilt swamped him. Swallowing it back, he hit the talk button. "Hi, Dad."

"You busy, son?"

"Working a case, but I've got a couple of minutes. What's up?"

"You mother wanted me to call and invite you to dinner Sunday night. Can you make it?"

Jordan ran through his schedule in his head as Katie

walked toward him. She climbed in, and he said, "I can make it."

"Great. Around five-thirty?"

"Sure, Dad. I'll be there."

Katie buckled her seat belt and checked her phone. Jordan hung up. Katie looked at him. "Your dad?"

"Yeah."

She nodded.

"What are your parents like?" he asked. She blinked and a deep sorrow crossed her face. Then she smiled. A smile so forced it nearly broke his heart.

She sighed. "They're good people. I get along better with my father than my mother." The smile slid off. "Ever since Lucy's disappearance, she's battled depression, has trouble getting out of bed most days." She shrugged and looked out the window. "People in their church have tried to reach out and help, but she doesn't respond much."

"I'm sorry." Jordan cranked the car and made a mental note not to go there again.

"Thanks. I am, too." She looked back at him and he could make out anger mixed with the sorrow. Then she lowered her gaze. "Is it wrong that I get really angry with her sometimes?"

Her voice was so low he had to strain to make out the words. "No. I can imagine fourteen years of depression would be very tiring."

"It's not just that. I don't even know that she can help it, but I needed her, too—" She flushed and shook her head. "Never mind." She took a deep breath and cleared her throat. "Speaking of my mother—" She pulled her phone from her pocket and dialed a number. "Hi, Mom." Jordan heard the woman's muffled answer, then Katie said, "Your dinner is being delivered. They're coming around five-thirty, all right?" She listened a moment. "No, Mom, you won't have to worry about washing or returning any pans. They'll all be disposable, okay? I hope you enjoy it."

More indistinguishable words and then a sigh from Katie as she said goodbye and hung up.

He couldn't help it. "What was that about?"

"Dad called me the day before yesterday and said my mom had a doctor's appointment today. My partner's sister, Christi, has a catering business. I asked her to deliver dinner to my parents tonight so they wouldn't have to worry about it. In all the excitement, I forgot to let them know."

"That's really thoughtful." Jordan eyed her.

She shrugged and flushed. "I don't know if thoughtful is the right—" She bit the words off and nearly chewed a hole in her lower lip.

"What?"

"Never mind. It's not important."

But it was, he could tell. However, he dropped the subject as he turned in to the parking lot of Jake's Diner. Dropped it, but didn't forget it. The woman intrigued him, and he wanted to know what it was she hadn't said. But that would wait.

They climbed from the vehicle, tugging their coats tighter against the wind. Katie walked at a fast clip toward the door and Jordan followed her.

The diner looked like a throwback to the fifties. A well-preserved throwback. With her hand on the door handle, Katie said, "Nice."

"Yeah. How come I didn't know about this place?"

She shrugged. "I've heard it mentioned in conversation, but never bothered to drive out here. I'll have to make sure I do that sometime soon. Just for fun."

"Maybe I'll come with you." He gave her a slow smile and she flushed.

Then lifted her chin. "Maybe I'll let you."

Cars zipped past on the highway. Several slowed and turned in.

One slowed almost to a stop in the middle of the road, catching Jordan's attention. "Look."

Katie looked. The car sped up and was soon gone from sight. She frowned. "What do you think that was all about?"

"I have no idea, but I've got the make and model."

They entered the diner and walked up to the bar area. Multicolored lights hung above and blinked in time with the Christmas carol coming from the speaker to her right.

Katie slid onto one of the silver, red-cushioned stools and Jordan sat beside her. For a few minutes, they watched the waitress scurry about taking orders, her red-and-white hat tipped with a bell that jingled at every shake of her head. Now she stood in front of Katie. "What'll it be?"

"I'll have a coffee."

Jordan said, "Same here."

Katie pulled out the picture of her sister that had been splashed all over the news when she'd disappeared fourteen years ago. When the waitress came back with their coffee, Katie eyed her name tag and asked, "Celia, how long have you been working here?"

Celia tilted her head and lifted a hand to hold the hat in place. She snapped her gum and said, "About six years now, I guess."

"Is there anyone that's been here for at least fourteen or fifteen years?"

"The owner. Been here twenty-seven years, as she likes to remind us on a regular basis."

"Who's the owner?"

"Betty June Clark."

"Is she here?"

"Somewhere." Her gaze darted to the newcomers walking in.

Katie flashed her badge. "You mind telling her we'd like to ask her a couple of questions?"

Now she had Celia's full attention. With wide eyes, she backed toward the kitchen. "Hey, Betty! You got company out here."

"Thanks," Katie said and sipped her coffee. Jordan dumped three things of flavored creamer into his. Katie nearly choked when he took the silver-topped sugar jar and dumped at least the equivalent of ten tablespoons into the steaming brew. "You like a little coffee with your cream and sugar, huh?"

He grinned and took a sip. "Yep."

In the mirror on the opposite wall, Katie watched the crowd behind her. She normally liked to sit with her back to the wall, but the place was packed and with the mirror she felt a little less like a target.

A woman in a black skirt, navy blue button-down shirt and white tennis shoes came from the kitchen. She eyed Jordan and Katie with wary curiosity. "Can I help you?"

Katie introduced herself and Jordan and studied the pretty woman. "You don't look old enough to have been here twenty-seven years."

Betty's tension lightened. She smiled. "Started working here when I was sixteen. I'm forty-three now. Took over when my daddy retired seventeen years ago."

Jordan asked, "Do you remember a local kidnapping case fourteen years ago? Lucy Randall?"

Betty stilled and her brow furrowed, eyes narrowed. "I remember. Very well, actually. Was all over the news for weeks."

"That's the one."

Betty nodded. "My baby sister was the same age as Lucy when it happened. That kidnapping has haunted me and my family for more reasons than one."

Katie perked up as her blood started to hum in anticipation. "Why's that?"

"Because I believe Lucy and her kidnapper stopped here to eat."

Katie jerked and felt the blood drain from her face. That would be a good enough reason for the woman to recall the details so clearly. "Why do you say that?"

"The guy had on a baseball cap and sunglasses and didn't take them off the whole time they were in here. The little girl's hair was whacked off like it had been done in a hurry without any care for style. When I cleaned the bathrooms, I saw a few strands of hair that looked like the same color as hers around the toilet in the men's bathroom. Our floor is dark wood. That hair stood out. And besides, that little girl just wasn't acting right."

"How was she acting?"

"She was jumpy and scared. At least that's what I thought."

"What color was her hair?" If it stood out against a dark floor, Katie had a good idea what the answer was.

"Blond. That fine white blond that comes naturally to the lucky few."

Katie swallowed hard. Lucy had had that kind of hair. Katie's hair was blond, too, but not like Lucy's. Lucy's had been so blond it had almost been white.

"Why didn't you call the police?" Katie forced the words past the lump in her throat.

"I did."

"You did?" Katie stared.

Jordan jumped in. "What happened?"

"They came out here, and I told them the same thing I told you."

"Did they get a crime scene unit over here?" Katie asked. She hadn't seen anything in the file to indicate one had checked the place out. At the very least, they should have gotten a sample of hair to compare to something of Lucy's—like a piece of hair from her hairbrush.

At the very least.

"No. It was just a couple of detectives who came out and asked a few questions. One looked at the bathroom, the other talked to me for a few minutes. When the one in the bathroom came out, he just said he'd be in touch if he had any more questions."

Katie drew in a deep breath and exchanged an incredulous look with Jordan. "Unbelievable," he muttered. His napkin fluttered to the floor. He and Katie bent at the same time to retrieve it.

A crack sounded. Betty screamed as the sugar jar in front of Jordan exploded.

Jordan spun, grabbed his weapon even as he ducked for cover. From the corner of his eye, he noticed Katie doing the same. Another blast came from outside the diner and hit the mirror over the bar. Katie screamed, "Get down! Get down! Call nine-one-one!"

The deafening chaos surrounding him, Jordan hit the floor, then scrambled to one of the unoccupied booths. Betty yelled into her cell phone as she crouched behind the bar.

A squeal of tires, a burst of horns and one sickening crunch followed by two more sent Jordan racing for the door of the diner. Katie followed. Outside, he saw the wreckage on the busy road. Katie turned to the patrons and hollered, "Everyone stay back and stay away from the windows!"

"You see him?" Jordan asked, scanning the area even as he moved toward the pileup. A car peeled away.

"There he goes!" Katie yelled.

"He'll just have to go," Jordan said between clenched teeth. "We've got to make sure no one's hurt. Come on." He got on the phone and called in the direction the shooter was heading.

A woman stumbled from the three-car wreck, holding her bleeding head. "He stole my car!" Katie bolted over. She gripped the young woman by her upper arms and led her away from the vehicles. "He had a gun and he hit me with it."

The woman's tears flowed while Jordan called back to let them know the vehicle was stolen. "I need CSU here, too."

Kate settled the distraught woman on the curb. She looked to be in her early twenties. Petite and soft. Defenseless. An easy target. "What's your name?" Katie asked.

"Miranda."

"Did you get a good look at him, Miranda?"

"No. He came from behind and pulled me out. I never

saw his face. But he had a rifle strapped to his back and a pistol in his right hand. I saw those real clear."

"Stay here."

Sirens sounded in the distance. Jordan left Katie with Miranda and went to see who else needed help. He asked a young woman with a toddler strapped into a car seat in the back of her minivan, "Are you all right? Your child?"

Oh, Lord, please, not a child.

But the woman nodded as she unbuckled the crying little one, her scared, pinched features doubling his determination to catch the person who'd caused this.

An older gentleman in a gray Taurus held his neck. Jordan jogged over to him. "Sir? Don't move, help's on the way."

"I'm all right. Did you see that idiot? Pulled right out of the parking lot and wrecked his car, then stole another one."

"You saw him?"

"Clear as day."

"What's your name?"

"Bobby Young."

"We'll get you checked out and then I'll need to get a statement from you, all right? We'll want you to meet with a sketch artist, too."

"Sure, sure. Whatever I can do to help catch that maniac."

Four police cruisers pulled into the area, blue lights flashing. Two officers made their way to him, and Jordan flashed his badge then gave them a rundown on what he'd done.

"We'll take it from here. Thanks."

Three ambulances arrived, and the paramedics got to work.

Jordan found Katie taking statements and keeping people clear of the wreck. She glanced at him. "CSU on the way?"

"Yes, along with everyone else."

Three fire trucks screamed onto the scene. Katie nodded. "Good."

Jordan knew he might be overstepping his bounds. Technically, while he was employed with the FBI, the FBI didn't handle car wrecks or local shootings, but he figured since one of those bullets came mighty close to having his name on it, he'd just work as though he belonged there. At least until someone told him otherwise.

Katie grabbed his arm to get his attention in all the chaos. She held up her phone. "Just got a call. He got away. They can't find any sign of him anywhere."

Jordan nodded. He wasn't surprised.

The crime scene unit van pulled into the diner parking lot. Jordan followed Katie and waited as the vehicle parked on the edge of the lot.

Katie watched Faith Nelson climb from the van. "I'm glad you're here."

"What happened?"

Katie filled her in as the woman grabbed her gear from the back of the van. To help process the scene, Faith had brought three of her team. Two headed for the diner; Faith and her other coworker started in the parking lot. "Where was he parked?"

"I'm not sure." She pointed to the street where Jordan directed traffic around the crunched vehicles. "But he ended up in that wreck before he stole another car that wasn't involved in the accident."

Faith delegated assignments to her team and headed

over to the shooter's vehicle. Katie followed. Jordan tucked his phone in his pocket and looked at her. "The car's stolen."

"Naturally."

Faith shrugged. "I'll do the best I can do here. Will be able to do more once we get it to the lab." She glanced at Katie. "I'll have Mariah work on it."

Katie nodded. "Thanks."

The crime scene photographer had his work cut out for him between the wreck and the diner. She noticed he had someone with him to help. For the next two hours, Katie worked the scene and listened as Jordan offered his opinion and expertise. He kept a low profile and didn't try to take over, although he might have wanted to. That bullet had come awfully close to his head. If she hadn't dropped her napkin—

"You ready to get out of here?"

Jordan's low voice cut into her thoughts.

"I'm ready."

Katie looked back at where the wreck had been. Broken bits of glass that had escaped the sweep-up were the only sign of the chaos from just a few hours earlier. The diner was another matter—crime scene tape and broken windows were evidence of the reality of what had happened.

She climbed into Jordan's truck and put on her seat belt. He said, "The car that the shooter was driving was the one that slowed down right before we went in the diner."

"You sure?"

"Pretty sure. Same color, make and model. A red Toyota Camry."

"So you think he followed us, let us go in and then came back to shoot the place up?"

"Yes."

She mentally chewed on that for a minute. "If you hadn't ducked, that bullet would have hit you in the back of the head."

He grimaced and reached up to rub the back of his neck, as though he needed reassurance it was still in one piece. "We're making someone uncomfortable. Someone who knows we're investigating your sister's kidnapping."

For the first time in a long time, hope sprouted. "If we're making someone uncomfortable in regards to Lucy's kidnapping, we must be onto something."

"I think that diner was a huge clue."

"So why wasn't it in the report?"

"That's a question for Detective Miller." He gave her a grim smile. "Plus we have an eyewitness. Bobby Young said he saw the man clear as day."

"Is he on his way to the precinct to work with the sketch artist?"

"He is."

Katie pulled out her phone and dialed the number she hadn't used in a year. He answered on the third ring. "Miller here."

"Hi, Frank. It's Katie Randall." Silence greeted her. "Lucy Randall's sister."

"I know who you are. What can I do for you?"

"I was wondering if you'd have some time to discuss my sister's case with me."

He grunted. "You're back on that, are you?"

She didn't let his gruffness deter her. "I am."

"You working with that guy from Finding the Lost?"

"Yes."

He huffed a sigh. "All right. Sure. I don't know what else you think I can tell you that I didn't tell him, but how about four o'clock tomorrow afternoon here at the station?"

"I'll be there."

She hung up and filled Jordan in. "Do you mind if I come along?" he asked.

"Not at all."

"I wonder what he'll have to say about the diner."

"Good question. But until then, I'm curious to see if Mr. Wray has anything to add to his story about why he was in my house."

"Shall we find out?"

She glanced at her watch. "Let's see if we can catch him before he heads to dinner."

Jordan followed Katie into the jail. The usual chaos—ringing phones, chattering of law enforcement and curses from recently arrested criminals—filled the air. It reminded him of his detective days before he'd applied to the FBI and gotten the case that had turned his life upside down.

But he wasn't here to think about that. Right now he wanted to know if Mr. Wray had anything else to add to his story.

Katie had called ahead and asked for him to be brought into one of the private areas where prisoners met with those involved in their legal activities. Katie paced the length of the small room while Jordan leaned against the table.

She said, "I wonder if he's retained a lawyer yet."

"Probably a public defender. I looked a little deeper

into his past last night. He was on probation. His latest crime will land him here for a good long while."

"Then maybe he won't have anything to lose by talking to us now."

"Maybe."

She shot him a glance and then looked at her watch. "Wonder what's taking so long?"

"He's probably at dinner."

She grimaced. "Is it already that time? I forgot how late it was."

"Your headache gone?"

"The one from this morning is. However, I have a feeling Mr. Wray may spark another one."

The door opened and Jordan straightened.

An officer said, "Mr. Wray won't be coming in."

"Why's that?" Katie asked.

"Because he's being transported to the hospital. There was a fight on the way to the dining hall. He was stabbed in the throat."

FIVE

Katie pushed the rotating door of the hospital and stepped into the emergency department waiting room. She flashed her badge to the woman behind the desk. "Wesley Wray. He was just brought in from the prison. Stabbing victim."

The woman got on the phone. She looked up. "I'm sorry. He died in the ambulance."

Katie let out a breath she hadn't realized she'd been holding. She nodded. "All right. Thanks." She looked at Jordan. "Great. Just great."

"Yeah." He placed a hand on her lower back as he directed her to the door. Now that her adrenaline rush was ebbing, disappointment flooded her. As did her awareness of the man beside her. Their moments together flashed in her mind. He'd been nothing but kind and considerate with her, thoughtful and selfless. Spending time with him was giving her a new perspective of him and she liked it.

"What are you plans tomorrow?" he asked.

"Thursday. I plan to have breakfast with my parents and then work late. You?"

He gave her an amused look. "Something along those

lines. I probably won't see my parents, but I'll definitely be working late."

"Do you see your parents often?"

He paused. "Most Saturdays. You?"

"Most Thursday mornings."

He opened the car door for her and she lifted a brow in surprise. He shrugged. "Chivalry's not dead, in spite of what most people think."

She smiled. "I like chivalry." She slipped into the passenger seat and buckled up. When he settled behind the wheel, she said, "Probably because I don't get much of it."

"Because you're a cop or because you just pick the wrong guys?"

She shot him a perturbed look. "Partly because I'm a cop, I suppose. I've chosen what was once a male-only field. My feminine side gets ignored mostly."

He turned the key and pulled from the parking lot. "Does that bother you?"

She hesitated. "Only sometimes. Depends on the circumstances."

"Like?"

"If I'm on a date and it gets ignored, yes, it bothers me. Working a case with a fellow officer, I don't even think about it."

"Do you go on dates often?" he asked.

His casual tone gave no hint as to the purpose behind the question. Was he asking because he was just curious or was there something more? Like personal interest.

"No. I haven't been on a date since my fiancé died a few years ago." As soon as the words left her lips, she wanted to recall them.

He stiffened and shot her a brief look. "What happened?"

"He was shot. He was a detective and walked into the wrong building at the wrong time. He and his partner were set up and ambushed. They never had a chance." She kept her words short, hoping Jordan would back off the line of questioning she'd opened up. "So, are you ready to call it a night?"

He didn't say anything and she wondered if he'd let her change the subject. The he said, "Who do you think killed Wray?"

"Someone who didn't want him talking to us."

"Which means Wray didn't pick my house randomly. He had a purpose in being there and I want to know what it was."

Jordan said, "It seems like he was looking for something."

"Like my laptop," she mused. "Remember? He asked if it was in my case."

"So what's on the laptop that would be of interest to someone?"

"Nothing. I don't keep work stuff on there, just personal stuff, mostly."

"And notes about Lucy's kidnapping?"

She stilled then nodded. "Yes. There are notes about Lucy on there."

"Interesting."

"Isn't it, though?" She sighed. "Are you ready to call it a night?"

"Yes, I guess I am. What time are you available tomorrow?"

"I'll be done by midmorning. I'm just running a few errands for my mother."

"All right. You like Chinese food?"

"Love it."

"Where do you want to meet?"

"Why don't you come to my house?" She held up Lucy's paper file. "I think I have this thing memorized, but I'm going to work on it tonight. I'm also going to check in with Mariah and see if she got anything from the diner."

"Will you let me know what you find out?"

"Of course."

Jordan dropped her at her car and Katie watched him drive away, wondering at the ball of tension in the pit of her stomach.

As she drove home, she couldn't get her mind off the handsome FBI agent. Why had she mentioned her fiancé? As a way of letting Jordan know she was single? He already knew that. A way of telling him she was ready to move on?

Was she? Maybe. But not with him. At least not while his parents still held so much animosity toward her. So what had mentioning her fiancé been all about?

Headlights in her rearview mirror captured her attention. The driver had them on bright and kept creeping closer. Katie adjusted the mirror and alternated keeping her eye on the lights behind her and the road before her.

Her phone rang, and she snatched it from the cup holder. "Hello?"

"Hey." Mariah's soft alto came over the line. "I've been working on the evidence the team gathered from that shooting at the diner."

"And?"

"The car had tons of fingerprints. Lots of little ones belonging to children that I can probably rule out. The others will take time to go through."

"Well, it was stolen, so that's to be expected."

"Right, it was reported stolen three days ago, but I

did find a receipt for gas you might want to check out. Someone filled up early this morning."

"Cash or credit?"

"Cash."

"Naturally." She chewed her lip and glanced at the lights in the mirror again. Still on bright and so close they helped illuminate the road in front of her. "All right, text me the address. Maybe they've got some video I can look at."

Mariah said, "Done."

The phone beeped, confirming Mariah's text.

"When are you coming home? I'm on my way there now."

"I'm not. I'm going back over to Grandma Jean's. She's come down with a nasty virus, so I told her I'd stay with her at night. My mom's there now."

"Uh-oh. I'm sorry."

"Yeah. Just pray I don't catch it."

"You're never sick."

"True," Mariah said happily. "I've got to go. I'll call if I come up with anything else."

Katie hung up and took one more look in her rear-view mirror. Enough was enough. Checking around her, she turned her signal on and pulled over to the side. She muttered, "Go on, then, if you're so impatient. But if you speed, you're mine."

But the car pulled up behind her.

Okay, so this wasn't about someone in a hurry.

She looked around. Darkness coated the area. Uneasiness crawled up her spine as she debated what she was going to do. Crawl out of the car and confront him? Wait for him to approach her?

But he was just sitting there and she couldn't see enough to figure out who he might be.

True, she was a cop and she had her weapon, but no way was she going to be caught alone on a relatively empty road after dark with someone intent on playing a dangerous game. She gunned the engine, grabbed her phone and dialed Gregory's number.

No answer.

She hung up and punched in Jordan's. The car followed her into the street, rammed his gas and bumped her. Hard. Katie jerked against the seat belt and lost her grip on the phone. It tumbled to the floorboard. She left it there and grasped the wheel to control the vehicle.

Katie gripped the wheel and put some of her defensive-driving skills to work. She slammed on the brakes and spun the wheel to the left. The tailgating vehicle roared past. Cars approached from behind. Her possible assailant took off. Katie gripped the wheel to go after the disappearing taillights, but by the time she got back on the road and headed after him, he'd vanished.

She slapped the wheel in frustration. She didn't even have a tag to call in.

Katie pulled to the side of the road once again and reached down to feel for her phone. She grasped it and noticed Jordan had called her five times. She hit redial.

"Are you all right?" he shouted.

"I'm fine." She relayed the car incident. "He's gone and I'm going home."

"Are you sure you're okay?"

"Yes. But I'll be sleeping with my gun tonight."

Jordan paced his den, knowing he was going to wear a groove in the floor if he didn't sit down. But he couldn't.

His nerves hummed and his adrenaline still flowed from the excitement with Katie.

"You okay?"

He spun to see his roommate, Brandon Hayes, standing in the door. "Yeah. I'm okay. Had a scary moment a few minutes ago, but it's all good now." When his phone rang with Katie's number popping up on the screen, he'd had a leap of gladness, a thrill he hadn't felt in a long time.

When he'd heard nothing but the squeal of tires, Katie's yell and then silence as the phone went dead, his elation had quickly turned to fear. He'd been halfway to his car, with no idea of where he was going or how he was going to find her, when she'd finally called him back.

"What happened?"

Jordan filled him in.

"Whoa. But she's all right?"

"Yeah. At least she says she is."

"Can I help with anything?"

Jordan paced the length of his den, debating whether or not to go over to her house. But she'd sounded fine. A little shaken maybe, but unhurt. Indecision made him hesitate.

"No. I guess not."

"Let me know if you need something."

An idea occurred to him. "If I need help with some surveillance, would you have some time?"

Brandon nodded. "Just not tonight. I'm already doing some for a case."

"Great. Thanks."

Jordan's phone rang, and Brandon walked back down the hall toward his bedroom. Jordan glanced at the phone display. His new boss with the FBI, Special Agent in Charge Ruby Parker. "What can I do for you, ma'am?"

"I need you to look into something for me."

"What's that?"

She hesitated. "It's a predator and a missing kid."

"No."

"Excuse me?"

"Look, the FBI asked me to be available for some contract work. I agreed, but one of the conditions was no missing children."

She huffed. "I don't understand you, Jordan. You work for an organization that finds missing children. I need you on this one." Her frustration came through loud and clear.

"I handle the adult cases only. Or children's cold cases. Cases where the victim's probably already dead and the family just wants closure. I don't do anything else. That was the agreement with Finding the Lost. That's the agreement with the FBI. Nothing's changed."

"Then I don't see that we need to keep you on."

"Look—"

"I'll be in touch."

She hung up, and Jordan slowly lowered the phone, visions of his past coming back to haunt him. Missing children. He simply couldn't do missing kids. Not anymore. Not since he'd let little Regina Palmer die. Even though no one blamed him for the child's death, Jordan couldn't seem to find a way to get past the guilt.

He drew in a ragged breath.

He wasn't worried about Ruby getting rid of him. She knew the deal.

And right now he wanted to focus on helping Katie. His gut told him they'd asked the right questions of the right person. Only he wasn't sure which questions had sparked the panic in whoever seemed to be targeting Katie.

Which meant they could narrow the list. Sort of. He'd already talked to over forty people.

He wondered how Mr. Young had done with the sketch artist and made a mental note to ask Katie about it first thing.

Jordan glanced at the clock once again. Seven o'clock. She should be home by now. Without waiting to talk himself out of it, he grabbed his phone and texted her.

You all right?

Within seconds, her reply buzzed him.

I'm home and going over the file. Trying to figure out who we've made nervous.

He chuckled.

Great minds think alike.

LOL. You, too?

Yes. Any news from the sketch artist?

No. And that's weird. I'll give her a call.

Let me know what she says. See you tomorrow.

Nite.

Jordan set the phone aside, feeling a little better now that he knew she was safe in her home. Still...

Brandon reentered the room, dressed in a heavy coat, gloves and a warm cap. He had a scarf thrown over his left shoulder. "I'll be gone until morning."

"How does it feel to be a full-time detective again?"

"Feels good. I needed to take the time off to help Erica with Finding the Lost, and I'll always be available, but being back on the job feels like I can breathe again, you know?"

He knew. Once a cop, always a cop. Exactly how he felt about being back on the FBI payroll.

"Be careful."

"Always."

Brandon left. Jordan grabbed his phone again and hit a number he had on speed dial.

Katie checked the locks on her doors and windows one more time, then settled on the couch with the file she nearly had memorized. Only this time she had new material to work with.

Jordan's notes.

She flipped the pages and studied the tight, neat words. Names of her parents' neighbors leaped out at her. One after the other. She finished Jordan's notes then started again. She'd talked to everyone he had—and they all said the same thing.

With one exception: the McKinneys. Her heart picked up a little speed.

The McKinneys had been in their early thirties when Lucy disappeared.

Mr. McKinney had been in a car wreck the week before. Mrs. McKinney had brought him home about three hours before the kidnapping, but stated she hadn't heard or seen anything out of the ordinary. However, she'd wanted to know if anyone had looked into the car she'd seen several days in a row, parked down the street from the Randall household. Mrs. McKinney thought it strange that she never saw it again after the kidnapping.

Katie's heart picked up speed.

Jordan had noted it was a gray sedan. A Buick, possibly, but Mrs. McKinney just wasn't sure of the make and model.

Katie pondered the idea that the car might mean something. Might somehow be an important piece of information. Could be. Then again, it could have belonged to someone on the street. Someone who had family visiting. Could have been a rental. Could have been anything.

Or it could have been the kidnapper staking out the area.

She reached for her phone to call Mrs. McKinney then looked at the time again. She blinked. Four hours had passed since she'd sat down with the file. Reading and rereading.

Exhaustion swamped her, only slightly lessening the excitement she felt at a possible new lead. Katie rubbed her eyes and set the file aside.

She needed sleep. Mrs. McKinney could wait until tomorrow. She checked the doors again, peered through the windows and checked her weapon one more time.

Was she safe?

Probably not, but she'd done everything in her power to give herself a fighting chance should she need it.

Jordan woke from a nightmare. One he'd had since the little girl had died on his watch. She kept calling for him to save her and he couldn't. Sweat coated him and he knew he wouldn't sleep again for a while. Katie instantly came to mind. He picked up his phone and dialed his buddy Cortland Buchanan, a retired FBI agent who'd settled in the area. He'd agreed to keep an eye on Katie's house tonight.

"Hey, Cort. Any activity going on over there?" he asked.

"Not a thing. Quiet and uneventful."

"Good."

"What are you doing up? Another nightmare?"

"Yeah." Only Brandon and Cortland knew about the nightmares.

"Sorry."

"I know."

"I'll let you know if anything happens."

"You staying awake all right?"

"I am. Coffee is my friend."

"And a few doughnuts?"

"I hate to admit to being a stereotype, but…"

Jordan felt the nightmare leaving him, felt his muscles relax their death grip and ease into a less painful state. "All right, buddy, call if you need me. I'll be up awhile."

"Drink some hot tea. Decaf. Does wonders for me."

Jordan grimaced. "Right." Not likely.

He hung up and grabbed his remote. Then tossed it on the bed. Why make Cort lose any more sleep when Jordan wasn't going to be closing his eyes any time soon?

He picked up the phone again.

Katie choked and sat upright in her bed, blinking the sleep from her eyes. And still her vision was hazy. What had awakened her? Her ears rang and she shook her head.

Only to realize the screech wasn't inside her mind, but coming from the house.

Her fire alarm. Awareness shot through her. She stumbled from under the covers and knocked the lamp over. The crash resounded as smoke continued to fill the air. Katie groped for the light switch in her closet. Flames shot up around the bedroom door she'd closed and locked as an extra measure of protection.

She grabbed her cell phone from the bedside table and punched in 911. She raced to the window and stopped to stare. A hole in her glass pane in the shape of a perfect circle stunned her. She blinked and realized she wasn't seeing things. Someone had cut the glass.

Mariah! Relief crashed through her as she remembered Mariah had stayed with her grandmother again.

"Nine-one-one, what's your emergency?"

"My house is on fire," she gasped.

"What's your address?"

Katie told her. She glanced back at the spreading flames and thought she saw an object, but she wasn't sure. The flames grew as though on steroids, biting, grabbing at everything in their path. Soon it would be her.

But she had to know. Katie dropped to the floor where she was able to grab some air. She moved toward the flames until the heat became unbearable. She gasped, choked on the lungful of smoke and scrambled back, but not before she caught a glimpse of what looked like a soda bottle resting against her door. As she moved back toward the window, she mentally filled in the blanks as to what had happened.

Someone had cut a hole in her window and tossed in a Molotov cocktail. Would he be waiting on her when she was forced to leave the room?

Smoke thickened, closing her lungs and burning her eyes. Light-headed, she forced back the panic and sent prayers heavenward. She didn't have a choice.

She stood and shoved the window up. Fresh cold air blew in and she sucked in a lungful, but she didn't climb out as she considered her options.

Her hesitation saved her as a gunshot shattered the window just above her head. Heart pounding, she ducked back to the floor and lifted the phone. "Officer in trouble. I need help now!"

"Help is en route, ma'am."

"How far away?"

"Two minutes."

"I don't have that long!" She took a shallow breath of the air near the floor. *Just keep breathing. Don't pass out.*

Nothing to do but get out. And not through her bedroom door. Or the bedroom window. On hands and knees, she spun, her brain whirling. The bathroom. Flames crept toward the door. Once she went in, she wasn't coming out. Katie took a deep breath, coughed until she thought she might lose a lung and darted inside. She slammed the door shut and raced toward the window.

She pushed it up and kicked the screen out of the way.

Smoke filled the bathroom and stars danced before her eyes even as another breath of fresh air wafted over her. With a prayer on her lips, she gripped the windowsill and hauled herself over. As she hit the bushes below, she heard the crack of a gunshot and felt the bite of the bullet.

SIX

Jordan heard the gunshot as he stepped out of his car. His heartbeat kicked into overdrive. "Cort!"

Cort was already racing for the back of the house. The next crack came seconds later. Jordan came to the edge of the house, weapon in hand, wrists pressed to his chest, the muzzle of the gun aimed toward the night sky. With one swift move, he swung around. And found the area empty.

But Katie's house on fire.

"Katie!" Jordan flinched at the sight of the flames roaring from her bedroom window. "Oh, no," he whispered. "Katie!"

The moon revealed a dark figure running the length of the back fence, a rifle clutched in his left hand. Cort bolted after him while Jordan raced toward the broken window of Katie's bedroom. Smoke gushed from the opening and he couldn't get close. Terror shot through him. *No, God, no. Don't let it be. Please, Lord.*

He heard the sirens coming. But it was too late. There was no way Katie would survive. He sank to his knees as firefighters rounded the house and turned their hoses on the blaze. He knew more were out front doing the same.

Movement caught his attention. He turned, weapon ready—and nearly dropped it in shock. "Katie!"

She stumbled toward him, face pale, blood soaking her left arm. He raced to her, yelling, "I need a paramedic!"

Then, worried no one would hear him over the roar of the water, he scooped her up and headed for the front of the house. Her head lolled against his shoulder. "I'm okay," she whispered. "I think it looks worse than it is." A deep cough racked her and Jordan held her even tighter. "Hurts to breathe." Her rasp told him she'd inhaled her share of smoke.

He was as worried about that as he was the wound in her left shoulder.

Jordan raced to the nearest ambulance. Two paramedics leaped from the vehicle. "Set her on the gurney." Tall, with wavy blond hair pulled into a functional ponytail, a woman who looked to be in her mid-thirties was the first to speak. Her confident, professional manner gave Jordan a small measure of relief. He laid Katie on the gurney just as Cort rushed up.

"He got away. Had a motorcycle stashed just up the road. She all right?"

Jordan stepped back out of the way as the paramedics took over, however, he didn't take his eyes from her still form. "I'm not sure." Anxiety twisted his insides. "What happened? How'd he get past you?"

Cort swiped a gloved hand over his salt-and-pepper hair. "He knew I was here and set up a distraction. I heard a bunch of pops. Turned out to be a whole string of firecrackers about two doors up." Cort's lips tightened and his jaw flexed. "I went to investigate and I guess he slipped around to the back of the house while my attention was diverted." Cort gave a disgusted sigh and muttered, "Can't believe I fell for that. As soon as I saw those things popping in the street, I knew what he'd done. I raced back and saw you climbing out of the car." He looked at Jordan and frowned. "What are you doing here, anyway? How'd you know there was trouble?"

"I didn't. I was going to come tell you to go home since I couldn't sleep." He stepped back up and grasped Katie's hand. Her eyes flickered and she shoved aside the oxygen mask with her good hand. The fact that she was conscious encouraged him.

He looked at the paramedic. "What's your name?"

"Christine."

"How is she?"

Christine moved the mask back into place. "She needs to be checked out by a doctor and get that wound on her shoulder stitched up. The bullet dug a nice groove, but missed anything major. CSU will probably find the bullet embedded somewhere inside."

Thankfulness washed over him. She wasn't hurt as badly as he'd feared. Jordan squeezed her hand. "I'll follow in my car."

He looked back to see Faith Nelson step out of the CSU van. She spotted him and rushed over. "Is Katie all right?"

He nodded to the ambulance. "She's okay for now. She's headed over to the hospital to get checked out." He shook his head. "He shot at her. There are bullets in there somewhere."

Faith looked at the house and the firefighters who worked hard to put out the blaze. "Might be a while before I can get in there to look."

"Yeah."

"But I'll find the bullets if they're in there."

"I'd be interested to know if they match the ones from the diner."

"She's stable," Christine told him. "We're ready to transport her."

"She needs a bodyguard." He had an idea. He dialed Gregory Lee's number. In short, concise sentences, he filled the man in. "Can you meet us at the hospital? Do you have anyone that can watch out for her?"

"Yeah. We've got buddies who'll take vacation days if they have to to help keep her safe."

Jordan had figured that would be the case. "Thanks. I'm on the way to the hospital with her now. Uniformed officers are on the scene. Some are searching for the shooter, others are going door to door telling the neighbors what happened and to lock up tight until this guy is caught."

"Good." A pause. "Does this have to do with her sister's case?"

"It's looking more and more like it."

"Man." A sigh filtered through the line. "All right. I'll see you at the hospital."

The ambulance doors slammed shut and Jordan ran to his car and climbed in to follow behind.

Katie woke, drew in a deep breath, choked and gave a ragged, hacking cough. When she opened her watery eyes, she saw Erica on one side of her bed and Jordan on the other. "What's going on?" she rasped.

Erica pushed Katie's hair from her eyes. "You don't remember?"

Katie frowned. The fire. So that's why her throat,

her chest, her eyes...everything hurt. "I remember. My weapon!"

Jordan said, "We found it behind the bush under your bathroom window. I've got it locked in my glove compartment." He didn't even blink at the fact that her weapon was her first thought. Erica looked slightly bemused, but she had been around law enforcement enough to know no cop wanted their weapon in the hands of the wrong person. Katie must have dropped hers when she fell out of the bathroom window and behind the bushes.

She wilted back against the pillow. "My house..."

"Your bedroom is destroyed," Jordan said, "but it looks like they were able to save the rest of it—other than the water damage. Gregory said you kept a copy of all your major personal records at the office. He found your home insurance number and they'll be out there first thing Monday morning."

For some silly reason, Katie felt tears fill her eyes. She blinked them back. "Thanks. And Mariah?"

"I've filled her in," Erica said. "She said she'd be by to see you soon."

"And these are for you." Jordan reached behind him and picked up a large vase that held a gorgeous bouquet of flowers. "Oh, my," she breathed. "Who are those from?"

Jordan shuffled his feet and she thought she saw a red tint creep into his cheeks. "Me. I thought they'd brighten things up around here."

Her heart skittered, skipped a beat then pounded into overdrive. "They're beautiful. Thank you so much."

He shrugged and ducked his head in a gesture of shyness that touched her. And made her appreciate the gesture all the more because she could tell he was uncomfortable.

Erica cleared her throat and held up Katie's purse. "Your partner found this in the den and brought it for you. It was a little waterlogged, but I think it might survive." She placed another bag on the bed beside Katie. "And these are some clothes for when you leave. I don't think you want anything to do with your wardrobe right now."

"Thank you. That's helpful."

Katie moved and winced at the fire racing through her shoulder. "He shot at me. Feels like he hit me. How bad is it?"

"Not bad at all." The voice from the door dragged her attention from her visitors. A tall woman with dark skin and even darker eyes approached the bed.

She held out a hand and Katie shook it. "I'm Dr. Sterling." She opened the chart. "You've got a nice wound, and it'll take a while to heal. You've also got about sixteen stitches. We've got you on an antibiotic drip and have treated you for smoke inhalation. That handy little device next to you is a morphine pump for the pain, but we'll give you a prescription you can take at home if you need it. You should be good to go first thing in the morning."

Katie blinked. She'd escaped relatively unscathed. *Thank You, Lord.* Exhaustion swamped her. All she wanted to do was sleep. "No more narcotics," she whispered. "What time is it?"

Jordan glanced at his watch. "Eight forty-five."

"Thursday morning?"

"Yes."

She gasped. "My parents. They'll be worried that I haven't shown up or called or—" She struggled to sit up but Jordan placed a hand on her arm with a glance at the doctor.

"Erica called them."

"Oh." She lay back against the pillow as reality sank in. Her parents knew she was hurt and in the hospital, but they weren't here. Hurt seared her. She would have thought her father would come by even if her mother refused. Then again, maybe it was better if he didn't.

Katie swallowed hard and wondered if she'd ever get to the point where she could just accept her mother's rejection and get on with her life. Maybe. Maybe she would just have to let God's love be enough. But she wasn't sure she knew how to do that.

Even though the pain of her parents' absence swirled within, her eyelids drooped. Dr. Sterling smiled. "Get some rest. I'll check back with you in a few hours."

Erica patted her hand as the door closed. "Why don't you listen to your doctor and get some rest? I'm going to sit here for a while."

"And I'm going to be around," Jordan said.

"What are you doing here? How did you know to show up last night?"

"I couldn't sleep."

"So you thought you'd come watch my house?"

"You need a bodyguard."

She forced herself to focus on him. "And you're taking on that job?" she rasped.

His eyes narrowed, then his face softened. "Can't think of any other job I'd rather do right now."

Katie wanted to respond, but let the drugs and fatigue take over. She felt a smile curve her lips before the darkness crept in.

She opened her eyes at the sound of the knock on the

door. Erica was nowhere to be seen. Jordan stood from the chair where he'd been dozing. Katie blinked, wondering how long she'd slept, but noticed with relief she didn't feel so drugged now.

When Jordan opened the door and her father stepped into the room, her heart gave a fast beat of joy. He'd come.

"Katie?" Concern knit his brows almost together at the bridge of his nose. "Are you all right?"

Her father's fifty-six-year-old face had aged a bit since she'd seen him last week. How was it possible to think he had a few more lines around his mouth, a bit more gray in his hair? "Hey, Dad. I'm all right."

He walked over to stand next to her. "Erica called us."

"Us?" She couldn't help it. She looked behind him, but knew her mother wouldn't be there. Katie's mother couldn't be bothered with the daughter who'd let her youngest child be taken. It didn't matter that Katie had been only fourteen years old. It didn't matter that she'd been asked by an adult to help carry groceries into the house. What her mother couldn't get over was the fact that Katie simply hadn't made Lucy go with her. That Katie had taken her eyes off her sister for approximately ten minutes and the girl had vanished while on Katie's watch.

Her father cleared his throat. "Me. Your mother wasn't feeling very well and—"

"You don't have to make excuses for her, Dad. I get it."

He flushed and shoved his hands deeper into his pockets. "Yeah. I guess you do."

And that was all that would be said about it. She sighed as fresh pain ripped through her. Would her mother never forgive her? "I sent her some chocolates for her birthday. Did she get them?"

"She did. And ate every one of them." He smiled and Katie thought it looked a little forced. "We enjoyed the meal you sent over, too. Not necessary, but she appreciated it."

"I just wanted to do something for her. And you." Only she was getting the feeling no matter what she did, it would never be enough. She swallowed hard and motioned to Jordan. "This is Jordan Gray. He's with Finding the Lost. Jordan, this is Bryce Randall, my father."

The two men shook hands.

"Glad to meet you," Jordan said. He looked from her father to her, his curious, watchful gaze making her want to squirm. If it wouldn't hurt her shoulder too much.

"Thanks for coming, Dad. Hopefully, I'll be out of here pretty soon."

"Does this have to do with a case you're working?"

Her gaze met Jordan's. She wasn't ready to tell her father anything yet. "We don't know for sure. We haven't really had time to figure that out."

He looked at Jordan. "Do you mind if I have a moment alone with Katie?"

"Of course." Jordan moved toward the door, and Katie wanted to protest, grab him back and make him stay right beside her. The panicked need for his presence, his protection, stunned her. This was her dad. She could talk to him. And she certainly didn't need Jordan's protection.

Once Jordan let the door close behind him, her father turned to her and swallowed hard. "Are you still looking for Lucy?"

Katie jerked at her sister's name. It had been so long since she'd heard either parent say it. She gave a short nod. She wasn't going to be the one to bring it up, but she wouldn't lie about it either. "Of course I am."

He sighed and rubbed his eyes. "I thought so."

Katie fidgeted with the blanket. "Is that a problem?" She couldn't help the challenge in her tone.

"It could be." He paused and gripped her hand. "Maybe you should just…let her go."

Her head snapped up. "Like you and Mom have let her go?"

He flinched and she wished the words back. And yet she didn't. His jaw firmed and his eyes narrowed. "Katie, I'm serious. She's been gone for fourteen years. She's probably…d-d-dead." Tears appeared and he blinked them back before they could fall. He took a deep breath. "Just…let her go, get a life. Find a man who loves you and give your mom and me some grandkids." He gave her a faint smile. "I think that would go a long way toward your mother's healing."

I don't deserve to get married, have a child. Be happy. She bit her lip on the words, shocked at how loudly they rang in her mind. She'd tried falling in love once and he'd died. The whole thing with her fiancé had just reinforced the fact that her purpose here on earth was to find Lucy. Then she could be happy. Maybe even be forgiven. "I can't do that, Dad," she whispered.

His hand reached out and grasped her shoulder. "You have to."

She cried out, the harsh tone and his hard grip on her injured shoulder so out of character. She stared at him through the fog of pain and medication. He jerked back at her cry, the stricken look on his face apology enough.

"Dad, please. Stop. You're scaring me." Not really physically, but she didn't recognize this man. He was usually a man who abhorred violence of any kind, but now he curled his fingers into a fist and punched it into his other palm. Sorrow—and fear?—filled his gaze, and he leaned over and kissed the top of her head. Another shock to her system. He hadn't displayed much affection toward her in the last fourteen years. *Maybe because you haven't let him.* She ignored the taunting voice and pulled back to look up at him. "What is it, Dad? What else is going on? You're not telling me something."

His face paled. "Nothing. I just want to see you happy, Katie. Believe it or not, that's all I want. Let Lucy go."

And then he was gone.

SEVEN

Jordan leaned his forehead against the smooth wall and took a deep breath. He needed to go jogging or put in a good workout in the gym. But Katie came first. It was obvious to him that someone didn't want her—or him—nosing around asking about a fourteen-year-old kidnapping.

Why? And who?

The why was easy to figure out. The who was a little more difficult. Was it the kidnapper himself, afraid of what they might find? Or someone who knew who'd taken Lucy and was protecting the kidnapper?

He slowed and considered the two questions. If it was the kidnapper, how did he even know they were investigating again? The answer to that was the person was someone Katie interacted with on a regular basis. Or was it someone he'd interviewed from the neighborhood?

One thing gave him hope—and scared him to death. If any of the above were true, that meant the kidnapper was still around. Somewhere close. On the one hand, that was good. On the other, it could mean Lucy was dead and the kidnapper was afraid their digging would bring evidence to light as to his identity.

Jordan paced the length of the hallway in front of Katie's room. The door opened and her father stepped into the hall, nodded to Jordan and turned to walk away. He stopped midstride and spun back to meet Jordan's gaze.

Jordan lifted a brow. "Everything all right?"

A sigh filtered between Bryce Randall's lips as he walked toward Jordan. "No. Not really."

"May I help in some way?"

Mr. Randall rubbed his palms against his khaki-clad thighs. "How close are you to Katie? How much influence do you have with her?"

Jordan grunted. "Not much, I'm afraid."

The man's face fell. "Oh."

"Why?"

He blew out a sigh and blinked as though holding back tears. "I want her to stop looking for Lucy."

Not what he'd expected to hear. "Again, why?"

Mr. Randall rubbed a hand over his lips. His nails had been chewed to the quick and a fine tremble ran through his fingers. "Look, it's been fourteen years. If Katie keeps letting this…obsession…control her life, pretty soon she's not going to have a life. And I really don't want to lose another daughter."

Jordan shoved his hands in his pockets and rocked back on his heels. "I see."

"Do you?"

"Yes. I think I do. I don't want her in danger any more than you do."

Bryce's shrewd eyes narrowed. "You might not have a lot of influence with her, but she means something to you, doesn't she?"

"She's…a friend. As well as a partner. Of sorts."

"Uh-huh."

Jordan changed the subject. "Where's Katie's mother? I would think she'd want to be with Katie at this time."

Bryce Randall winced. "Katie's mother isn't well. Hasn't been since Lucy disappeared." He swallowed hard. "In some ways I lost my wife that day, too." He drew in a shuddering breath. "If I lose Katie, I won't live through it and neither will her mother."

A debate raged in Jordan's head. Should he say what he was thinking or keep quiet? His mouth made up his mind. "Katie really needs to hear that from you."

"I told her. Sort of."

"But more importantly, I think she needs to hear it from her mother." Jordan debated whether to say anything more, then went for it. "She's trying to win her mother's love back. She thinks constantly doing for you and her mother is the way to get her to love her again."

Raw pain glittered from the man's eyes. "I know. And that's a topic for another day. For now, please, do your best to convince Katie it's time to let Lucy go. To let her rest in peace."

"Then you think she's dead?"

Bryce's sad eyes met his. "Don't you?"

Katie wanted nothing more than to crawl in bed and shut the world out. Between Gregory and Jordan, they'd made sure she had ample security for her overnight stay at the hospital.

Though she had been sure that Wednesday night would never end, Thursday morning had finally come. And so had the doctor, followed by the nurse bearing her discharge papers. Now she sat in the passenger seat of Jordan's car and pulled the seat belt across her shoulder to click into place. "I could have gotten Erica to come get me."

"I know. She offered, but I told her I wanted to take you home."

Curious, she looked at him. "Why? You have something more about Lucy's case?"

"Maybe, but that's not the only reason."

"What else?" Katie thought she saw a light shade of red bloom on Jordan's cheeks and blinked, sure she must have imagined it. "What else?"

He glanced at her. "Because I wanted to be with you."

Katie swallowed hard. "Oh."

He gave a restrained laugh. One without humor. "Come on, Katie, I know we're working together, but you've got to admit there's a certain…something…between us." He pulled out of the parking lot, his eyes active, roaming between all the mirrors, and she knew he was worried about being followed.

"A something?" she asked.

"A something."

"Ooookay."

"Now, we can either address it. Or ignore it."

Katie chewed on her lip, flashes of the confrontation with his father at the morgue running through her mind. "I'm hungry."

Jordan gave a half laugh, half groan. "Okay. We're going to ignore it, then?"

"For now."

"Right. What are you in the mood for?"

"A cheeseburger. A good one, not a frozen one."

"How about Randy's?" Her stomach growled, and he shot her a smile. "I guess that was approval."

"Definitely." His smile sent her heart pounding in a

wild dance, her pulse skittering, the butterflies fluttering in the pit of her stomach. Even though she was afraid to acknowledge the attraction to him, she couldn't very well deny it to herself.

But it scared her.

And thrilled her all at the same time.

But she wasn't going to do anything about it yet. She still had to find Lucy and couldn't let her feelings distract her.

Besides, his parents hated her.

He pulled into the parking lot at Randy's and she climbed out of the car, moving slowly in order not to tear her stitches.

"You were very lucky, you know." He stared at her shoulder.

"I'm not sure I attribute it to luck." She touched the bandage. "Right now, I'm giving God the credit."

"Yeah."

They entered the restaurant with Jordan watching her back. Katie kept her eyes open for anything that made her uneasy. The smell of grilling burgers and fried potatoes greeted her, making her stomach growl once more. She licked her lips, ready to eat. She didn't mind hospital food, but there was no way she was going to turn down Randy's burgers.

Once settled, she set the menu aside, already knowing her order. "What are you getting?"

"I'll get what I always get. Breakfast. Eggs, bacon, grits and sometimes a steak. But the grits are my favorite. I don't know what Randy does to those grits, but I've yet to find anyone to match him for the flavor."

"You come here a lot?"

"Weekly. Sometimes daily. And I always get the grits."

She laughed as the waitress approached with their water. She gave a flirtatious wink at Jordan. "It's been a while since you've been in, Jordan. Good to see you haven't forgotten us." She turned to Katie and gave her a sweet smile. "What can I get you?"

Once they'd given their order, Katie leaned back with a grimace.

"Sore?" Jordan asked.

"In spades."

His lips tightened. "I should have taken you home."

"And miss Randy's? Not a chance." She sipped her water. "I'm on medical leave for the next week," she said softly.

"Why do I get the feeling you have something other than resting and healing on your agenda?"

She lifted a brow. "Nothing gets past you, does it?"

He smiled at her. Within a few minutes, their food was in front of them. Jordan paused like he might be waiting on her to say a blessing. Even as disappointed with God as she was, she found she couldn't ignore Him. He still gave her hope and she found strength in leaning on His promises.

So she still prayed, and she still wanted to say grace over her food. Katie bowed her head and Jordan followed her cue. His low voice reached her ears. "Lord, we thank You for this food and for Katie's safety. Please guide us as we continue to search for Lucy. Let us bring her kidnapper to justice and give her family closure. Amen."

"Amen," she whispered. "Thanks."

Katie dug into her burger. The first bite sent her taste buds dancing. They ate in silence until Jordan's phone rang. He glanced at the number and set his fork down. "Hello?" He listened, the furrow between his brows easing as he nodded. "Great. Great. Thanks so much." He hung up.

"What was that all about?" Katie asked.

"That was one of your former neighbors I'd managed to track down. She no longer lives in the neighborhood, but she's still friends with Elaine Johnson. I'd left a message for her to call me if she knew anything about Mrs. Johnson. Apparently, Mrs. Johnson is now a resident of White Oak Manor's assisted-living program."

"Oh, what a shame. I guess that means her health is failing."

"Look like that's the case."

"But at least we know where she is now."

"Exactly. I suggest we get over to White Oak as soon as possible and see if she can tell you anything more."

Katie nodded but frowned. "I really don't think there's going to be anything for her to tell me, but I'm ready to give it another go."

"I'm assuming you haven't heard anything back from your sketch artist?"

She blinked and grabbed her phone. "In all the craziness, I forgot to call her back. I saw her number on my phone this morning."

Her phone buzzed, and she snagged it. "Hello, Gregory."

"Hey, just thought I'd let you know that we've got the guy who killed Wesley Wray."

"Who is it?"

"An inmate by the name of Charlie West."

"Did he say why he killed Wesley?"

"Just that Wray was on his last nerve so he decided to get rid of him. Charlie's in for the rest of his life. He had nothing to lose killing Wray."

"Someone paid him to do it. Will you check his family members' bank accounts and see if we can find a money trail to follow?"

"Already thought of that. West is married with kids. His wife just had five grand deposited into her account this morning."

"So that's what a person's life is worth these days," Katie muttered.

Gregory said, "I'll keep you updated as I get information. I'm working on tracking the money."

"Okay, thanks."

She hung up and brought Jordan up to date. He thought about it. "I guess we need to question Mr. West."

"I guess so."

"Then let's—"

His sharply indrawn breath snagged her attention from the phone. "What is it?"

He shot her a look full of apology. "My parents. Heading this way."

Katie's stomach dipped to her toes. The last time she'd seen Paul and Lisa Gray, they'd been staring down at the body of their dead son and blaming her for his death. She swallowed hard, suddenly having to fight to keep the hamburger down.

Jordan fought the knot of dread from in his gut. He shouldn't have brought Katie here. Not when his parents ate here almost as often as he did. What had he been thinking?

His father's eyes lit up when he saw him and he and his mother made their way toward him. And Katie.

His mother's eyes landed on the back of Katie's head and a smile lifted the corners of her lips because she didn't know who Jordan was eating with. Yet. Jordan bit back a groan. He stood, desperate to cut them off.

He stepped forward and held out his hand. His dad shook it while his mother tried to get a glimpse of the woman sharing her son's table.

His father asked, "You're still planning on coming to dinner Sunday, right?"

Jordan nodded. "Yes, I'll be there."

"And who is this lovely—" Lisa's shocked gasp could be heard around the restaurant. Jordan closed his eyes and said a quick prayer. His father frowned and stepped around his wife to see what had her pale and trembling.

"You!"

Katie stood and wiped her mouth with her napkin. She shot Jordan a look full of apology. "Hello." The word trembled on her lips, and he wanted to hug her for the effort.

A strangled sound came from Paul's throat and his wild, stunned gaze landed back on Jordan. "Her? What are you doing here with her? You would sit at the same table with her?"

Jordan saw they had the attention of the restaurant and he rested a hand on his mother's elbow. "Why don't you get a seat? Katie and I were getting ready to leave. I'll come by later and explain everything."

"Explain? What's there to explain? I can see exactly what's going on." With a scathing glance at Katie, Paul took Lisa's elbow. "I won't breathe the same air as her. We'll find somewhere else to eat." He escorted his wife from the restaurant.

Katie sat with a thump, her face pale and pinched.

Jordan sat across from her and reached for her hand. He squeezed it and she pulled away from him. Still looking at the door where his parents had made their sudden departure, she asked, "Will you please just take me home now? I'm not feeling well."

"Katie, I'm sorry."

"No." She finally looked at him and the anguish there tore at his heart. "It's not your fault."

"It's not anyone's fault but Neil's and the killer who attacked him."

She sighed and pushed her plate aside with a trembling hand. "Just take me home." She blinked. "Then again, I guess home is out of the question. Will you take me to a hotel?"

"I thought Erica said you could stay with her."

"She did, but I refuse to put her and Molly in danger. A hotel will be fine."

Jordan didn't like it, but he nodded and she rose, dug into her purse and dropped a ten-dollar bill on the table. He grabbed it and pushed it back into her hand. "I got this one."

It said a lot about her fragile state of mind when she just took the money and walked to the door without another word.

Jordan almost asked her to stay inside and wait for him before walking to the car, but he didn't have to. She stood by the door, ignoring a few of the still-staring patrons. As the cashier handed him his change, he stole another glance in her direction. She'd squared her shoulders and planted her hands on her hips as she stood to the side of the door and examined the parking lot.

Jordan pocketed the money and walked over to her. "See anything?"

"No. I don't see him, but he's watching."

"All right then, let's go find him."

EIGHT

Katie set her small bag of borrowed clothes on the sofa. She looked around. "It's a nice room."

A small suite, it had a mini kitchen that opened into a sitting area complete with a full-size couch and a flat-screen television. The work area was next to the sliding glass doors that led to a small balcony. A king-size bed and bathroom in a separate room rounded out the suite.

Jordan went through it as though he thought her attacker would be waiting. He'd retrieved her weapon and the comforting weight of it at the small of her back allowed her to breathe a little easier. Using the shoulder holster was out of the question with her injury.

She glanced at the clock on the microwave. Twelve forty-five. It felt like it should be a.m., not p.m.

"Cort will be watching your room tonight," Jordan said as he walked back into the main living area. "He feels guilty for letting that guy get so close to you."

"It wasn't his fault."

"He doesn't feel that way."

"I really don't think there was anything he could have done differently."

"That's what I keep telling him." His phone rang. "Hello?"

Katie placed the rescued file on the desk and started pulling the papers out one at a time as she listened to his side of the conversation.

"Thanks, Max." Jordan hung up. "Max said he parked your car four doors down from your room."

"Good."

"He also said he doesn't think he was followed, but can't vouch for that a hundred percent."

"I trust him."

"But you'll still give the car the once-over before you get in it, right?"

She lifted a brow. "Of course." Katie turned her attention back to the papers. "They're dry now. Might be a little hard to read, but…"

"You really don't need the file at this point, do you?"

He took a seat at the table.

She shrugged. "No. The only thing I didn't have memorized was your notes, but I read them."

"I've got copies." He paused. "I'm sorry about my parents."

Pain darted through her. She met his gaze for a brief moment, then dropped her eyes to the file. "You don't have to apologize for them. They're entitled to their pain."

"But they're not entitled to lash out at you."

"They have to have someone to blame. I suppose I'm the best choice for that. I arrested their son and he died." She paused then asked, "Do they even acknowledge the fact that he was drinking and driving?"

"No. They're convinced it was all just a mistake, a misunderstanding." She stared at him and he shrugged with a sad frown. "They're not in touch with reality when it comes to Neil's death."

"Have you tried to tell them?"

He gave her a shuttered look. "I've tried. A little."

She gave a trembling sigh. "Why don't you feel the same as your parents?"

He flushed and shook his head. "I did for a while. But working with you, even in a limited capacity, on Molly James's kidnapping transformed my opinion of you. I realized for the first time that you weren't some egotistical cop who had something to prove by teaching a drunk kid a lesson. You can't predict the future. You put a drunk man in a cell with other drunks. It happens every day. It's what cops do."

"I know, I just wish…" she rasped. Emotion choked her almost as much as the smoke she'd inhaled. She cleared her throat and stood, walked to the window and placed herself to the side so she could see out, but anyone watching wouldn't be able to see her. The parking lot was half full. No one loitering in the shadows that she could tell.

"And—"

When he broke off, she looked at him. "And?"

"And there's stuff about Neil they don't know." He glanced away, then back. "Stuff I haven't told them."

She lifted a brow. "Like what?"

"It doesn't matter at this point. Suffice it to say I'm not sure I'm doing them a favor and am praying about it."

Completely baffled, she stared at him. He shook his head. "Never mind."

Okay, then. When—if—he decided to share with her whatever he was talking about, she'd listen. Until then…

Katie asked, "What about this neighbor, Mrs. McKinney? I talked to her twice but didn't get much."

At first he didn't answer and she wondered if he was ready to change the subject. She let out a small breath of relief when he did. Talking about Neil and his parents caused a hard knot to form in her stomach. She needed to talk about something different. He finally said, "She'd brought her husband home from the doctor about three hours after Lucy disappeared. When they got home, they saw all the commotion, but no one really talked to them because they weren't there when it happened. I thought about going to see her." He shrugged. "And while I doubt she can tell us anything, I don't want to leave any stone unturned."

She nodded. "First I have a stop to make."

"Where to?"

"I want to go see Frank and ask him a couple of questions. He told me to come see him at four, but I'm going to see if he'll be willing to just talk to me if I walk in. If he's there."

"Ah." He pursed his lips and looked like he might argue the wisdom of that. Instead, he stood and she followed him down the steps to his car. "I'm going to hunt down Tracy, too, and see if she's got a composite of our shooter."

As she slid into the passenger seat, she supposed she ought to get her own vehicle. In fact she was quite surprised at her rather passive agreement in letting him be her chauffeur. The truth was, she liked the man. Liked being with him, liked his sense of humor, liked bouncing the case off of him and getting his feedback.

And that worried her. Jordan was very easy to be around, but somewhere in his eyes, there was a pain that never really went away. She wondered about it. Wondered if he'd ever share it with her.

Then wondered why she wanted him to. They had no future together. His parents had already lost one son because of her. There was no way she'd cause them any more pain by falling in love with the other.

"You okay?"

He pulled her out of her disturbing thoughts and she nodded, turning to stare out the window. "Just thinking."

"Yeah. I know what you mean."

Her phone rang. Gregory. "Hey."

"Hey. I tracked the money that landed in West's account."

"Great. Where'd it come from?"

"It was a cash deposit, so I don't have a name, just a video snapshot of the guy who made the deposit. Trying to get a name to match the face."

"Send the face to Jordan's phone. He can use his resources with the FBI and put their facial recognition software to good use."

Jordan nodded. Within seconds, his phone dinged and he pulled over to shoot the email to his buddy at the FBI. Katie hung up with Gregory feeling like they were making baby steps, but at least they weren't going backward.

The rest of the drive to the station didn't take long. Jordan drove with practiced ease while Katie kept her gaze glued to the mirrors.

"You see anyone that makes you twitchy?"

"No. Not yet."

"Me, either."

"Doesn't mean he's not there," she muttered.

"Yeah."

He pulled into the parking lot, and Katie stared at

the building that had become her second home. "Should have just brought a sleeping bag and slept in my office."

He laughed. "Might be the safest place in the city for you."

She shook her head and climbed out of the vehicle. Katie led the way into the station, eyes scanning the familiar area. Fellow officers called out well wishes and a few even offered hugs. Jordan tapped her arm. "I'm going to be in the evidence room. I want to take a look at the original file on Lucy again."

"There's nothing in it that you haven't seen. I copied everything."

He shrugged. "You're probably right, but I just want to take a look."

"Sure." Katie passed her desk and went straight to Frank's.

He looked up and jerked in surprise. "Hey, I didn't expect to see you."

"We had a four o'clock appointment, remember?"

"Yes, of course. I just figured after last night…" He shrugged. "Glad you're okay." He glanced at his watch. "It's not four."

"I know." She smiled. "Do you have few minutes? I've got some other things I need to do. I'm not planning on coming back here after I leave, so I would appreciate it if you'd just talk to me now."

"You still want to go over your sister's case?"

"If you don't mind. I have a question or two I still need answered."

He sighed. "Have a seat."

Katie sat and reached in her bag to pull out Lucy's file. She opened it on the desk in front of her and turned it so it was right side up for Frank. She pointed to the small slip of paper with the diner's address. "Jordan and I went here yesterday and talked to the owner. It's also where we were shot at."

Frank frowned at her. "You've had a rough couple of days."

"I have, but that's not important right now. I talked to Betty June Clark, and she said she remembers the case. And the two detectives who worked it."

"Really?" He leaned back and crossed his arms. Then sat forward. "Wait a minute, I remember her. Pretty blonde?"

"Yes."

He nodded. "She thought the kidnapper had come in with Lucy and eaten there. Called us to check it out."

"Right."

"At the time, there were no surveillance cameras working. The place was pretty run-down. We talked to her and the other workers, but came up with pretty much nothing."

"What about the hair in the bathroom?"

"What hair?"

Impatience licked at her. "Betty said the girl had chopped hair and she found hair around the toilet in the men's bathroom. Said she told you and Danny Jackson about it."

"Yes, I remember something about that, but if I remember correctly, it had already been cleaned up by the time we got in there." He rubbed his eyes. "Come on, Katie, it's been fourteen years. I haven't looked at that case since we filed it with cold cases." He spread his hands, palms up, in a helpless gesture. "I can't remember everything."

She held her temper in check. He was right. It had

been a long time. "Then maybe you remember this. Why wasn't your visit there documented in the folder?"

He frowned. "It was. Both Danny and I filled out reports."

She tapped the file. "Nothing but that little scrap of paper with the address."

He sighed and rubbed his eyes. "I don't know, Katie, you know how it is. You have ten cases going at the same time and sometimes things might…" He trailed off.

"Slip through the cracks?" she asked softly, her tone deadly.

"No, no, not that, just—you're talking fourteen years ago."

She got up before she said something she shouldn't.

"Katie, stop. Come on. I didn't mean we didn't do our jobs. We did. We wrote the reports. I don't know why they're not in the file."

She kept her back to him and took a deep breath. "If you remember, give me a call, will you?"

"Of course."

"Thanks." She started to leave then turned back. "Have you seen Tracy?"

"Uh…yeah. She was near the break room right before you came over."

She left, the file clutched tight, thankful it hadn't been destroyed in the fire.

Katie had another idea. She found Jordan in the break room studying the file. "Find anything?"

"Nothing really. You?"

She shook her head and took a deep breath. "I've had this feeling before, but today sealed it."

"What feeling?"

"That the investigation was botched. Whatever word

you want to use, Frank Miller and Danny Jackson did my sister and my family an injustice."

He frowned. "What did he say about the diner?"

She told him. "I want to go talk to his former partner, Danny Jackson."

"He's on my list, but I haven't talked to him yet."

"I talked to him briefly about a year ago, but he was more interested in his golfing handicap than he was in rehashing a cold case."

"That's unusual. Most retired guys relish talking about their cases."

"Yeah, the cases they've solved. Not the ones that got away."

"True." He closed the file. "You were right. You copied every last teeny, tiny piece of information in this file, didn't you?"

"I did."

He stood. "Let me put this back and we can go."

"I'm going to see if I can find Tracy." She told him where the woman's office was.

He said, "I'll meet you there."

Katie left him to return the file and headed down a long hallway and to the second floor. She leaned against the wall to catch her breath and realized her lungs still hadn't fully recovered from her bout with the fire. The burning in her shoulder was aggravating, but nothing she couldn't ignore. Once she got her breath, she knocked on the door.

"Come in."

Katie stepped inside to see Tracy at her desk, phone pressed to her ear. When she saw Katie, she hung up. "I was just dialing your number." She frowned with concern. "How are you feeling?"

"Like I need an oxygen tank strapped to my back, but other than that, I'm all right."

"Have you heard anything back about the fire? How it started?"

"A Molotov cocktail through my bedroom window."

"Ouch." Her friend winced. "You've made someone a little angry?"

"Yeah, a little."

"Who?"

"I've no idea." She didn't want to discuss the fire or the fact that someone wanted her dead. "Hey, do you have the composite for the shooter at the diner? Bobby Young is our witness."

Tracy blinked at her. "No, I don't have it. He never came in, and he hasn't answered my calls."

Unease crawled up Katie's spine. "What do you mean he never came? He was coming as soon as he could after he got his car towed, got checked out at the hospital and changed his clothes. I think he had some blood on them and wanted to change. You're saying he didn't come over?"

"Right. I left a message on your voice mail at home yesterday morning." She grimaced. "Which means you probably didn't get it."

"No. It's been so crazy, I haven't even called to check my messages. Why didn't you leave one on my cell?"

"I started to, but the captain walked in just as I went to voice mail, so I just hung up. I figured you'd get the message at home anyway. Or see my number and call me. Which you did."

Katie nodded. "Thanks. I'm going to find Jordan and we'll see if we can track down Mr. Young." As she talked, she backed toward the door. And came up against what felt like a brick wall. She spun to find herself nose to chin with Jordan. His hands came up to cup her elbows. She jerked back and he gave her a crooked smile. But the glint in his narrowed eyes said he'd enjoyed the brief proximity.

Her pounding heart said she had, too.

Not going to happen, Katie, remember? His parents hate you.

She took a deep breath and filled Jordan in on the latest. His half smile dipped into full frown. "You have his address?"

She turned and looked at Tracy. "You have it?"

Tracy turned back to her computer and with a few clicks of her keyboard, she had Bobby Young's driver's license on the screen. Another click sent her printer humming. She handed the paper to Katie.

"Thanks."

"When you find him," Tracy said, "let me know."

"Count on it."

Katie walked beside Jordan as they headed down the steps and toward the exit. "Will you take me to pick up my car?"

"Now?"

"Yes. I prefer to have it."

"You sure you're feeling all right? You just got out of the hospital. You were shot, remember?"

She shot him a sardonic look. "Really? And besides, it was just a graze."

He gave a short laugh and said, "Sure."

In Jordan's car, as they headed back to the hotel, Katie's phone buzzed. "Hi, Erica."

"Hey, how are you feeling?"

"I've felt better, but I'm doing all right."

"Max and I want you and Jordan to come to dinner tonight. Do you think you can make it?"

"I don't know. I don't think that's very safe for you."

"It will be if you just make sure you're not followed."

Katie sighed. "You know I can't guarantee that."

"You don't want to stay here—I get that. But I think coming to eat will be fine."

Uneasiness twisted Katie's stomach into a knot. She probably should say no, but she hadn't seen Erica in a while and would love to spend time with her and Molly. But Erica wasn't finished. "I want to discuss your case, anyway. Might as well do it here as at the office."

"We're on our way to talk to a witness from the wreck."

"Then come after. It's all right if it's late. I'll get Molly settled with her favorite movie so we can talk uninterrupted."

Katie caved. "All right, then, let me ask Jordan." He glanced at her and she relayed the invitation. He nodded. "We'll be there," Katie said. "I'll call you when I'm on the way."

"Great. See you when you get here."

Katie gnawed on her lower lip. When a warm finger reached over to pull it from the clench of her upper front teeth, shivers ran through her. Jordan glanced at the traffic light then back to her. "You're going to chew right through it if you're not careful."

She swallowed hard and then gathered her wits as he pulled into the hotel parking lot. She grabbed her keys and said, "I'll meet you there."

"Watch your back."

"I always do."

Ten minutes later, she pulled behind Jordan to the

curb of Bobby Young's house. As far as she could tell, no one had followed.

The clock pushed toward two o'clock. She climbed from the car and looked around. Jordan approached and she asked, "I didn't see anyone following, did you?"

"Not a soul."

"That almost makes me nervous."

"I understand that completely."

Mr. Young's neighborhood was on a cul-de-sac with five other houses. Large lots and a lot of trees gave it a feeling of privacy and community at the same time. Katie nodded. "Nice place."

"Very."

Jordan walked up the steps to the porch of the traditional ranch and rang the bell. Katie kept an eye on the area around them. Right now, she didn't like being too exposed. The middle of her back between her shoulders itched.

No one answered the door.

"Not answering his phone, not answering the door. How old is he?" Katie asked.

"Sixty-four."

"He could be working or retired. Do we know?"

"I have his statement on my phone. Let me see if that information came up. Hold on a second." He pressed a few buttons. "Retired."

"Retired usually means not at work, but never at home if the retiree is in good health and active." She pointed to the flag hanging from the porch. "A golfer's flag. Might be on the course. We have another number for him?"

"Nope. That's his cell phone. He doesn't have a landline."

Katie pursed her lips and walked to the garage. The

double door was closed, but had four windows at the top. "I'm too short to see in. Wanna take a look?"

Jordan obliged. "A single car parked on the right side closest to the entry to the house. It's not the car from the wreck. Can't see the tags, but I'm willing to bet it's a rental."

"Then if his car is in the garage, why isn't he answering the door or his phone?"

Before Jordan could answer, his phone rang. He listened for a few minutes then hung up. Katie lifted a brow in silent question. Jordan said, "We got a hit on the guy at the bank who made the deposit into West's wife's account."

"Who is it?"

"A guy by the name of Norman Rhames."

"Never heard of him."

"Apparently he's got some ties to a terrorist group, but basically keeps his nose clean except for crimes that don't keep him behind bars for very long."

"We need to track down this Mr. Rhames and find out who had him deposit that money."

"Help you folks?"

Jordan turned to see a well-groomed lady in her mid-seventies standing in the drive next to Mr. Young's. She shut her mailbox and headed their way.

Jordan said, "We're looking for Mr. Young."

"He should be there. Although I didn't see him take his usual morning walk."

"He walks every day at the same time?" Katie asked.

"Pretty near every day. He's got a touch of arthritis but even when it's acting up, he doesn't let it keep him down for long." She pushed her glasses a little farther up on her nose. "You're not his daughter, are you?"

Katie said, "No, ma'am. I'm Detective Katie Randall with the police department. Mr. Young was involved in a wreck a couple of days ago. We just needed to ask him a few more questions." She flashed her badge and the woman placed a hand over her heart.

"He told me about that when he got home. He looked awful. I'd come outside for a short walk, and he pulled into the drive. His son Hunter picked him up from the hospital. Bobby had blood all over his clothes and everything. I asked if he needed anything and he said no, he just wanted to change and get to the police station. He'd seen the carjacker and needed to meet with the sketch artist. Sounded like something right off the television."

So he'd arrived home from the hospital and had planned to meet with Tracy.

"You're pretty good friends then?"

The woman smiled, her white teeth straight and even. "I'm Janice McDowell. And yes, Bobby and I are friends as well as neighbors. We try to look out for each other since we both live alone."

"How did Mr. Young plan to get to the police station?" Katie asked.

"He has another car. It was his wife's. He's never been able to sell it. Thankfully he wasn't hurt more than a scratch and a couple of bruises. And that carjacking! Why, what this world is coming to—" She shook her head.

"Do you have Hunter's number?" Katie asked.

"I might have it somewhere. Would take me a while to find it, probably." She looked at the phone in Jordan's left hand. "Or you could look it up on that fancy toy of yours. I even know the name of his street because it's my daughter's name. Laurel Street."

"Hunter Young. Laurel Street. Got it." Jordan hit dial. "Nate, hey, I need some information." Jordan had bypassed the white pages and gone straight to his information specialist at Quantico. Nate gave him what he needed within seconds. Jordan dialed the number that flashed up in his text message box.

"Hunter Young."

"Hi, Mr. Young, this is Special Agent Jordan Gray with the FBI. I met your father when he was involved with the wreck a couple of days ago." Had it only been two days? "He was supposed to come down to the police station to meet with a sketch artist, but he never showed up and we're having trouble getting in touch with him."

Silence greeted him.

"Mr. Young?"

"I'm just thinking. I'm working at home today. I can run over and check on him and let you know."

"We're actually at his house."

"Oh. Stay there, I'm on the way."

Jordan hung up and passed on the information.

"Oh, dear. I do hope everything is all right."

Katie gave the woman a reassuring smile. "We can let you know if you'd like to wait in the comfort of your home."

"That's a very nice way of saying I need to stay out of the way, hmm?"

Katie gave a low chuckle. "Yes, ma'am."

Mrs. McDowell nodded and gave a light laugh, but it didn't cover her worried glance at Bobby Young's house.

"Does he have any animals?" Katie asked.

She shook her head. "No. He likes to travel too much. Said an animal would tie him down."

"Thank you, Mrs. McDowell, you've been very helpful."

"Please let me know when you talk to him?"

"Of course. We'll have him call you."

She nodded and walked slowly back up her driveway.

Jordan looked at Katie. "I'm going to walk around to the back and see if I see anything."

Katie nodded. Jordan headed around the side of the house but turned back at the sound of a vehicle approaching. A classy white convertible Mercedes with a black top. Hunter Young must do well for himself. The Mercedes pulled to the curb and a tall man in his early forties climbed from the car. A worried frown creased his forehead. "I'm Hunter Young."

Jordan shook the man's outstretched hand. "FBI Special Agent Jordan Gray. This is Detective Katie Jacobs."

He blanched. "Since when does the FBI investigate a car wreck?"

Katie flashed her badge and said, "He was with me working another case when it happened. He's not officially investigating, but we were both concerned when your father didn't show up like he promised, so thought we'd check on him."

Hunter nodded. "You've every reason to be concerned. If Dad said he'd be there, he would have been. I brought him home from the hospital, and that's all he talked about. Once all the excitement was over and everyone was okay, he thought it all a great adventure. He was excited about working with the sketch artist to find the guy responsible." Hunter walked toward the house, pulling a set of keys from his pocket. "I tried calling his cell all the way over here. He rarely doesn't answer. And usually calls me right back if I do get his voice mail." He opened the front door. Cold air rushed out at them. "Dad?"

Jordan had a bad feeling growing in his gut. Why was the house so cold? It was the middle of December. Everyone had the heat on. Especially with the temps dropping into the low teens at night. He placed a hand on the man's arm. "Do you mind waiting here and letting us check it out?"

"Yes, I mind." He stepped inside. "Dad?" He looked at them. "Why is it so cold in here?" He gave a shudder. "He didn't say anything about the heat pump giving him trouble. Dad?"

"Sir," Katie said. "If we find something, this could be a crime scene. We need to keep it as undisturbed as possible. Wait here."

Her words were an order. Hunter flinched, but stopped in his tracks. "Crime scene? You think—"

"I don't think anything," Katie said with a more gentle tone. "I just want to cover all my bases. For your father's sake."

Hunter swallowed hard and Jordan could tell the man wanted to go tearing through the house. He didn't blame him. If it were his father, he'd feel the same way. But Hunter stood still and clenched a fist. "He could be lying hurt or sick. Hurry. Please."

Katie stepped lightly, wishing for crime scene booties. Bobby Young might not even be here, but her gut cried out that he was and it wasn't going to be good. She stepped into the den and noticed the wide-open French doors that led to the back deck. Cold air blew in.

"Jordan."

"Kitchen's clear." He came up beside her. Spotted the doors. "Uh-oh."

"Mr. Young?" Katie called. They cleared the first floor, then headed for the second. "Bedroom one, clear," she called.

"Bedroom two, clear," Jordan echoed.

Katie stepped into the next room and came to a halt. Even through her heavy down coat, she felt the cold in the house to her bones.

This was his office. The desk faced the window, looking out to the wooded area behind the house. Katie stepped closer and walked around for a view of the chair.

Katie sucked in a deep breath and dropped her chin to her chest in despair. "Jordan!"

She heard his footsteps on the hardwood. "What is it?"

"I found Mr. Young."

NINE

Jordan hated this part of the job. And this wasn't even officially his job. But Katie had asked him to do it while she secured the scene. She already had a crime scene unit and the medical examiner on the way as well as uniformed officers who would canvass the neighborhood, questioning everyone they could find.

When Jordan escorted Hunter from the house and told him the news, the man broke down, his sobs heart wrenching. Jordan didn't blame him. He simply stood there, hand on Hunter's shoulder, until the man could gain some control.

It didn't take him long. Jordan had a feeling Hunter's personality wouldn't let him be emotional for any extended period of time. Within minutes Hunter had wiped his face with his expensive silk tie and hardened his features. Pure fury now blazed from his green eyes. "Who did this?"

Jordan had his suspicions. Unfortunately, he didn't have a name to go with those suspicions. "I don't know, sir, but I promise we'll find out." He paused. "Did your father have any enemies that you know of?"

Appalled, Hunter looked at him. "No. None."

"Did you notice anyone following you home from the hospital?"

Hunter blinked. "No."

And why would he? He had no reason to even think about being followed.

Jordan nodded and as law enforcement arrived. He asked Hunter a few more questions, then did his best to fade into the background. After all, this wasn't his case.

He had to keep reminding himself of that. His case was Katie's case. And while he had a feeling Mr. Young's murder had everything to do with the fact that he'd seen the shooter from the diner, Jordan wasn't going to put his nose any further into the investigation unless he was invited.

He sent a text message to Erica to let her know what was going on. She shot one back.

Come when you can.

An hour later, Katie emerged from the house and veered toward the Mercedes, where Hunter was sitting. He got out of the vehicle, shoulders stooped and looking shell-shocked, his initial fury overshadowed by his crushing grief. For the time being. The anger would return. Jordan knew this from experience.

His phone rang and he recognized the number as the McKinneys'. "Special Agent Gray."

"Hello, Mr. Gray, this is Eileen McKinney. You left a message for me to call you."

"Yes, ma'am. Thanks for calling me back."

Jordan explained what he wanted and Mrs. McKinney clucked. "I don't know what more I can tell. I told that detective the day of the kidnapping everything I could think of—and trust me, that wasn't much."

"I understand, but sometimes talking to a different person can spark something."

"Well, if you want to come on out, I'll be here for the next forty-five minutes or so."

Jordan hesitated, then said, "I'll be there in about fifteen minutes."

"I'll be looking for you."

Jordan hung up. Katie still talked to Hunter, who leaned his head back against the headrest and scrubbed his eyes. He saw Hunter nod, and Katie gave his shoulder a squeeze.

She walked toward him. He said, "You look like you've been hit by a truck. You're not doing yourself any favors by pushing yourself like this. You're supposed to be on leave."

She grimaced. "Tell me what you really think."

"Sorry. I'm concerned." Her gaze warmed for a minute and she looked like she might like to fall into his arms and let him shelter her from the world. He almost held them out to her so she could do it. She blinked and the moment was gone. "You think he was killed by the shooter?"

"I do."

"Because he saw him at the wreck. He was the only one who got a really good look at him, but I'm worried about the others."

"I've contacted my lieutenant, and he's putting extra patrols on the others involved in the wreck. The young mother and the girl, Miranda." She glanced around. "I'm going to be here a little longer. I've got a few more things to take care of. Why don't you head on over to Erica's?"

"I just got a call from Mrs. McKinney. She wants me to come talk to her now."

Hope dusted her expression. "Good. I'll meet you at Erica's as soon as I'm finished here."

"Leave you to come alone? I don't think so."

She rubbed a hand down her face. "Seriously, I'll be fine. I'll get in my car and head over there as soon as we're done. I'm surrounded by cops. The killer is long gone."

Jordan looked around. Strange faces lined the sidewalks, neighbors vying for a glimpse of the action. "You hope."

"I've got the photographer discreetly taking pictures of the crowd. We'll take a look at the pictures and see if anyone jumps out at us. Now go on. I'll be fine."

"I can ask her if tomorrow would be better."

Katie sighed. "Jordan, I've got a job to do. You can't be with me twenty four–seven. Your job is to find out about Lucy. It's what I've hired you to do, not babysit me. I'm a police officer. I'm trained to take care of myself."

Frustration filled him. She was right, but he didn't have to like it.

Gregory stepped from the house. "Katie, can I see you for a minute?"

"Sure." She looked back at Jordan. "Go. I need to know if she has anything to add to Lucy's kidnapping."

Against his better judgment, he nodded. "All right, text me when you're leaving, what route you're taking and anything else I should know."

Katie nodded. "All right. If it will make you feel better."

"It would."

Jordan headed for his car. Reluctantly. But she was right. She was a cop. She was surrounded by cops. He sent up prayer for her safety and pulled away from the scene.

Katie watched Jordan go and prayed he'd come back with some answers. Something. Anything that they could grasp and run with to find Lucy. For the next hour, Katie finished working the crime scene and kept an eye on her back.

By the time she texted Jordan, she was exhausted. All

she wanted to do was go to the hotel room and collapse in a heap. In fact, she seriously considered just staying where she was and sleeping in her car.

A tap on her window made her jump. When she saw Gregory's concerned face staring at her, she ordered her pulse to slow down. She lowered the window. "Hey."

"You all right?"

"Hanging in there."

He nodded, his brow still creased. "You heading over to Erica's?"

"I'm thinking about canceling and going to crawl into bed."

"You need an escort?"

Katie tried to discern if there was any sarcasm in his tone, but didn't detect any. He was concerned. And she was too touchy.

"No. I'll be extra careful."

He pursed his lips. "I like working with you, Katie. See that you stay in one piece, will you?"

She shivered as a gust of cold wind blew across her face. "I'll do my best."

Gregory nodded. "Text me when you're locked in your hotel room, okay?"

Katie smiled. She was glad to know she had people who cared whether she was safe or not. Too bad her parents weren't nearly as concerned. She frowned and ordered herself not to go there. She was tired and didn't need to get maudlin. "Sure."

Gregory walked toward his vehicle and she wondered why the tall, handsome detective didn't spark any romantic interest in her. Immediately Jordan's face came to mind and she knew why she wasn't attracted to Gregory. Jordan was the one who set the butterflies loose in her stomach. He was the one who made her palms sweat and her heart race.

Gregory was a great guy, but he wasn't Jordan.

She sighed and sent a text to Jordan.

I'm going back to the hotel. I'm going to call Erica and tell her I'm not coming.

He replied in a moment.

All right. I'm almost done here. Let me come back and take you back to the hotel.

She ditched the texting and dialed his number. "Hey. You're all the way across town. I'll be at the hotel and locked in my room before you get back here."

"Katie—"

The exasperation in his voice made her smile. She was glad he was concerned. "I'll be fine. I'll text as soon as I get there. I do have a gun, remember? And I'm trained in self-defense. And I'm alert and know someone's after me. Should be enough, right?"

"Wasn't enough when someone tried to burn your house down, was it?"

Ouch. "Hmm. Okay, I'll give you that point," she muttered. "However, I'm leaving now." She pulled away from the curb and waved to Faith as the woman packed her van. The M.E. was still with Bobby Young. Hunter Young had left the scene, claiming he had to go break the news to his family. She didn't envy him that job.

He sighed. "Then stay on the phone with me."

She paused. "All right."

"I'm still going to Erica's. She really wants to talk about this case."

"Fill me in tomorrow?"

"Bright and early. Cort's going to be outside your hotel room all night."

"Poor guy."

"He never sleeps. If he gets four hours a night, he's as fresh as though he's had eight."

"Not fair."

"Tell me about it."

She paused. "Hey, Jordan?"

"Yes."

"Thanks for caring."

"You're welcome, Katie."

The warmth in his voice made her cheeks start to heat. She cleared her throat. "What did Mrs. McKinney say? Anything helpful?"

"Yes. I think we may have something to work with."

Not what she'd expected to hear. She sat a little straighter. "What?"

"She remembers seeing a car, a gray sedan, parked several doors down. She also remembers seeing the car there every day for about two weeks before your sister disappeared."

"Someone staking the place out," she whispered.

"It's one theory, of course, and that's what I think. I could be wrong, but…"

"We need to ask the other neighbors specifically about that vehicle."

"I'm already compiling the list. Get this, though. Mrs. McKinney took a picture of the car."

"What?" Her blood started humming. "Why?"

"Well, it wasn't a picture of the car per se. She was taking pictures of her kid on his skateboard. He'd just gotten the board as a birthday present and was up and down the street showing off while she was snapping pictures."

"And of course she had those pictures in an album somewhere." Excitement tripped through her.

"Of course. The car was fuzzy in a few of them, but she let me take the best one of the lot."

"Take a picture and text it to me, will you?"

"Sure."

New hope sizzled. The car wasn't much, but it might turn into something big. "There wasn't any mention of a strange car in the case file."

"No."

"Right."

Anger filled her. "What were Frank and Danny *doing* while my sister was in the hands of a kidnapper, maybe fighting for her life—" Her voice cracked on the last word and she cleared her throat.

"We'll figure it out."

"We sure will." Resolve hardened and she sent up a silent prayer for God's blessing. *Help me find her, Lord.*

They chatted until she reached the hotel. "Cort's waiting on me, just like you said. Parked right outside my room."

"Good. Sleep tight, Kate."

"Bye, Jordan."

Katie hung up and let a smile linger on her lips. She climbed out of her car and was greeted by Cort. "Glad to see you looking good. Sorry about the night of the fire."

She patted his arm. "Don't you worry about that. I appreciate your willingness to do this."

"I miss the job. Being retired ain't all it's cracked up to be."

Katie bid him good-night and entered her room. The text from Jordan came through and she clicked on the picture. A young boy, about twelve years old, looked like he was having a blast as he rolled down the street on his skateboard, arms wide to help with balance.

The screen was small so she couldn't get much detail on the car behind him, but zooming in helped. And she had a picture she could show when they questioned more neighbors about seeing the vehicle. *Thank You, God, for this small step.* Her adrenaline ebbed and exhaustion swamped her.

As she prepared for bed, her stomach rumbled. She'd forgotten to eat. A glance at the clock said she was going to bed at 5:49 p.m. So what? She was exhausted.

She shut the light off and within minutes was asleep.

Jordan inhaled the scent of home-cooked food. Fried chicken and macaroni and cheese. His stomach rumbled. He would be forever grateful that Erica and Max often took pity on him and invited him to share their meals.

He was disappointed Katie had backed out, although he had to admit he was surprised she'd lasted as long as she had. Her body had taken a beating over the last couple of days and was bound to give out before much longer.

Brandon walked into the den, grabbed a red-and-green Christmas pillow from the seat and flopped onto the couch. Erica's brother had become almost a permanent fixture around the place. So much so that Jordan thought Max might be a little worried about what was going to happen after his and Erica's wedding in a little less than three weeks—on New Year's Day. He couldn't believe Christmas and the wedding were coming up so fast.

Brandon asked, "When are we eating? I'm hungry."

Max laughed. "You're always hungry." He looked at Jordan and sobered. "So, how's it going with Katie these days? I know she was avoiding you for a while there. How's it going now that you two are working together?"

Jordan grunted and set his tea on the coaster. He settled onto the couch. "It's going much better now, but you're right when you say Katie wasn't happy Erica assigned the case to me."

"I know. Strange. Do you know why she was perturbed you got the case?"

"Yes." He didn't say any more.

Brandon and Max exchanged a look. Brandon shrugged and Max rolled the glass between his hands, then said, "I think it's because she's attracted to you."

Brandon snorted.

Jordan jerked then choked a laugh. "What?"

Max shrugged. "That's Erica's deduction."

Jordan lifted the glass of tea to his suddenly dry mouth. He knew she was attracted to him. The feeling was mutual. But that wasn't the reason she hadn't wanted him on the case. "She said something to Erica?"

"Nope. Not a word."

He hadn't thought she would. Then again, she and Erica were tight, so… "Oh."

"But women notice these things, you know?"

"Especially Erica," Brandon said, his lips curving into a sardonic smile. "Now that she's found the love of her life, she's determined everyone in her path will do the same."

Max grinned. "Poor Brandon. And yet you keep coming over and giving her opportunities to set you up with her friends."

Brandon patted his trim belly. "If she wasn't such a good cook, you wouldn't see as much of me."

Jordan knew that wasn't true. The man was crazy about his niece, Molly, and was very protective of his sister. When she'd almost been killed by the woman who'd kidnapped her daughter, Brandon and Erica had grown even closer, watching out for one another and pulling together as siblings often did when a crisis hit a family. He looked at Jordan. "But if Erica says she's attracted to you, she is."

"Maybe." He wasn't going to debate his romantic life. Or the lack of. He glanced at his watch and wished they'd get onto another subject. Katie was fine, safely in her hotel room and most likely sound asleep. And he wanted to hurry up with the dinner and discussion and get back to her. In fact, if his invitation to dinner hadn't felt more like a business invitation over a personal one, he'd just go ahead and leave.

But Erica wanted to talk about the case, and Jordan appreciated her willingness to feed him a home-cooked dinner while she did it.

Max pulled at his lower lip. "I hate that Katie didn't feel like coming, but she probably needs the rest more than she needs the food."

"She's definitely had a few long days."

"Max, are you two ready to eat?" Erica asked from the door. Molly stood behind her, flour streaks covering her face and clothes. Jordan's gut clenched like it did every time he was around small children. It wasn't that he didn't like them—he did. They just brought back bad memories. Memories he fought off on a daily basis. Memories he kept at bay most of the time by avoidance. He found working himself to death was better than alcohol. He had enough issues and didn't need to add to his troubles by becoming a drunk.

And prayer. Sometimes prayer helped, too.

He tuned back in as Max said, "We're more than ready. Bring it on." Max stood and Jordan followed him into the kitchen.

He hated that Katie wasn't there, either. He missed her presence. How odd. He shot a text to Cort.

How is she?

Cort responded,
Fine. Sleeping, I think. Lights have been off for about half an hour now. Quiet.

Great. Keep me updated.

Will do.

Jordan put his phone away and bowed his head as Max led the blessing.

Erica looked up after Max said "Amen," and said, "Fill me in on Lucy Randall's case and the progress you've made, will you?"

Max choked on his laughter. "Let the man eat, Erica."

She flushed. "Sorry."

Jordan cleared his throat and dug in. While Max and Erica discussed whether or not Erica should hire another person for the Finding the Lost agency, he could feel Molly watching him. When he looked up, he saw her slide Nellie a green bean. The dog ate it.

When Molly realized she'd been caught, her gaze flew to her mother and then to Max, then back to Jordan. She lifted a finger to her lips, and Jordan couldn't help it. He bit back a smile and gave her a slow nod. No way would he rat her out.

Her eyes sparkled with mirth, and she happily plopped a bean in her own mouth. The knot in his belly eased, and he breathed a sigh of relief. Maybe the past could fade after all.

"Don't you think, Jordan?"

Erica's question made him blink. "Huh?"

"You weren't listening to a word we said, were you?"

"Ah, no, sorry. I was…um…thinking."

Erica narrowed her eyes. "I'm sure I can guess what you were thinking about."

Jordan felt a flush start to creep up the back of his neck. "Hmm. I won't argue with a woman who feeds me."

Erica laughed and backed off. Jordan enjoyed the food and the company, and even some of the teasing, but he was ready to get down to business. Erica seemed to sense his restlessness and said, "Max, why don't you and Jordan take your coffee into the den. I'll get Molly settled and be there shortly."

Max stood. "Why don't I get Molly settled and you and Jordan can start talking?"

"Guess that's my cue to shove off," Brandon said. He looked at Jordan. "I'll see you later."

Jordan nodded.

"Don't forget, we're having Christmas dinner here," Erica said.

Brandon frowned. "Right. I may have to work. We'll see." He left and Erica sighed then stood and gave Max a smile that made Jordan ache to have someone look at him that way. No, not someone. Katie.

He swallowed hard and followed Erica into the den. The coffee warmed his hands.

"So tell me the latest. What have you learned from Mrs. McKinney?"

* * *

Katie sat up and looked at the clock. She'd been asleep for an hour and fifteen minutes. Now her nerves hummed and her senses spun. Knowing it would be a futile effort to try to go back to sleep, she tossed aside the covers and turned on the light.

She wanted her house back.

She wanted whoever was trying to kill her behind bars.

She wanted to find her sister.

She wanted a relationship with Jordan.

That last admission wasn't easy, but it was one she couldn't deny.

And she wanted her mother to love her. It seemed that no matter what she did or how hard she tried, it was never good enough.

Tears threatened at the thought, and she pushed them back. She couldn't dwell on that or she'd go nuts. For the next fifteen minutes, she paced the room. Then picked up the phone and dialed her parents' number.

Her mother answered on the second ring. "Hello."

"Hi, Mom."

"How are you, Katie?"

She swallowed. "I'm doing okay. I wanted to let you know that I hired a maid service to come clean your house for you next week."

Silence echoed for a brief moment, then her mother said, "Well, that's very nice. Thank you."

"Sure." Katie took a deep breath. "I was wondering if you'd like to meet for breakfast one day soon. I'm working a rather complicated case right now, but—"

"I don't think I'll feel up to that, Katie, but thank you

for the invitation." The oh so proper politeness made Katie want to weep.

"Okay, well, maybe another time. Is Dad around?"

"Hold on."

Katie bit her lip. She almost wished her mother would yell at her. Anything would be preferable to the cold, polite attitude.

"Hello?"

"Hi, Dad."

"Hi, sweetie."

"She's not warming up at all, is she?"

His sigh echoed. "I'm working on her. At least she's speaking to you."

"True." It was only in the last few years that her mother had climbed far enough out of her depression to even interact with Katie. And every once in a while Katie thought she caught a glimpse of longing and love in her mother's eyes. But before she could act on it, her mother shut it off and shut her out.

It broke her heart. "I'm doing everything I can to make her love me, Dad. What else can I do?" Her voice cracked on the last word and she wanted to call the words back. "Never mind. You don't have to answer that."

"Katie—" His voice wobbled and he cleared his throat. "Your mother loves you, honey. She loves you so much."

"No, I don't think she does," she whispered. "I think she hates me."

"Oh, baby…"

"I'm sorry, Dad, I shouldn't have brought it up. Forget it." She took a deep breath. With an effort, she shoved aside the hurt, wondering if she'd ever get used to it.

"Dad, I need to ask you something and I want a straight answer."

"What's that?"

"You asked me to drop Lucy's case."

"Yes." She heard his wariness, but appreciated he didn't push the subject of her mother.

"Why?" He sighed and didn't answer. "Dad?" Katie prompted.

"Because it's dangerous," he blurted. "I don't want anything to happen to you. Please, Katie, don't put yourself in any more danger."

Katie sat stunned. Hearing the worry in his voice nearly undid her as much as her mother's coolness.

"How do you know I'm in danger?"

"Landing in the hospital isn't enough? That fire was deliberately set. The police officer I talked to said you were shot at. You need to stop looking for Lucy."

"Dad, I don't even know that the fire or anything else going on is related to looking for Lucy." She suspected it, of course, but had no real evidence of it.

"Well, I do," he snapped.

Katie paused. "You do? How?"

A heavy sigh filtered through the line. "I…"

"You what? Tell me."

"I got a phone call. Someone with a low voice told me to warn you to stop looking for Lucy—or he'd make sure I had another daughter disappear."

Katie sat frozen. Shock raced through her. "When was this?"

"Right after the fire."

"That's why you came to the hospital. To tell me to stop looking for Lucy."

"Yes." She closed her eyes at his husky admission.

"Why didn't you tell me about the phone call?"

"He said not to. Said he'd come after your mom and me if I said he called, so you can't say anything."

As she absorbed the shock that someone related to Lucy's kidnapping had contacted her parents, she said, "He probably didn't want me to try and trace the call."

"Katie, please, drop it. Lucy's gone. It's not worth your life."

"Dad, this is the whole reason I became a detective." She paused. "If I stop looking for her, he wins," she whispered. And her mother would never forgive her. She had to find Lucy. "You really want that?"

"Of course not," he snapped. Katie bit her lip and waited. He finally said in a softer tone, "Of course I don't want him to win, but honey, I can't lose you, too."

Heart in her throat, Katie finished the call with her father with promises to be careful. For a moment she sat there, marveling. Her father loved her enough that he didn't want her looking for Lucy if it put her in danger. She swallowed hard at the realization and wished her mother felt the same way.

Clamping down on her emotions, she called Gregory and filled him in. "Will you try and trace the call and see if the officers on duty in that area will ride by my parents' house more often?"

"Sure."

"Thanks."

Phone calls finished, her mind in a jumble of thoughts, she was debating her next move when her stomach rumbled.

Katie dialed one more number.

"Hello?"

"Do you have any leftovers? I'm starving."

Erica laughed. "Of course. I was just sitting here with Jordan talking about your case. We'd love for you to join us."

In the background, she heard Jordan's low rumble. "Tell her I'll come get her."

Erica started to repeat it, but Katie said, "I heard him. Let me talk to him a minute, please."

She waited while Erica passed the phone to Jordan. "Hey."

"Hey, you don't need to come get me. I'll get Cort to follow me."

He paused. "I suppose that would work. Or you could just let him drive you."

"No. I want my car." She didn't know why she did.

"But Cort's perfectly capable—"

"I want my car, Jordan." He went silent and remorse for snapping at the man who was only trying to help washed over her. "I'm sorry. It's probably a control issue. Everything in my life is out of control. The least I can do is drive myself." She hadn't meant to be quite that blunt. Hadn't even planned on using those words. But there it was. Some subconscious need to be in control had surfaced.

A sigh reached her. "I get it. Just be careful. I'm calling Cort now."

Katie hung up and shrugged on her heavy coat, wincing at the pull in her shoulder and ignoring the various aches and pains she was going to have to live with for a while. She grabbed her weapon and keys and walked out the door.

A light rain fell, and she wondered if it would cause problems on the road. The asphalt didn't feel slick beneath her feet and the temperature hovered just above freezing. She'd be all right.

Katie said, "He wants you to follow me."

Cort waved his phone at her. "I know. No problem."

"You don't have to do this."

"I don't mind." Cort's dark eyes twinkled at her. "You have him wrapped, my girl."

"What are talking about?"

"You two'll figure it out. Now go get in your car in case someone decides to play target practice with your head."

Katie smirked and climbed into her car. She set her phone in the cup holder and waited for Cort to pull behind her.

With his headlights in her rearview mirror, she made her way out of the parking lot and turned left, staying in the right-hand lane. Cort pulled in behind her. Regret filled her that her search for Lucy had caused such disruption in so many lives. She flexed her fingers around the steering wheel and clicked her blinker to turn right even as she pressed the brake to slow for the approaching light.

A car flashed past her then slowed. Her stomach clenched into a knot. She gripped the wheel tightly and kept her eyes on the guy. His brake lights winked at her just before she pulled up beside him.

She turned right on red. Cort's headlights disappeared for a brief moment, then were there again. Her phone rang. She glanced at the number on her caller ID. Jordan.

Katie grabbed the phone. "Hello."

"Just checking on you."

"I'm fine."

"Where are you?"

"Holcombe Street. I'll be there in about ten minutes."

"All right. Cort still behind you?"

She checked the mirror. Bright lights behind her about two car lengths back. "Right behind me."

"Be careful, Katie."

"I am. I'm going to check in with Gregory and get the latest on Mr. Young. I'll see you in a bit."

He hung up and she bit her lip. Her heart was doing things it shouldn't be doing. Not for him. Jordan Gray was off-limits, but she couldn't seem to keep her distance. He was exactly the kind of man she wanted. And his parents would probably never be able to accept her.

And that was a big enough obstacle for her to put the brakes on her emotions. Shut them up tight and throw away the key.

Or at least try.

Jordan's phone rang. Cort. "What's up?"

"I lost her."

"What? I just talked to her. She said you were right behind her."

"I got cut off when she turned right on Holcombe. Some dude cut in front of me. By the time I got around him, she was gone. Which route would she take, left or right at Henry?"

Jordan thought but didn't know. "I have no idea which way she'd go. Let me call her and ask her where she is."

He hung up and punched in Katie's number.

Then groaned when it went to voice mail.

TEN

Katie ignored Jordan beeping in as she talked with her roommate on the phone.

"Unfortunately, I don't have a lot to tell you on Mr. Young. He had no defensive wounds, so he trusted whoever he let in his house. And that person took him by surprise and shot him execution style. He was killed sitting in his chair," Mariah told her.

"Yes, I knew that. Do you have a time of death?"

"You said the house was cold when you entered due to the open doors, and that messes up my timeline. As best I can determine, he died the day of the wreck, but I can't be a hundred percent sure. The shooting at the diner happened at one-oh-four p.m. He was at the hospital for a good wait."

"His neighbor saw him come home with his son. That was around five-thirty p.m."

"As far as I can tell, he was killed shortly after that."

"The killer was waiting for him," she whispered. "But how did he get his information? How would the killer have known who it was?"

"Maybe he got the license plate and got someone to figure it out."

"Or maybe when he raced off and lost the police chasing him, he circled back and watched everything."

"And followed the man to the hospital."

"And then home."

"It could've happened that way."

"Maybe." Katie heard her phone beep again. "I've got to go. Thanks."

"See ya."

She glanced at the screen of her phone. Jordan. She'd missed him again. She smiled. It felt rather nice to have someone worry about her.

Then she frowned. She just wished he didn't have a reason to. She'd call him back as soon as she got on the straight road. He could wait sixty seconds.

Katie turned off the main highway and took the road that would lead her to Erica's home. Erica and Max had bought the property three months ago, shortly after they'd found Molly and brought her home. Max and Erica's wedding was in a few weeks, and Katie couldn't be happier for her friends.

Max had decided to give his house to his sister, Lydia, whom he'd bought it for, anyway. Katie knew he was anxious for the wedding so he could move into the new place and he, Erica and Molly could be a family at last. She started to dial Jordan's number when she noticed the lights behind her.

Cort seemed to be following a little too close. She tapped her brakes. The road was getting slick, and he needed to back off a little.

Cars passed her on the left going in the opposite direction. Streetlights were sparse and the darkness pressed in on her. She shivered and sent up a prayer for safety.

Cort backed off for a few minutes, then he was right

back on her tail. What was he doing? Was he trying to get her attention?

She cleared the screen of Jordan's number and started to punch in Cort's when the device rang. Jordan. "Hello."

"Katie, Cort got cut off and lost you. Do you have anyone behind you?"

A frisson of fear shot up her spine. Along with a surge of anger. "Yes, and he's riding my bumper."

"Tell me where you are and I'll call for backup."

"I'm on—"

The car slammed into her bumper and she lost her grip on the phone. It flew to the floorboard. "I'm on Sunset!" She prayed the phone was still on. She didn't dare lean over to retrieve it.

Katie tightened her grip on the steering wheel as she glanced in her rearview mirror and tried to get a look at the face of the person following her. This was not happening again. Hadn't her attacker learned his lesson the first time?

Apparently not.

Under one of the few street lamps, she caught a glimpse of the car. A late-model silver Mustang. It hung back and she slowed.

The Mustang slowed more.

Katie kept her foot on the brake and with her right hand made sure she could reach her weapon easily. She didn't want to remove it from the back of her waistband lest it end up like her phone.

She slowed until she was going twenty miles per hour. The Mustang stayed back. Then shot forward. Katie pressed the gas and the Mustang fell behind.

"Why are you playing with me? Who are you?" she whispered to the image in her mirror. Headlights approached and the car zipped past on her left. Still she kept her eyes on the Mustang.

Icy patches had formed on the road. With the additional rain and now below-freezing temperatures, the roads could be dangerous. She'd worked in this kind of weather for years and driving in it had ceased to bother her. Crime didn't care what the weather was like, and she'd had to learn fast how to drive on the slick roads. However, she'd never had someone trying to kill her while she navigated them.

Katie sped up again, praying she wouldn't hit a sheet of black ice.

The Mustang stayed right with her. Close enough not to lose her and far enough back not to be identified. Not that she would be able to see anything in this darkness.

She shivered as the cool evening air blew through her cracked window. She couldn't afford for the windows to fog up, so she'd lowered it slightly. December in the South. One year it would be in the eighties, the next, freezing. Apparently this was the year for the cold. She loved it.

What she didn't love was someone following her. Being a potential threat. The headlights fell farther and farther behind. Had he given up?

Keeping her eyes on the rearview mirror, she took the turn that would take her to Erica's house. Trees bordered her right and lined her left. Pastureland stretched behind a white picket fence.

Secluded. Peaceful. Serene.

Longing filled her. What would it be like to find that one person she would feel comfortable enough with to share her life?

Jordan immediately popped into the forefront of her

mind. Handsome, strong, quiet. Mysterious. A man with a past. A man that made her blood hum a little faster, and her heart twist with something she refused to acknowledge. Her jaw firmed. *Stop thinking those kinds of thoughts. That's not your life.*

She obeyed the mental order and pondered the strangeness of the Mustang, watching for it, wondering if she should turn around and go after it. She thought about stopping and retrieving her cell phone, but that would leave her vulnerable should her attacker still be back there.

Which he was.

Headlights zoomed up behind her. She pressed the gas pedal. And still they came closer. Katie took a deep breath, pictured the twists and curves to the road ahead of her. She came up with a plan just as the car behind her rammed into her once again.

She jerked into the seat belt, tightened her fingers around the wheel and brought forth all of the defensive driving techniques she'd ever learned.

Katie slammed on the brakes and spun the wheel to the left. The vehicle came at her again and this time caught her on the driver's side. She kept control, stayed on the road.

Until she hit the patch of black ice that sent her spinning, crashing toward the trees lining the side of the road. The seat belt tightened; her head hit the window. Her car bounced off the first tree, careened into the second and came to a stop, nose down, against the third.

Blackness threatened, her head throbbed. Nausea churned.

Don't pass out, don't pass out.

Katie took a deep breath, fought off the dizziness and encroaching darkness.

Get out of the car. Now. Now.

Night had fallen. A light drizzle dampened her broken windshield. Katie unhooked the seat belt and caught herself on the steering wheel. She pushed against the driver's door with no results.

Stuck. She'd have to get out the passenger side.

With effort, ignoring the throbbing in her head and the nausea churning in her gut, she released the seat belt. She gave a quick glance in the rearview mirror. Saw the headlights at the top of the gently sloping hill.

A shadow outlined by the lights.

A shadow headed her way.

Jordan paced the length of Erica's den. "Where is she? She was getting ready to tell me where she was and I got cut off. Why isn't she answering her phone?" Max came in and Jordan filled him in. "I'm going to look for her."

"I'll go with you."

Jordan slipped into his jacket and followed Max out the door into the frigid, wet weather. The foreboding in his gut bothered him and he offered up a short prayer for Katie's safety.

ELEVEN

With a grunt, Katie shifted. Ignoring her shoulder's screaming protests, she'd managed to crawl over the armrest into the passenger seat and shove open the door. Her cell phone. Where was it? She turned back to the car and searched the passenger-side floorboard. Nothing. She glanced up. The shadow had disappeared. Her eyes darted from one side of the car to the other. Through the windows and behind her.

Where had he gone?

Leaves crunched, and she froze. Looking up, through the driver's window, she could see his head and shoulders, moving closer, slowly, as though he was hesitant to approach the car but compelled to do so.

Katie's stomach lurched and she swallowed hard. The throbbing in her head didn't help the nausea churning her gut. And it felt like the seat belt had left a permanent bruise across her left shoulder, exacerbating the already sore area. Absently, she wondered if she'd pulled her stitches loose. She rolled out of the car onto the frozen ground and bit her lip as pain raced through her.

The cold felt good at first, reviving her a bit, clearing

her mind. Then the rain came harder, slithering under her collar, leaving a freezing streak down her back.

Cold seeped through her coat and into her bones.

Her teeth began to chatter as shivers wracked her. She kept an eye on the figure, listened to his footsteps as he crept closer. She wrapped stiff fingers around her weapon and then released it. She wasn't sure she'd be able to pull the trigger. And didn't want to. Yet. Not until she knew who the man was.

She slipped her right hand into her left armpit, desperate to warm her fingers. Shudders racked her. Shock, cold, adrenaline and fear. A combination that sent her body into a tailspin. Trying to control her shakes, she took another look through the window.

The man coming toward the vehicle was not her friend. He was not here to help her. She knew he was the reason her car now kissed the tree. Katie inched her way toward a large tree trunk.

If she hadn't been wounded and nearly frozen stiff, she would have been tempted to pull her weapon and confront him once her fingers warmed up. But right now she felt like fleeing and hiding were her best options.

Decision made, she scooted faster toward the tree. She worried the headlights would illuminate her like they did the man coming after her if she stood. Through the passenger window, she could see the shadow's head and shoulders. Familiarity tugged at her. There was something about his silhouette, like she should know him....

Ribs protesting, head throbbing, shoulder hollering, she kept her lips clamped against any escaping sound. The pain raged through her, but she figured pain was better than death.

And she had no doubt the man who'd run her off the

road didn't plan to leave her alive. He was taking his time to investigate the car. Taking the time to make sure she was dead.

She reached the tree and shifted herself behind it. A curse reached her ears, and she clenched her teeth together to keep them from chattering. He'd just realized she wasn't in the car. Shivers racked her. Shock and cold. A deadly combination. But she'd be all right as long as she stayed conscious.

Katie peeked around the tree. Her attacker stood still, his head swiveling from side to side, as though undecided which way to search first. A hard fist slammed against the roof of the car and she flinched.

"Where are you? You're dead, Katie. It's time to give it up. Show yourself and I'll make it quick." The harsh, guttural growl sparked more fear in her belly as reality and disbelief hit her. Having her house burn down around her had been horrifying and scary, but to have him come after her face-to-face with the full intent to kill her without hesitation...

That was just plain terrifying.

Jordan peered into the darkness, his head aching with the strain of trying to see. "You're sure this is the route she would take to get to your house?"

Max said, "It's the only route."

Jordan supposed that was good. "What if she wasn't headed over to your house? What if she changed her mind? What if—" He clamped his mouth shut. No sense in what-ifs.

Max said, "It's possible, but I don't know what else to do except—"

"There. Headlights."

"Yeah. Pointed into the woods."

Max accelerated and flashed his lights at the vehicle. A figure darted through the beams and jumped into the car. Tires spun on the slick asphalt, but caught and sped away. Soon the vehicle's taillights disappeared from sight. "I don't like that," Jordan muttered.

"What kind of car, could you tell?"

"No, it's too dark. This road needs some street lamps."

"Let's check out what that guy was in such a hurry to get away from." Max pulled near to where the other car had been parked and pointed his lights into the wooded area. "This is only about a mile from my house. I've got a flashlight in the glove compartment."

Jordan had the flashlight and his door open before Max put the car in park. His feet hit the asphalt as a car approached, then slowed and pulled to the side. Jordan and Max exchanged glances. Jordan got a good look at the vehicle. "Cort," he told Max.

Cort burst from the car, eyes frantic and furious. "Where is she?"

"That's what we're trying to figure out." Jordan swung the high-powered beam around. "Look at that tree." He pointed to a tree with limbs and bark torn off. "Something hit it pretty hard." He started down the hill. "Katie? Katie, are you down there?"

He waved the light and noticed a rough path that had been cut by something heavy. The rain picked up speed, and the cold seeped through his heavy coat. He ignored it, his only concern for Katie.

"Katie?" Max added his voice from the top of the hill. No response. He called, "I'm going to call Gregory and see if he's had any luck."

Jordan moved farther down the hill and his light

bounced off metal. "Get down here, Max, Cort. I found her car."

Within seconds, they stood beside him. Max held a second flashlight in his left hand. They made their way to the vehicle. Jordan felt his heart shudder at the sight. "That doesn't look good."

"Is she in there?"

Jordan flashed the beam on the interior. "No. But I see blood." *Lord, let her be okay, please.* "Katie?"

A low groan reached his ears. He paused. "You hear that?"

"Yeah. Back there." Max aimed his light toward the trees on the other side of the vehicle. Jordan stomped through the soggy leaves and underbrush toward a large tree. Another sound.

He rounded the tree. And there she was.

Pale as death.

Katie was cold. So cold. She'd never been so cold in her life. She groaned and reached for the blanket she kept at the end of her bed.

"Katie? Katie, wake up."

She tried, she really did. Her eyes wouldn't open, but she felt the sensation of being lifted, cushioned. Movement. Jordan murmuring in her ear.

A prick in her left arm. Warmth. Finally warmth.

"Let's get her to the hospital."

She tried again to open her eyes. This time she managed to pry her eyelids up to half-mast. What had happened?

Memories rushed at her. The man in the Mustang. He'd run her off the road. Or had it been him?

She noted she was in an ambulance. A paramedic hovered over her. "Katie? You with me?"

"Yeah," she croaked.

Relief relaxed the man's features a fraction. Slowly her muscles lost their rigid tenseness. A blood pressure cuff on her left arm tightened and released. Her nose itched. Heavy blankets weighted her down.

And everything hurt. She gasped.

A warm hand covered hers. She slid her eyes to the right. Jordan. "Hey, what are you doing here?" she whispered.

"Thought I'd come along for the ride." The concern in his eyes stirred something within her. She tried to scowl but couldn't stop her heart from doing that little fluttering thing it did every time she thought about the man. Or heard his name. Or smelled his cologne. It was downright annoying. She did not want to be attracted to him. It would only lead to a broken heart.

But she was. And had been since she'd started to really get to know him almost six weeks ago. And now, with his gentle hold on her hand, she felt her heart slipping even further down the slippery slope she'd put it out on.

"Car. Ran me off the road." It was almost too much of an effort to talk. Now that she was warming up, sleepiness invaded her body. Not the sleepiness like the cold where she knew if she went to sleep, she might not wake up. This was different. Comfortable. Welcoming. She drifted.

Jordan's voice jerked her back. "I know. Max and I think we came up on the vehicle."

"He got away."

"Yes. He did."

She sighed. And frowned. She needed to think, to figure out who wanted to see her dead. Why the man's shadow had seemed so familiar. Later. She was so tired. Her eyes drooped.

Katie woke with a start. Her eyes popped open and awareness hit her hard—along with a headache. She ignored the pain and forced her brain to cooperate. Someone had tried to kill her. Again. Jordan had ridden over in the ambulance and she was in the hospital. Again. This really was getting to be a really bad habit.

And Jordan was now sitting in the chair next to her bed. Snoring softly.

Her heart stirred with an emotion she wasn't sure she could identify, but she found herself blinking back tears. She sighed. Just because he was good-looking and intense didn't mean she had to act like she'd never seen a good-looking and intense man before. She needed to stop thinking about her attraction and worry about who was out to kill her.

She blinked and licked her lips. Dry. She spotted the cup of water with the straw on the tray and tried to reach for it. Sore muscles protested and she couldn't hold back a gasping whimper as pain rippled through her.

Jordan stirred, lifted his head and leaned forward. "Hey, welcome back."

Her heart ignored her lecture of only seconds ago and fluttered at his sleepy concern. "What are you doing here?" He handed her the cup and she took a sip of the cool water.

He smiled. "You already asked me that question." Had she? Oh. Right. In the ambulance. He reached for her hand and squeezed her fingers. "You scared us all to death."

She grunted. "Sorry. Scared myself pretty bad, too. Where are Max and Erica?"

"Keeping all of your cop friends from invading your room and demanding a statement."

She almost smiled but was afraid it would hurt. "And Gregory?"

"Pacing like a caged tiger while he tries to track down who ran you off the road. Last time I talked to him, he had a crime scene unit on the way and a wrecker to pull up your car."

"It's raining—or at least it was. I'll be surprised if they're able to find anything."

"They'll give it a try. I called your insurance company. I'll be surprised if they don't total the vehicle."

"Lovely," she murmured and grimaced at the thought of dealing with everything that awaited her when she was released from the hospital. Again.

A knock on the door interrupted them. Jordan stood and went to open it while Katie closed her eyes and wondered why Jordan was allowing himself to care when he knew as well as she did that they didn't have a chance of working out romantically. But he did care. She could see it in his eyes. More tears surfaced because she was going to have to put the brakes on her emotions, the feelings that were rapidly developing for this man.

Because she just wasn't up to a broken heart.

TWELVE

Jordan frowned and gazed at the crowd still in the waiting room.

He'd answered several questions from Gregory, who looked annoyed with Jordan for asserting himself as Katie's protector. But he frankly didn't care.

Jordan didn't understand his need to be with Katie, but the thought of losing her last night had done something to his heart that he couldn't explain and wasn't sure he even wanted to try. He just knew he'd never felt this way about anyone before and wasn't going to let it slip through his fingers without putting up a good fight for it.

Which was why he'd planted himself in her room: to make sure she wasn't bothered by anyone she didn't want to see. To check and double-check that she was going to be all right.

She needed her rest, not the hounding of her detective friends. And so he'd appointed himself her guardian. Her protector. And so far she'd let him step into that role.

However, he knew she needed to give a statement. He motioned to the detective and Gregory shot to his feet. Within seconds, they were back in her room. She had her eyes closed, her head tucked against the pillow.

The pale cast to her skin said she was getting close to being wiped out.

"Don't be long," he said to Gregory.

Gregory grunted, and Katie opened her eyes. She gave a wan smile to her partner. "Glad to see you."

"Not as glad as I am to see you. Twice in one week? You keep landing in this place, they're going to put your name on a room."

She grimaced. "I'm going to hear jokes about this for a long time to come, aren't I?"

"Since you're going to live, yeah."

She gave a little laugh and grimaced. "I figured."

"Don't worry, something will happen to take the heat off you in a couple of months."

Katie gave a pained laugh and a low groan. "Stop making me laugh, it hurts."

Gregory pulled out a green notebook. "I need a statement."

"Someone tried to kill me again. How's that?"

Gregory pursed his lips then said, "It's a start." He flipped to a blank page. "So what are the details?"

"Nothing. I was on that little road that leads to Erica's house. I was driving slow, being careful of the possibility of black ice, thinking Cort was behind me. Then Jordan called and said he wasn't. The guy rammed me, and I dropped my phone." Jordan handed her cell to her.

She placed it on the bed beside her. "Thanks. Headlights came up behind me, and I sped up. The car behind me did, too, and rammed me again. I hit a couple of trees and managed not to die."

She kept her tone light, but Jordan could see the thread of tension in her jaw. A muscle began to tic. She rubbed her hands down the sheet covering her legs. "He got out of the car and came looking for me. I managed to crawl out the other side of the vehicle, facing away from him. When he realized I wasn't in the car, he was mad."

Gregory's gaze turned serious. "He's been after you. He arranged to have Cort cut off so he could follow you without interruption."

"Yeah." She paused. "So does that mean there are two of them after me?"

"Definitely someone who has help. You think the guy who ran you off the road had something to do with Bobby Young's murder?"

"I don't know, Gregory. I really don't know. Probably. Everything seems tied together." She gave a hard smile. "But that's good. That means we're getting closer. It means someone's nervous."

"So you think this has something to do with your sister's case?" Gregory asked.

"Yes. Definitely," she said.

Gregory raised a brow. "You're still chasing that?"

Katie eyed him, steel in her gaze. "You know I am." She would never have been able to keep that a secret from him. And she hadn't tried. Had no reason to. Gregory understood her need to find Lucy and had even offered to help if she wanted.

He nodded. "Let's just assume that this doesn't have anything to do with Lucy. Is there anything new you've been digging around in? Anything out of the ordinary?"

Katie's eyes shot to Jordan's. "No. I've been thinking along those lines, too. The only thing I've done different is hiring Finding the Lost and getting them involved."

"Then maybe that's the answer," Gregory said. He looked at Jordan. "Someone is nervous about the questions you've been asking. Looks like you've kicked over a beehive."

"Looks like," Jordan murmured.

Another knock on the door caught their attention. Jordan opened it, and Erica and Molly stepped inside. Erica rushed over. "Are you all right? I tried to see you earlier, but you were still out cold. Max and Jordan have been keeping me updated."

Molly moved close enough to lean against the edge of the bed. "Aunt Katie, are you gonna die?"

Erica flushed and clapped a hand over the seven-year-old's mouth. She shot an apologetic look at Katie. "No filters, as you know very well."

Katie grinned, grateful for the lighthearted moment in the midst of the thick tension. "I'm not going to die. At least not today. I'm very glad you came to see me, though."

"Me, too. And guess what?"

"What?"

"I'm getting another puppy. A friend for Nellie, only this one's gonna be a baby dog. And I get to walk him and feed him and give him a bath whether he wants it or not, and—"

"All right, kiddo," Erica interrupted. "The puppy's not a done deal, remember?"

The little girl's face dropped, and Katie wanted to hug her. "I'll talk to her," she whispered.

Molly's face lit up, and she shot a triumphant look at her mother, who in turn sent Katie an exasperated frown. Katie shrugged and a pang hit her as she realized her interaction with Erica was one she might have had with Lucy had her sister not disappeared. She blinked away the sudden moisture and tapped Molly's nose. Composed once again, she looked up at Erica, whose eyes had turned serious.

She said, "This hospital thing is starting to be a habit with you."

Katie grimaced. "So I've been told. Don't worry, I plan on breaking it, and fast." She knew she would be sore and achy for a couple of days. She supposed she should be used to it by now. A yawn caught her off guard. Embarrassed, she said, "I think my painkillers are catching up with me."

Erica squeezed her hand. "Get some rest. I'm serious, though. I would love for you to come stay with us if you need to."

Katie swallowed. "Thanks, Erica. But—" she shot a glance at Molly "—I'd never put your family in danger." Erica squeezed her hand and Molly gave her a gentle hug.

They left and Jordan said, "You should take her up on it."

Katie shut her eyes. "You know I can't do that."

"Yeah."

She heard Jordan leave just before sleep claimed her.

Jordan decided to grab a few hours of sleep. The exhaustion pursuing him had finally caught up, and Katie had pushed him to go home and rest. Jordan caved, realizing he wasn't going to be any good for her if he was punchy and less alert than usual. After assessing the security situation, he had agreed he should take advantage of the willingness of others to help and get some sleep.

She had a guard on her door in case the guy who had tried to kill her decided to come back and finish the job. Plus a few of her off-duty police officer buddies milled in the waiting room. Most had gone home, but the ones she was close to remained, determined to watch over one of their own.

It was obvious Katie was well-liked and respected by those she worked with. She was good at her job. She cared and yet managed to keep her sanity. Not everyone did.

When he woke, it was Friday morning. As he dressed, he debated his feelings for Katie. He remembered the sense of loss he'd felt when he realized Cort wasn't behind her and she was in danger once again.

He swallowed hard. He could have lost her. Almost had. The fact that he was even debating pursuing a romantic relationship with a woman his parents held such animosity for told him he was in way over his head.

And he knew he was going to have to talk to his parents. Tell them the truth about Neil. And not for the first time, he second-guessed himself in withholding the truth from them. Was he being selfish? Allowing them to put their youngest son on a pedestal? He hadn't wanted to tarnish their memories by telling them, but was that the right thing to do?

He grappled with the questions until a headache started to build. He grabbed his keys and headed out the door to climb into his car. He dialed Katie's number at the first red light. "I'm guessing you had a quiet night?" he asked.

"I did. No one was getting in this room with all of my volunteer bodyguards outside. Gregory sent them all home around midnight, then he stayed outside the door the rest of the night."

"Glad to hear it." She sounded better. Stronger. "Have you gotten a clean bill of health yet?"

"Somewhat. Erica's on her way to take me home."

"I was on the way to do that, but I can catch up with you later if you prefer." If she had a ride, he could go by his parents' house.

"Erica's bringing me some clothes and other items, but I appreciate the offer."

"Of course. Do you have an escort?"

"Max. And I think Gregory was going to come, too."

"Good." She should have enough help if someone tried anything. He paused and made a decision. "I've got an errand to run. Should take me about an hour. After that I was going to talk to Mrs. Johnson and see if she remembered anything about a strange car in the neighborhood. I thought if you felt up to it, you could go with me."

"Oh. Okay. Right."

He wondered if she was fidgeting with the sheet like she'd done yesterday when she was uncomfortable. "What's going on, Katie?"

A sigh greeted him. "I'm considering dropping the investigation."

For a moment, he wasn't sure what to say. "Those are the last words I expected to come out of your mouth."

"I know." He pictured her rubbing her forehead. "My father called me again this morning. He keeps trying to convince me to stop investigating. He's really worried. And I'm...torn." She blew out a sigh. "It's so odd. I never thought I'd hear him say anything like that. When I became a detective and started looking for Lucy, he was so...hopeful. And now—" He heard commotion in the background. She said, "Erica's here."

"All right. I'll meet you at your hotel in thirty minutes. I can run my errand a little later. We'll go see Mrs. Johnson first."

"Okay, sure."

"I'll be right there." He hung up and took the next left. His parents needed to know what had happened to Neil. He didn't want to tell them—in fact he dreaded doing so. But he'd been a coward for long enough. It was time to lay the truth on the table. He wasn't going to let a lie keep him from finding happiness with Katie. He didn't want to hurt his parents or taint their memories of Neil, but if he was ever going to be able to have a relationship with Katie, his parents had to hear the truth. He just had to find the words to do it.

As for Lucy Randall, she was a missing child who would now be an adult if she was still alive. But fourteen years ago, she'd been a child who had lived and breathed, had hopes and dreams. Just like the child Jordan had failed to find, just like the one he'd let die. The emotions that came with the memory came hard and swift and he gasped.

No. He was going to find Lucy. It didn't matter that fourteen years had passed. She needed to be found. She deserved to be given justice. And no matter what Katie said, Jordan was determined to make sure Lucy got what she deserved.

THIRTEEN

Friday, midmorning, Katie stood at the window of her hotel room. Jordan pulled into the space in front of her door, and Cort climbed from his vehicle to greet him. He crossed the parking lot to shake Jordan's hand. Katie stepped outside. "You made good time."

"You look like you've been hit by a truck." His soft-voiced concern dispelled any indignation that might have risen at his words. And he was right. She looked awful.

Cort shot Katie a guilty look. "I guess I'm losing my touch. That's twice now he's gotten to you."

"It's not really your fault. I'm beginning to think this guy is trained and has inside information."

"What do you mean?"

She nodded to her room. "Why don't y'all come in and we'll talk a little before Jordan and I go see Mrs. Johnson."

The men followed her inside and planted themselves at the round table in the corner. "What kind of inside information?" Jordan demanded.

She shook her head. "I don't know. He knew what hotel I was staying in because he was watching for me to leave. He knew Cort was helping me and he had someone working with him to cut Cort off so he could get behind me. And they worked it at just the right moment so I wouldn't know what happened. Sure, it was a gamble as to whether it would work or not, but they tried it. And almost won."

She paced in front of the table. "This guy doesn't have any trouble finding me. He seems to know my every movement. He didn't try to strike at me in the hospital either time—he catches me on the road or in my house, places with no cameras and a good chance for him to get away. And he threatened my parents anonymously."

"He doesn't want to get caught," Cort said.

"Absolutely not."

Katie's phone rang and she ignored her aches and pains as she moved to get it from her purse. "Hello?"

"Hey, it's Mariah. Are you okay?"

"Yes, I'm fine." She paused. "Well, I'm still alive, so I suppose that qualifies as okay."

"I'm sorry I haven't been around. I've been working almost nonstop over the last few days and taking care of Grandma Jean in the interim."

"Don't worry about it. It's probably safer for you not to be around me right now."

Mariah blew a raspberry. "I'd help fight back, you know that."

Katie smiled. She appreciated her friend's willingness to fight on her behalf. "Well, the lab is much safer. Speaking of…"

"Right." Mariah turned all business. "Your guy got a little careless. I just got my hit from IAFIS and we have a fingerprint from your Molotov cocktail bottle."

"Who does it belong to?" Her stomach tightened in anticipation of hearing the name of the person who wanted her dead.

"He's a parolee. His name is Norman Rhames."

"Norman Rhames!"

"I take it you've heard of him?"

"Yes. I have. He's the guy who made that deposit into Lisa West's bank account. Her husband is the one who killed the guy who broke into my house."

"Never a dull moment for you, is there?"

"You're funny. But no, never a dull moment." She bit her lip. "Okay, this is an interesting twist."

"Well, I hope you find him. That's my home, too, and I want this guy stopped." Fury seeped through her words and Katie empathized.

"Thanks for the information. I'll pass it along to Gregory and let him work with it. I'm chasing another lead. Maybe one of us will come up with something."

"Sounds good."

"How's Grandma Jean and her cold?"

"She's better and so far I haven't gotten it." Mariah paused. "Of course, I've only been there to sleep at night. I've hardly been around her. My poor mother is not faring so well, I'm afraid."

"Glad she's better. And I'll say a prayer for your mom." Katie blew out a sigh. "I'll let you know what happens with Mr. Rhames."

"Be careful, Katie."

"Yes, ma'am."

She hung up and passed on the information to Jordan and Cort, then called Gregory and filled him in.

"I'll track him down ASAP," Gregory said. "I'll call you as soon as he's in custody."

Katie said, "Please do. I have a few questions for him."

Like why someone who deposited five thousand dollars in the account of the wife of a felon was the same person who tried to kill her the other night.

"I'm sure. Are you all right? Need a hand with anything?"

"No, but I appreciate everything you've done so far."

Gregory snorted. "Haven't done much."

"You're not complaining about my absence, you're helping me track down information and you're picking up the slack on our cases. I can't tell you how much I appreciate that."

"You'd do the same for me."

"You know it."

"What's on the agenda for today? You going to take it easy, or is that a dumb question?"

"What do you think?"

He laughed. "I figured."

"We're going to talk to Mrs. Johnson at the nursing home. See if she remembers anything about a gray sedan being parked in the neighborhood."

"Be careful, Katie."

"You know it." She hung up, grateful for a partner she trusted and one who supported her efforts in finding Lucy.

Jordan stood. "Thanks for your help, Cort. Having you watching is the reason Katie is alive. If you hadn't been behind her and called…" He shrugged.

Cort shook hands with Jordan and gave a disgusted snort. "If I had been a little quicker with the steering wheel, I wouldn't have lost her."

Jordan turned to Katie and said, "Do you feel up to visiting Mrs. Johnson now?"

"I'm sore, of course, but yes, I'm up to it."

"Do you mind if I drive?"

She gave a low chuckle. "Unless you want to hitch-hike, that's pretty much our only option right now." She sighed. "I guess I need to put car shopping on my list of things to do."

"Are you getting a rental?"

"It should be ready by the time we finish with Mrs. Johnson. Erica lined it all up for me."

"She's a good friend."

"She is."

Cort stood and said, "Guess I'll be going, unless you want me to follow and watch for a tail?"

Jordan nodded. "That'd be great."

They filed back out of the room, and Katie joined Jordan in his car. She clicked on her seat belt. "Have your parents said anything more about us working together?"

The abrupt question didn't faze him. "No. And I haven't exactly gone out of my way to talk to them since the confrontation in the restaurant. I was thinking about that earlier and I've decided I'm going to have to make some time to do that."

His low words had a tightness to them, and she almost regretted bringing the subject up, but she and Jordan were growing closer by the day. And if it wasn't for his parents' hatred of her, she'd encourage the relationship. As it was…

"They don't know the whole truth," Jordan said.

"What do you mean?"

"That night you arrested Neil. They don't know everything he was doing that night." He cleared his throat. "I kept it from them."

Katie gaped. "Then I don't know the whole story, either. I thought it was just a DUI. Are you telling me there's more?" She glanced in the rearview mirror and saw no one behind them.

"Yes."

"Do you mind sharing?"

He sighed. "Apparently, Neil was a drug mule."

Katie gasped. "What?"

"When they did the autopsy, they found bags of heroin in his stomach."

"Oh, no."

Jordan's lips twisted. "He'd just gotten back from Mexico. From what I can figure out, you stopped him on his way from the airport to deliver the drugs."

"How did you find all this out?"

He slanted a glance at her. "I have my sources."

"But I smelled alcohol on him. He registered twice the legal alcohol limit on the Breathalyzer."

"I know. I'm not saying he wasn't drinking. In fact, he probably had a few on the plane, as he always hated flying. But there was more to it than that."

Katie blew out a breath. "Wow. And you never told your parents this?"

"No." He pinched the bridge of his nose. "Dad's in his late fifties. But about two years ago, he had a mild heart attack."

"Oh. I'm sorry."

"He seemed to bounce back from it pretty well, but my mother is a worrywart. She keeps telling me we need to spare him as much stress as possible."

"Is she right?"

"I don't know. The day of Neil's funeral, he had another heart attack. This one more severe. So…" He shrugged. "I'm sure all the stress didn't help."

"So you kept all of this information to yourself."

"Yes."

"So why tell him now?"

"Like I said, I've been thinking. All of the anger and resentment and bitterness he's harboring toward you surely can't be good for him, either."

"True."

"I think what I'm going to have to do is tell my parents about Neil. It's time."

"What if he has another attack?"

He blew out a heavy sigh. "His last check up was good. No sign of any more damage. He's going to have to face what Neil was into if he's going to have any kind of peace. Right now he's in such denial, he's simply adding stress to his life—and his heart."

Jordan pulled into White Oak Manor's parking lot. He shut off the engine and turned to face her. "This isn't something I just came up with. I've been contemplating it for the last six months."

"I see." She looked at her fingers. "And you've decided now is the time?"

"I think so. I've been praying about it."

"And?"

"I don't know. God hasn't said yes or no in a way that's loud and clear."

"So why do it now?"

"For reasons I've already stated, but I won't deny part of it's because I want to explore whatever is developing between us. And I can't do that as long as my parents are planted firmly in the way."

Katie blinked. Shock zipped through her, followed by surprise and then…hope. "What do you think is developing?"

Jordan moved in closer and placed a hand at the base

of her neck. "This," he whispered. And covered her lips with his. Warm honey moved through her veins, making her languid and giddy with the thought that she could kiss this man forever. She reached up and cupped his chin as he deepened the kiss, and she wanted to protest when he pulled away with a gentle smile. He gazed down at her. "That. And more." He stroked her cheek. "I've never met anyone like you before, and I want to see if we have something special." He tilted his head. "Correction. I think we do have something special, and I want the freedom to explore just how special it is."

She swallowed hard and let out a breath. "Wow." He wasn't holding anything back right now and his openness, his vulnerability stunned her.

"Exactly."

"Okay."

"Okay what?"

"Talk to your parents if you think that's what you need to do." Then she frowned and tried to ignore the effects of his kiss. With just one kiss, he'd stirred up the longing for a relationship with him, the hope for a possible future together.

She thought for a moment, trying to figure out the best way to say what was in her heart. Finally, she said, "I'll be straight with you, Jordan. As much as I'd also like to see where this could go between us, I don't know if I can do it if your parents hate me." She bit her lip, then said, "In fact, I'm pretty sure I can't." She heard the anguish in her last two words and when he flinched, knew he'd heard it, too.

Jordan and Katie walked into the lobby of the assisted-living home and stopped at the front desk. Katie flashed her badge and asked for Mrs. Johnson's room while Jordan stood by a window and watched the parking lot.

"Who was here?" Katie asked.

Jordan tuned in to the conversation.

The lady behind the desk said, "I think it was her son. He came in and she seemed confused as to who he was. That happens a lot these days, poor dear. She is almost ninety, you know."

"Yes, I know, thanks. Do you think it would be possible for us to just speak to her briefly? I promise we won't keep her long. It's really urgent that I talk to her if she feels up to it."

The woman hesitated then said, "Let me check with her nurse. She was apparently pretty agitated when her son left."

Katie shifted beside him. "She's going to say no."

"Why do you say that?"

"I just have a feeling. Come on."

"Where are we going? We don't have her room number."

"Sure we do. I can read upside down. She was documenting something in the chart and snapped it shut when I walked up, but not before I saw the name and a number I'm guessing is her room."

They made their way down the hall to Mrs. Johnson's room. Jordan held the door for Katie, then slipped in behind her. The dark room held the odor that seemed to be indigenous to nursing homes and hospitals: antiseptic, bleach and air freshener.

"Mrs. Johnson?" Katie's soft voice brought his attention to the woman in the bed. A night-light burned in the corner. "Mrs. Johnson?"

Jordan turned on a small lamp and the low-wattage bulb bathed the room in a soft glow.

The woman on the bed stirred. Katie sat in the chair next to her and took her hand. "Hi, Mrs. Johnson. Do you remember me? Katie Randall?"

Mrs. Johnson blinked owlishly, and Jordan picked up a pair of glasses and slipped them on her nose.

"Oh, Katie," Mrs. Johnson said, her voice paper thin and wispy. "Yes, of course I remember you. Will you help me sit up? I must have dozed off." She clicked her teeth and sighed. "I seem to do that a lot lately."

Katie pressed the button, and soon Jordan heard the bed whirring as it lifted its occupant into a sitting position.

"What are you doing in here?"

Jordan spun to see the woman from the front desk. "We decided to come on back and visit."

"Why didn't you wait on me? Her son asked that she not be disturbed."

"That man wasn't my son."

The nurse hurried in. "Now, Mrs. Johnson, you know you sometimes get confused. Of course that was your son."

"Young lady, I do get confused, but I have never not known my own son. I don't have dementia, and I don't have Alzheimer's, so I would appreciate you not trying to make it sound like I do. I'm old and occasionally forgetful, but that was not my son. Now, please go away and let me enjoy my visitors."

The long speech seemed to wind her, but Jordan saw a twinkle in Mrs. Johnson's eyes. A twinkle that blasted hope through the room. The nurse blew out a breath of exasperation but turned and left the room without another word.

Mrs. Johnson looked at Katie. "Did you ever find your sister?"

Katie blinked. So Mrs. Johnson did remember. Katie had almost decided fourteen years would be too much for the elderly woman. "Do you remember the day she was taken?"

"Like it was yesterday." She snorted and coughed. "Can't remember what I had for breakfast, but I'll never forget that day. If only I hadn't asked you to help me carry in those groceries." A tear leaked down her lined cheek. Katie grabbed a tissue and wiped it away.

"It's not your fault, Mrs. Johnson."

A trembling hand lifted to rub her nose. "Well, sometimes I feel like it was."

Jordan shifted. "We think the man who took Lucy was watching, just waiting for an opportunity. If it hadn't been that day, it would have been another time."

That seemed to settle her. "He was watching?"

Katie said, "We think so. Do you remember seeing a strange car parked on the street a couple of weeks before the day of the kidnapping?"

"A strange car? No, I don't think so." She sniffed. "I remember wondering what that police car was doing out there day in and day out, but that's the only car I remember thinking was strange."

"Police car?"

"Uh-huh. Lucky it was so close that day, wasn't it?"

"Yes, very lucky. Mrs. Johnson?"

"Hmm?"

"Who was the man that came to see you, and why did they think he was your son?"

"Guess he told them he was."

"What did he want?"

Her eyes clouded and drooped. "To tell me to be quiet, but I'll talk if I want." Her words slurred, her eyes closed and a snore slipped out.

Katie's eyes met Jordan's. "I think she's done."

He tapped Mrs. Johnson's shoulder. She snorted and her head lolled over to her left shoulder. Jordan sighed. "I think you're right."

Katie stood and winced as her sore muscles protested. She ignored the pain and made a mental note to take some more ibuprofen. "Why hasn't anyone else said anything about a police car being there?"

They walked from the room together. Jordan shook his head. "There were so many police cars there that day most neighbors probably didn't think anything about it."

"Maybe."

"And maybe the police car wasn't really parked. Maybe it was just doing drive-bys, you know?"

"That's possible, I suppose, but she did say 'parked there day in and day out.'"

"You think it's the same car Mrs. McKinney saw?"

"I don't suppose there's any way to know. Mrs. McKinney didn't identify it as a police car, though. Just a gray sedan. And the picture is too unclear to determine if the vehicle is actually an unmarked car."

"You think the man who came to see Mrs. Johnson was the man after me?"

"I don't see how. He wouldn't know we were coming today."

"Right."

"It does seem strange to me, though, that she would get a visitor telling her to keep quiet."

"Did you tell anyone that we were coming here?"

Katie thought about it. "Just Gregory."

"You don't think that was him at the home, do you?"

She frowned. "No way. He was tracking down Norman Rhames. And besides, why would he do that?"

"I don't know. It's just weird. I think we should get the video footage and see who Mrs. Johnson's visitor was."

Katie nodded. "Good idea." She made the required calls and was promised a return call when she could go see the videos.

Once outside the building, Jordan hovered, placing his arm around her shoulder and tucking her close to his side. While she relished the proximity, his touch set her bumps and bruises to screaming. She eased away from him and he shot her a look with a big question mark in his eyes. "Sorry, it hurts."

Realization dawned and regret flickered. "Stay next to me then." Warmth flickered in her midsection. She liked being close to him, wanted his arm around her. He glanced around. "If someone's going to shoot, I want to make you as small a target as possible."

Laughter burst from her before she could choke it back.

Jordan helped her into the car and shut the door, then climbed in his side. He looked at her. "What in the world are you laughing about?"

"I'm sorry. I was just thinking how I was enjoying being close to you, that it was sweet you wanted me tucked up under your arm and you're just worried about me getting shot." She laughed again until tears formed.

She swiped them away. "I think I'm hysterical, because it's really not that funny."

He kissed her. She leaned in and felt her emotions even out. Her tears stopped and she hitched a breath and kissed him back.

When he pulled away, his eyes held soft compassion as well as other emotions she wasn't sure she could identify. He said, "I want you close, Katie."

She bit her lip, then gave him a watery smile. "Good."

"I'm taking you back to your hotel room. You need some rest."

Katie leaned her head back against the seat. Exhaustion swamped her. "I think I won't argue with that."

Jordan slept in the car outside her hotel room from 3:00 a.m. to 7:30 a.m. Saturday morning. Gregory had taken the first shift. Jordan's five hours of protection duty gave him time to think. And he'd made a decision. One he had to run past Katie. He texted her.

Sitting outside your room. Ready when you are.

Coming. Slowly.
Sore?

To say the least. Be there in a few min.

Ten minutes later, Katie emerged from her room, and he smiled in sympathy as she climbed into the car with a grimace.

He handed her a mug and poured her a cup of coffee from the Thermos. She took a sip and sighed, a grateful sound that made him glad he could do something for her. "You're my favorite person this morning," she murmured.

He laughed. "Glad I could help you out." He turned serious and gripped the steering wheel. "I want you to go with me somewhere."

"Where?"

"You know that errand I said I needed to run yesterday?"

"Yes."

"I want you to run it with me."

Wary now, she glanced at him from the corner of her eye. "And where might that be?"

"To talk to my parents. I'm going to tell them what really happened with Neil."

A long pause. She finally said, "I don't think that's a good idea, Jordan. If their reaction at the restaurant is any indication of how they still feel—"

"Please." His fingers tightened on the steering wheel. "It *is* how they feel, and it needs to be addressed. I think they need to see you're not some monster."

"I don't know. They may never speak to you again if you bring me around."

"It's something I think we need to try."

"Jordan, they're hurting. It's only been a year."

"I know, but they're not healing. That's the problem. I understand it's only been a year. I still hurt when I think about him, too, but the anger they still hold toward you…." He shook his head. "At the restaurant, you would have thought Neil died two weeks ago, their anger was so fresh and raw. It's not right."

"Exactly. Which is why I don't think it's a good idea for me to go."

"Please." He kept his voice low, his tone convincing. "I've already thought about the safety issue. Max is going to follow us."

"Jordan…" She drew his name out and he sensed capitulation.

Jordan took her hand and squeezed her fingers. "I want them to see you as you. Not as the woman they believe killed their son." He drew in a deep breath. "I think they need that as much you do."

She sat still and looked at him. "I'm still not sure it's the best idea, but if it's that important to you, I'll do it."

He lifted her hand to his lips and pressed a kiss to her knuckles. Her eyes met his. "Thanks," he whispered.

She nodded and he dropped her hand. "I've already called them. They're expecting me."

"They're early risers."

"Obscenely early. Mom's already started baking."

As Jordan drove, Katie stayed quiet, lost in her thoughts. He left her alone and silently rehearsed how he wanted to break his news of Neil's drug involvement to his parents. Nothing he came up with sounded right. He had a feeling nothing would.

Jordan pulled into his parents' drive, but didn't cut the motor. From the vehicle behind them, Max waved, indicating they were in the clear. No one had followed. Jordan waved back. For several long minutes he simply sat there, staring at the house he and his brother had grown up in.

"It's nice," Katie said.

The house was a modest two-story cottage-style home. His favorite feature was the wraparound balcony on the second floor. Christmas lights wove in and out of the spindles like kudzu. A white wreath hung on the door and bright-eyed reindeer graced the lawn.

"Yes. I had a great childhood. Ideal, really." He gave a slight smile.

"What are you thinking?"

"That my mother always worried we'd play airplane or try to parachute off that balcony and break our necks."

"But you didn't?"

"No way. I had a pretty good sense of self-preservation." He frowned. "Too bad Neil didn't." Neil had found another way to break his mother's heart.

Jaw clamped against his rising emotions, he pulled all the way into the two-car carport that was enclosed on three sides. He twisted the key and silence fell between them. Jordan opened the car door and climbed out. "Could you wait here for a few minutes?"

Katie slid him a glance from the corner of her eye. "You did tell them I was coming, right? You said you'd already called them, that they were expecting us." He moved to the back of the carport, and Katie climbed out of the car to follow him. "They know, right, Jordan?"

"I said they were expecting me."

Her face lost all color. "You can't spring me on them."

"I know. But I didn't want to tell them over the phone. I couldn't think of a good way to explain it. Could you hang back a little until I tell them?" He glanced around. "And stay down. We weren't followed, but that doesn't mean you're safe."

"That's why you parked in the carport? To give me cover while you broke the news to your parents?" She shot back into the car and slammed the door, glaring daggers at him.

He grimaced and didn't blame her. He'd taken the coward's way out by not telling his parents she was coming with him and not telling Katie he hadn't told his parents. "I'm sorry. You're right. I'm a big coward when it comes to this kind of thing."

Her eyes softened slightly. "I'll just make some phone calls."

"Thanks, Katie."

Jordan went around to the front door and tried the knob. Locked. His lips twisted into a smile in spite of his roiling emotions. Maybe all of his preaching about safety had sunk in. He knocked, and his dad opened the door. Pleasure lit his features. "Jordan, good to see you, son. Come on in."

Jordan entered the small foyer and breathed in the scent of his childhood. Depending on the season, he always knew what his mother's house would smell like: December meant homemade chocolates, pies and cakes. His mouth watered. "I need to talk to you and Mom, but first I'm going to have a taste of whatever she's cooking in there."

His dad grinned at him, and Jordan felt a surge of remorse at the pain he was about to put them through. He studied his father. In his late fifties, Paul could still pass for mid-forties, in spite of his heart issues. Jordan hoped he aged as well—without the heart problems. He shucked his coat and hung it on the rack by the door as he wrestled with the reason he'd come over.

Jordan's mother stood at the oven, placing another pan of goodies on the rack. "Hi, Mom."

"I thought I heard you." She turned and crossed the room to give him a hug and a peck on the cheek. "How are you doing?"

"I'm doing all right."

Jordan snagged a sweet treat from the cooling rack and popped it in his mouth. The sugary concoction melted on his tongue. "Mmm. Delicious as always." He smiled. "I heard you were in your Christmas baking mood. I could smell this stuff all the way from my apartment."

Her eyes twinkled up at him. Jordan noticed time hadn't been quite as kind to her as it had to his father. Fine lines radiated across her forehead and around her mouth and eyes. Grief had added more than her fair share, he supposed.

Anger at Neil surged and he bit his lip. "I need to talk to you and Dad. Do you have a minute to sit down?"

"Sure I do." She pulled off the red-and-white checked apron with the big red heart that said *50 and Fabulous.* He'd given it to her four years ago when she'd bemoaned her fiftieth birthday for six full months. He noticed she wore it every time she worked in the kitchen.

The three of them sat at the kitchen table. Jordan snagged another chocolate, scrambling to find the words he'd practiced on the way over. They'd deserted him.

He took a deep breath and for one frantic moment wondered if he was being selfish. Were his words necessary? Would they do more harm than good? Would his parents even believe him?

Maybe not at first. But eventually they would. And that was when it would hurt the most. When the truth of Neil's actions finally sank in.

"What is it, son?" His dad clapped him on the back.

Jordan rubbed his forehead. "I need to tell you guys something and I'll just tell you straight up, it's not going to be easy for you to hear."

Matching frowns immediately appeared on their faces. His mother covered his hand with hers and her eyes narrowed, searching his expression. "What is it you don't want to tell us?"

She could always read him. Jordan shook his head. "I've been thinking—and praying—long and hard about telling you this, but the fact of the matter is, I don't think you—" he looked at his father "—most especially you, Dad, are healing from Neil's death."

"Healing?" His father's eyebrows came to a V at the bridge of his nose. "Healing? How are we supposed to heal when the cop who helped kill your brother is out there free to kill other kids?"

Jordan held on to his temper with effort. He hadn't come here to argue with his parents. He knew just mentioning Neil's name was enough to set his dad off on a tangent.

"They did an investigation, Dad, thanks to your insistence. There was nothing to prove she'd been negligent. Neil was drunk. He was arrested for driving under the influence and he was placed in a holding cell. End of story." He clasped his hands between his knees and prayed for wisdom.

"It's not the end! She placed him in a cell with a killer!"

Jordan thought his head might explode with the effort of holding in his temper. "She didn't do anything wrong. Neil was drunk when he chose to drive. He ran a stop sign going fifty miles per hour right in front of Detective Randall. What else was she supposed to do? She did her job. It was Neil's stupid choices that killed him, not her."

His father stood and jabbed a finger at Jordan. "I refuse to sit here and listen to you defend her. I can't believe you would come into my house—"

Jordan slammed his palm onto the table. His father jerked, and his mother gasped. Jordan took a deep breath. "Stop. Okay? Just stop." He looked at his dad. "And sit down, please. I'm not done." His father, still staring at Jordan's uncharacteristic outburst, slid back into his chair.

"Why do you say she didn't kill him?" his mother whispered, her stricken expression zinging straight to his heart.

"Because I know the truth about Neil. Truth I've kept from you, thinking to spare your feelings, your memories." He looked at his dad. "Your heart. But I—"

"What truth?" His father's voice was low, the question, wary.

Katie sat in the car and felt her anger dissipate with each passing moment. She understood Jordan's reluctance to tell his parents over the phone that she was coming along. If Jordan had told his parents he was bringing her by, most likely they would have flipped out. His father would have stewed and stressed over it. She wasn't exactly sure how his mother would have reacted.

She understood Jordan's thinking. When he told his parents she was sitting in the car outside, they might be a little more likely to see her. If only out of good manners.

Although good manners hadn't stopped Jordan's father from heaping his grief and anger on her head in the morgue. Or at the restaurant.

Katie moved the rearview mirror to give her a good view of the area behind her. Max and Jordan seemed confident they hadn't been followed, but Katie wasn't going to relax her guard. She called Gregory, who'd followed up on the receipt they'd found in the shooter's wrecked and abandoned car.

"Are you in or out of the hospital?" he answered by way of a greeting.

Katie grimaced. "Out."

"Try and keep it that way, will you?"

She heard the concern in his voice and appreciated it. "I'll do my best. It's been so crazy, I haven't had a chance to track down that receipt. Did you?"

"I did."

"And?"

"And our shooter had on sunglasses and a ball cap along with a scarf wrapped around his neck."

"Video footage?"

"Yes. But my guess is he was familiar with the camera placements, because he kept his back to them as much as possible."

"And he paid in cash."

"At the pump. He never entered the store."

"Of course." She sighed and watched the door leading into the house. No sign of Jordan. "So that's another dead end."

"Maybe. I mean, we're looking for a guy who's about five feet eleven or six feet tall. He's a little overweight and is Caucasian. Couldn't get hair or eye color, of course, but this information might help."

"What about his hands? Could you do any close-ups?"

"He was wearing black gloves."

Of course he was. "All right. Thanks. Let me know if you come up with anything else."

"Will do."

She hung up then dialed her mother's number. Voice mail. She left a message about stopping by soon and hoped she was well. Katie avoided mentioning her stay in the hospital and her mother's noticeable absence.

And the hurt that it caused.

She winced and glanced in the mirror. Nothing. Another look at the door to the house. Another nothing. Jordan sure was taking a long time.

Even though it was Saturday, Katie knew Mariah was working. She called her roommate for an update on the diner evidence. Mariah said, "Bullet casings came from a semiautomatic .308 Winchester rifle. It's not a hard weapon to get your hands on, and there's nothing really special about it. Lots of hunters use it."

"Lovely. Anything else?"

"Trace evidence such as hair and other fibers that don't add up to anything right now, but will be available for comparison if you come up with a suspect."

"Okay."

"So what are you doing on your medical leave?"

Katie glanced at the house and caught Jordan's eye, staring at her from behind the window of the kitchen door. "Getting ready to walk into the lion's den, I think."

Jordan met Katie's eyes through the glass and shook his head. He paced back to the table and sat again, wishing he could take out his agitation on the patterned linoleum floor. Instead, he shifted and cleared his throat. "Neil was into drugs. Not just using them, he was a mule." He paused at his parents' blank expressions. "Someone who transports drugs over the border for a lot of money by swallowing packets of drugs."

His mother blinked at him, her audible gasp making Jordan grasp her hand. She pulled away and stared at him as the color in her cheeks drained away.

"How dare you?" His father jumped up, face red, eyes blazing. "She's brainwashed you! How dare you come into this house and malign your brother's memory? How dare you!" He strode from the kitchen.

"Dad—" Jordan moved to follow. His mother's hand on his arm stopped him. Her white, pinched face sent sorrow racing through him. "I'm sorry. I shouldn't have…" He shook his head.

"No. It was time."

Her quiet response had him looking into her eyes. "What do you mean?"

She wiped her hand on her apron and clasped them in front of her. "About six months before Neil died, I heard him being sick in the bathroom. I knocked on the door and he told me to go away, that he was fine. He was in there a really long time. I thought he might have the flu or something. I took a phone call and then came back to check on him later. He was unconscious in his room. I called nine-one-one and got him to the emergency room, where they said he'd overdosed."

"One of the packets had leaked. Or ruptured."

She nodded. "He almost died."

"Why didn't you ever tell me?"

"You were working like crazy, your father was on a business trip and—" she held her hands up as though beseeching him to understand "—Neil swore me to secrecy. Said he'd never do it again. Begged me to think about Dad's heart. Said if your dad died because I told him about the drugs, it would be on my head."

She gave a sad smile. "I didn't let that last part sway me, but it did make me think." She swallowed hard. "I was very worried what this information might do to Paul." His mother twisted a napkin between her fingers, shredding it, piece by piece. "And Neil promised. Took my hands, looked me in the eye and promised."

"And you believed him?"

She nodded. "He was scared. Truly terrified when he

found out how close he came to dying. He said he was done with that and he'd stay away from the people he was involved with."

"People like that don't just let you walk away."

She swiped a few stray tears. "I made him go to counseling. Told him I'd tell your dad if he didn't. Neil didn't like it, but he did it. I thought he was doing better." She flicked a glance at him and shoved the napkin pieces away. "I searched his room every day and never found anything else. He had that good job at the construction company. He was going all over the city working and he seemed happy enough. Every once in a while he'd get an out-of-town job. He was doing well. I thought."

School had never been Neil's strong point, and their parents hadn't pushed the issue when he'd dropped out to work full-time. As long as he was working, they were happy to let him live with them until he saved enough to go out on his own.

"Then one afternoon, he'd just come home from an out-of-town job. I checked the bathroom and found a little pouch of white powder. When I asked him about it, he took it and said it wasn't what I thought. He was just holding it for a friend." Tears clouded her blue eyes and she swallowed hard. "I'm not stupid, Jordan. I figured he was using again. He denied it, of course, but I knew."

"Oh, Mom, why didn't you say something?"

"I hadn't said anything to your father the first time. This time I was going to say something, and Neil knew it. He stormed out and I never saw him again." Her voice cracked on the last word. Jordan squeezed her fingers and she took a steadying breath. "He left to go on that trip to Mexico. I was trying to figure out how to tell your father before Neil came home. The next call we got was from

Neil saying he was in jail, that he was being wrongly held. And then later, from the police saying he was dead."

"You kept that from me?"

Jordan and his mother swiveled as one to see his father standing in the doorway, face pale. The sick look in his eyes shouted his betrayal. Jordan's stomach sank.

His mother sighed and nodded. "I did. And before you say anything, I thought long and hard about it before I did it. I was scared your heart couldn't take it."

"Then we have a lot to talk about."

"I guess we do."

Jordan rose. "I'm sorry."

"Why did you decide to tell us this now?" his mother asked.

Before Jordan could answer, his father asked, "It's because of Katie Randall, isn't it?"

Jordan considered acting like he didn't know what he was talking about, but couldn't do it. "Part of it's about her. I won't lie, I'm interested in dating her and getting to know her better." He paused and rubbed his eyes. "I've been debating whether to say anything to you since I read the autopsy report."

"Wish you'd said something before now," his dad said.

Jordan looked him in the eye. "No, you don't."

Tears filled his father's eyes, and he blinked them back. "I'm not sure I believe it."

"I know. It's hard to swallow." He glanced at his mother, who stared at her hands. "Talk to Mom. Work it out. Don't let Neil's death destroy you two. He may have been into some bad stuff, but he loved you guys." A sob broke from his mother's throat, but she nodded her agreement.

Jordan hugged each parent, letting them cling a little

longer than usual. "I'm sorry." He couldn't seem to stop apologizing. Because he really was sorry. Sorry Neil had gotten into drugs. Sorry his mother had carried such a burden. Sorry his dad was feeling betrayed by his new knowledge. And sorry Neil was dead.

"Could we pray together?"

His mother's shaky question rattled him. Of course they needed to pray. He nodded and pulled his father to his feet. The man stood silent, refusing to say anything, but Jordan's mother gripped his hand and he didn't pull away. Jordan prayed from his heart, asking God's divine intervention in this painful way. And forgiveness for all involved.

"Amen."

"Amen," his mother whispered.

Jordan looked at his parents. "I was wondering if Katie could come in."

His mother looked startled. "What?"

"She's in the car."

"All this time, you've left her there?"

Jordan felt heat rise from his neck. "I needed to talk to you first."

"No." Jordan's father took a deep breath. "I'm not ready to see her."

"But Dad, I told you what happened. It's not Katie's fault."

"She still arrested him and put him in that cage with those animals." Stubborn pain glinted in the man's eyes and Jordan knew it might be hopeless to argue, but he had to try.

"Because Neil was driving drunk. He even took a swing at her. You're still in denial, Dad. You've got to realize that continuing to blame Katie for Neil's decisions isn't going let you heal. It's just going to keep your bitterness boiling until one day it's out of control and you have nothing left except that bitterness." Jordan knew he sounded harsh, but coddling his parents and handling them with kid gloves hadn't helped them move on. Still, he took a deep breath and softened his tone. "Think about it, Dad. You're going to grow into a bitter old man if you don't let this go."

His father jerked as though Jordan had reached out and punched him. He turned on his heel and left the room.

"Give us some time." His mother took a deep breath. "I have a feeling we're going to be talking a lot over the next several hours. Probably days."

Jordan nodded. Maybe she was right. Seeing Katie right now wouldn't be good. They both needed to process what they'd just learned about their dead son.

He gave his mom another hug. "Call me if you need to. I'll check on you later."

She nodded and Jordan headed for the front door, hoping Katie wasn't ready to kill him for making her wait so long.

FOURTEEN

Katie was ready to kill the man. She was sore all over and had a headache that wouldn't quit. Thankfully he'd left the car running with the heat on, or she'd be freezing, too. It was only the fact that she was warm that kept her from biting his head off when he slipped into the driver's seat and gripped the steering wheel.

Then she got a glimpse of the pain on his face, and her anger melted like ice cream on a hot summer day. She reached over and placed a hand over his. "Are you going to be okay?"

In one move he pulled her into a hug, burying his face in her neck. Stunned, she sat there, then wrapped her arms around his shoulders. A shudder went through him. "That was one of the hardest things I've ever done, but I'll be all right. I just pray they will be, too."

The need to comfort him swept over her and she just let him cling to her in spite of the physical pain his embrace caused her.

He shifted to place lips over hers. A light kiss at first, as though he was saying thank you. She felt his deep sorrow, the tightly leashed control on his grief—and his unspoken need for comfort. She kissed him back and let time stand still.

When he lifted his head, he sighed and closed his eyes. "Thank you for being here."

Katie cleared her throat, trying to dislodge the lump of tears that had gathered. "Sure."

"They're not ready to see you yet."

"So you don't want me to go inside?"

"No. I think it's better if we let them digest everything I told them and try again another day."

She swallowed hard. "All right."

"Mom knew about Neil." The words sounded forced, painful. Then they registered.

"She knew?"

He nodded. "And she kept it from my dad. He's not happy with her."

"Oh, dear. I'm so sorry. Are they going to be all right?"

"I hope so."

He cranked the car and backed out of the carport. Katie touched his arm and pointed at his mother, who was walking toward them. He stopped the car in the driveway. "She's got something."

Jordan's mother approached the vehicle, carrying two cups with lids. Her smile was strained, but at least it was there. Jordan rolled the window down and she handed him the cups. "Hot apple cider."

Jordan passed one to Katie. Stunned, she took it. "Thank you, Mrs. Gray."

Jordan's mother bit her lip, then sighed. "You're welcome." Then she leaned in and pressed a kiss to her son's forehead. "Please be careful." She flicked a glance to Katie and once more offered a wobbly smile. "Goodbye."

"Bye."

Then she was back in the house and Katie was left staring at the front door. "Wow. Didn't expect that one."

"Tell me about it," Jordan murmured. But Katie could see the hope in his eyes and for the first time since Neil's death, she thought forgiveness might come from his parents.

Katie's phone rang as they pulled away from the house. She glanced at the number and did a double take. Her lieutenant. "This is Detective Randall."

"Katie, how are you feeling?"

"I'm sore and banged up, but nothing that will keep me down for long."

"Good, good, I'm glad to hear it. I was wondering when you plan to come back to work."

Katie swallowed. She'd planned to take advantage of every minute of leave she could get to work on Lucy's case, but... "I have four days of medical leave, but do you have something you need me to cover?"

"We're having a rash of crime here and I'm short staffed because of the flu. If you're able to help at all, I'd appreciate it. I'll give you some time off later. If the doc says no go, I understand. I don't want you to push it."

She was going to push it, whether it was working on Lucy's case or one he had for her. "Tell me what you need."

"I've got a dead body dumped off the highway along I-85 North. Gregory's already on his way. Can you meet him there?"

Katie bit her lip. She didn't want to be interrupted, but she knew she needed to do this for her boss. "I can be there in ten minutes."

"Thanks, Katie. I owe you."

"Sure." She hung up and looked at Jordan. "I need you to drop me off."

"Leave is up, huh?"

"Yes. For now. If I was truly incapacitated, it wouldn't be an issue, but I'm not."

"You'll be with your partner and a whole slew of other law enforcement personnel, right?"

"Right."

"It still may not be safe. I mean if he's got a sniper rifle—"

"Doesn't matter. I've got to do my job. I'm not going to let him take this from me, too. You can stay, if you want."

He narrowed his eyes as he thought, and at first she thought he might decide to stay. Then he shook his head. "You should be safe enough at the crime scene, and your buddies won't want me hanging around."

"We're not a territorial group." He scoffed, and she laughed. "Okay, okay. I wouldn't mind you there, but you might get a few looks from the others."

"I may go back to my office and look at the pictures from the neighborhood again."

"Call me if you come up with anything?"

"Absolutely."

Jordan dropped her at the crime scene, scoped out the area for the next twenty minutes, and when he didn't find anything or anyone that posed a danger to Katie, he headed for the office. He had an idea he wanted to implement.

Once in the office, he pulled Lucy's file and went straight for the pictures. He studied them one by one and gave a grunt of satisfaction when he thought he found what he was looking for. He picked up the phone and called Danny Jackson.

"Jackson here."

"Jordan Gray. I was wondering if you'd have a few minutes to talk about Lucy Randall."

A heavy sigh filtered through the line. "You still gnawing on that one like a dog with a bone, aren't you?"

"Yes, I guess I am."

"Then all right. But you gotta come to me. I'm down at McGee's Café."

Jordan grimaced. A thirty-minute drive. "All right. Don't leave, it'll take me half an hour to get there."

"I'm not going anywhere. Got nowhere to go."

Jordan gathered the photos and slid them back into the file. Then he grabbed his phone and sent a text to Katie, letting her know what he was doing. And begged her to stay with someone in order to ensure her safety until he got back.

She sent him a text assuring him she was surrounded by law enforcement and would let him know when she was finished. He tucked his phone into his pocket and sent up a prayer for her safety. And for God to bring closure to this search for Lucy—one way or another.

FIFTEEN

Katie did her best to keep her back from being exposed to any place she thought might be a good spot for a sniper to draw a bead on her. Out on the highway, trees lined the road for miles. Lots of hiding places. She noticed Gregory keeping an eye on her and the area around them, too. He said, "You all right?"

"I've been better, but I'm making it."

"Mom wanted to have flowers delivered, but you'd already been released. I told her to send them on to the hospital, you'd probably be back tomorrow."

She gave him a light punch on his arm. "You're hilarious." She pointed. "Who do we have here?"

He turned serious, all business now. "You're not going to believe it."

She lifted a brow. "Try me."

"It's Norman Rhames."

Katie gaped for a full two seconds, then snapped her mouth shut. She rubbed her head and stared down at the body. "You're right. I don't believe it. I take it the lieutenant didn't know who he was when he sent me out here?"

"Nope. We just got confirmation on his identity about a minute before you drove up."

"I'll keep my hands off the investigation since there's a possible connection to Wray, but since I'm here, will you tell me what you know?"

"He was shot in the back of the head. Execution style."

Katie narrowed her eyes. "Now that's just shouting for an investigation. I want to know the connection between Norman Rhames and Wesley Wray."

Gregory pursed his lips. "You don't think it's a coincidence?"

"There's no way this is a coincidence."

He nodded. "I agree."

Katie got on her phone and called Jordan. He answered with, "Are you okay?"

In spite of the seriousness of the situation, Katie almost had to smile at his instant question. "What makes you ask that?"

"Cute."

"I'm also fine. Guess who our dead guy is?"

"Who?"

She filled him in. "You want to use your FBI contacts and see if you can find a connection between Wesley Wray and Norman Rhames sometime before Christmas?"

Katie felt a little disloyal to her department, but the FBI had more resources than a local department. With one phone call, Jordan would probably find what she wanted to know within the hour.

Her phone buzzed and she lifted a brow at the name that popped on the screen. "Hello, Detective Miller, what can I do for you?"

"You working that dead body on the highway?"

"I am."

"Heard it on the scanner. Thought you were on medical leave."

"I did, too."

He gave a half laugh, half snort. "Flu's swept through this department like a tsunami." He paused. "I got to thinking about your sister's case."

She stepped to the side out of the way of the crime scene unit that had just arrived. "Why's that?"

Gregory shot her a curious look that she ignored. She kept her back to a tree and let her gaze probe the area. Nothing set off her alarms. No rustling leaves, no shadowy figures. Nothing. Her muscles relaxed a fraction.

"Because you won't leave it alone and…" He paused.

"And?"

"And I might not have put some things in the notes that should have been there."

Her stomach knotted. "Why would you do that?"

"I didn't do it on purpose," he snapped. "I was going through a bad time that year. But that wasn't your sister's fault, and she deserved a better investigation than she got." He paused and she thought she heard him swallow. "If you'll meet me somewhere, I'll do my best to tell you everything I remember. I don't know if it'll do any good, but I'll tell you. And give you the notes that I made. I only have one copy and I don't want to fax them or email them anywhere. I don't want anyone stumbling across them."

The rough edge to his voice captured her attention one hundred percent. She looked around. "When and where can we meet?"

Another pause. "This can't get out, Katie. If it's known I didn't exactly do my job, my name will be mud around the department. No one will look at me the same. I don't want anyone to know we're meeting. This has to be completely confidential or it's going to come back to bite me."

"I won't say a word, Frank. I just want to find my sister." She stuffed down the anger she wanted to heap on this man's head. She couldn't blast him. Not yet. Not when he might have more information on Lucy. She looked around. "Give me another thirty minutes. Where do you want me to meet you?"

He gave her the address, and she memorized it. "I'll see you shortly."

Jordan pulled into the parking lot of the local pub. His buddy at Quantico had promised to get back to him within an hour with the connection between the two parolees. If he could find one. Jordan figured he would.

Katie sounded like she was fine, and Jordan offered up a prayer for the Lord to keep her that way.

He stepped inside the restaurant and spotted Danny Jackson at the bar nursing a drink and watching a football game on the television hanging from the wall. Jordan slipped onto the stool beside him. "Thanks for waiting for me."

"Like I said, I didn't have anywhere else to be. My wife died last year after a two-year battle with cancer, and I've just been going through the motions until I can join her."

"Sorry to hear that."

Danny shrugged. "I always thought I'd be the one to go first, you know?"

"Yeah. In our line of work, odds aren't exactly great for us to reach retirement age."

Danny grunted. "You didn't come here to chew the fat with me. What are your questions?"

Jordan didn't take offense at the man's gruffness; he figured that was just part of his personality. He'd seen too much, lived through some bad stuff and watched his wife die. The man had a right to be a little rough around the edges, he supposed. But he couldn't just let it go. "You think God's finished with you? That you don't have purpose anymore?"

Danny stilled. Then took a sip of the drink. "Funny you should say that."

"Why's that?"

"Because I was just wondering that very thing last night."

"So you believe in God?"

"More now than I used to. My wife was a believer." He shook his head. "She didn't want to leave me, but had no doubts where she was going when she took her last breath."

"I'm glad you can take comfort in that."

"I do. Not everyone can say the same for someone they've lost."

Jordan thought about Neil. While his brother had made some really rotten choices toward the end of his life, he'd given his heart to God at a middle school summer church camp. Jordan had no doubt that Neil was in heaven; he just wished he hadn't gone quite so soon.

He shoved thoughts of Neil away and focused on the man next to him. "But the Lord's left you here. Guess there might be a reason for that."

"Might be."

"And that reason might have something to do with Lucy Randall." He phrased it as a statement and waited.

A heavy sigh escaped the man and he rubbed a callused hand over his eyes. "It might."

Jordan took a stab in the dark. "Why don't you tell me what's been bothering you for the last fourteen years?"

Danny jerked like he'd been shot.

Bull's-eye.

Danny stared at him a minute, then finished his drink. "Come on."

"Where are we going?"

"To my truck, where we can't be overheard because the conversation we're getting ready to have never happened. Understand?"

"Gotcha."

Jordan followed Danny out to the man's oversized pickup truck. He had a fishing rod hanging on the gun rack on the back window of the king cab. Jordan climbed in the passenger seat and shut the door.

Danny cranked the truck and turned the heat on, but didn't move to put it in gear. "Ask me your questions."

"What is it you don't want to tell me? What are you afraid of?"

Danny barked a harsh laugh. "I'm not afraid of anything, son. Fear isn't keeping my mouth shut. Haven't you ever heard of a thing called loyalty?"

Jordan blinked. "Loyalty? To whom?"

Katie glanced at her watch and headed for her car. She was running later than she'd expected, especially with Gregory harassing her about needing an escort to wherever she was going.

She felt bad about putting him off, but she needed to talk to Frank, and Frank obviously didn't want an audience. If she had someone with her, he might clam up and she'd never learn what he wanted to tell her. However, she could let Jordan know what was going on. She shot him a text and waited for it to send.

Glancing around, she wondered if she was being

watched, if someone planned on following her. With a shudder, she climbed into her vehicle.

If someone followed her, she and Frank would take care of it. Thirty-eight-year-old Norman Rhames hadn't had a chance. The medical examiner's off-the-record deduction had been that in all likelihood Rhames died from the gunshot to the back of his head. The lack of defensive wounds on his hands said he hadn't put up a fight. Katie wondered if he'd trusted whoever it was that had killed him.

Possibly.

But it wasn't the same person who'd killed Wesley Wray, because that had happened while the man was locked up.

She checked the area one last time. Gregory waved to her and stood watching with a frown on his face as she pulled from the gravel edge of the highway and merged with the traffic.

Nerves danced along the top of her skin and she kept her eye on the rearview mirror.

Jordan sat back as the answer hit him. "Loyalty to your former partner. Frank Miller."

"Yeah. Frank."

"What was Frank's problem?"

Danny ran a hand over the gray stubble on his chin. "His problem was his personal life. More specifically, his wife and family."

Jordan nodded. "It happens."

"His wife was going to leave him. Gave him the whole line of grief about how he's always working and never home, yada yada."

"I feel for him. He sure didn't need that on top of the

stress of the job." Jordan shook his head. Not every officer's wife felt that way, but too many of them did and those in law enforcement had a high rate of divorce.

Danny seemed to relax a fraction at Jordan's understanding words. "Well, she wasn't a prize when he married her, but she was a looker, and I guess that's what attracted him to her."

Jordan thought about Katie's beauty. While he appreciated the outward package, it was her heart and inner beauty that drew him like a magnet. "So Frank was a bit distracted from the investigation."

Danny nodded. "*Distracted* is a kind word. It was weird, too, because he pushed for the case. It had originally been assigned to two other detectives, but Frank wanted it. The other detectives sure didn't care. As overloaded as we all were, they gladly passed it on to us."

"Why was that?"

"He said he needed all the work he could get. Said he couldn't shut his brain off so he might as well do some good." Danny rubbed his chin. "And he did. He worked a ton of hours, slept at his desk, solved a lot of cases."

"But not Lucy Randall's."

"No. Not Lucy's." He frowned. "I'd never seen Frank so messed up. He finally told me what was going on. His wife had filed for divorce six months prior and then just four months before we got Lucy's case, his niece drowned at summer camp. Frank loved that little girl like she was his own. His sister and her husband had let him stay with them until he could get set financially, and he and Jenny really bonded during that time."

Danny took a swig of his drink and sighed. "He and his wife didn't have any kids, which turned out to be a good thing in the end. So not only was he struggling with the demise of his marriage, but his sister turned into a raving madwoman, wild with grief."

Jordan swallowed and pinched the bridge of his nose, his heart going out to the man. "That's awful."

His phone vibrated, indicating a message. He'd check it in just a minute. He didn't want to do anything to cause Danny to clam up.

Danny said, "I told him to focus on the case, that if he just put all of his energy into solving Lucy's kidnapping, he could get his mind off of his troubles for a while."

"Did it work?"

"Seemed to. For a while." Danny chewed a toothpick and stared out the window.

"What else?"

A heavy sigh left the man. "We questioned a witness, and she talked about a car being at the scene."

"A gray sedan?"

Danny lifted a brow. "Yes. I documented it and put it in the report, then in the file. The next day it was gone. When I asked Frank about it, he just shrugged and said he didn't know what I was talking about. I documented it again and put it back in the file. A week later it was gone again. I demanded an explanation, and Frank dodged it. Said he didn't know and to quit bugging him about it."

"What'd you do?"

"I dropped it for the moment. We weren't getting anywhere on the case, anyway. Didn't seem like a big deal."

Jordan pulled out the picture Mrs. McKinney had given him, then the ones taken the day of the kidnapping. "Take a look at this." He handed Danny Mrs. McKinney's picture. "This was shot a few days before Lucy was taken. The lady who took this picture spent a lot of time outside while the car was parked there. On this particular day, it was her son's birthday and they'd given him a skateboard. He was out there having a blast while his mom took pictures to put in her scrapbook." He handed him another picture. "This was taken by the crime scene photographer the day of the kidnapping."

Jordan tapped the photo. "This is one of the officers' vehicles. It's parked in the drive, but tell me that's not the same car in both pictures. The one on the street and the one in the drive."

Danny set them side by side and studied them for a full minute. "Yeah, they could be."

"The woman who took this picture said that the car behind the kid was parked there for hours at a time for two weeks. She even called the cops and they blew her off."

Danny looked at the pictures again. "It looks familiar." He swallowed hard. "That's a cop car."

"That's what I thought. I just want to know which cop was driving it."

His phone buzzed and he checked the caller ID. "I gotta take this. Why don't you see if you can pull the driver of that car from your memory."

Danny grimaced and Jordan turned his attention to the caller. "Seth, what do you have for me?"

"You wanted a connection between Mr. Wray and Mr. Rhames and I've got one for you."

Excitement quickened his pulse. "What is it?"

"The only connection I could find is that they have the same arresting officer."

Katie pulled into the parking lot of the warehouse and cut the engine of her rental. Gregory pulled in behind her and she rolled her eyes.

Katie slipped her phone into the back pocket of her jeans and walked up to Gregory. "What are you doing?"

"I was concerned." He crossed his arms and frowned down at her. "You wouldn't tell me where you were going. I was concerned."

"Look—" She had to get rid of him. If Frank showed up, he'd be mad as fire. And she might never learn what he knew about Lucy. "I need you to disappear for a while. I'm meeting a CI and I don't want you scaring him off."

"A confidential informant? For which case?"

"Which case do you think?"

The light went on for him. "Ah."

"Now go, will you?" She glanced at her watch. "He'll be here any minute."

"Are you sure? Let me stay as backup."

"I don't need backup with this one." She hesitated. "All right. But get out of sight, will you?"

Relief crossed his features. "Okay."

He left and Katie leaned against her vehicle. She checked her phone. No response from Jordan. That was weird. She texted him again.

A black sedan pulled into the parking lot. Frank pulled up beside her and climbed from his car.

"I guess this is as private a place as any," she said.

Frank shook his head. "Move your car out of sight. I'm going to do the same. I don't need someone saying they saw us meeting."

Katie sighed and dropped her arms. "Fine."

Once the vehicles were moved to Frank's satisfaction, he said, "Let's go inside, I'm freezing."

Her phone buzzed and she pulled it from her pocket. Frank looked back. She said, "It's a text from Jordan wanting to know if I'm all right. We must have crossed texts."

"So tell him you're fine. You're a cop, Katie, and you act like you need a babysitter."

Katie's head shot up. "Someone's tried to kill me, Frank. Not once, but several times. Excuse me for appreciating friends who want to help look out for me."

Frank shrugged and entered the warehouse. Katie rolled her eyes and followed.

Jordan tucked his phone back into his pocket once he finished the call with Seth and checked for any messages from Katie.

Meeting a CI at warehouse on Buckley. Says he has info on Lucy. Will call when I'm done.

Satisfied she was still all right, Jordan processed what he'd just learned. Before he told Danny what Seth had just revealed, he wanted an answer from Danny. He pushed. "Whose car, Danny?"

"I can't say for sure."

"But it looks like…" He waited.

Danny slammed a fist on the steering wheel. "Frank's, all right? It looks like the car Frank and I used to drive."

Jordan pulled his phone back out and texted Katie, asking her who the CI was. Then he decided to forget the texting and dialed her number. When he got her voice mail, he said, "Frank knows more about Lucy's kidnapping than he's letting on. Be careful and let me know you got this message." He looked at Danny. "I just learned that Frank was one of the many arresting officers of Wesley Wray and Norman Rhames. Both of whom are dead."

"That's odd."

"Very. Everything is coming back to Frank Miller and I want to know why. Call him and tell him you need to meet him."

"No."

"Do it or you'll go down as an accessory."

"Accessory? Accessory to what?"

"Kidnapping."

"Kidnapping! He didn't take that girl. Sloppy police work maybe, but not kidnapping. You're crazy!"

Jordan leaned in. "I don't know if he took her or not, but I think he did." He shrugged. "Even if I'm wrong and he didn't take her, he covered up something in relation to it and you helped him. Now call him!"

Danny flexed his fingers on the wheel, then reached for the phone he'd tossed in the cup holder. He dialed the number.

"Put it on speaker."

"It's his number."

"Just put it on speaker and do it now."

Danny did. Frank's voice came on the line. As a message. "You know what to do." Beep.

Danny hung up.

Jordan sighed. "Call his office, please."

Danny dialed the number. Voice mail again.

Jordan pinched the bridge of his nose. "Will you show me where Frank lives?"

"Yeah. You want to follow me?"

"That would be great, if you won't try to lose me."

Danny shot him a perturbed look. "I won't." But he didn't move.

"What is it?"

"You really think Frank had something to do with that kidnapping?"

"It looks that way."

Danny swallowed hard and looked at the streetlight. "I thought he was just stressed out. He wouldn't have any reason to kidnap a kid. Where would he keep her?"

"Let's see if he's home. When we find him, we can ask him."

Jordan climbed out of the truck and into his vehicle. His mind centered on Katie and what her reaction would be if Jordan was right. He sent her another text asking her to call when she could, then pulled out onto the two-lane road to follow Danny.

Katie looked around. The warehouse had been empty for about four months. She remembered when this particular shoe business shut down. The machines still stood as though frozen in time. Or waiting for someone to start them up again.

Crates and boxes stacked to the ceiling had letters and numbers on them that probably meant something to the previous workers.

"Frank? You find anything?" She spun to look behind her, wondering where he'd gone.

A loud crack sounded and sparks flew from the nearest machine. Stunned, yet moving on reflex, Katie dove behind the nearest stack of crates. "Frank! Are you okay?"

Katie yanked her weapon and her phone. Fumbled the phone and watched it skitter under the crate. She dropped to her knees and shoved a hand after the device. Her fingers found it as another bullet pierced the wood about chest high.

"Frank! Frank, are you all right?"

When he didn't answer, Katie's blood ran cold. Had

something happened to him? Was he lying hurt? But both shots had been in her direction. Had she been followed to the warehouse? With a smooth move, she slid the phone from under the crate and into her palm. She pressed 911.

The phone rang, then the call dropped.

"Stupid metal buildings," she muttered.

Her ears strained to hear the slightest noise that would indicate her attacker was near. She needed to move. She needed to find Frank.

"Katie, I'm over here."

Katie headed in the direction of his voice.

SIXTEEN

Jordan pulled to the curb behind Danny and climbed out of his car. Danny walked up to the door and rapped on it.

Nothing.

"Use your key," Jordan said. It was a wild guess, but one he was gratified to see paid off. Danny lifted a brow, then without another word, flipped the keys on his chain to the one that fit the door.

He pushed the door open and Jordan stepped inside. Neatness and order greeted him.

"I'm only doing this because if you're right, then I've been aiding a kidnapper all these years."

Jordan grunted. "You didn't know."

"I knew something was up, but I didn't bother to find out what."

True, the man had let things slide, but if he'd been aware of the real story, he would have probably done things differently.

And Lucy Randall might have grown up with her family.

Jordan pushed those thoughts aside and started looking for something…anything…that would give him a hint about what Frank had done with Lucy. "You going to help me search?"

"Yeah." The big man sighed and started down the hall. He disappeared into the first bedroom on the left.

Jordan searched the den, scoped the kitchen, then walked down the hall to the bedroom Frank had set up as an office.

A big executive-type desk sat against one wall with a leather chair pushed to the side, like Frank had just gotten up to get a cup of coffee and would be right back. His laptop screen saver flipped family pictures. Jordan jiggled the mouse.

The screen saver disappeared and a box popped up asking for a password.

Jordan left the computer and went for the drawers, checking his phone. No return text from Katie yet.

"You know if we find anything, it's not going to be admissible in court."

"I know. I'm not planning on taking anything, but Katie doesn't have enough for a search warrant yet." He paused. "I don't think. They might issue one based on the pictures of the cars, but I doubt it."

"I tried Frank's phone again. It went straight to voice mail."

Jordan opened the next drawer and pulled out a file labeled *Jenny*. "Who's Jenny?"

"His niece. The one who drowned."

Jordan opened the file and stared at the picture on top. "Danny, how old was Jenny when she died?"

"Seven. Or eight. I forget."

"Have you ever seen a picture of her?"

"Yes. He used to have a picture of her on his refrigerator and one on his desk. After she drowned, he removed all the pictures. Like it was just too painful for him to see them." He scratched his head. "I don't even remember what she looks like now."

Jordan flipped the picture over. "Her obituary's taped to the back." He turned back to the picture, then pulled out his cell phone and scrolled until he came to the picture of Lucy Randall. "Look at this."

Danny looked. And sucked in a deep breath. "They could pass for twins."

Jordan looked at Danny. "You think you could find the address of Frank's sister?"

"Probably."

Jordan's phone buzzed. Katie's answer, FRANK, sent fear exploding through him.

Katie ducked as another shot came her way. "Frank!"

Chills of fear raced all over her. Frank was shooting at her.

She had to get out of the warehouse to get a cell signal or she was going to die.

She had to move, change locations. Find a better hiding place. *Something.* She took a deep breath and darted for the next stack of crates, expecting to feel the burn of a bullet entering her flesh. The shot came, but he missed. When he moved to get a better angle, she got a glimpse of him.

"Frank, stop! Why are you shooting at me?" She flipped her phone on silent.

"Because you keep sticking your nose where it doesn't belong!"

Lucy.

"She's my sister. Why don't you want me to find her?"

Another shot. She ducked, noticed she had one bar and punched in 911 on her cell phone again.

It rang once, twice. "Nine-one-one, what's your emergency?"

"I'm—"

The phone blipped the sound of the dropped call and Katie bit back a groan. She quickly typed a text to Jordan, then one to Gregory. A footstep squeaked to her left. She caught her breath and moved toward the edge of the crates.

"Where's my sister? Where's Lucy?" she called and moved as silently as she could down a passageway made of crates toward the window to her right.

Another shot cracked the wood where she'd just been. But Frank wouldn't answer. She figured he was doing his best to hunt her down and didn't want to give away his location by opening his mouth. Fine. Two could play that game. She did her best to regulate her breathing, control the fear racing through her. If she could get to the window, maybe she could find a signal.

Jordan's phone beeped, indicating a text message. He read aloud, "Need help. Two-four-five-six Buckley. No signal." Terror shot straight through him.

Danny glanced at him and frowned. "Katie?"

"Yeah." Immediately, he dialed her number. Straight to voice mail.

"That doesn't sound good," Danny said.

Jordan punched in the number for Katie's partner. Gregory answered on the second ring. Jordan snapped, "Katie's in trouble." He gave the man the address.

Gregory said, "I got her text. I'm on the way. I just got a report about shots fired there."

Jordan punched a text back to her.

On the way.

A sick feeling engulfed him. *Please, God, let her be all right.*

Katie fired back in the direction the last shot had come from and thought she heard sirens in the distance. It was hard to tell. It might just be the ringing in her ears. She prayed it was sirens. Her nose itched. The smell of gunpowder filled the air and she had to hold her breath to ward off a sneeze.

A crate fell to her right and she spun, then darted toward it and to the right behind the crates next to it. Had Frank pushed one over trying to trap her into exposing her location? Or was it an accident?

Either way, she stayed put, breathing in through her nose and out through her mouth. She looked at her phone. Still not a good enough signal to make a phone call. The window was too far, with too much open space between her and it.

And where was Frank?

Another shot sent shards of wood raining down on her. One piece sliced the skin on the back of her hand and she bit her lip to keep from crying out. Blood dripped. Another hard piece grazed her forehead and she blinked as she hit the cement floor.

Come on, come on, where are you, Gregory? Jordan?

She couldn't hold Frank off forever. She scuttled toward what had once been a break area with a kitchen. The appliances were gone, but the granite countertops were still there, as well as the cement base they sat on.

Her phone vibrated. She glanced at the screen.

On the way.

Relief filled her. Blood dripped from her hand and she pressed it to her jeans, trying to stop the flow.

Gritting her teeth, she did her best to ignore the pain that bit at her. Her entire body still ached from all the trauma it had been through in the last few days. She'd pushed herself hard and was paying for it.

God, please. Don't let this man kill me.

Jordan led the way to the address Katie had texted him. When he pulled up, he flashed his FBI badge to the officer on crowd-control duty. Knowing a gunshot came from the warehouse, all he wanted to do was rush the place. Common sense and training held him still. Worry for Katie ate a hole in his belly.

Danny raced toward the doors, ignoring the shouts for him to stop. Jordan flashed his badge again and took off after the man. "Danny! Wait!"

Danny ignored him. He pulled open the door and stepped inside the warehouse. Jordan pulled his weapon as the SWAT team descended. He followed Danny inside and let the door close behind him.

"Frank!" Danny's voice held a desperation that made Jordan wince. "Frank, are you here?"

"Get out of here, Danny! This doesn't concern you." His voice echoed, but Jordan thought it originated from the left. He started moving in that direction, using the crates as shelter.

"There're cops all over the place," Danny called out. "They have evidence placing you at the kidnapping. I don't want you to die, and that's how this is going to end if you don't come out."

"Mind your own business, Danny."

"Why'd you do it, Frank? Why'd you take her?"

"Shut up! Just shut up!"

Jordan glanced around. Frank was hiding, but he had a good idea of where the man was. While Danny kept Frank's attention, Jordan slipped behind the nearest crate and stopped to listen.

Katie froze at the new voice. Danny Jackson. She moved to the left and found herself closer to the window. When Frank had answered Danny, his voice had been scary close. She backed up, stepping carefully, her goal no longer the window, but Frank.

Help was here. She needed to help them help her.

She turned, silent and watchful. Where was he? Her fingers gripped her weapon. The safety was off. Step by slow step, she moved.

A scuff from behind. She turned and came to an abrupt stop when a vise dropped over her head and closed around her throat. Adrenaline rushing, Katie dropped her phone, but years of training sent her into defense mode. She stepped backward into her attacker, jabbing with her elbow.

He deflected the blow and jammed his gun into her ribs. She gasped and stilled. Her heart beat with fear and anger.

"I took those courses, too, remember?" he hissed into her left ear.

"So what now, Frank? You know how this is going to play out. You either let me go or we're both going to wind up dead."

"I'm not ready to die yet."

"Then let me go."

"I'm not going to prison, either."

Terror curled in her belly.

"Frank!" Danny Jackson's voice again.

Frank stiffened and tightened his grip on her throat. She choked and he loosened it slightly. "Now we're going to walk out of here and get in the car and go."

"They'll just follow."

"Then we'll lose them."

"What did you do?" she whispered. "What did you have to do with her kidnapping? Why did you botch the investigation?"

Jordan could hear Katie's pained questions. Frank didn't answer her. He peered around the edge of the crates, could hear the negotiator on the megaphone. Frank didn't answer. In fact, he acted like there wasn't a whole city of cops outside the building.

He had a tight grip on Katie's throat, and Jordan could see the man's weapon pressed against her side. His heart thudded, and he took a deep breath. One shot. He'd only get one shot. He'd better make it count.

The SWAT team was useless without windows. If they couldn't see the perp, they couldn't shoot him.

"Frank, come on, man, talk to me."

Danny was in full cop mode, shrugging off his retirement like he'd never left. Jordan just prayed the man could talk some sense into his former partner while Jordan figured out a way to disarm Frank. Or shoot him.

"Frank! They've got evidence that you kidnapped Lucy Randall," Gregory joined in.

Jordan spun back and stepped around the crate so he

could see the door. Gregory had slipped into the warehouse along with four SWAT members. He turned his attention back to Katie. She had gone perfectly still. "You? You kidnapped her?"

Whispered curses slipped from Frank's lips. "I had to."

To Jordan, it looked as though Frank's grip wasn't quite as tight. Everyone talking to him had distracted him.

Jordan raised his weapon and closed one eye as he centered the muzzle on Frank's lined forehead. But the man had a gun on Katie. If Jordan shot, would Frank's hand spasm and pull the trigger?

Frustration gripped him.

He shifted and tried to catch Katie's eye.

She saw him and her eyes widened.

Then she wilted straight to the floor, as though her legs had given out.

Frank cursed and held her by her chin. He looked up just as Jordan pulled the trigger.

SEVENTEEN

Katie felt Frank jerk and dropped the rest of the way to floor. She rolled and kicked out, clipping his knees and bringing him down beside her.

Before she could blink, Jordan was on the man and rolling him to his stomach, yanking his hands behind his back. "You're under arrest."

"You shot him. Oh, please tell me you didn't kill him," Katie said.

Frank groaned, and Katie felt a giddy shot of relief.

Jordan grunted as he clipped the cuffs onto Frank and hauled him to his feet. "I was going to, but figured we'd never find Lucy if I went with a head shot. You dropped at just the right time and I caught him in the shoulder. Nice moves."

"Thanks. Glad he didn't pull the trigger when I slumped." She stood in front of Frank and felt a strange mixture of emotions. And detachment. "Where's my sister?"

Frank shook his head and grimaced. The amount of blood covering his shirt said the shoulder wound probably needed to be looked at pretty fast.

Law enforcement had them surrounded. Gregory looked at her. "You all right?"

"I'm alive, so I guess that means I'm just fine."

He nodded. Katie waved paramedics over and Jordan helped Frank onto the gurney. None too gently, she noticed. Frank cried out and sucked air between his clenched teeth.

Katie noticed Danny Jackson staring at Frank. When he saw her watching, he shook his head. "I didn't know, I promise."

Katie stepped up to the gurney and looked down at the man who'd ripped her family apart. "Why?"

He opened his eyes and glared. "It doesn't matter now, does it?"

"Of course it matters!" Her fist balled and she was ready to slug him. "Where is she? Is she alive?" The question ripped from her. Frank looked away and Katie grabbed his good shoulder and shook it. He gasped. "Is she alive!"

He met her gaze. "No. She's not."

Her knees buckled, and she felt Jordan's hands catch her on her way to the concrete. "No. No, no, no. Please…"

Jordan helped her back to her feet and away from Frank. She couldn't stop the sobs that choked her. Jordan held her, then shook her. Why wouldn't he just let her give in and have a moment of grief?

"Katie! Listen to me!"

She hiccupped and shuddered. "What!"

"I don't think she's dead."

Katie drew in a ragged breath and stared. "Why?"

"Because of what we found at his house."

"You searched his house?"

"Yeah. And now that we got him on all kinds of

charges including attempted murder, we won't have any trouble getting a search warrant."

Katie wiped her eyes and sniffed. "What'd you find?" She watched the ambulance pull away from the parking lot.

"Evidence that he took Lucy." He gripped her hands. "His niece died a few months before Lucy was snatched. Danny talked about how inconsolable the family was and how Frank nearly fell apart, but that the job was the only thing that kept him going."

"So he took Lucy as an attempt to replace his niece?"

"That's what we think."

"So where is she?"

"I'm going to take a wild guess and say he took her and gave her to his sister."

"Where do they live? Let's go."

Jordan checked his phone. "I've got her address right here." He placed a hand on her arm to stop her from heading to the car. "Let me call and see if she's home." He looked around. "Plus, you're not done here."

Katie took another breath and closed her eyes. She had to get herself together. Hope flared like a spotlight, bright and piercing. Lucy might be alive. If she was, she'd just celebrated her twenty-first birthday two weeks ago. And she might even be somewhere close by. Her fingers itched to pick up the phone and call her parents, but she couldn't do that until she knew for sure. She wouldn't dare take a chance on raising their hopes only to have them dashed.

It seemed to take forever, but Katie managed to get through the wrap of the crime scene, giving her statement and chugging a bottle of water.

Impatience zipped through her. She looked at Jordan. "Are you ready?"

"She apparently still lives with her par—" He shot her a look. "The family that she—" He held his hands up.

Katie bit her lip. "I guess they're her parents now, aren't they?"

Jordan nodded. "I'm sorry. I know this is a hard one, but she's lived with them for fourteen years. If they raised her as their own, then yes, she probably thinks of them as her parents."

"Okay. I know you're right. I'll just have to remember that." She paused. "In fact, we probably should talk to her parents first and ask them the best way to approach telling Lucy the truth about her past."

Jordan pressed the phone to his ear. "She's not answering her phone."

"Then I'll sit outside her house until someone comes home."

The four-hour drive to Raleigh, North Carolina, passed mostly in silence broken by Katie's phone calls to the Banks residence every thirty minutes.

Katie was glad for Jordan's company. He drove to the address he'd gotten from his buddy at Quantico. Bill and Lindsay Banks lived in an older middle-class neighborhood with a lot of ranch-style houses on one-acre lots. The Banks' still hadn't answered when Jordan pulled to the curb of the house.

Katie's phone rang, and she glanced at the ID, then at him. "It's my parents' number."

"Go ahead and answer it. We're just going to be doing a waiting game for the next little while. I'll step out of the car and give you some privacy if you want."

Katie shook her head and clicked the phone off. "No.

I don't want to talk to them yet. I want to be able to tell them I found Lucy and when they can see her."

"You think finding Lucy is going to make your mother love you again?" He asked the question softly and she winced. He grimaced. "Never mind. I'm sorry."

"No," she said, her voice low. "It's a valid question. The answer is—I don't know."

"But you keep trying."

She gave a sad smile. "I don't know how to stop at this point." She took a deep breath. "However, I do think I'm going to have to come to terms with the fact that my mother may never change, and I'm going to have to figure out a way to accept that."

"And forgive yourself for Lucy's kidnapping?"

Another wince. "Yes." She shot him a look. "Just like you need to forgive yourself for the death of that little girl."

Jordan's fingers flexed on the steering wheel. "I know it wasn't my fault. In my head I know that."

"I understand. I've finally come to see that Lucy's kidnapping wasn't my fault. I didn't cause it. Someone else chose to do that and blaming myself is exactly the wrong thing to do. God doesn't blame me. My mother may blame me, but God doesn't, and that's what I have to get through to my heart."

"You've been doing a lot of thinking."

"I have." She gripped his hand. "Jordan, that little girl's death wasn't your fault. God doesn't blame you."

His throat worked and he nodded. "I'm starting to see that." He glanced at her. "Thanks to you."

Her phone rang and she jerked. "My dad again."

"Answer him, Katie. Talk to him."

With a deep sigh, Katie pressed the button. "Hello?"

"Hi, Katie, I hope this is a good time." Her mother's voice echoed in her head. For a moment, shock held Katie speechless. Her mother had called her.

She cleared her throat. "Hi, Mom. I have time. What can I do for you?"

After a slight hesitation, her mother said, "I wanted to know if you'd like to come to lunch on Sunday."

Katie felt tears spring to her eyes. "I would love to, but—" She bit her lip. No sense in pushing things too soon. She'd ask her father about her mother's out-of-character behavior later.

"But why am I calling?"

"It doesn't matter. I'm just glad you did." She swallowed hard against another rush of tears.

"It does matter and maybe this isn't the time or the way to handle it, but to put it bluntly, I'm tired of being afraid."

"What?"

Her mother cleared her throat. "Your father told me what happened with you. How someone threatened to hurt you if you didn't stop looking for Lucy." A sob and then a shaky breath filtered through. "And it was like a slap in the face. Since the day you decided to become a cop, I've been preparing myself to lose you, too. When your father told me what you were going through, with the fire, then the car wreck, it was a wake-up call. I've been consumed by fear and I refuse to live that way any longer. And I needed to tell you."

Katie sat stunned, unable to think, breathe, move. She finally let out a small gasp.

"I owe you an apology, Katie, and I didn't want to tell you this over the phone, but I didn't want to wait another minute, either. I love you and I'm so sorry for not being the mother you needed."

Tears rolled down Katie's cheeks. How long had she waited to hear those words? A car pulled into the Banks' driveway and Katie sucked in a deep breath.

"I love you, too, Mom. Thank you for calling and telling me. I needed to hear it."

They hung up with promises to get together soon. Katie looked at Jordan, still in shock. "Did that just happen?"

"Sounds like it."

"Could you hear?"

A light flush highlighted his cheeks. "Sorry, but yes. Every word."

"She loves me," Katie whispered. "I did all I could to earn her love, but she didn't care about all that stuff."

"You can't earn love, Katie. And I think that's a hard lesson for all of us to learn sometimes. Love is a gift and you can't earn a gift."

"Ephesians two, verse eight," she whispered.

"What does it say?"

"'For by grace you have been saved through faith, and that not of yourselves; it is the gift of God.'" Katie lifted her eyes to his. "She just offered me the gift of her love, a love I was trying so hard to earn, and I'm about to explode."

Jordan reached out and placed a hand under her chin. Her eyes met his very intense and direct gaze. "What's not to love?" he asked softly.

Katie wondered if she'd ever be able to draw a deep breath again. Her heart felt too full. Like it had grown several sizes and was squeezing her lungs. "What are you saying?"

"I'm saying…we have a lot to talk about. After you figure out if your sister is here."

Katie almost started laughing at the timing of everything. Instead, she gave a hiccupping sniff and took the tissue Jordan handed to her. "Let me get myself cleaned up and then we can go in." She mopped and scrubbed, then inspected the damage in the visor mirror. "It's a good thing I don't normally wear makeup," she muttered.

Jordan smiled and opened his door. "Ready?"

"As I'll ever be."

She climbed out of the car and walked toward the house.

Jordan took a deep breath as he stood beside Katie and watched her rap on the front door. This was it. They had no idea if Lucy was here or not. But someone was home.

Footsteps sounded and then they were face-to-face with a woman in her late forties. Jordan thought about the profile Seth had sent him. One he'd had to skim fast. But he recognized Lindsay Banks.

Katie smiled. A quick twitch of her lips. "I'm Katie Randall. I was wondering if I could have a moment of your time."

"What's this about?"

"It's about your daughter."

"Lucy?"

"Um…yes, ma'am. Lucy." Jordan heard her choke on the name, but she forced it out.

"Is she all right?" Stark terror stood out in the woman's eyes.

Jordan said, "She's just fine as far as we know, but we have some information we need to share with you. Is she here?"

"No. She's at work."

Jordan could tell they were scaring the poor woman to death. Katie apparently sensed it, too. "Mrs. Banks, could we just come in and sit down?"

"I'm sorry, I don't let strangers in my house."

Katie sighed and flicked a look at Jordan. She pulled out her badge and showed it to the woman. Mrs. Banks sucked in a deep breath and pressed a hand to her lips. "Do I need to call my husband?"

"If you'd like to. He needs to hear this, too." It might be better to have both of them there. Were they in on the kidnapping? Did they know what Frank had been up to? Her gut said no, Frank acted on his own, but Katie wanted to know that for sure.

Mrs. Banks stepped back and opened the door. Jordan followed Katie and the woman into a formal living area. She gestured to the couch, but didn't sit. Katie took one end of the sofa and Jordan slid into one of the straight-backed wooden chairs. He figured Mrs. Banks would feel better without him looming over her.

She crossed her arms and let her gaze swing back and forth between them. "Now, what's this all about? Is Lucy in trouble?"

"Not at all," Jordan said. "Are you going to call your husband?"

She hesitated. "Tell me what this is about first."

Katie ran a hand through her hair and sent up a silent prayer for the right words. "Mrs. Banks, we know you lost a daughter when she was seven years old."

The woman's eyes went wide and she sank into the nearest chair. "Yes. That's right."

"And we know soon after that you took in a young girl about the same age."

"Yes. Lucy. Her parents were killed in a fire and there were no other living relatives." She gave a small laugh and rubbed her head. "It's just amazing how it all happened, really. I was grieving for Jenny." Her eyes teared up. "I still do, but—" a tremulous smile curved her lips "—my brother, Frank, is a detective in Spartanburg. Frank appeared on my doorstep with little Lucy, saying she needed a home. When I saw her, I couldn't say no." She sighed. "She saved my life." She twisted her fingers. "You see, I couldn't have any more children after Jenny, so…she was my world and when she died…"

Katie reached over and patted the woman's hand. "I'm so sorry, Mrs. Banks. I can't imagine how awful that was for you and Mr. Banks."

Katie had a sneaking suspicion that the Banks' had no idea that Frank had kidnapped Lucy. "Did you not see news reports on Lucy? I know she made CNN and other major news networks."

Mrs. Banks grimaced. "We don't watch the news. Too depressing."

A fact Frank would have known.

Mrs. Banks closed her eyes. "I don't talk about Jenny's death very much, simply because it was a horrible time." When she opened her eyes, her grief faded and she smiled. "But Lucy was—" She paused. "Lucy was our gift straight from God."

EIGHTEEN

Katie cleared her throat, but the knot that had developed refused to budge. She talked around it. "Mrs. Banks, we have reason to believe that your Lucy is really Lucy Randall."

The woman's forehead creased. "Who's that?"

"A young girl who was taken from her home fourteen years ago."

"Taken." Mrs. Banks gaped. "And you think—"

"Ma'am, I know this is hard to process, but we have evidence that Frank Miller kidnapped Lucy Randall and gave her to you."

Jordan's soft words filled the room.

"Evidence?" she whispered. "No. Oh, no, please..."

"Would you like to call your husband? There's more."

With a shaky hand, Mrs. Banks pulled a cell phone from her jeans pocket and dialed a number. "Bill, there's a bit of an emergency at home. I need you to come." She listened. "No. I'm not hurt. Just come and drive carefully. You don't need to speed." She hung up and looked at Katie, then Jordan. "What's this evidence?"

Katie exchanged a glance with Jordan and decided to just be honest. "Frank's been arrested for murder and attempted murder. We have someone who puts his unmarked car at the scene of the kidnapping, and he basically admitted to taking her."

The woman's face went a pale gray. Katie had to contain herself from demanding Mrs. Banks get on the phone and call Lucy and tell her to come home. First she had to help these people deal with this shock. Then she could see Lucy.

"Frank? Arrested?" She sounded dazed.

Katie bit her lip. The news was too much. She should have had Mrs. Banks call her husband right away. She slid over and took the woman's hand. "We'll wait for your husband to get here to finish this."

She nodded and for the next twenty minutes, they sat. Just when Katie thought she couldn't bear the silence a minute longer, the front door opened and Mr. Banks bolted into the house. "Linds? Where are you?"

"Here, Bill." Mrs. Banks stood and her husband whirled. His salt-and-pepper hair was askew, as though he'd run his hands through it repeatedly on the drive home. "What is it? What's wrong?"

"They think Lucy is—" She couldn't say another word as sobs overtook her.

Bill Banks looked at Katie and Jordan. Katie introduced herself and began the story once more.

When she finished, the couple simply stared at her in shock.

"So you're saying my birth family is still alive?" A soft voice from the dining room grabbed their attention. Katie jumped to her feet.

Mrs. Banks cried out. "How much did you hear?"

"All of it. Daddy called and said there was something wrong at home and he wasn't sure what, but it sounded serious. I came right here. I heard you talking and didn't want to interrupt and—" she spread her hands "—I heard everything."

Katie stared at the young woman. A stranger and yet... familiar, too. "Lucy," she whispered.

Lucy looked at her. "So I was kidnapped?" She stared at her parents. "You told me they were dead. That they all died." She wrinkled her brow. "I remember them, you know. In snatches and bits and pieces, but I remember them."

Mrs. Banks sobbed against her husband's shoulder.

Katie sucked in a deep breath. "Lucy, what do you remember about that day?"

"He took me from the yard. He was very nice, but very firm. He was a police officer and told me I had to go with him. So I did." She swiped a hand through her hair. "He became my uncle. Uncle Frank. I remember being sad and missing my family. My sister. Katie." She whispered the name, and Katie bit back a sob.

"That's me. I'm Katie," she said softly.

Lucy's brow rose and her eyes narrowed as horror entered them. "You're my sister?"

"Yes."

"I was kidnapped."

Katie nodded. "And I've been looking for you ever since."

Lucy's gaze flew from Katie to Jordan to her parents and back to Katie. "I need to sit down."

She slid to the sofa next to her mother, and Katie restrained herself from reaching out and touching the girl. Lucy hugged her mother, then crossed the room to her father and wrapped him in a tight hug. She looked at Katie. "I want to see your evidence. If what you say is true, I want to know beyond a shadow of a doubt."

Katie nodded. It seemed to be all she could do.

Tears in her eyes, Lucy smiled, then moved to wrap Katie in a tight hug. "I've missed you."

Katie let a sob slip out as she hugged her sister back. "And oh, how I've missed you."

Lucy drew in a deep breath and looked at her parents. Katie followed her gaze. They looked shell-shocked. Katie knew what she had to do. She looked at her sister. "Take your time and reassure them, then call me." She pulled a card from her pocket and slid it in her sister's hand.

Lucy's tears spilled over, but she simply nodded as Katie turned to leave.

Jordan slipped his hand over hers and gave her a squeeze. She squeezed back and made it out the door and into the car before she turned, wrapped her arms around his neck and cried her happiness into his shoulder.

And bless the man, he let her do it.

After about ten minutes, he started mopping her face with a tissue. "Come on, Katie, I'm going to need an oar to steer the car if you keep this up."

She sniffed and sat away from him, taking the tissue and finishing the job. "I'm sorry, I'm just so happy and almost unwilling to believe it's true. We found her."

He handed her a bottle of water. She eyed it suspiciously. "How long has this been in here?"

He laughed. "Since last night. It won't kill you, I promise."

She took a swig and sighed. "I need to call my parents."

"Yes."

Katie took out her phone and dialed her parents' number. Her mother answered on the second ring. "Hi, Mom. I've got some news for you."

"News? What kind of news?"

"We found Lucy."

EPILOGUE

Katie looked around the dinner table. Christmas Day had arrived with snow flurries and cold temperatures, but inside her parents' warm house, Katie marveled at her mother's bright eyes and happy smile. She kept coming back to the sight of Lucy sitting between her birth parents, with the parents who'd raised her sitting across the table.

Jordan sat to her right. And wonder of wonders, his parents had agreed to join them. His father wasn't falling over himself to be pleasant to Katie, but at least he could be in the same room and not cast blame.

Jordan said his parents had spent many hours working out the fact that his mother had chosen to keep Neil's secret. They were going to counseling to deal with everything, including accepting that Katie didn't deserve Paul's blame. And he was beginning to see the light.

Katie just shook her head. Never in a million years would she have pictured this scene. And yet here they all were.

Tears threatened and she rose on the pretense of carrying some empty dishes into the kitchen.

Jordan followed her. She put the dishes into the sink

and felt his hands fall on her shoulders. He turned her to face him. "All you all right?"

She looked up into his eyes and felt her heart kick into overdrive. "I'm more than all right. I don't have the words to describe how I feel right now. I feel overwhelmed with how everything worked out." A tear slipped down her cheek and he brushed it away. "This isn't the normal ending to a kidnapping." She blinked. "I really believed she was dead, Jordan."

"I know. I did, too."

"And I keep having trouble wrapping my mind around the fact that we found her."

"I know."

"You know how Lucy's other mother said that Lucy was her gift from God? Well, reuniting our family is another gift."

"God's done some amazing work over the last few weeks. One of those things was keeping you alive to enjoy this moment." He pulled her to him and buried his face in her neck. "I don't know what I would have done if you'd been killed."

She pushed him back and cupped his cheeks with her palms. "I think I love you, Jordan."

He blinked, then gave a laugh and grabbed her around the waist to lift her so they were nose to nose. "I know I love you, silly woman."

He kissed her, a long, thorough kiss that left her breathless. She grinned. "I'm so thankful God sent me to Finding the Lost."

"Will you marry me?"

She gaped. "Marry you?"

"What? Too soon?"

"No. Yes. Maybe. No."

He grinned. "So which one do I pick?"

She laughed through her tears. "Yes."

"Soon?"

"Soon."

"Awesome."

He planted another kiss on her lips, and she clung to the happiness and blessings God had chosen to bestow upon them.

She pulled back. "Not every day is going to be this wonderful, you know."

"I know, but let's enjoy while it lasts."

"I'm good with that."

She kissed him again, knowing her future was bright and God's love was enough to get them through whatever came their way. God's unconditional love. A love she couldn't earn, but which was freely given.

A love she accepted with a grateful heart. A love she planned to pass down to her children and her children's children. Children. The thought made her weepy again. Oh, yeah, she wanted children. Jordan's children.

Jordan pulled back and kissed her nose. "Merry Christmas, Katie."

"Merry Christmas, Jordan."

* * * * *

Laura Scott is a nurse by day and an author by night. She has always loved romance and read faith-based books by Grace Livingston Hill in her teenage years. She's thrilled to have published over twenty-five books for Love Inspired Suspense. She has two adult children and lives in Milwaukee, Wisconsin, with her husband of over thirty years. Please visit Laura at laurascottbooks.com, as she loves to hear from her readers.

Books by Laura Scott

Love Inspired Suspense

Justice Seekers

Soldier's Christmas Secrets
Guarded by the Soldier

Callahan Confidential

Shielding His Christmas Witness
The Only Witness
Christmas Amnesia
Shattered Lullaby
Primary Suspect
Protecting His Secret Son

True Blue K-9 Unit: Brooklyn

Copycat Killer

Visit the Author Profile page at
Harlequin.com for more titles.

HER MISTLETOE PROTECTOR

Laura Scott

Rejoice in the Lord always.
I will say it again: Rejoice!

—*Philippians* 4:4

This book is dedicated to my sister, Michele Glynn. I know Madison is only an hour away, but I still miss you so much. I love you!

ONE

"Ms. Simon, wait! I have a letter for you."

Rachel Simon, CEO of Simon Inc., froze, despite the fact that she was running late for her nine-o'clock meeting. The sick feeling in her stomach swelled with dread as she forced herself to turn and face the receptionist.

"Here you go," Carrie Freeman said with a wide smile.

Rachel stared at the thin envelope with her name typed neatly on the front, the dread congealing into a mass of fear. The letter looked exactly like the one she'd received in her mailbox at home last night, and she instinctively knew there was another threat inside. She swallowed hard and took the envelope from the receptionist, being careful to hold it along the edges. Then she cleared her throat. "Who dropped this off for me, Carrie?"

"I don't know… It was sitting on my desk chair when I came back from the restroom. There was a sticky note, telling me to deliver it to you first thing."

Rachel tried hard to keep her fear from showing as she cast a worried gaze around the lobby. Was the person who had left the note watching her right now? "Do you still have the sticky note?" she asked.

Carrie's expression turned perplexed. "I tossed it in

the trash bin." Rachel glanced over the receptionist's shoulder at the large stainless-steel trash container standing near the lobby door. "Do you want me to go through the garbage to find it?" Carrie's tone indicated she wasn't thrilled with the idea of pawing in the trash although Rachel knew she would if asked.

As much as she wanted to see the note, she shook her head. Asking Carrie to search through the bin would only bring unwanted attention to herself. She wasn't ready to go public with the weird phone calls and the threatening letter she'd received. The last thing she needed was some sort of leak to the media, as if her company hadn't been through the wringer already.

"No thanks, just curious to see if I recognized the handwriting, that's all. Thanks again, Carrie."

Rachel turned back toward the elevators, her mind focused on the contents of the letter rather than on her upcoming meeting with the two top research scientists in her pharmaceutical company.

The ride to the tenth floor, where her office suite was located, seemed to take forever. She smiled and chatted with various employees as if the envelope in her hand didn't matter.

"Good morning, Rachel," her senior administrative assistant, Edith Goodman, said as she entered through the glass doors. "Dr. Gardener and Dr. Errol are waiting for you in the conference room."

"I'm sorry, but please tell Josie and Karl that I'll need to reschedule our meeting."

Surprise flashed in Edith's eyes, but she quickly nodded and crossed over to the conference room next to Rachel's office. As her assistant delivered the news to the two researchers, Rachel ducked inside her office and closed the door, dropping the envelope on her desk as if it might burn her fingers.

She didn't have any gloves, so she put another piece of paper over the envelope and used her letter opener to slice beneath the flap. Inside was a single piece of paper with a computer-printed message, exactly like the one she'd received at home. Her stomach knotted with anxiety as she carefully opened the paper and read the short message.

"You will scream in agony, suffering for your past mistakes."

She shivered, the words searing into her mind. She opened her purse and drew out the letter she'd received last night, when she and her son, Joey, had come home from basketball practice. The wording was similar, yet different.

"You will repay your debt of betrayal."

The two letters, spread out side by side on her desk, seemed to mock her. She couldn't ignore the threat any longer, not when she knew, with grim certainty, the source of the veiled threat.

The only person she'd ever betrayed was her ex-husband, former State Senator Anthony Caruso. A few months after they were married, the joy of discovering she was pregnant was marred by learning Anthony had ties to organized crime. At first she couldn't believe he was involved in anything illegal. She was embarrassed that the man she'd fallen in love with was nothing more than an illusion. His fake charm covered a black soul.

All too soon, Anthony was openly talking about his Mafia association as if nothing she did could touch him.

But he'd been wrong. She'd lived in fear for months, but one night, he'd lost control and hit her hard enough to give her a black eye and a minor concussion. The evidence of physical abuse, along with her father's money—and the fact that her father's best friend was a judge—helped her buy her freedom.

And Joey's, too. She received sole custody of their son and a no-contact order. Joey was nine years old now, and she was eternally grateful Anthony hadn't seen his son since Joey's first birthday.

But since Anthony's untimely death last year during a crime bust, it was obvious he couldn't have sent these letters. So who had? She could only assume they'd come from someone inside the Chicago Mafia. Most likely from Anthony's uncle, Frankie Caruso.

She buried her face in her hands and fought the rising wave of helplessness. How long would she continue to pay for her naive mistake of marrying Anthony? This past year, since her ex-husband's death, she'd thought she was finally safe. But now it seemed the Mafia wasn't going to leave her alone.

Ever.

Taking several deep breaths, she did her best to control her fear. When she raised her head, she knew she had to take action. With trembling fingers, she went through her files to find the business card of a Chicago police detective who'd questioned her about Anthony last year. She needed to talk to someone who knew the truth about Anthony. Someone who understood how deeply infiltrated the Mafia was in this city.

Someone who would believe her—like Detective Nick Butler. They'd only met a few times, but she remembered him well. He was tall, broad shouldered with light brown hair and amazing blue eyes. In so many ways, Nick was the complete opposite of her ex-husband.

To be honest, Detective Butler hadn't been very happy with her last year during his investigation of Anthony, but that knowledge wasn't enough to stop her from picking up her phone and making the call.

If there was one thing she knew about Detective Butler, it was that he sincerely cared about justice. He'd worked against the Mafia before. She could only hope that he wouldn't turn his back on her now.

Nick stared at the various reports spread over his desk as he tried to figure out a way to breathe new life into his dead-end cases. With his partner out on medical leave and the upcoming holidays, he hadn't been assigned anything new. But working their old cases felt pretty much like beating his head against a brick wall.

When his phone rang, he answered it absently. "Detective Butler."

"Good morning, Detective. I don't know if you remember me, but my name is Rachel Simon."

Nick straightened in his chair, his instincts on full alert. "Of course, I remember you, Ms. Simon. How are you and your son, Joey, doing?"

"Fine. Well, sort of fine. I, uh, have a problem I'd like to discuss with you. I think it's linked to your past investigation...."

The subtle reference to the Mafia wasn't lost on him. He was surprised to hear from Rachel after all this time, yet he couldn't ignore the underlying hint of fear in her tone. He rose to his feet and glanced at his watch. "I can meet you now, if that works."

"That would be great. Do you remember where my office is located?"

"Yes. I can be there in fifteen minutes."

"Thank you."

After ending the call, Nick slid his cell phone into his pocket and strode to the door. He remembered Rachel Simon very well, as he'd questioned her last year related to a missing-person's case. Her ex-husband had been the prime suspect in the twenty-two-year-old model's disappearance.

Rachel hadn't been much help to his investigation, because she claimed she hadn't seen or spoken to her husband in seven years. Which, based on the divorce settlement and the no-contact order he'd uncovered, was likely true. But at the time he'd felt certain she was holding back on him, that she knew far more about her ex-husband's connection to the Mafia than she'd let on. And even then, her fear of her ex had been palpable.

Ironic how she'd contacted him now that she needed his assistance. And he couldn't deny being curious as to what was going on.

The ride to the office building of Simon Inc. took less than his allotted fifteen minutes. He walked into the lobby and smiled at the perky redhead sitting behind the receptionist desk. "Good morning, I'm here to see Ms. Simon."

"Yes, she mentioned you were coming." The redhead wore a name tag that identified her as Carrie Freeman and she was young enough to make him feel ancient at thirty-seven. "Just take these elevators here to the tenth floor."

"Thanks." He pushed the elevator button, already knowing Rachel's office was on the tenth floor. Once he arrived up there, he was greeted warmly by Rachel's assistant, Edith Goodman. A far cry from the last time he'd been here, when the sixty-something-year-old had protected her boss like a mama bear hovering over her cub.

"Rachel's waiting for you in her office," Edith said. "Is there something I can get for you, Detective? Coffee? Soft drink?"

"Coffee would be great."

"Black, no sugar, correct?"

He shouldn't have been surprised she remembered, considering Edith Goodman ruled Rachel's office with an iron fist. "That's right."

Rachel's office door was open, and she met him halfway, offering her hand as he strolled toward her. "Detective, thanks for coming on such short notice."

Her slender fingers were firm as they gripped his. She was as beautiful as he remembered, with her sleek blond hair framing her face and distinctive green eyes. But despite her smile, dark shadows hovered in her eyes. "I have to admit, I was intrigued by your call."

Her smile faded, and she waited until Edith had handed him a mug of coffee, before inviting him inside her office. "Please, have a seat."

He sat in the chair facing hers, and his gaze immediately landed on the two pieces of paper lying on her desk. They'd been turned toward him. He took a sip from the steaming mug before setting his coffee aside. He leaned forward and read the messages.

"You will repay your debt of betrayal."

"You will scream in agony, suffering for your past mistakes."

The threats were all too real and his protective instincts jumped to the forefront. He was angry at the idea of Rachel being stalked by some lunatic. He lifted his gaze to meet hers. "Who sent these to you?" he demanded roughly.

"Isn't it obvious?" Rachel scowled and crossed her arms protectively across her chest.

"Not to me," he said, striving for patience. "An ex-boyfriend? A disgruntled employee? You must have some idea."

Her scowl deepened. "I don't have a boyfriend, ex or otherwise, and a disgruntled employee would more likely try to sue me rather than send threats. I've received a few phone calls, too. The caller never speaks, but I can hear heavy breathing on the other end of the phone. Don't you see?" She spread her hands over the letters. "These have to be from someone within the Mafia."

He stared at her for a long moment, trying to figure out what was going on in her mind. Their last interaction hadn't been entirely cordial, since she'd avoided discussing anything related to her husband's ties to the Mafia. He sat back and reached for his coffee mug. "So you're admitting that Anthony Caruso was involved with the Mafia?"

Her cheeks turned pink and she avoided his gaze as if embarrassed. "I told you that much a year ago," she said defensively.

"But you claimed you didn't know any details," he reminded her.

"Look, Detective, my goal last year was to do whatever was necessary to protect my son. And I never lied to you about that missing woman. At the time we spoke I hadn't seen Anthony in seven years, so I had no idea who he was seeing or who he was associating with."

"But you knew what he was capable of," Nick said, capturing her gaze with his.

She stared at him for a long moment before breaking the connection. And when she spoke, her voice was so soft he could barely hear her. "Yes. I knew exactly what he was capable of. I believe he murdered that woman. But my belief is a far cry from actual hard-core evidence. There was nothing that I knew that would have helped your case."

The simple admission helped squelch his lingering anger. He was a bit ashamed that he'd spent time rehashing the past instead of moving forward. He caught sight of the photo of her son, Joey, that was displayed proudly on her desk. The kid had blond hair, green eyes and a smile that matched his mother's. Nick could understand her need to keep silent if it meant protecting her child.

For a moment, he thought about how much he missed his wife and daughter. He would have done anything to protect them, too. But unfortunately, they both died in a terrible car accident two years ago. And while he knew they were in a much better place in heaven, he still missed them every day.

He pushed the painful memories aside. "Okay, maybe someone within the Mafia sent them, but at this point, we don't have any proof. We can't go after anyone in the syndicate without evidence. I'll take these notes and have them dusted for prints. Maybe that'll give us a place to start."

She grimaced. "Well, to be perfectly honest, the first one probably won't help much. I treated it normally since I had no idea that it was a threat. The second letter I was very careful with, although the envelope was handled by my receptionist." She went on to describe in detail how she'd received the letters.

He made notes in his notebook. "Do you remember

when the phone calls came in?" he asked. "Was there a common number?"

"The calls came from a blocked number, and they started three days ago."

Three phone calls and two written threats in the past three days. Hard to tell if the danger was escalating. He'd known some stalkers who called their victims twenty or thirty times a day. These messages seemed to be aimed at keeping Rachel off balance and afraid. "You haven't noticed anyone following you? Or watching you?"

"No. Nothing like that." Her gaze rested on her son's photograph. "Right now, the threats are centered on me, but I called you because I need to be sure Joey is safe."

"I understand. I'll see what we can get from these letters, but at this point, our hands are tied." As much as he wanted to order protection for her, they needed more than just her suspicion that the Mafia was behind the threats. He took out his business card and slid it across the desk. "I want you to be extra vigilant. If you see anything suspicious, please call me on my personal phone regardless of the time of day or night."

She took the card and nodded. "Thank you."

He rose to his feet, wishing there was more that could be done. After donning a pair of gloves, he placed both notes and the envelopes in a plastic evidence bag, even though he knew the odds of getting a decent set of prints were slim. And they'd have to get Rachel's fingerprints as well as the receptionist's on file to cross match them.

Having a new case to work on would help keep him busy. But first he needed to see what the forensic team came up with. Otherwise, he'd have nothing to go on, which wouldn't help keep Rachel and her son safe.

And he wasn't about to lose another mother and child on his watch.

* * *

Rachel managed to get some work done before heading out to take Joey to his last basketball game before the Christmas holiday. The drive to the school, located on the outskirts of town, was uneventful. The game turned out to be a lot of fun and her son scored four points, edging their team to a ten to eight victory. Joey and his teammates were loud and rambunctious as they celebrated, and Rachel felt more at ease as the night unfolded. But as she and Joey headed home, she noticed a big black truck keeping pace behind her. No matter what speed she chose to go, the truck remained right behind her.

Detective Butler had warned her to be on the lookout for anything suspicious. At the moment, the truck certainly seemed suspicious, but maybe she was letting her imagination get the better of her. She didn't recall seeing a truck behind her on the way to the basketball game or parked anywhere along the long country road outside the school.

So how would the driver of the black truck know where to find her? How would anyone have access to Joey's basketball schedule? Maybe this was nothing more than a coincidence.

She did her best to keep her expression neutral as Joey relived every moment of winning the basketball game.

"Did you see my last basket? The coach said it was amazing and that without my score we might not have won the game. Isn't that awesome, Mom?" he asked for the third time. "I can't wait until our next tournament. Coach said I can be in the starting lineup!"

"The game was awesome," she agreed, looking once again in her rearview mirror. Was the truck gaining on them? Darkness came early in December so it was hard to gauge the distance. She tightened her grip on the steering wheel and pressed down on the accelerator. For the first time she bemoaned the fact she'd traded in her high-powered sports car for a four-cylinder eco-friendly hybrid last year. The hybrid's engine chugged as she fought to increase her speed.

The truck edged closer, and she glanced helplessly around at the winding country road she'd taken to avoid the traffic on the interstate. Was the driver of the truck behind her the same person who'd sent her the threatening letters? Was he working for someone linked to the Mafia?

Swallowing hard, she drew her cell phone out of the front pocket of her sweatshirt and pushed the preprogrammed number for Nick Butler. He'd told her to call day or night and, thankfully, seven-thirty in the evening wasn't too late. She held her breath until he answered.

"Butler."

"It's Rachel. We're being followed by a black truck license plate number TYG-555. We're on Handover Road, just past Highway 12."

"Mom? What's going on?" Joey swiveled in his seat, finally realizing that something was wrong.

"Hang tight, I'm not far away. I'll be right there," Nick said in a calm, reassuring tone.

"Hurry," she urged, before sliding the phone back into her pocket and returning both hands to the wheel. She increased her speed more, wondering why Nick would be so close, when suddenly, the truck rammed into her from behind, causing the steering wheel to jerk in her hands as the car swerved dangerously. She and Joey were wearing their seat belts, but she wasn't sure the restraint would be enough to prevent them from being harmed. "Hang on, Joey!" she shouted as she fought to stay in control.

"Mom!" Joey screamed as the truck rammed into them again, and this time, she couldn't prevent the car from slamming into the guardrail with a sickening lurch. She tried to ride against the rail, but the car spun out of control, doing a complete three-sixty before hitting the side rail again, thankfully on the driver's side.

The impact caused the airbags to explode in their faces. Pain radiated through her face and chest. "Joey!" she shrieked, frantic to know her son was all right.

The car came to an abrupt halt, but the driver's side door was bent inward to the point of pinning her left foot. She batted away the air bags as she frantically reached over for her son. "Joey? Are you all right?"

"Yeah," he said, between hiccuping sobs. "I think so."

Coughing as air bag dust filled her lungs, she tried again to get her foot out from the twisted hunk of metal. When that didn't work, she reached over to help Joey get out of his seat belt. "I need you to get out of the car, Joey. Run away and get help. Find Detective Butler. Do you understand me? You need to get away from here and find Detective Nick Butler."

"Not without you," he cried.

"I'll be right behind you," she said, even though she wasn't sure she'd be able to wrench herself free. "Now go. *Hurry!*"

Somehow, Joey managed to crawl out of the passenger-side window, which was completely busted open. She pulled, gritting her teeth against the pain as she tried to yank out her pinned foot.

Through the open window she saw Joey stagger a bit before he managed to pick up his pace enough to run. She heard the distant wailing of a police siren and hoped that was Nick, as she shifted in her seat again, determined to find a way to get free.

But then she saw a large man dressed completely in dark clothing, recognizing him as the driver of the big black truck that had caused her to crash. Through the glow of her headlights, she saw him take off running after her son. "No! Joey!" she screamed, ripping her foot out of her shoe, finally gaining freedom. *"No!"*

Too late. The tall stranger easily scooped up her son and dropped a black hood over Joey's head before taking off with him thrown over his shoulder like a sack of potatoes. Joey struggled against him, but the guy never hesitated, ignoring her son's kicks and punches.

"No!" she wailed, scrambling to get out of the crushed car. She threw herself across to the passenger seat and wiggled her way through the broken window. "Stop! Joey!"

But the moment she fell from the window onto the paved road, the big black truck engine rumbled to life and pulled away, tires screeching, with her son trapped inside.

TWO

Nick slammed his foot down hard on the accelerator, racing to Rachel's location, his heart pounding in his chest. Earlier that day, he hadn't been entirely convinced her stalker was really someone from the Mafia. But the threats had been enough that he couldn't bear to leave her totally on her own, so he'd followed Rachel to her son's basketball game without telling her he was nearby.

Now he realized his instincts had been right on. The panic in her tone gripped him by the throat and he couldn't help feeling that this was his fault for not doing more to keep her safe. He saw Rachel and Joey leaving the school after the game, but at that moment he'd taken a call from his boss, questioning why he'd taken on Rachel's stalker case. He'd explained about the possible mob connection, which had eased his captain's concern. But in the time it had taken him to placate his boss, Rachel and Joey had disappeared from sight.

His fault for not telling her he was there. And if something bad happened to Rachel and Joey, he'd never forgive himself. As he drove, he silently prayed for their well-being.

Please, Lord, keep Rachel and Joey safe in Your care. Amen.

The closer he got to the location she'd given him, the

more his gut tightened with fear and worry. And when
he saw her mangled car wedged against the guardrail, his
stomach dropped. He was surprised to see there weren't
any police cars or ambulances at the scene. As he pulled
over, Rachel was there, limping and crying, making her
way down the road. He bolted from his car and ran toward her. "Rachel, what is it? What's wrong?"

"He took Joey!" She grabbed his arm in a tight grip.
"You have to do something! Right now!"

"Which way did they go?"

"N-north."

"All right, let's go." He took her arm since she was
shaking so badly he was afraid she wouldn't be able to
stay upright. She managed to hang on long enough to
climb into his car. He slid quickly into the driver's seat.

As he drove he reached for the radio. "I have to call
my boss, tell him to send a chopper. The truck will be
easier to find from the air at night."

"Wait! I have a text message."

He froze, watching as she pulled her cell phone from
the pocket of her pink hoodie sweatshirt.

"Oh, no," she whispered.

"What is it?"

"Don't call the police or I'll kill him." She lifted her
tortured gaze to his. "I knew it! I knew the mob was after
me. And now they've kidnapped Joey!"

Every instinct he possessed told him to radio for
backup, but Rachel had grabbed his arm again, squeezing so tight he winced as her nails dug painfully into
his skin. "We have to find him. We have to get to Joey!"
she sobbed.

"Rachel, I know you're scared, but let's calm down

and think this through. We need to get the helicopters to go after that black truck."

"If that guy sees the police he'll kill Joey. You don't know how ruthless the Mafia can be. Please don't do anything that will hurt my son. *Please!*" Her green eyes implored him to listen.

He pressed harder on the accelerator, going well above the speed limit. He wished a cop would try to pull him over, because then they'd have their badly needed backup.

"This is all my fault. They have Joey and it's all my fault," Rachel moaned.

He glanced over at her, wishing there was something he could say to make her feel better. But he knew only too well what it was like to lose a child.

"There!" Rachel's excited shout drew him out of his depressing thoughts. "That's the black truck that hit me."

He couldn't believe they'd found the black truck here, on the side of the road. But as they came closer, it was clear that the vehicle had been abandoned. Was it possibly a different truck? No, the damage to the front bumper convinced him they had the right vehicle. The passenger-side door was left hanging wide open, as if someone had grabbed Joey and taken off running without bothering to shut the door behind him.

He scanned the area, but there wasn't much he could see in the darkness outside the glow from his headlights. He could tell that beyond the open cornfield was a subdivision full of houses, many of them twinkling with various holiday lights. The kidnapper could be anywhere. Either on foot or—if he wasn't working alone—in another vehicle.

"Where are they? Where's Joey?" Rachel barely

waited for him to stop the car before she was out and racing over to see for herself.

He followed hot on her heels, ready to prevent her from disturbing any evidence. But he needn't have worried.

She simply stood there, staring inside the empty truck, her eyes welling with tears. "They're gone," she whispered.

He curled his fingers into helpless fists, knowing there wasn't any way to put a positive spin on this latest turn of events.

Joey was gone and Nick didn't have a clue as to where he might be.

Rachel shivered, ice creeping slowly through her bloodstream like a glacier. She'd been so certain they'd find the black truck. Find Joey.

But her son was still missing.

"Come on, Rachel. I have to call my boss," Nick urged, putting a hand beneath her elbow to nudge her away from the truck.

She didn't move, couldn't seem to tear her gaze from the empty truck. Joey had been in there, with a hood over his face. She couldn't bear to think of how frightened her son must be. "Hang in there, Joey," she whispered, as if he could hear her. "I'm coming to get you."

"Rachel, there's nothing more we can do here. Not until we get a forensic team to go through the truck to pick up trace evidence."

"No cops," she said weakly, even though she knew it was too late. Nick was a cop and she'd called him right before the crash. And obviously they needed all the help they could get to find Joey. Her frozen brain cells finally put a few pieces of the puzzle together. "How did you get to me so quickly?" she asked with a frown.

He shrugged and ducked his head before he abruptly turned away, heading back to his vehicle. She forced her legs to follow him, wincing as she stepped on a stone with her foot that didn't have a shoe.

"Wait," she said, stopping him once again as he reached for the radio. "Can you call this incident in as a hit-and-run? Without mentioning Joey?"

"Rachel, you know that's not smart," he said with a heavy sigh. "I get that they have you running scared, but the more people searching for your son, the better."

Logically, she could agree, but there was nothing logical about her feelings regarding the mob. And she was convinced that her husband's uncle, Frankie Caruso, was the mastermind behind Joey's kidnapping. "You don't understand," she said brokenly, wishing she could convince him. "If they get any sense that the police are involved there's nothing to stop them from killing him."

"Why would they kidnap your son in the first place?" he asked. "You have to admit, kidnapping is a huge leap from stalking."

She drew her arms across her jacket, trying to maintain some warmth in the cold December night. Her left ankle throbbed, but she shoved the pain aside. No matter how much she hurt, she wouldn't allow anything to stop her from finding her son. "Maybe the Mafia is looking for money from my company? Money that will help them rebuild their organization?"

"It's possible, since the Mafia has taken several big hits lately," Nick mused. "And you think they targeted you because of your marriage to Anthony?"

"Yes. Don't you see? It all fits! My father's money helped me escape Anthony all those years ago, so now they want me to pay them back. That's basically what those threatening notes said, right?"

Grimacing, Nick nodded slowly. "I guess in a twisted way, that makes sense."

She was dizzy with relief, knowing she'd finally managed to convince him of the Mafia link. "The mob fights dirty and plays for keeps," she murmured. "If you call in reinforcements, the dirty cops might find out and let Joey's captors know. I just can't take that chance."

"Not all cops are dirty, Rachel," Nick said, a hard edge to his tone.

She sensed she was losing the battle. "During my brief marriage to Anthony, I knew of several Chicago cops who were on his payroll. None of them would lift a finger to help me. Can you honestly say that there isn't the possibility of dirty cops still on the force?"

He scowled as he twisted the key in the ignition. "No, I can't tell you that as much as I wish I could. I hate knowing that some of the very men and women who are supposed to put criminals away actually join forces with them, instead. Kidnapping is a federal offense, so we could call in the FBI."

Fear tightened her chest to the point she felt she couldn't breathe. "Are you sure there isn't any possibility of someone linked to the Mafia working inside the FBI, too?"

Nick let the car idle as he scrubbed his hands over his face. "No, I can't tell you that, either. Because there was a dirty FBI agent involved in a case I worked on last summer. We arrested him, but I always wondered if there weren't others, too. Others that we missed."

The thought of losing her son was making bile rise

to her throat. "Please, Nick. All I'm asking for is a little time. Please keep Joey's involvement out of this for now."

He turned his head and stared at her for a long moment. "I'm going to at least let my boss know what's going on. I know he's not dirty and we need someone to trust." She wanted to protest but knew that he had a job to do. Nodding stiffly, she dropped her hand from his arm so that he could call in a crime team to investigate the crash scene and the abandoned truck.

She didn't relax a single muscle until he disconnected the call, without once mentioning Joey. Unfortunately, her relief was short-lived when Nick punched in another number.

"Hey, I think we have another link to the Mafia angle," he said into the phone.

She strained to hear the other side of the conversation, which she assumed was with Nick's boss. "Yeah? Like what?"

Her heart squeezed when Nick briefly explained what had transpired. "I'd like to keep this quiet for now, while we wait for some more evidence. If the Mafia is behind this, there isn't much to stop them from doing something drastic if they sense we're onto them."

"I'm not sure I like that plan, Butler." She could hear Nick's boss's weary tone. "The feds won't be happy if we don't follow protocol."

"Yeah, but you and I both know that there have been far too many dirty cops, both locally and at the federal level. Just give me a little time to see what we can shake out, okay?"

"All right. But keep me posted."

"Will do." Nick hung up the phone and then put the car in gear.

"Thank you, Nick," she murmured softly.

"Don't thank me," he said in a harsh tone. "We don't have Joey back yet. And you need to know this may not turn out the way you want it to."

"We'll get him back." She wasn't even going to consider the possibility of failure.

He let out an exasperated sigh. "I hope so, but you have to understand that we don't have a lot of time. If we don't hear from the kidnappers soon, I won't give you a choice. We will call in the FBI."

She wanted to argue, feeling deep down that calling in the FBI would be the worst thing they could do. After all, she knew from personal experience how the Mafia worked. The members of the mob were cruel and ruthless and wouldn't hesitate to kill her son just to prove their point.

The threatening notes she'd received were right. She had screamed in agony when they'd kidnapped her son. And if they demanded a ransom, she would repay her debts in order to get him back.

Panic bubbled in her throat and she had to swallow the urge to start screaming all over again. She needed to stay calm, to think this through logically, if she was going to have any chance in finding Joey.

After several long deep breaths, she felt somewhat calm. "You never did mention how you reached me so quickly," she said, glancing over at Nick.

There was a long silence before he admitted, "I followed you and Joey. I guess I was hoping to catch the guy in the act of leaving another note for you."

He'd been sitting in the parking lot of the elementary school? She tried to grapple with that revelation. "I didn't see you," she said. "And believe me, I was on alert, searching for signs of Frankie or one of his thugs."

Nick shifted in his seat. "I stayed in my car, a little ways down the road, just close enough to watch your vehicle."

She wasn't sure that news was reassuring. If she hadn't seen Nick, maybe she'd missed the driver of the black truck, too? She couldn't bear the thought that she may have led the kidnapper straight to her son's location.

More deep breaths helped rein in her fear. She tried to find comfort in the fact that Nick had cared enough to try to protect her, but the image of her son being kidnapped by the driver of the truck was seared in her mind.

Helplessly, she gazed down at her phone, looking at the text message again. Don't call the police or I'll kill him.

Why hadn't they already demanded money? That had to be the reason they'd kidnapped Joey. Nothing else made sense.

"We should probably stay in a hotel tonight," Nick said, breaking into her grim thoughts. "Especially because you received those threats at both your office and your home."

She pressed her fingertips against her aching temples, trying to think. "I guess a motel would be okay."

"It's our best option. For now."

She understood the warning implication in his tone. This was a temporary plan at best. She stared down at her cell phone for another long moment, willing the kidnapper to contact her again. The sooner they told her how much money they wanted, the sooner she could get her son back, safe and sound.

"Tell me what you know about Frankie Caruso," Nick said quietly.

Her stomach twisted into painful knots. "I'm afraid I don't know much. I only met him for the first time at our engagement party and then again at our wedding. I knew he'd raised Anthony after his parents died, but I didn't know about their link to the Mafia. Not until after we were married."

Nick glanced at her, and she wondered if he thought she was an idiot for not figuring out what was going on sooner. She'd often asked herself the same thing. She didn't like to think about how naive she was back then. She graduated college early and by twenty-five had worked her way up in her father's company to vice president. Hours of studying meant she hadn't dated much. Anthony had swept her off her feet with his dashing good looks and his charm.

It was only after they were married for a few months that she caught a glimpse of his dark side. But by then she'd discovered she was pregnant and tried to make the marriage work.

Until she was on the receiving end of his violent temper.

"Has Frankie been living here in Chicago?" Nick pressed.

"Early on, he did, but after Anthony won his second term as state senator, Frankie moved down to Phoenix. Anthony told me that his uncle was tired of the brutal Chicago winters."

"But you think Frankie's back in the area?"

She lifted her shoulders in a helpless shrug. "Honestly, I haven't kept track of Anthony's uncle in the years since our divorce. I was lucky to get away from Anthony early in our marriage, shortly after Joey's first birthday." Two years of marriage that had seemed like a lifetime. "I suspect that since Anthony is dead, Frankie might have come back to take his place within the Mafia."

"Rachel, there isn't much of the Mafia left for him to return to," he said. "I happen to know that Bernardo Salvatore and his right-hand man, Russo, are both dead."

The news surprised her. "Really? How?"

He pressed his lips into a grim line. "I can't go into details other than to tell you that I was there when they were killed. You have to consider there might be someone else besides Frankie Caruso after you."

"I'm telling you there's no one else I can think of," she said, wishing he would believe her. "Besides, if Salvatore and this Russo guy are dead, then it makes even more sense to me that Frankie came back to Chicago. Clearly he wants to pick up the crime syndicate where Salvatore left off."

"Maybe. I'll try running a search on him," Nick murmured. "It's possible we'll get lucky."

She didn't bother to tell Nick that she didn't feel lucky. The thought of her son being held by the Mafia, alone and afraid, made fear clog her throat to the point she could barely breathe. Outside the passenger-side window, she stared at the holiday decorations lighting up people's houses. Would Joey be back in time for Christmas? She couldn't even imagine the possibility that he wouldn't be.

Nick pulled up to a low-budget motel and secured two connecting rooms. She reluctantly took her room key from his hand, knowing she couldn't relax, couldn't rest.

Not until she found her son.

"Rachel?" She glanced up when she heard Nick call her name from the open doorway between their rooms.

"What is it?" she asked, rising to her feet and crossing over to meet him in the doorway.

"Are you hungry?"

She grimaced and shook her head. "No." The mere thought of food made her nauseous. "You mentioned doing a search on Frankie Caruso. Do you have a laptop with you?"

"Yeah, I have my laptop," Nick replied. "So far, I haven't found much."

Frankie Caruso was too smart to leave an obvious trail. She kept her phone gripped in her hand, unable to bear the thought of losing the small link that she had with Joey's kidnapper. She hated to think of what her son might be suffering through right now. Why hadn't they contacted her again? What were they waiting for? "We have to keep searching. We have to find something!"

"Rachel, I know you're upset, but there isn't much more I can do. If we don't hear something soon, we'll have no choice but to pull in the FBI."

"No. We can't." The very thought of bringing in the authorities nearly made her double over in pain. "Your boss promised us some time, right? I'm sure the kidnappers will contact me soon."

"All right." There was a hint of disappointment in his gaze. She told herself she didn't care what Nick thought of her. He couldn't possibly imagine what she was going through. Or what she'd already suffered at the hands of the Mafia. She'd lived with Anthony for two long terrible years and had learned early on that confronting the Mafia directly only made them angry.

She didn't want the man who'd kidnapped Joey to take his anger out on her son.

"I'm going to get something to eat," Nick said over his shoulder. "Stay here and don't let anyone in except for me."

"Can I use your laptop while you're gone?" she asked.

He shrugged. "Sure, why not?"

She waited for him in the doorway, gratefully taking the computer from his hands. "Thank you."

"I'll be back soon," he said huskily, and he closed the connecting door on his side.

She opened the computer and tried to think of what little she remembered from those early days with Anthony—the places he went, the people he considered friends. She'd purposefully pushed all those bad memories out of her mind after she escaped, so dredging them up again wasn't easy.

Typing Frank Caruso's name into the search engine didn't bring up many hits. She tried using Luigi Gagliano's name too, as he was a distant cousin to Anthony.

Still nothing. And as she stared blankly at the computer, a terrible thought occurred to her.

Here she was, waiting for Joey's kidnappers to call with some sort of ransom demand, but what if she was on the wrong track? What if Frankie didn't want her money, but simply wanted her son?

Frankie had raised Anthony, bringing him into the world of crime at a young age. Was it possible he wanted to use Joey as a surrogate for Anthony?

Was it possible that Frankie was, right now, driving far away with her son?

Rachel's heart rate soared as she surged to her feet. Nick had been right! They should have called the police and the FBI right away! If Frankie had kidnapped Joey for personal reasons then he already had a head start on them.

She grabbed her phone, intending to call Nick, but then forced herself to stop and think. Why would Frankie send her threatening letters, saying she would repay her debts, if he didn't want money?

Pacing the length of the small motel room helped calm her ragged nerves. Her ankle throbbed, but she ignored it. She'd never had a panic attack like this before, not even in the dark days after Anthony had beaten her. She had to stop overreacting to every thought. Every remote possibility.

Somehow she had to be smarter than Frankie Caruso or Luigi Gagliano.

She sat down at the small desk and clicked on the mouse to reactivate Nick's computer. There was one angle she hadn't considered, and that was Frankie's ex-wife, Margie Caruso. Frankie and Margie had divorced the year Rachel was pregnant with Joey, but, surprisingly, they'd stayed on friendly terms. She'd often wondered if Margie had also been involved in illegal activities; otherwise, why wouldn't Frankie have tried to silence his ex-wife? After all, Anthony had often threatened to kill Rachel if she ratted him out.

Anthony's threats hadn't been empty ones, either.

And if Margie was part of the Mafia, it wasn't a stretch to think that she could be in cahoots with Frankie on this kidnapping scheme.

A quick search revealed that Margie was still living in the Chicago area. She wrote down the address, determined to convince Nick that they needed to pay the woman a surprise visit.

THREE

Nick couldn't stop thinking about Rachel and Joey as he ran a few errands. He understood what Rachel was going through—he'd been inconsolable after his wife and daughter went missing, too. He knew he shouldn't let his emotions get in the way of doing what was right, but seeing the pain etched on Rachel's face was impossible to ignore.

After picking up some new clothes he'd put a call in to his FBI buddy, Logan Quail, only to find out his friend was out of the country on his honeymoon. No wonder Logan hadn't returned his calls. The timing was unfortunate, since Logan's expertise would have been perfect for Rachel's situation.

But he'd just have to use another way to help Rachel find her son.

As he was picking up some fast food, his phone rang and he was surprised to discover that the caller was his boss, Ryan Walsh. "Hi, Captain."

"Butler. We have some news from the crash scene you called in earlier."

"You do?" He juggled the phone as he handed over

cash and accepted the bag of food from the bored teen at the window. "What do you have?"

"We got a hit on one of the fingerprints. Perp's name is Ricky Morales and he's got a rap sheet, largely for drug busts, but, most recently, he was arrested for armed robbery. He just got out on bail about six months ago."

Nick pulled away from the drive-through window and parked in the first open slot he saw. "Do you think Morales has found a home working as a thug for the Mafia?"

His boss grunted. "Don't see why not. It's a lead worth following since the truck is registered in his name, too. Explains why he dumped his ride as soon as he did. I'll send his last-known address to you in an email. Where are you right now?"

"Getting something to eat." Nick didn't want to say too much. "We also have a possible suspect in Frankie Caruso, who happens to be Anthony Caruso's uncle. Ms. Simon is convinced that Frankie is back to take over the Mafia."

"What do you think?" Walsh asked.

"I think she could be right. You might want to see what you can find out about Caruso's activities. In the meantime, we'll start looking for leads related to Ricky Morales."

"Sounds like a plan." He could hear his boss scribbling notes. "Good work so far, Butler. Keep in touch."

"I will." Nick disconnected from the call and stared at his phone for a moment. He debated searching for Morales right now, but then decided he needed to get back to the motel. At least he had some positive news to give Rachel.

The drive didn't take long. He grabbed the clothes and the bag of food, his mouth watering at the aroma of burgers and fries, and swiped his key card. The moment he closed the motel door behind him, he heard Rachel knocking on the connecting door.

"Coming," he called as he reached for the door. He smiled at her. "Don't argue, but I brought food for the both of us."

"There's no time to eat," Rachel said in a rush. "Look what I've discovered." She gestured to the computer screen. "Margie Caruso, Frankie's ex-wife still lives outside of Chicago. We have to get over there right away."

Her excitement was palpable. "Good news, but I have something to follow up on, too." He pushed the laptop out of the way so he could haul the food out of the bag. "I'll search while we eat."

Rachel frowned, but he noticed she was staring at the burgers and fries as if her appetite may have returned. He bowed his head and gave a quick prayer of thanks. Rachel didn't say anything, respecting his silent prayer, until he finished and dug into his food. "What are you following up on?" she asked.

"Sit down and eat," he suggested.

She grimaced, but came over to sit beside him. As if she couldn't help herself, she popped a French fry into her mouth. He waited until she surrendered to her inevitable hunger by unwrapping the second sandwich and taking a bite before telling her what his boss had uncovered.

"You think this Ricky Morales is the guy who kidnapped Joey?" she asked, her green eyes filled with hope. "I mean, that seems to be the most logical conclusion. And we should be able to find him, right?"

He nodded, even though he knew tracking Morales down wouldn't be quite that easy. As he ate, he pulled up his email and jotted down the information his boss had sent. "Here's his last-known address. It's on the opposite side of town from Margie Caruso's place."

"It's only eight-thirty...there's plenty of time yet to head over to see what we can find. I need to keep busy, searching for Joey. We have to find him as soon as possible!"

"We'll check both addresses out tonight," he assured her.

"Thank you," she murmured.

He shook his head, not wanting her gratitude. He was beginning to identify with Rachel on a personal level. Her fear tugged at his heart. He knew, only too well, what she was going through. Those hours his wife and daughter were missing had been the longest, darkest hours of his life. And when the news came in that they were both found dead in their mangled SUV at the bottom of a ravine, his grief had been overwhelming. Without his faith, he never would have survived the dark days following their deaths.

Grimly, he hoped and prayed that Rachel's outcome would be different. *Please, Lord, keep Joey safe in Your care and guide us in finding him. Amen.*

Rachel pushed away her half-eaten sandwich and the remaining cold French fries, her patience wearing thin. She couldn't bear the thought of sitting here another minute. If she didn't take some sort of action to help find her son, she'd go stark, raving mad.

She tapped her fingers impatiently on the table, as Nick finished his meal. "I bought a dark sweatshirt for you, since that pink one is too easily seen at night, and a new pair of athletic shoes," he said between bites. "Also hats and gloves. Why don't you change while I finish up?"

"Okay, thanks," she said, reaching down for the bag of clothes. The shoes were a welcome sight, and while she loved her pink sweatshirt, she realized Nick was right about how it stood out. The black sweatshirt beneath her jacket would blend far better with the night.

She disappeared into the bathroom and quickly changed. Her left ankle was swollen, but she managed to get that shoe on by loosening the laces. The pain in her foot was nothing compared to the gaping hole in her heart.

When she emerged from the bathroom, she was grateful to see that Nick had finished his meal, disposing of all the garbage in the trash can by the door. He'd pulled on the matching black sweatshirt, too, before zipping up his jacket. He shut down the computer and then turned to her. "Ready?" he asked, rising to his feet.

"Yes." She was more than ready. She tucked her room key into her back pocket and followed Nick out to the car. Once she was buckled in, he set his phone in the cradle where he could easily read the GPS directions.

"Where are we going first?" she asked.

"Morales lives closer," he said, glancing over his shoulder as he backed out of the driveway. "We'll go there, first."

She didn't argue with his logic. Granted, it wasn't likely that Morales would abandon his truck and take Joey to his home address listed on the registration, but, then again, criminals weren't always known for being smart.

The minutes ticked by with agonizing slowness as Nick drove through the night. She tensed when she noticed they were heading straight into a seedy part of town. Her stomach roiled at the thought of Joey being kept in a place where he was likely to be assaulted, or worse even, if he managed to escape.

"There it is," Nick murmured. "Second apartment building on the right."

"Do we know which apartment might be his?" she asked, leaning forward to see better. The dilapidated building sure wasn't comforting. "Do you really think he would have brought a kidnapping victim here to his place?"

"Doubtful, especially if he's working for someone else," Nick said. "I'm going to get out here to see if I can find out if he's still living here. Slide into the driver's seat and head around the block. This won't take long."

"All right." As soon as Nick pulled over and climbed from the vehicle, she slipped over the console and adjusted the seat so she could drive. "Be careful," she added before he shut the door.

He nodded and then pulled his sweatshirt hood over his head and hunched his shoulders as he loped across the street to the apartment building. As much as she wanted to watch, she forced herself to put the car in gear. At the end of the block was a stop sign and she turned right. There was a small group of tough-looking kids smoking cigarettes as they gathered at the street corner, beneath a streetlight where a small Christmas wreath was hanging. As she watched them she saw the gleam of silver. A knife? Or a gun? Several of them hid their hands in their pockets as she went past, giving her the distinct impression they were hiding something. Drugs? Maybe. Swallowing hard, she made sure the doors were locked before she gripped the steering wheel tightly.

As she came around the last corner to the street where Morales's apartment building was located, her heart sank when she saw the group of teens had moved down closer to the apartment building. Had they noticed Nick getting out of the car and going inside? What if they planned to rob him when he came out? This was a bad neighborhood, where crime ran rampant. She knew Nick carried his service weapon, but the odds were still stacked against him, especially since all six of them were likely armed, too.

She was fumbling with her cell phone, intending to call Nick to warn him, when he slipped out of the apartment building and headed down the steps. Her heart hammered in her chest as the group of kids stepped forward, cutting him off.

Nick kept his hand in the pocket of his jacket and she assumed he had his gun ready. He sidestepped the kids, but they crowded closer and once again, she caught sight of a flash of silver.

Rachel unlocked the car and leaned on the horn. The group of kids swung around in surprise, and in that split second, Nick ran around them and jumped into the car. "Go!" he shouted as he slammed the door shut.

She stomped on the accelerator and the car leaped forward. In her rearview mirror she saw the group of kids begin running after them. Did they still intend to rob them? Or worse? As she approached the stop sign up ahead, she glanced frantically both ways before ignoring the sign and going straight through the intersection without stopping.

"Take it easy," Nick said, putting a hand on her arm as she took another turn a little too fast. "They flashed a few knives and demanded money, but we're safe now."

She couldn't speak, could barely calm her racing heart enough to take a deep breath. Her entire body was shaking in the aftermath of their close call.

"Pull over up ahead," Nick instructed.

She knew he wanted to drive and couldn't blame him. She did as he requested, trying to hold herself together. She dragged herself out of the driver's seat as Nick came around to meet her. He lightly clasped her shoulders, peering down at her. From the streetlight behind her, she could see the concern etched on his handsome face.

"Are you all right?" he asked.

She tried to speak, but her throat felt frozen. It abruptly hit her how much she was depending on Nick to help find her son. If anything had happened to him, she'd be lost.

As much as she longed to lean against his strength, she forced herself to step back, putting distance between them. "I'm fine, but I was afraid they were going to hurt you," she confessed softly.

"Me, too, and I didn't really want to shoot any of them. Thanks to your quick thinking, I didn't have to. Now let's get going, okay?"

She nodded and went around to the passenger side of his car. "Did you find anything?" she asked, hoping the stop at the apartment building hadn't been in vain.

"Yeah. Morales still has a place there, apartment number 210 according to the mailbox. I spoke to the manager, but he claims he hasn't seen Ricky in weeks."

She tried not to be too discouraged by the lack of information. Truthfully, he'd found out more than she'd hoped. "I guess that means he's not likely keeping Joey there."

"I doubt it. There are too many nosey people around, like those thugs back there."

"I hardly think they'd be the types to turn Ricky in to the police," she said with a sigh.

Nick didn't say anything to the contrary, which only made her more depressed. "Are you still up for heading over to the ex-wife's place?" he asked, changing the subject.

"Yes." Granted she'd been terrified back there at the apartment building, but nothing was going to stop her from searching for Joey.

Nick glanced over at Rachel, marveling at the depth of her strength. Granted, she'd been scared to death back there at the apartment building, but that hadn't stopped her from doing what needed to be done.

He used his radio to request a search on the Morales apartment related to the hit-and-run case. The dispatcher agreed to send a couple of uniforms over. He didn't really think they'd find anything useful, especially since the manager had been all too willing to talk once he'd seen Nick's badge.

If Morales had been around, the manager would have told him so.

The trip to Margie Caruso's house took about twenty minutes. Her neighborhood was several steps up from where Morales lived. At least the houses were neat and clean for the most part, several decorated with Christmas lights.

The address indicated the house they were looking for was the third one on the right. Nick slowed down as he drove past the modest red brick home with the tan trim and black shutters. The entire place was dark, not a single light on inside the place that he could see.

"What do you think? Is anyone home?" Rachel asked.

"I don't know. It's about nine-fifteen, so I suppose Margie could already be asleep...." But it wasn't likely.

Maybe they were on the wrong track? Could be that Margie Caruso was living a normal peaceful life that had nothing to do with the Mafia or kidnapping Rachel's son.

"What's the plan?" she asked, keeping the house in sight as he drove by.

"Don't have one yet. It's not as if we can simply walk up and demand to search the place, even if someone answers the door."

"Why not? I could try talking to her," Rachel said impulsively. "We're both ex-Carusos and I can use that connection to feel her out."

He wasn't sure he liked the idea, but couldn't come up with anything better so he reluctantly nodded. "All right. I'll park on the street, in front of the neighbor's house. If anything seems off, you need to get out of there right away."

"I will." She hesitated for a moment before reaching for the door handle. Extremely bright lights bloomed in his rearview mirror as a car headed straight for them.

"Wait!" Nick shouted, reaching out to grab her arm. She paused, half in and half out of the car, so he yanked her back inside at the same time gunfire echoed through the night.

FOUR

"Get down!" he yelled, stomping on the gas and peeling away from the curb. He kept a hold on Rachel while she managed to get her legs tucked inside the car. He let go long enough to take a sharp right-hand turn, which caused the half-open passenger-side door to slam shut.

"What's going on?" Rachel asked.

"Stay down," he barked. Glancing at the rearview mirror, he could see the vehicle was keeping pace behind them. He could tell by the high yet narrow set to the headlights that it was a Jeep.

He had to figure out a way to lose it and fast.

"Why is he shooting at us?" Rachel gasped, her eyes wide with fear.

He shook his head, unable to answer as he concentrated on losing the gunman. He took several more turns, dodging around various vehicles in his way. Thankfully, traffic was relatively light this far outside the city, or escaping the shooter would have been impossible.

When there was a gap in traffic, he jerked the steering wheel to the left, taking the car up and over the curb, making an illegal U-turn. It wasn't easy keeping his eyes on the road while watching the Jeep behind him. The other car didn't make the turn right away, which was reassuring.

He immediately took another right-hand turn, putting even more distance between them. When he found an on-ramp for the interstate, he took it and pushed the speed limit as hard as he dared until he found the next exit. On that road, he switched directions, heading left.

Fifteen minutes later, he was convinced he'd lost the Jeep. "Are you all right?" he asked, as Rachel eased upright and reached for her seat belt. "He didn't hit you, did he?"

"I don't think so," she said, patting her arms and legs as if she wasn't entirely sure. "Did you get the license plate number? Do you think that was Joey's kidnapper?"

"I didn't get the plate number because I was blinded by his high-beam lights." He tried to figure out what had just happened. The whole event was weird. "Don't you think it's odd that he took a shot at us, but didn't keep firing? And that he didn't target anything important?"

"What do you mean nothing important? He almost hit us!" Rachel protested.

"Not even close," he argued mildly. "We were practically sitting ducks and he didn't hit either of us, or any significant parts of the car, like the gas tank or wheels. It's almost as if he wanted to scare us more than kill us."

"So it must have been Joey's kidnapper!" Rachel's tone had a note of excitement. "He didn't want to kill us, because he still wants the money."

"Maybe," he agreed, although the scenario didn't quite feel right. This entire case wasn't like anything he'd experienced before. He knew crooks, had investigated them for years and they always had a reason for what they did.

Only this time, nothing made sense.

He took the next exit off the freeway, slowing his speed to the posted limit.

"We have to go back there," Rachel said urgently, interrupting his train of thought. "To see if we can find Joey. We must have been close if they were so desperate to scare us away."

"Rachel, calm down for a minute and think this through. How did they find us outside of Margie Caruso's house in the first place? I made sure no one followed us when we left Morales's apartment building."

"I don't know, maybe it was all just a big coincidence? Morales could be working for Margie Caruso, and maybe he just pulled up as we got there."

"I don't think so." Nick hated to burst her bubble, but she wasn't thinking rationally. He pulled off onto the side of the road and turned in his seat to face her. "Even if he saw us there, how could he know we were the ones in the car?"

"Maybe he recognized your car from the crash site?"

"I came in from the south and you said he went north," he reminded her gently. "Rachel, they have your cell phone number. They sent you a text, threatening to kill Joey if you called the police. Don't you see? The only thing that makes sense is that they've tracked us through the GPS in your cell phone."

Rachel swallowed hard as she stared down at her cell phone. Was Nick right? Had they really tracked them through her phone? She wasn't a techno-geek so she had no clue how to even do something like that.

But she knew the possibility existed.

And if Nick's hunch was correct, then Joey's kidnapper already knew she wasn't alone.

Fear swelled in her throat, choking her as tiny red dots swam before her eyes.

"Breathe," Nick commanded, giving her shoulder a shake.

She didn't even realize she was holding her breath. She took a shaky gasp of air and lifted her tortured gaze to his. "They're always going to know where we are, aren't they? We're never going to be able to escape."

"Not unless we ditch your phone," he said grimly.

She clenched the phone so hard she was surprised she didn't break it in half. "No. No way. This is the only connection I have to Joey. This is the number they're going to use in order to contact me for the ransom demand. I'm not giving it up, Nick. I'm not! *I can't!*"

He stared at her for a long moment before releasing a heavy sigh. "Okay, if you're not getting rid of it, then we need to figure out our next steps. Because the kidnappers are going to be able to find us, no matter what we do or where we go."

"What if we buy a new phone, but keep the same number?" she asked suddenly. "Wouldn't that work? I mean, the GPS is linked to the device, not to the actual phone number...right?"

Perking up, Nick flashed her a smile. "You're brilliant, Rachel. That's exactly right. Now we have options."

"Do you think the stores are still open?" she asked.

"There are plenty of twenty-four-hour superstores. Here, use my smartphone to find the nearest one...."

"Okay." She took the phone and used the search engine to find the closest superstore. "There's one about seven miles away," she told him.

"Perfect."

They arrived at the superstore and quickly made their

way over to the electronics section. She stayed back as Nick purchased the phone, along with a car charger, explaining to the clerk how they wanted to keep the same number.

"We can do that," the clerk said. "But it can sometimes take up to twelve hours to get the number transferred over."

"Twelve hours?" she echoed in shock.

The clerk shrugged. "It might be quicker, but I can't say for sure when."

Nick's expression was grim but he purchased the new phone and car charger, paying for a full year so that there wasn't any way to trace the contract fee. He gave her the phone and she stared down at it.

Twelve hours. She had to hang on to her old phone and evade the kidnappers for the next twelve hours.

And they were no closer to finding Joey.

She wanted to scream in frustration but forced herself to take several deep breaths to fight off her rising panic instead. She had to believe the kidnappers would keep Joey alive in order to get the payout. They had to.

She followed Nick to the car. When he started the car and pulled out of the parking lot, back onto the road, she plugged the new phone into the charger and then glanced at him. "Where are we going?"

He shrugged. "I think it's better to stay in the car and keep moving for now. We'd only be sitting ducks in a motel."

She couldn't argue his logic. "Would you be willing to split up so one of us could go and check out Margie's house? I need to know for sure Joey's not in there."

Nick was silent for so long she thought he was ignoring her. "Rachel, you're not a cop...so no, I'm not willing to split up. Let's just worry about staying alive tonight, okay? Unless you're having second thoughts about going to the FBI?"

She shivered. "No, I'm not having second thoughts. I heard what you told your boss about dirty cops at the local and federal level. I can't risk losing my son, Nick. I just can't."

He sighed. "I know what I said, but I can't help wondering if God isn't trying to tell us something the way these obstacles keep getting thrown in our way."

She was a little uncomfortable by his reference to God, but just the thought of calling in the police made her sick. "Your boss is willing to give us some time, so why are you still pushing the authorities on me?" When he opened his mouth to protest, she held up her hand. "I trust you, Nick, and I don't have much choice but to trust your boss, too. But I can't take the chance of trusting the wrong person. It could end up costing my little boy his life."

Truthfully, it was hard enough to trust Nick. But the fact that he'd been so angry with her for not giving him details about Anthony's involvement with the Mafia a year ago had gone a long way in convincing her that he was one of the good guys.

However, that didn't mean she wanted to open the circle of trust to include anyone else. Not unless there was no other choice.

Nick pulled into a mall parking lot, and she wasn't surprised when he positioned the car in a way that they'd be able to escape in a hurry if need be. She shivered a little, burying her face in the collar of the dark sweatshirt beneath her jacket. Her jean-clad legs were cold, and she rubbed her hands on her thighs to try and warm up.

"I have a blanket in the trunk," Nick said gruffly, before sliding out of the driver's seat. He returned a few minutes later with a wool blanket. "Why don't you stretch out in the backseat?"

"I won't be able to sleep," she protested. "Besides, we should take turns keeping watch."

"I'll keep watch first while you try to get some rest." His tone indicated there was no point in arguing.

Resigned, she opened the passenger door, pausing for a moment as she realized there was a bullet hole near the bottom of the window. The reminder of being used for target practice made her shiver again. Clutching the blanket, she climbed into the backseat and huddled down, grateful for the added warmth from Nick's blanket. She vowed to give him the blanket when it was her turn to keep watch.

The backseat was hardly comfortable, but that wasn't the reason she couldn't sleep. Images of Joey kept flashing through her mind, haunting her to the point where she almost couldn't stand it another moment.

"Nick?" she said softly, breaking the silence. "You don't think the kidnappers will hurt Joey, do you?"

"Try not to torture yourself thinking the worst, Rachel."

"I'm not trying to torture myself, but every time I close my eyes I picture that man grabbing Joey and slinging him over his shoulder. Don't you see? I'm the one who told Joey to get out of the car and run. It's my fault he was kidnapped."

There was a long pause, then Nick said, "Rachel, it's not your fault. I'm sure he would have gotten Joey even if you hadn't told him to run."

"Stop trying to placate me," she said sharply.

There was another brief silence. "Look, Rachel, I don't know if you believe in God, but if you do, praying can help you get through this."

She remembered how Nick had prayed before eating their fast-food dinner. Maybe he believed but she wasn't sure she did. "My parents weren't very religious. When I was growing up the only time we went to church was at Christmas and Easter." She hadn't thought about church or God in a long time. "I'm not sure I believe there really is a God, or that He cares anything about me or Joey."

"There is." Nick's voice exuded confidence. "And He does care about you and Joey. If you keep an open mind and an open heart, you'll be rewarded."

"Rewarded?" She couldn't hide the sarcasm in her tone. "I hardly think having my son kidnapped is anything close to rewarding."

"You're twisting my words, Rachel," he said quietly. "I meant that God can help you through difficult times."

"There's nothing more difficult than having your child in danger." She fought the rising anger. Who was he to preach to her at a time like this? Her son was missing and he wanted her to pray?

"I do know a little about what you're going through, Rachel. Two years ago, I lost my wife and my daughter in a terrible car crash. I nearly went crazy during the hours they were missing, before they were found dead in the bottom of a ravine. And trust me, I wouldn't have made it through those dark days without God's strength and the power of prayer."

His blunt statement surprised her and caused her to feel ashamed. Why was she taking her anger out on Nick? None of this was his fault. Clearly, he knew what it was like to lose someone he loved. Losing his wife and a daughter had to have been horrible. But prayer? She wasn't sure she was buying that idea.

She couldn't remember the last time she'd prayed, if ever. And she wasn't sure that prayer alone would make her feel better about losing her son.

She wouldn't survive if Joey died. Everything inside her would die right along with him.

"I've been praying for Joey's safety," Nick went on in a low voice. "And I want you to know, I'll keep on praying for Joey and for you."

Tears pricked her eyes and her throat swelled, making it hard to speak. Knowing that he would pray for her son brought a surprising level of comfort. And she suddenly realized that he was right. She did need to keep an open mind. Because if Nick's prayers could really help, she would gladly take them. She would take anything she could get if it meant keeping Joey safe.

She cleared her throat, trying to hide the evidence of her tears. "Thank you, Nick. And I'm sorry I snapped at you. I didn't know you lost your wife and daughter. I guess you really do know what I'm going through."

"For a long time I wanted to join them up in heaven," he admitted. "But God chose another path for me, so I've decided to dedicate my life to putting bad guys away and leading a Christian life, until God calls me home to be with my family."

She wasn't sure what to say in response to that, since truthfully, his plan sounded a bit lonely. Although who was she to argue about being alone? She wasn't interested in having a relationship again, either, especially not while she was raising her son. She was too afraid to trust her instincts about men after the way she'd messed up with Anthony.

Was Nick subtly warning her that he wasn't interested in being anything more than friends? If so, she was happy to oblige.

Right now, she didn't care about anything except getting her son back safe and sound.

As the minutes passed slowly, she stared out through the car window at the stars scattered across the night sky. And suddenly, she found herself uttering a simple prayer to a God she wasn't even sure existed.

Please keep my son safe.

FIVE

Rachel must have dozed in spite of herself, because, when she opened her eyes, dawn was breaking over the horizon and she didn't recognize the area. She assumed Nick had driven somewhere else at some point in the middle of the night. It took a moment for her to realize the beeping noise that woke her up came from a phone. She scrambled around, searching for her phone as Nick twisted in the driver's seat to look at back at her.

"Another text message?" he asked.

She pushed the button on her old phone and her heart leaped into her throat at the message that bloomed on the screen.

Ten million dollars will buy your son's freedom. Details on the exchange to follow. Remember, no police or your son will pay the price.

She tore her gaze from the message and held up the phone to show Nick. "It's the ransom demand," she said in a choked voice. She wasn't sure if she should be relieved or worried that the message had come so early in the morning.

She stared at the phone, wanting desperately to believe that some sort of contact from the kidnappers was better than nothing.

"Text them back that you need proof that Joey is still alive," Nick ordered, starting the car and driving out of the parking lot. "Tell them you want to talk to your son."

She hesitated, afraid that if she made the kidnappers mad they might hurt Joey.

"Rachel, you have to know Joey is alive, or there's no point in agreeing to the demand."

Although she hated to admit it, she knew he was right. She took a deep breath and texted back, No money until I speak to my son.

The moment she pressed Send, she wanted to call the message back. She stared at her old phone for several long moments, hoping the kidnapper would respond. With every minute that ticked by, raw fear rose in the back of her throat, suffocating her.

"What if they don't let me talk to him?" she asked, unable to hide the quiver in her voice. "What if they hurt him, instead?"

"You have to insist on it," Nick said, a hard edge of steel lining his tone. "Please trust me on this, Rachel."

"I do, it's just that I don't care about the money," she whispered in agony. "I just want them to give me Joey."

"I know that, and believe me, they know that, too. They're playing on your fear, Rachel. They're doing this to keep you off balance. You have to be strong. For Joey."

She nodded, but the vise grip around her heart wouldn't loosen. She wanted to talk to Joey. Desperately needed to hear his voice.

Please, God, please keep Joey safe.

Just when she was about to give up all hope, her old

phone rang, from another blocked number. She pushed the button and lifted the device to her ear. "Hello? Joey?"

"Mommy? Are you there?"

Hearing her son's voice made her eyes well up with tears. "Yes, Joey, I'm here. Are you okay? They didn't hurt you, did they?"

"No, but I'm scared," Joey said, and she could tell he was crying, too.

"Ask him something that only he knows," Nick whispered from the front seat. Belatedly, she realized he'd pulled off to the side of the road. "To prove it's him and not some other kid playing the part."

She nodded, indicating she'd heard him. "Joey, sweetheart, listen to me. Everything's going to be okay. But I need you to tell me who your favorite basketball player is. Can you do that for me?"

"K-Kirk Hinrich."

Yes! The starting point guard for the Chicago Bulls was Joey's favorite player. "That's good, Joey. I love you. I'm going to get you out of there soon, okay?"

"That's enough." A mechanically distorted voice broke into her conversation with her son. "We will give you details about the exchange soon."

"Wait!" she shouted, but nothing but silence was on the other end. She stabbed the button on her phone to call the blocked number back, but all she heard was a weird click then nothing. It took every ounce of willpower she possessed not to scream in frustration. But nothing could stop her tears.

"Don't cry, Rachel," Nick said in a low, soothing voice. "We're better off now than we were a few minutes ago. At least we know Joey's alive and that they're going to set up the exchange."

Nick was right, but she couldn't seem to stem the flowing tears. Just hearing Joey's voice made her furious with the kidnappers all over again. Her son was alone and afraid. "We have to find him," she sobbed.

He reached over the back of the seat to gently squeeze her shoulder. "We will. Remember God is watching over him, too."

Despite how she'd already prayed twice for her son's safety, Nick's words were far from reassuring. Because suddenly she couldn't understand why, if there really was a God, He would put an innocent nine-year-old boy in this kind of danger.

"I don't believe that," she said abruptly, pulling away from his reassuring touch. She used the bottom of her sweatshirt to mop her face. "I don't trust a God who allows my son to be in danger. And I can't understand how you could believe that, either."

Nick stared at her for a long minute, his gaze shadowed by a deep sorrow, before he wordlessly turned away and began driving again.

She ducked her head, swiping away the moisture from her cheeks. She shouldn't feel guilty for hurting him, but she did. Yet, at the same time, she couldn't bring herself to apologize, either.

Right now, nothing mattered except Joey. That was how she'd lived her life since leaving Anthony. A woman on a mission to provide a normal life for her son, keeping him safe from harm.

This wasn't the time to allow herself to get distracted. By Nick or by the God he believed in.

Nick drove to the truck stop he'd passed earlier, so they could use the restrooms and get something to eat. He tried not to be hurt by Rachel's anger as he understood, better than most, what she was going through. He'd been angry with God, too, at first when he'd discovered his wife and child had died. Anger was a normal part of the grief process, but that didn't mean he was giving up on her.

He'd continue praying for both Joey and Rachel.

Besides, she needed to cling to the knowledge of her son being safe and sound. There was still hope that they could figure out a way to get him back.

Rachel didn't say anything when he pulled into the truck stop parking lot, bringing the car to a halt between a pair of twin semitrailers. He climbed out of the driver's seat and then glanced back at her. "I thought we'd clean up in the restrooms first. I'll meet you in the diner in about fifteen minutes or so, okay?"

She nodded and pushed her way out of the car to join him. Wordlessly, they walked inside together before splitting up.

His stomach growled and the scent of bacon and eggs caused him to hurry. He scrubbed his hands over his rough stubble, wishing he had a razor. When he finished up in the restroom, he slid into a booth next to the door and perused the menu while he waited for Rachel.

She joined him a few minutes later and he didn't waste any time in placing their orders. Once they were alone with their coffee, he leaned forward and said firmly, "We need to figure out what to do from here, Rachel. Ten million is a lot of money."

"I know." She stared at her coffee, her hands huddled around it for warmth, but she didn't drink any.

"I know you're the CEO and president of your company, but are you really going to be able to get that much together?"

Slowly, she shook her head. "The economy has been

tough, and we've had a large class-action lawsuit that has eaten away a significant portion of our profits."

Lawsuit? How come she hadn't mentioned this earlier? "What was the lawsuit about?"

She grimaced before answering. "We put a new diabetes medication on the market about two years ago. In clinical trials it was superior in performance to the medication that almost two-thirds of the diabetes patients are currently taking." She hesitated for a moment. "But something went wrong, and several people suffered very bad side effects and two patients died. The FDA mandated that we pull the drug off the market, and the lawsuit was filed shortly thereafter."

He stared at her in shock, mentally kicking himself for not investigating this angle earlier. "Rachel, isn't it possible that Joey's disappearance could be linked to this lawsuit rather than the Mafia?"

She sighed and lifted her gaze to his. "I don't see how the lawsuit could be related. I authorized a large settlement for those patients and their families. They deserve to be compensated for our mistake. What reason would they have to come after me now?" She gripped the mug tighter in her hands. "Besides, does it really matter who took Joey? All we need to do is to figure out a way to get him back."

It did matter, but he didn't say anything as the waitress headed their way with two plates of food. She plopped them down on the table, and then glanced at the two of them. "Need anything else?"

He forced a smile. "No thanks, we're fine."

The waitress turned on her rubber-soled heel and strode away. He bowed his head and prayed. *Thank You, Lord, for this food we are about to eat, and please keep Joey safe in Your care. Guide us in our journey to find*

*him and help Rachel open her heart and her mind to
Your peace and Your glory. Amen.*

When he opened his eyes, he realized Rachel had her
head down, waiting for him to finish before eating her
breakfast. She didn't join him in prayer, but she didn't
lash out against God again, either, which he chose to believe was a good sign.

He dug into his bacon and eggs, savoring every bite.
When the knot of hunger in his stomach had eased, he
glanced up at Rachel again, noting with satisfaction that
she was doing a good job of demolishing her own meal.
"Tell me more about this lawsuit."

She lifted one shoulder. "There's nothing to tell."

"How is it that you didn't find the side effects of the
medication during the clinical trials?" He didn't know
much about the pharmaceutical industry, but surely there
would have been an indication of the dangerous side effects long before the medication was released to the public.

Rachel tapped her fork on the edge of her plate.
"That's one of the things I've been working on with my
research team. We don't know why the blood clots only
showed up after the medication was approved. The FDA
wants a full investigation, and we're actually in the middle of pulling everything together." She sighed, and then
added, "At least we were. Until all this happened."

The timing couldn't be a coincidence. "Who benefits
if your company goes out of business?"

"No one." She set her fork down and pushed her half-
eaten plate away. "My company employs well over three
thousand people, who would all be out of a job if something happened. I can't see how this could be connected
to Joey in any way."

He found it impossible to ignore the sliver of unease.

"Rachel, be honest with me. Is your company in danger of going under?"

"Not yet, but we can't afford to take another hit like the one we took earlier this year. So far, we've managed to weather the storm."

Relieved by that news, he continued to finish his breakfast. "What about your competition? Wouldn't they benefit if you went belly-up?"

"I can't imagine any company going to these lengths to get rid of the competition. You're on the wrong track, Nick. Those threatening notes have the Mafia written all over them."

She could be right. "You better eat," he advised. "There's no telling when we'll get our next meal."

She picked up her fork. "As soon as we're finished here, I need to call Gerry Ashton, my vice president of Operations."

"Why?"

"Because he's my second in command and owns forty percent of the company stock. I'm fairly certain he'll be willing to buy my shares. And I know his wife has a significant amount of money."

His stomach clenched at hearing her plan. "Do you think something that drastic is really necessary?"

She shrugged and toyed with her food. "Yeah, I do. Besides, I'd give up my company in a heartbeat if it meant getting Joey back safe and sound."

As Nick finished up and paid their bill, he couldn't help wondering if this was exactly what the lawsuit victims had planned all along. Forcing Rachel to give up everything she owned in order to save her son.

Rachel glanced at the clock, wondering if she dared call Gerry this early on a Thursday morning. They were both generally early risers, but it was barely seven-fifteen. She couldn't deny the deep sense of urgency. What if the kidnappers called right away, wanting the exchange? What if she didn't have enough time to pull the money together?

Logically, she knew that they would give her some time—after all getting the money was the end goal. Wasn't it?

She wished Nick hadn't questioned her about the lawsuit, because now uncertainty gnawed away at her. But those messages *had* to be from Anthony's uncle Frank, or from someone else within the Mafia. Nothing else made sense. Once they were back in Nick's car, she scrolled through her old phone's list of contacts until she found Gerry's cell number. Just as she pushed the button to call him, another text message came through. Another message from the kidnappers?

No, it was the text message stating that her phone number had been successfully transferred to her new phone. "Finally," she muttered.

"What?" Nick asked.

After she filled him in, Rachel got busy activating the new device. She had to click on a link first and then wait another few minutes for the phone number to be registered before she could use her new phone. When that was finished, she typed in Gerry's number and waited anxiously for him to pick up.

There was no answer, so she left a message. "Gerry, it's Rachel. Call me as soon as you get this. It's urgent."

Nick filled up the gas tank at the truck stop and dumped her old phone in the garbage before he slid behind the wheel and drove back out toward the highway. "Where does Gerry live?"

"About fifteen miles west of our corporate offices," she answered.

Nick glanced her way. "Okay, we're a good hour away, so I'm going to head in that general direction."

She nodded, hoping Gerry would call her back soon.

Forty-five minutes passed before her new phone rang, and she pounced on it when she saw Gerry's number come across the screen. "Hello?"

"Hi, Rachel, what's going on? What's so urgent?"

She relaxed a bit, hearing the sound of his voice. "Gerry, I'm so glad you called me back. I need your help. Would you mind meeting with me right away?"

"Of course, but why? What's wrong?"

"I'd, uh, rather explain in person."

"Okay, well then why don't you come to my house? We'll have plenty of privacy as Nancy is out visiting her mother, helping her recover from her hip surgery."

Nancy was Gerry's wife and she vaguely remembered that he'd mentioned Nancy's mother needing surgery. "That sounds perfect," she said, feeling relieved to know that Nancy wouldn't be there. "I'll see you in about fifteen minutes or so."

Asking Gerry for money wouldn't be easy—he'd been like a father figure to her since her own father had passed away from a sudden heart attack. She didn't like the thought of selling off her company, but she didn't have a choice. She'd give up everything she owned if it meant getting her son back safe and sound.

"You're not going to see him alone," Nick said, breaking into her thoughts.

She glanced at him in surprise. "I wasn't planning to."

He scowled as he navigated the streets heading toward Gerry's house. "But you didn't mention that you'd be coming with someone," he muttered.

"I didn't want to put him on guard," she admitted. "I'm not sure how much I should tell him."

"As little as possible," Nick responded. "No sense in dragging him into this mess."

"You're right. It's bad enough that I'm asking him to bail me out by buying my shares of company stock. And we still have to find a way to convince the bank to bypass their normal requirements to give me the cash immediately."

"One step at a time," he advised.

Gerry's house was much grander than hers, but then again, she preferred the family-friendly neighborhood she'd chosen to raise Joey in. There was nothing better than watching the neighborhood kids get together to play a quick game of soccer or baseball in the park across the street.

She had to shove the poignant memories aside. She needed to believe Joey would play again in the park, as soon as they got him away from the kidnappers.

"This is it," Nick said, as he pulled up into the driveway. There was a large wreath on the door and she could see the twinkling lights of a Christmas tree through the window. "Are you ready?"

She nodded and slowly climbed out of the car. She rang the doorbell and braced herself as Gerry swung open the door. He looked surprised to see Nick standing beside her. "Hi, Rachel, come on in."

She stepped across the threshold and then turned to make introductions. But before she could speak, Nick thrust his hand out. "Gerry, my name is Nick and I'm a good friend of Rachel's. I'm so glad we finally have a chance to meet in person, after all I've heard about you."

Her mouth dropped open, and she quickly closed it

again. Nick's message was clear—he did not want to be introduced as a detective.

Gerry accepted Nick's handshake. "Nice to meet you, too," he said, throwing a suspicious gaze at Rachel. "I have to say, Nick, you have the advantage here, because Rachel hasn't mentioned you to me at all."

The reproach in his tone was obvious and she swallowed hard, already hating the way she wasn't being completely up-front and honest with Gerry.

"Gerry, I'm sorry to bother you," Rachel said abruptly. "I'm in trouble. Financial trouble."

His eyebrows furrowed together as he gestured for them to come in and sit down in the living room. "What do you mean by financial trouble?"

She twisted her hands in her lap, unable to hide her nervousness. This was extremely important and she couldn't afford to have Gerry refuse her request. "I can't tell you, so please don't ask. I need a lot of money, and I'm hoping you'll be willing to buy my shares of stock in the company."

The stunned expression on Gerry's face would have been comical if the situation wasn't so grim. "Rachel, I'm happy to loan you whatever you need. There's no reason to sell your stock."

His offer was humbling, but she knew she couldn't take him up on it. Gerry was in his late forties and his two sons were currently enrolled in college. She couldn't take advantage of his generosity. "I insist on selling them to you. That way, if anything happens…" She couldn't bring herself to finish her thought. "It's just better this way, because I need ten million dollars."

"Are you kidding me?" Gerry leaped to his feet and began to pace. "Rachel, that just about covers all your stock! And how are you going to get the bank to give you that much money?"

"I'm hoping Edward Callahan, the bank manager, will bend a few rules for me," she said. "He knows the company is worth far more than that."

Gerry let out his breath in a huff and then turned to glare at Nick. "Can't you talk her out of this nonsense?" he demanded.

"I'm afraid not. Rachel is the one in charge here. I'm just helping her out as a good friend."

Gerry's gaze narrowed and he threw up his hands. "All right, fine. I'll help you. But, Rachel, please reconsider taking a simple loan. There's no reason to sell off your stock from your father's company."

His offer was generous, but she shook her head stubbornly. She'd never sleep at night with that heavy a debt hanging over her head. "I need you to buy the stock, Gerry. I want everything legal. Please don't fight me on this."

She couldn't explain that the likelihood of getting the money back was slim to none. And besides, if something happened to her during the exchange, she wanted the company to be in good hands. Gerry would be able to pick up where she'd left off without any trouble.

And even if she did survive, she knew full well that, after this was all said and done, she and Joey would have to start over, with a new job and maybe even a new house.

A price she was willing to pay if it meant getting her son back safe.

SIX

Nick watched the interchange between Gerald Ashton and Rachel with interest. There was no denying the gentleman, who he guessed was roughly ten years their senior, seemed to care about Rachel. There was a casual familiarity between them as they ironed out the details of obtaining the money. While they worked, he swept a curious gaze around the room.

Family photos featuring Gerald, his wife, Nancy, and their two grown sons were proudly displayed. The furnishings in the room, including the holiday decorations, were expensive and fancy—not to his taste at all but not awful, either. The place looked like something out of a fashion magazine, and he didn't doubt for a moment that a professional decorator had had a hand in the outcome.

He'd never been to Rachel's house and wondered if her style was similar to Gerry's. Not that he should care one way or the other. But somehow, he couldn't imagine Rachel raising Joey in a fancy, formal place like this.

Or maybe that was wishful thinking on his part.

He had to admit there was nothing to make him think Gerry was anything but what he seemed—a wealthy businessman who cared about his family and about Rachel. He told himself to relax and tuned back into the conversation.

"I'll call Edward," Gerry told Rachel, putting a re-assuring arm around her shoulder. Nick had to grit his teeth to stop from going over to forcibly remove it, even though the gesture was clearly intended to be reassuring and friendly. "I'm sure we can come up with some way to get you the cash you need. But the earlier I call him, the better."

"We appreciate your help, Gerry," Nick said, determined to make his presence known. He was more than willing to play the role of Rachel's boyfriend, if necessary. "Rachel said such kind things about you, I'm glad to see she was right."

Gerry actually looked flustered by the compliment. He removed his arm from Rachel's shoulders and pulled out his phone. "Give me a few minutes to talk this through with Edward, okay? We'll have to sign the paperwork in front of a notary, too, and he'll have someone at the bank we can work with, I'm sure."

"Thanks, Gerry."

While the older man was making the call, Nick crossed over to kneel by Rachel's side. "Are you okay?" he asked. As far as he could tell, she was holding up pretty well, considering.

"I will be once we have the cash," she murmured in a low voice. "At least we're one step closer to getting Joey back."

"Agreed. Just hang in there a little longer, okay?"

She nodded again but was still twisting her fingers together. He gently put his hand over hers, stilling her motions. "We'll get through this, Rachel," he said reassuringly. He wanted to invite her to pray with him but, after her outburst in the car earlier, settled instead on praying silently for her and Joey.

When Gerry returned, Nick rose to his feet. Rachel stood, too, and he stayed close by her side. Gerry's gaze was openly curious as it moved between the two of them, but he didn't comment. "Edward is going to do his best to pull the funds together. He's asked that you call him in two hours. We can meet him at the bank to finalize everything."

"Sounds good. Thanks again, Gerry." She set the drafted forms aside. "Bring these with you, okay? I'll see you in a little while."

Gerry hesitated before taking the documents she'd handed over. "I feel terrible about this, Rachel, and my offer still stands. If something changes, and you still have the money, I'd be more than happy to rip this agreement up as if it never happened."

"Thanks, Gerry." Rachel's smile was heartbreaking, and she reached up to kiss Gerry's cheek before turning away. Nick followed, as they made their way back outside.

In the car, he turned toward her, half expecting tears, but her eyes were dry and her expression was determined. "What now?" she asked, as if she hadn't just agreed to sign her life away. "We have two hours until we need to be at the bank."

"We'll find a coffee shop with free Wi-Fi so we can do some more research on Frankie Caruso. I also need to update my boss." He put the car in gear, backing carefully out of Gerald Ashton's driveway. At this moment, he didn't think he'd ever admired a woman more than he admired Rachel. She was beautiful, smart, sincere, and the one of the best mothers he'd ever known.

And the part of his heart that he'd sent into a deep freeze after Becky's and Sophie's deaths thawed just a little.

Rachel gratefully climbed out of the car at the coffee shop, hanging on to her new phone with a death grip. Nick purchased two large coffees and then found a small table near a gas fireplace. It was nice and cozy near the fire, and she sipped her coffee, gazing up at the wreath hanging above the mantel as he booted up the laptop.

"You can do some searching while I figure out a plan about handling the exchange," Nick said, turning the computer toward her. "Plus, I need to call a friend of mine to help with the exchange. Don't worry," he added, when he saw her dismay. "Jonah is someone I'd trust with my life. Unfortunately, we can't do this alone, Rachel. We need backup."

She nodded, her stomach twisting as she understood what he was saying. Getting the money from the bank was the easy part. Keeping her son alive during the exchange was going to be much tougher.

But failure was not an option.

As Nick made his calls, she sat there feeling numb. Even after he'd finished, she could only manage to stare blindly at the computer screen. For a moment she was tempted to start praying again. She regretted her harsh words to Nick earlier this morning. She'd been angry and had taken that anger out on him, wanting to hurt him the same way she was suffering.

Was she crazy to ask for God's help? Why would God listen to her? Her parents hadn't been religious, but she sensed they'd believed in God. At least they'd seemed to. Maybe she really was missing something important.

For a moment she bowed her head and opened her heart. *I'm sorry, Lord. I never should have said those hurtful things. Especially when they're not true. I know Nick believes in You and I want to believe, too. Please help show me the way. And please keep my son safe in Your care. Amen.*

As before, the moment she finished praying, a sense of peace settled over her. She looked up and caught Nick staring at her, and she forced herself to smile. "I'm sorry, Nick. I do want to believe in God. I want to believe He'll keep Joey safe."

"I'm so glad, Rachel," he murmured, reaching over to take her hand in his. "Looks as if my prayers have been answered. I've been praying that you'd allow the Lord to help carry your burden."

Nick's hand was warm on hers, and she found it odd that she didn't want to let go. Never before had she ever depended on a man to help her. Except for her father, especially when she'd needed to escape Anthony. She knew she was lucky to have Nick's help with this. She never would have been able to manage alone.

Her new phone rang, interrupting the peaceful silence. Startled, she glanced at the screen, half expecting to see the familiar blocked call.

But the call was from Edith Goodman, her assistant. She winced as she realized she had forgotten to let Edith know she wouldn't be in the office today. Or at all, considering she wouldn't be the owner of the company once she returned from the bank in a few hours. "Hi, Edith," she said to her assistant. "I'm sorry I forgot to let you know that I'm taking the rest of the week off."

"The rest of the week?" Edith's voice rose sharply.

"This isn't like you at all. What in the world is going on, Rachel?"

"I'm sorry, Edith, but there's something important I have to do." She wanted to reassure her assistant that Gerry would be there to take over the company, but Edith would find that out sooner or later. No need to spill the beans yet. "Just cancel my meetings and let everyone know I'm taking a personal leave of absence, okay?"

"If that's what you want," Edith replied slowly. "But that wasn't the reason I called. I just thought you should know what happened, before you read about it in the newspaper."

"Read what?" She had no idea what her assistant was talking about. She hadn't even thought about reading the newspaper since getting the threatening notes. Surely there wasn't another pending lawsuit? She'd feel guilty selling her shares of stock to Gerry if in fact they weren't worth the price.

"Dr. Josie Gardener is dead, Rachel," Edith said, her voice tinged with sorrow. "It looks like she may have committed suicide late last night."

Nick knew that, whatever the contents of the phone call between Rachel and Edith, it was bad news. Rachel went pale, her fingers gripping the phone tightly as she listened.

"Do you know anything else?" she asked. He couldn't hear Edith's response, but then Rachel said, "Okay, thanks for letting me know," and she disconnected from the call.

"Rachel? What happened?" He took her hand in his, trying to offer some sort of comfort.

"One of my top research scientists was found dead

in her home early this morning," she said in a whisper. "They think it might be a suicide."

Suicide? As before, the timing was too much of a co-incidence. "Was this the same research scientist who was responsible for the new diabetes drug going to market and then being recalled by the FDA?" She nodded. "Josie Gardener wasn't the only one involved in creating the new medication. She worked with Dr. Karl Errol, too."

Nick glanced around, not wanting to discuss anything further in a public place. "Let's go out to the car," he murmured.

Rachel seemed to move in slow motion as they packed up and went back outside, carrying their coffee. He felt better once they were safely settled in the car. "Is there any reason to suspect she was involved in covering up the side effects of the medication?"

"Of course not!" Rachel's denial was swift. "Her reputation was on the line with this new medication. And even if it wasn't, why commit suicide now? Why not back when the lawsuits were initially filed?"

She had a point, but he found he couldn't let it go. "Maybe she was afraid you'd find out the truth and couldn't bear to face the consequences of her actions?"

Rachel frowned for a moment, as if considering his idea. "I don't know, Nick. We have been working on releasing our research documents to the FDA, but if there was something Josie was trying to cover up, I'm sure Karl would have told me."

Unless Karl was in on it, too, he thought. Was it possible that Karl was responsible for kidnapping Joey? Maybe Karl's goal was to keep Rachel preoccupied while he swept the truth about the diabetes drug under the rug?

Once he had the money, he could disappear out of the country without anyone being the wiser.

The more he thought about the theory, the more convinced he became that he was onto something. But he didn't think Rachel was going to go along with his idea—she was too loyal to her coworkers to think anything bad about them. "Where does Karl live?" he asked, trying to sound casual. "Maybe we should pay him a visit? See what he knows about Josie's death?"

"He lives in a small house not far from the company," Rachel said, her forehead wrinkled in a deep frown. "I would say he'd be at work, but, with Josie's death, I guess I'm not sure. They were close, but only in a professional way as far as I know. Neither one of them is married. Josie has a brother and a twin sister, but no children."

Nick felt bad for Josie's family, but he was more interested right now in where Karl Errol was. "Do you know Karl's home address?"

Rachel rattled it off as he entered it into his phone GPS. He pulled out of the coffee shop parking lot and followed the directions with a sense of grim determination. Hopefully, the good doctor would be at home, playing the role of grieving colleague.

When they pulled up in front of Karl Errol's house, the small, brick Tudor appeared to be deserted. There were no holiday decorations adorning the home, and the yard had a shaggy look of neglect beneath the light dusting of snow. "Stay here," he advised Rachel. "I'm going to take a look around outside."

"Should I call Edith and see if he's at the office?" she asked, as he slid out from behind the wheel.

"Sure." He flashed a reassuring smile before heading up the cracked sidewalk leading to the researcher's front door.

No response from inside the home, which was pretty much what he expected. He peered through the windows but couldn't see much—the sunlight outside caused a glare that made it difficult to see. He walked around the house, crunching on leaves as he made his way to the garage, which was closed and locked up tight. He strode over to the back door and checked it as well. The screen door opened, and his heart quickened as he tested the interior door.

Locked, but with a flimsy, old-fashioned type of lock. He considered trying to jimmy it with a credit card, but was loath to do anything illegal.

He hesitated on the cracked stoop. What if Joey was inside the old house? What if his theory about Dr. Errol was right? That he'd kidnapped Joey to keep Rachel from uncovering his mistakes?

Wrestling with his conscience, he turned away from the door, but then caught sight of one of those fake rocks that were sometimes used to hide keys. Why people bothered with that sort of thing, he had no clue. Talk about being obvious. He reached down, opened up the fake rock and removed the key.

He accessed the house, wrinkling his nose at the stale air. When was the last time the doctor had been home? Either the guy simply lived like this, or he was holed up somewhere else—with Joey—biding his time until he could get his hands on Rachel's cash.

He quickly swept through the house, including the upstairs bedrooms but didn't find anything suspicious. There were only three bedrooms, and they were all empty. He even went down in the basement, which was dark and dank, smelling strongly of mold.

Nothing. Which he found a bit odd. Usually people left a bit of themselves strewn around, at least a bill or a coupon or something. But the place was so void of anything personal that he couldn't help wondering if he was on the right track. Granted, he hadn't found Joey here, but he wasn't willing to give up his theory just yet.

Back up in the kitchen, he searched for notes or anything at all that might indicate where Dr. Errol had gone. The garbage can was empty and there wasn't a single stray note to be found. He even went back to the master bedroom, but still didn't find anything.

Dr. Errol was either innocent or smarter than he'd given the guy credit for. And he was leaning toward the latter.

He left the house the same way he'd come in, returning the key to its hiding place in the fake rock. He hurried back around to the front, where Rachel was waiting in the car.

"What took you so long?" she asked, when he slid in behind the wheel. "I was getting ready to come out and look for you."

"Sorry, I was poking around and lost track of time. Did you get in touch with Edith?"

"Yes, she said that Karl called in saying he was staying home today." She stared at the house through the windshield. "Maybe we should try knocking at the door again?"

Time to come clean. "Actually, I found the house key hidden in a rock near the back door. I went in and checked out the house. Believe me, no one is home. And from what I saw, I don't think he's been home in a couple of days, either."

"He hasn't been home?" She stared at him incredulously. "But that's crazy. I know for a fact that Karl was at work the day we met in my office. I had a meeting scheduled with both him and Josie that I canceled."

"That was on Wednesday," he said thoughtfully, going back through the timeline. It was Thursday and he found it hard to believe that only twenty-four hours had passed since he'd sat in Rachel's office looking at the threatening notes she'd received. "That means he must have been planning this for a while."

"You don't know what you're talking about," Rachel said, crossing her arms over her chest. "I saw the guy who kidnapped Joey, remember? He was young, in his late twenties or early thirties. I can guarantee he wasn't Karl Errol. Karl is a short, rather nerdy type of guy with glasses and a half-bald head, although I don't think he's hit the age of forty yet."

She was clearly exasperated with him, but he couldn't just let this go "Rachel, it's best if we keep all possibilities open, okay? Errol could have easily hired Morales to kidnap Joey."

"Believe what you want," she said with a disgusted sigh. "I know that Karl isn't capable of doing anything like this."

There was no point in continuing the argument, so he concentrated on backing out of the driveway and heading back toward the city. They still had a good hour and fifteen minutes before they were due at the bank.

However, Rachel wouldn't drop the subject, even though he hadn't said a word. "Obviously you've forgotten how we were shot at outside Margie Caruso's house, which implicates the Mafia, not one of my employees."

He hadn't forgotten, but that incident had been more of a warning rather than an attempt to kill them. "Maybe we should head back over there, then?" he asked. "We have time."

"Great idea," she agreed enthusiastically.

He stifled a sigh and headed toward the freeway. They'd driven about twenty minutes when Rachel's cell phone beeped. He tightened his grip on the steering wheel because so far the only person who'd texted Rachel since this nightmare began was the kidnapper.

"He wants to know if I have the money yet," Rachel said, glancing up nervously. "What should I tell him?"

"Tell him that we'll have the money by one o'clock this afternoon. That gives us a little bit of a buffer since we're hoping to have this settled by noon."

"I don't know if that's a good idea," she protested. "I don't want to make him angry."

Nick understood her concern, but he wanted some time to react to the kidnapper's exchange plan. Since Logan was out of the country, he'd had no choice but to call his friend and fellow cop, Jonah Stewart, for assistance. Jonah lived with his wife, Mallory, in Milwaukee, but once he'd heard the story, Jonah had readily agreed to drive up to Chicago. "If this guy understands anything about banks, he'll understand the time frame is more than reasonable."

Rachel swallowed hard and sent the message explaining they'd have the money by one o'clock in the afternoon.

There was a tense silence as she waited for the kidnapper's response. When her phone beeped again, she picked it up with shaking fingers.

"Well?" he asked. "What was his response?"

Rachel lifted her tormented gaze to his, her lower lip quivering with fear. "He said to text him the minute we get the money and not a second later. He also said he'd hurt Joey and keep on hurting him for every minute we're late."

SEVEN

Rachel shivered, despite the bright sunlight streaming in through the windshield keeping the interior of the car toasty warm. She couldn't bear the thought of the kidnapper hurting her son. She didn't even want to think about what Joey may have already suffered.

She forced her frozen fingers to text back. I promise I'll call as soon as I have the cash. Please don't harm my son.

"Rachel, try not to panic. I'm sure he's bluffing," Nick murmured, reaching over to squeeze her hand.

"I'm not willing to take that chance," she snapped.

Nick didn't seem a bit fazed by her anger. "Remember, we've just purchased a new phone. There's no way for him to track us from now on. And it could be that he isn't even aware of that fact, yet."

Suddenly, the idea of getting a new phone didn't seem like such a good one. Her heart lodged in her throat and she gripped his hand tightly. "What if he gets mad about the switch and hurts Joey?"

"Don't worry, Rachel," Nick said in a soothing tone. "The kidnapper has come too far to turn back now. He wants your money, remember?"

Nick's theory wasn't at all reassuring. Yes, the kidnapper wanted her money, but it could be that he also had a sadistic streak and took some kind of perverse pleasure from hurting young children, too. She was tempted to beg Nick to return to the truck stop, so she could grab her old phone out of the garbage.

But he was already heading down the highway toward Margie Caruso's house, so she bit her tongue and tried to relax. At least for now, the kidnapper couldn't track their movements, which was a good thing. She hoped and prayed that they'd find Joey there.

This time, Nick didn't pull up in front of the house, but drove around the block, parking on the opposite side of the house. It was broad daylight, so it wasn't exactly easy to hide from curious eyes.

"Remember, I'm the one who's going to do the talking here," she reminded Nick as they slid out of the car.

He grimaced and nodded, keeping a sharp eye out as they walked down the street. Margie Caruso's house was the third one in from the corner, so it didn't take long to get there.

She could hear the faint hint of Christmas music coming from one of the houses, and she couldn't help quickening her pace, eager to see if Margie was home. Nick hung back as she walked up the sidewalk and rang the doorbell.

The seconds passed with agonizing slowness, but soon the door opened, revealing a well-dressed and nicely groomed woman who didn't look anything close to her fifty-some years. But the moment Margie saw Rachel standing there, she frowned. "No soliciting," she said abruptly.

"Wait! My name is Rachel Caruso. I'm not selling anything, I just want to talk to you for a minute."

Margie paused in the act of closing the door, her gaze raking over Rachel from head to toe. "You're Anthony's wife?" she asked.

Hiding a wince, she nodded. She tried to think of a way to forge a bond with the woman. "We divorced a long time ago, but I was hoping you wouldn't mind talking to me for a few minutes."

The former Mrs. Frankie Caruso pursed her lips for a moment. "Who's he?" she asked, gesturing toward Nick.

"This is Nick, a good friend of mine." She twisted her hands together, hoping Margie wouldn't guess that he was a cop and refuse to see them. Rachel didn't exactly want to have this conversation outside. Not that she was even sure what she was going to say. The main reason they'd come to Margie's house was to make sure Joey wasn't being held here.

"I guess you'd better come in, then," Margie said, opening the screen door for them.

Nick held the door as she entered the house first. She glanced around curiously and was a little disheartened to find nothing unusual. There were some holiday decorations, including a small fake tabletop-size tree. Would Margie invite her in if she was hiding her son here? Somehow she doubted it. Yet she firmly believed Margie Caruso would be a link to her son. "You have a very nice home," she murmured as she stepped into the living room.

Margie let out a bark of laughter. "Yep. Bought and paid for by Frankie," she bragged. "Do you want something to drink? I have coffee and soft drinks."

"No thanks. I really hope you don't mind us just dropping in like this," she said, before Nick could respond. "It's just I need to find Frankie and I was hoping you'd know where he was."

"Have a seat," Margie said, waving at them as she dropped into a recliner. "What do you want with Frankie?"

Rachel's mouth went dry and she wished she'd agreed to take something to drink. "It's nothing major, I just need to ask him a few questions."

"Ms. Caruso, do you mind if I use your bathroom?" Nick asked, interrupting them.

"No problem, it's down the hall to your right," Margie said, waving in the general direction.

Rachel figured Nick was trying to give them some time alone, most likely thinking that Margie might open up more if he wasn't sitting there. She stared down at her hands for a minute trying to figure out a way to get Margie to speak openly about Frankie. "Last I heard, Frankie was in Phoenix," she said in a low voice. "I should tell you that I've received some threatening letters and phone calls." She glanced up, trying to assess Margie's reaction. "I guess I couldn't help wondering if your ex might be involved."

Margie let out a sigh. "I highly doubt Frankie's entangled in something like that," she said without hesitation. "It's not really his style."

"What is his style?" Rachel pressed. "I divorced Anthony a long time ago, so how do I know Frankie's not holding some sort of grudge against me?"

Margie tapped one long, lacquered nail against the end table. "Frankie has been splitting his time between Phoenix and Chicago, but I can't imagine he's holding the divorce against you. Why would he? Our divorce wasn't that big of a deal."

The news that Frankie Caruso could be right now in Chicago made her pulse race with a mixture of dread and excitement. Frankie had to be the one behind Joey's kidnapping…it was the only thing that made sense. "I have to tell you, I admired how you and Frankie seemed to get along, even after your divorce," Rachel said.

"Yes, well, we had some business ventures together, which helped," Margie replied evasively. Rachel tried not to show her distaste—certainly, those business ventures were likely Mafia related.

"Like I said, it's just amazing that you both managed to stay friends," Rachel added. "Obviously, that wasn't exactly the case with me and Anthony."

"I know. Anthony wasn't shy about telling us how upset he was at how you managed to keep him from your son." Margie's gaze was challenging, as if daring Rachel to disagree.

The mention of Joey kicked her pulse into high gear. So Frankie and Margie knew about Joey. Knew that she'd kept Anthony away from his son. Was this the motive behind the kidnapping? A way to show her the power of the Caruso name?

"Me and Frankie didn't have kids," Margie continued, clearly oblivious to Rachel's spinning thoughts. "I guess it was a good thing, considering how we didn't stay together."

Rachel couldn't decide if Margie was putting on an act for her benefit or not. She didn't dare glance at her watch, even though Nick had been gone for what seemed like a really long time. She didn't want Margie to wonder where he was, either. "I guess maybe you're right," she murmured. "Divorce is much easier without fighting over kids." Before the other woman could ask anything more, Rachel quickly changed the subject. "Are you going to see Frankie anytime soon?"

Margie's eyebrows lifted. "Maybe. Why?"

Flustered, Rachel strove to keep her tone light and casual. "I thought maybe you could just mention to him that I'd like to talk to him. If he has some time. Nothing urgent…"

Margie stared at her for a long moment, as if trying to gauge what Rachel really wanted. "Yeah, sure. I might see him. Maybe you should give me your phone number so that he has it if he wants to get in touch with you."

"Of course. Do you have a pen and paper handy?"

Margie rose to her feet at the same moment Nick walked back into the room. "Wait here for a minute."

After their hostess left the room, she looked at Nick. "Well?" she asked in a low voice.

"Nothing," he murmured with a slight shake of his head.

Nothing, as in he didn't get to search very much? Or nothing, as in he truly hadn't found anything?

Before she could ask anything more, Margie returned. Rachel hastily scribbled her number on the slip of paper the older woman handed her. "Thanks so much, Margie. I really appreciate you taking the time to talk to me."

"No problem." Margie walked them to the front door. "Take care."

"You, too," Rachel said, before slipping outside. Nick followed her, grabbing her hand as they strolled down the sidewalk to the street. "We probably shouldn't have parked far away," she murmured under her breath. "Margie will think it's odd that we didn't pull up right in front of her house."

"You might be right," Nick said. "But you did a good

job of convincing her that your reason for being there was related to Frankie. Maybe she'll think we're just paranoid."

Once they turned the corner, Rachel relaxed. "I *was* there because of Frankie. He's been here in Chicago, Nick. I think he must be involved in Joey's kidnapping."

Nick didn't say anything more until they were in the car. "Frankie might be involved, but as far as I could tell, Margie isn't. I looked around and didn't find anything. I even managed to sneak down the basement stairs. There weren't any hiding places down there that I could see, so I didn't spend a lot of time searching. I was afraid she'd hear me."

Rachel couldn't believe he'd managed to get all the way into the basement. "What would you have done if she had heard you?" she demanded.

He shrugged. "I would have claimed that I took a wrong turn."

She put a hand over her knotted stomach, glad she hadn't known what Nick was doing while she chatted with Margie. Her nerves were already at the breaking point. Time was running out; they were due to be at the bank in the next twenty minutes.

Soon, they'd be one step closer to getting Joey back, safe and sound.

Nick glanced at Rachel as he navigated the traffic, taking the fastest route to the bank. He couldn't say he was surprised that they hadn't found anything at Margie Caruso's house. He still believed that Dr. Karl Errol might be the missing link. But no matter what he thought, there wasn't enough time to keep searching for Joey. He knew that once they'd finished their transaction at the bank, Rachel would contact the kidnapper.

There was no way she'd risk anything happening to her son. Not that he could blame her. Easy for him to say the kidnapper was bluffing. If Rachel found a single mark on Joey, she'd never forgive him.

His phone rang and he picked it up, recognizing Jonah Stewart's number. "Hey, are you in town?"

"Yep, sitting in the parking lot of the hotel down the road from the bank."

Nick could feel Rachel's curious gaze on him. "Good. We'll be at the bank within the next ten minutes or so. I'll be in touch as soon as we're finished."

"Sounds good. I'll be waiting."

"Thanks, buddy." He disconnected from the call.

"Was that the cop buddy you told me about?" Rachel asked.

"Yeah, Jonah Stewart is a Milwaukee detective who helped build a case against your ex-husband. Anthony tried to kill him. Thankfully, Jonah and Mallory escaped, and Anthony was the one who'd died that night."

"So he was the one responsible for bringing down Anthony," Rachel mused. "I always wondered exactly what happened."

The last thing he wanted was for Rachel to hear the gory details. "None of that matters now. Just know that we really can trust Jonah."

Rachel nodded and looked away, staring out the window as if lost in thought.

He mentally kicked himself for reminding her of Anthony Caruso, especially at a time like this, when her son was still missing. Didn't she already have enough to worry about? Right now, she needed to stay focused on the task of getting the money together. That was the first step. The second was to exchange the money for her son.

With the kidnapper calling the shots, they'd be lucky to get Joey back without incident, even with Jonah's help. "Nick?"

He dragged his gaze to meet Rachel's. "Yes?"

"I want you to promise me something."

Uh-oh. He braced himself, certain he wasn't going to like this. "Promise you what?"

She locked eyes with him. "Promise me that you'll get Joey out of there safely. I don't want you to worry about me—I want you to focus on keeping my son safe."

Every instinct in his body protested, but he knew very well that if the situation was reversed, he'd ask the exact same thing. Children were a cherished gift from God and they deserved a chance to be protected. As much as he didn't want to lose Rachel, he knew he had to give her this much.

"I promise," he vowed, silently asking God to spare both Rachel and Joey so he wouldn't be forced to make an impossible choice.

Rachel rubbed her sweaty palms on the sides of her jeans before picking up the pen to sign over her shares of the company stock to Gerry Ashton. She couldn't help glancing at her watch, wondering if right now, the kidnapper was somewhere close watching them.

"Are you sure about this, Rachel?" Edward Callahan asked. The poor bank manager had been beside himself since they'd arrived. She wanted to believe he cared about her, but she suspected the large withdrawal of cash was the main source of his concern.

"Absolutely." She wasn't nervous about selling off her

company; she was worried about Joey. Because the moment Edward handed over the cash, she'd have to call the kidnappers.

Please, Lord, please don't let them hurt my son.

The transaction was completed with ridiculous simplicity—she was sure she'd completed far more paperwork when she'd bought her house eight years ago.

A house that she'd have to sell, once she had her son back. She shoved the thoughts away, refusing to dwell on her decision. She'd give up everything she owned to get Joey back.

"I have the cash pulled together in the vault," Edward said as Gerry finished his portion of the agreement. "It wasn't easy… I had to send couriers to several other branches to get what you needed. I—uh, put it all in a large duffel bag for you. I didn't want it to look too obvious as you left the building. A cashier's check would be much safer," he added, even though he'd already lectured her on the perils of walking around with so much money.

"I know, thanks, Edward." She forced a smile as she turned toward Gerry. "I haven't told anyone at the office yet, but I'd appreciate it if you'd tell Edith first, privately."

Gerry's forehead was puckered in a concerned frown. "I will. Rachel, I wish there was more I could do to help you…."

"You've helped more than you could ever know," she assured him. "Thanks again."

Gerry gave her a quick hug and then tucked his copy of the paperwork into his briefcase and made his way toward the door. She turned her attention toward the bank manager. "I'm ready."

Nick stayed close at her side as they walked into the bank vault. Edward used his ID to open the first door and then punched in a key to access the second door. Once inside the vault, she saw the duffel bag he'd mentioned, surprised to find that it was the size of a small suitcase.

"I promise it's all there," Edward said, as she opened the bag and went through the contents. She'd never seen so much money before, especially not such crisp one-thousand-dollar bills.

"I'm sure you'll understand Rachel's need to verify the amount," Nick said, standing over her as if worried the bank manager himself was in on the kidnapping.

"Of course," Edward agreed, discreetly wiping more sweat from his brow.

She focused on the task at hand. The thousand-dollar bills were bound in stacks of one hundred so it didn't take long to validate the amount was correct. "Thanks again, Edward," she said, as she rose to her feet, slinging the duffel bag strap over her shoulder.

"We'd like to leave through the back door," Nick announced.

Edward nodded and led the way back out the vault, pausing long enough to close and lock both doors before he took them to the back of the bank.

Nick stayed close to her side as they left the building and climbed back into the car. She crammed the duffel bag on the floor between her feet, too afraid to store it in the backseat. The minute they were settled, she pulled out her phone.

"Wait just a minute, okay?" Nick said, putting a hand on her arm. "Let me call Jonah first."

The image of her son being hurt was impossible to ignore. It took every ounce of willpower for her to wait for Nick to call Jonah. He hadn't even completed his call when she quickly texted the kidnapper, I have the money.

Within seconds, her phone rang. Before she could push the button to answer, Nick whispered, "Put the call on speaker."

With trembling fingers she did as he directed. "This is Rachel."

"Go to the abandoned barn located twenty miles outside the city near the intersection of Highway F and Highway 93 in exactly one hour," the mechanically distorted voice directed. "Come alone or your son will pay the price."

Rachel swallowed hard. "I'll be there," she whispered, never doubting for one moment the kidnapper would make good on his threat.

If he hadn't hurt Joey already.

EIGHT

Nick watched the blood drain from Rachel's face, leaving her pale and shaking. He wanted nothing more than to take her into his arms and offer comfort, but this wasn't the time or the place. Right now, they had to get to the abandoned barn as soon as possible, if they were going to be successful in getting Joey back.

He called Jonah, repeating the kidnapper's directives. "I'm not sure where this place is, but we need to take only one car, as it doesn't sound like there's a lot of cover," he told his friend. "And, if you don't mind, it might be best if we take your car to change it up a bit. Rachel and I have been driving around town in mine, and the kidnappers might recognize it. What do you think, buddy?"

"Sounds good." Jonah quickly gave him directions to where he was parked at his hotel on the edge of town and they agreed to meet there in less than ten minutes.

"It's almost over, Rachel," he said, reaching out to squeeze her hand before he put the car in gear and drove away from the bank. "We're going to get Joey back."

"I'm so scared," she whispered. "There are so many things that could go wrong."

"Try not to think of the worst-case scenario," he advised, knowing that was his job.

"I won't. But I'll be glad when this is over."

He didn't bother pointing out that even if they managed to get Joey back unharmed, the nightmare might not be over. There was no guarantee the kidnapper would simply disappear once this exchange was completed. Especially since Morales was nothing more than a hired thug, doing what he was told. Whether the source of the kidnapping was the Mafia or someone related to her company, Rachel and Joey could still be in danger.

And of the two scenarios, he still found himself leaning toward the possibility that this was all somehow connected to her company.

He slowly unclenched his hands from the steering wheel. He needed to keep a cool head. Right now, it was best to focus on the upcoming swap. Later, there would be plenty of time to think about who was behind this.

The moment he pulled into the hotel parking lot, they quickly switched vehicles. Rachel lugged the duffel bag of money and Jonah handed the keys to Nick, choosing to climb into the backseat.

Nick quickly introduced the two and then started the engine. "Pleased to meet you, Rachel," Jonah Stewart said as he buckled himself in.

Rachel tried to smile, but it wasn't much of one. "Thanks for helping us."

"I don't mind at all. We're going to get your son back, Ms. Simon," Jonah said reassuringly.

"Please, call me Rachel."

Nick listened to their brief conversation as he drove, pushing the speed limit as much as he dared while following the directions leading them to the designated meeting spot. The GPS took them directly out of town, into farm country. As the traffic thinned, he pushed his speed even further, wanting to make good time.

The kidnapper hadn't chosen the location or the tight timeline by accident. Clearly the guy didn't want to give them too much time to prepare. And Nick absolutely didn't want to get there after the kidnappers were already there. He was hoping that the perpetrators might have to pick up Joey first, before meeting them, which would give them the time they needed.

A half hour would be nice, but he'd take less time if he had to. They would need every second to get the lay of the land. And to get Jonah hidden someplace nearby where no one would see him.

"Dear Lord, please keep my son safe in Your care," Rachel whispered.

Her quiet prayer caught him off guard, but he quickly joined in. "And, Lord, please guide us and give us strength as we fight to get Joey back safe and sound."

"Amen," Jonah said from the backseat. Rachel glanced over her shoulder at Jonah in surprise.

Nick reached over and squeezed her hand. "Jonah is a believer, too."

"Good to know," she said in a soft voice. "I feel like I need all the help we can get." There was a slight pause before she asked, "Does praying always make you feel calmer?"

"Absolutely," he agreed. "Sharing my burdens with God always helps me feel better."

"I wish I knew more about God and faith and prayer," Rachel said. "I feel like I'm not worthy of His help."

"You are worthy, Rachel, and so is Joey. But if you'd really like to learn more, I'd be honored to teach you." He didn't want to push her too hard, but he was thrilled that she had opened her heart and her soul to God and faith. "Once we have Joey back, I'll be happy to study the Bible with you."

"After we have Joey back," Rachel repeated. "I'm going to hold you to that, Nick." She was twisting her hands together in the way he knew meant she was worrying again.

"We're going to be okay, Rachel," Jonah chimed in from the backseat. "God will guide us through this. We've been in other tight spots before, right, Nick?"

"Right," Nick agreed drily.

There was so much more he wanted to say, but off in the distance he caught sight of an abandoned barn at the end of what looked to be a hard-packed dirt road. That must be the meeting place. His heart sank as he realized it was out in the middle of a wide-open space, where it would be difficult to hide any backup.

"Take a look, Jonah," he said, gesturing toward the barn. "They sure didn't leave us many options."

"We'll find something," Jonah replied with confidence. "I doubt they're going to take the time to search the entire barn. I suspect they'll make this a quick exchange and get out of Dodge."

"I hope you're right," Nick muttered, pushing down harder on the accelerator. He couldn't help constantly looking at the clock on Jonah's dashboard. It seemed that time was slipping away from them.

The kidnappers would be there in forty-two minutes. Unless, of course, they decided to show up early. In that case, there was no way to judge how much time they had to prepare.

Rachel's stomach hurt so badly she feared she might be sick. She took several deep breaths and wrapped her arms tightly across her middle. She could do this.

She had to do this.

The big dilapidated barn loomed ominously as they approached. This was it. The moment she'd been waiting for and dreading at the same time. In less than forty minutes the kidnappers would drive up with her son, demanding money in exchange for his freedom.

Please, Lord, please keep Joey safe!

The calm she'd felt before after praying seemed to have deserted her now. Maybe because her prayers betrayed the depth of her desperation. Despite Nick's reassurances that she was worthy, she couldn't help feeling that maybe God thought she was a big fraud. But she hoped He wouldn't punish her son for her previous lack of faith. She took another deep breath.

Nick backed up the dirt road so that the car was facing outward toward the road. The minute he shut off the car, he and Jonah jumped out to see what they had to work with.

She was still trying to pull herself together. But when she stared down at the duffel bag, she realized she couldn't sit here. She had to be in the driver's seat, as if she'd just driven here by herself. Swallowing hard, she shoved open the door, hauled the duffel bag up so that it was on the seat, and then slammed the door.

Nick had Jonah's car keys, so she went to find him. She needed the kidnappers to believe she'd followed their instructions to the letter.

The barn door was open only about a foot, so she turned sideways to slide inside. The interior was surprisingly dim. She's expected it to be brighter considering there were several missing boards and glassless windows. The place reeked of fertilizer mixed with musty old hay, thanks to the piles that looked as if they'd been there untouched for years.

Nick stood, looking up at the loft. She followed his gaze and gasped when she saw Jonah carefully going up a rickety old ladder that didn't look strong enough to hold his weight.

"Are you sure that's safe?" she whispered.

"Not really, but he insisted on giving it a try."

There was a loud noise as Jonah's foot broke through one of the rungs of the ladder. Her heart lodged in her throat as he hung there for a moment before he regained his balance. In a few minutes, Jonah was safely on the loft.

"Wouldn't he be better off down here?" She couldn't imagine the rotted wood that made up the loft floor would be any sturdier than the ladder.

"I'll be down on the ground level, and he's going to try and get some leverage from up above. See that window up there?" He indicated the open space in the wall of the barn located above the loft. "It overlooks the front of the barn, and that's our best option."

She felt dizzy watching Jonah ease his way into position, so she lowered her gaze and tried not to sneeze. Despite the cold December air, the moldy hay was making her eyes water. "Where are you planning to be?"

"Outside, as close to you as I can manage," he said grimly. "There are several stacks of hay outside along the north side of the barn. If I drag a few more out there, I should be fairly well hidden."

She helped Nick carry a couple of stacks of smelly, musty hay outside. They had to open the barn door wider and it groaned loudly in protest. She froze, hoping it wouldn't fall off.

After two trips, they had a decent-size stack of hay along the side of the barn. Nick carefully closed the barn door and then used a bunch of hay like a broom to brush the dirt, covering up their footprints.

The north side of the barn seemed too far away for her piece of mind, but she bit her lip so that she wouldn't complain. After all, she couldn't very well expect Nick to hide in the backseat of Jonah's car. Truthfully, she was lucky to have any backup at all.

"You might want to give me the car keys, just in case they want me to go someplace else," she said.

Nick scowled and dug them out of the front pocket of his jeans. "Here you go. But don't follow those guys someplace else, Rachel. There would be nothing to prevent them from killing both you and Joey, while still taking off with the cash. Your best option is to stay right here, where Jonah and I can protect you."

"I know," she said, taking the keys from Nick. As much as she knew he was right, she wasn't sure she'd be able to say no if it came to the kidnappers giving her an ultimatum. Her greatest weakness was her son's safety. If they threatened to hurt him, she knew she'd go along with whatever they asked of her.

She turned to walk away, but suddenly Nick grabbed her hand to stop her. Glancing over her shoulder, she found him staring at her intently. "What's wrong?" she asked.

"Nothing. Just—be careful, okay?" he said gruffly. Then, before she could respond, he pulled her close and gave her a quick kiss.

The kiss was over before she had a chance to register what had happened. But she longed to throw herself into his arms, absorbing some of his strength. This wasn't the time or the place, though, so she said the first thing that came to mind. "Remember your promise," she blurted. "No matter what happens, save my son."

He stared at her for a long moment. "I won't forget my promise, Rachel. But my goal is to get both of you out of here safely." He turned away and began digging a hole for himself in the hay.

She turned and hurried back to the car. By the time she'd slid into the driver's seat, she couldn't hear him any longer. He must have gotten himself hidden very quickly.

Her lips tingled and she wondered if Nick had kissed her on purpose to distract her. If so, his ruse had worked. For a couple of minutes her stomach hadn't hurt, although now the pain was back with a vengeance. She took another deep breath and focused on the task at hand, anxious to be ready if the kidnappers showed up early.

The driver's seat was all wrong, so she scooted the seat up so that she could reach the pedals and adjusted the mirrors to accommodate her smaller frame. From the way Nick had parked the car, she couldn't see much of the north side of the barn, which was back and to her left. Using the rearview mirror, she could just barely catch a portion of the stacked hay.

Nick and Jonah were both armed and ready. She tried to find comfort in the fact that if she couldn't see Jonah or Nick, then the kidnappers couldn't see them, either.

The minutes ticked by with excruciating slowness, and she resisted the urge to turn on the car to warm up. If she was cold, surely Jonah and Nick were even more so.

Within five minutes of waiting, she spotted a black Jeep coming down the highway from the same direction they'd come. With a frown, she followed the Jeep's progress. If this one belonged to the kidnappers, they were fifteen minutes early.

Rachel clutched the steering wheel and strained her eyes in an attempt to catch a glimpse of her son. She thought there might be someone in the passenger seat, but the Jeep was too far away to be certain.

At the last possible moment, the Jeep slowed and then turned onto the dirt road. She held her breath as the vehicle approached. The driver was the same big dark-haired man who'd snatched Joey out from the car crash. There was a smaller person in the passenger seat and when the Jeep came closer, she could tell the small person had a dark hood over his head. The Jeep pulled to a stop about thirty feet from her vehicle.

Panic threatened to overwhelm her. What if the person in the front seat really wasn't Joey? What if this was nothing more than a horrible trick? What if they planned to kill her and take the money, while keeping her son to sell him in the black market of human trafficking?

Her pulse thundered in her ears as she pushed open the car door. She grabbed the duffel bag of money and dragged it over the console so that it was right next to her, as she stepped out of the car.

"I want to see my son!" she said in a loud voice.

The driver, who had to be Morales, reached over and yanked the hood off her son's head. Joey squinted and ducked his head, shying away from the light. He reminded her of a prisoner who'd been locked in a cell for days, unable to bear normal daylight.

Cold fury swamped her. It was all she could do not to rush over to grab Joey and yank him out of there. She narrowed her gaze and stared, waiting for direction.

Morales slowly and deliberately pushed open his door

and stood. Her heart dropped to the soles of her feet when he leveled his gun directly at her son. "One wrong move, lady, and I'll shoot to kill."

"I have the money," she blurted out. "You can have it. All I want is my son."

"Hold on, now," he said, sweeping his gaze around the area. She never flinched, trusting the men behind her to stay well hidden. "You'll get your kid soon enough."

"I'm not armed and I'm here alone, just like you asked," she said, drawing his attention back to her. "Here's the money. If you'll just let Joey out of the car, we'll make the swap."

His expression turned ugly. "Listen here, lady, *I'm* the one who's in charge. The kid doesn't move until I say so."

Her fingers clenched on the duffel bag as the seconds drew out to a full minute. He approached her with slow, deliberate steps, rounding the front of the Jeep. With every step closer, she grew more nervous. She came out from behind the safety of the driver's door, lugging the duffel bag.

"Set it down, where I can see it," he said in a low, guttural voice. So far, his movements had been slow and cautious, but the glint of excitement in his eyes betrayed his greed.

Ironically, that glimpse was enough to make her relax. She was certain he wasn't going to do anything foolish if that meant risking the money. But she didn't set the duffel bag down the way he told her to. "I will, but only if you let Joey open his car door."

He glared at her for a minute before giving a little wave of the gun. "Open your door, kid, nice and easy."

She tried not to divert her attention from the gunman, but she couldn't help sneaking a sideways glance at Joey. He was still squinting, as if he couldn't see very well but managed to open his passenger-side door. She could see his feet dangling outside the car, in the familiar basketball shoes she'd bought for him earlier in the school year. They were bright orange, his favorite color, and her eyes stung with the memory of how excited he'd been when he'd worn them for the first time.

The Jeep was high off the ground, and she wanted to call out a warning to Joey to be careful. But with the gunman so close, she didn't dare. Instead, she opened the duffel bag, holding it awkwardly against her chest, to show him the cash inside.

The gleam in his eyes got brighter, and she was struck by the fact that this guy obviously wasn't very smart. Nick was right—there had to be someone else acting as the brains of this operation. Morales was nothing more than a pawn. Right now, though, all she cared about was her son.

"Get out of the car, kid," Morales shouted. When she glanced over at her son, the thug lunged forward in an attempt to grab the money, but Rachel was faster. She snatched the handles of the bag, whipped it around and threw it at Morales, hitting him directly in the chest. "Run, Joey!"

While Morales was grappling with the bag, trying to make sure he didn't lose any of the cash, she leaped forward and grabbed her son. With a herculean effort, she hauled him up and ran toward the car, using her body to protect him as best she could. "Get inside," she urged.

"Stop!" Morales shouted. The sound of gunfire erupted and she ducked behind the open driver's door and threw herself over Joey, squashing him against the front seat.

"Stay down!" Nick shouted, coming around the corner of the barn, looking like a madman with straw sticking out of his hair and clinging to his clothes.

Morales turned and fired again. Panic-stricken, she glanced sideways and caught a glimpse of Nick hitting the ground. "Nick!" she screamed.

More gunfire, this time from up above, but Morales had already thrown the duffel into his Jeep and taken off, his tires churning up clouds of dust as he barreled down the dirt road.

NINE

Nick ignored the burning pain in his left arm as he crawled across the ground to reach Rachel and Joey. She held her son in a tight hug as if she might never let him go. Every instinct in his body was clamoring for him to follow Morales, but he couldn't bring himself to leave Rachel and her son. Or take them along, putting them in more danger.

"Are you all right?" he asked, pulling himself upright and leaning against the car. "Any injuries?"

"No injuries," Rachel murmured as she lifted her tear-streaked face from her son's hair. She barely glanced at Nick, her attention focused solely on her son. She brushed his hair away from his forehead. "Joey? Are you sure you're not hurt anywhere?"

Joey shook his head but didn't say anything, burrowing his face once again against his mother. The boy's silence was a bit concerning, but not completely unexpected considering the trauma he'd been through.

"Nick, you're bleeding!" Rachel reached out to touch his arm. "He hit you?"

"Winged by a bullet, nothing serious," he said, glanc-

ing around for Jonah. His buddy shoved open the barn
door and came out, limping.

"I tried to take out the Jeep, but I fell through a hole
in the floor," Jonah said with disgust. "I'm sorry I let
him get away."

"Nothing more you could have done, Jonah," Nick assured his friend. "And the way you shot at him from up
in the loft obviously scared him off, which is probably
a good thing. He was armed, and the way things were
going down, I doubt he intended to leave any witnesses
once he got the cash."

"Yeah, I got that same feeling," Jonah muttered. He
looked at his car and scowled, fingering the bullet hole
in the back door along the driver's side. "Now I know
why you wanted me to take my car. Hope he didn't hit
anything in the engine."

The bullet holes in the back door of the driver's side
were sobering, proof of how lucky they were to get out
of this with a gouge in his arm and nothing more serious. "I'll reimburse you, Jonah."

"No biggie," his friend said, waving him off. Joey
lifted his head and gazed at both him and Jonah with
suspicion. Nick belatedly realized they were both strangers to the child, so he dropped to his knees and smiled
over at the boy. "Hi, Joey, my name is Nick Butler and
I'm a detective with the Chicago Police Department.
And that's my buddy Jonah Stewart, who is a police detective, too, from Milwaukee. We've been helping your
mom find you."

"Thank you," Joey said in a wobbly voice, his curiosity apparently satisfied. "Can we go home now? I'm
hungry."

Nick was trying to figure out a way to let the boy

know it wasn't safe to go home yet, when Rachel interrupted. "You're hungry? Did they give you anything to eat or drink?"

Joey shook his head. "No. They kept me in a room in the basement. It was dark and I think there were big hairy spiders, too. The door was locked and I had a mattress and a toilet but nothing else," he admitted, his lower lip trembling with the effort not to cry.

Rachel's eyes filled with tears. "I'm so sorry, Joey. So sorry..." Once again, she hugged him close as if she could erase the horrible memories by will alone.

"We'd better get out of here," Jonah said quietly. "In case they decide to come back."

Nick couldn't agree more. "Rachel, do you have the car keys?"

She sniffled and used the sleeve of her jacket to wipe away her tears. "Here you go," she said as she handed them over. "Joey and I will take the backseat."

He understood she couldn't bear to let go of her son. "You'd better drive," Nick told Jonah, as he loped around to the passenger side of the vehicle. "I'm going to call my boss and put an APB out on that Jeep. And I don't suppose you have a first-aid kit in here somewhere?"

"In the glove box," Jonah said. He slid behind the wheel and grunted as his knees hit the steering wheel. He adjusted the seat back and then started the car.

Nick called Ryan Walsh, quickly filling his captain in on the details. "I'm fairly certain the driver was Ricky Morales and the Jeep's tag number is JVW-555."

Walsh wasn't entirely thrilled to hear what had transpired. "I'm glad you got the kid back, but we need to keep looking for the link to the Mafia," he said. "When are you coming in to file your report?"

"Soon," Nick hedged. "Just let me know as soon as you hear anything about Morales or the Jeep, okay?" He disconnected from the call.

"Where to?" Jonah asked, as he turned off the dirt road and back onto the highway.

"That's a good question," Nick muttered, as he rummaged around for the first-aid kit. "We should probably pick up my car first."

"No, we need to stop for something to eat, first," Rachel said from the backseat. "Joey's hungry."

"Is he all right? Or should we get him checked out by a doctor?"

"Physically, he looks fine," Rachel said after a moment's pause.

He knew she was already worried about the emotional trauma Joey may have suffered. "You're right, eat first and then pick up my car."

From there, he wasn't sure, other than he wasn't going to take Rachel or Joey back to their home.

Not until he knew for sure they were safe.

Rachel knew she was smothering Joey, but she couldn't seem to stop touching him—his hair, his arm, his knee—to remind herself that he was actually sitting right here beside her.

Thank You, Lord, for keeping my son safe!

There was a tiny voice in the back of her mind telling her that there was a good chance God didn't have anything to do with getting Joey back safely, but she was too emotionally drained to listen. Right now, she found an odd comfort in believing God had been with them through those horrible moments when she'd faced Morales.

"Can we eat at Mr. Burger's?" Joey asked in a soft, hesitant voice. His lack of confidence broke her heart.

"Of course," she agreed, even though she normally avoided those types of fast-food joints like the plague. "Nick, let me know if you see a Mr. Burger's."

"There's one up ahead," Jonah pointed out. She wasn't surprised, as they were everywhere. A few minutes later, they pulled into the parking lot. Jonah swiveled in his seat. "Inside? Or drive-through?"

"Drive-through," Nick said, before she had a chance to respond. "All of us going inside would draw too much attention."

She belatedly remembered his bloodstained jacket. "The drive-through is fine."

Nick warned her to go light on Joey's food, as they placed their order. She went with both a chocolate shake and a soda for her son, along with chicken pieces. No one else ordered anything to eat, including Rachel. The nausea that she'd lived with for the past few hours had dissolved, but she still wasn't hungry.

Jonah kept driving as Joey ate. He only ate about half his food before declaring that he was full. The thought of her son going hungry gnawed away at her, although she was grateful he didn't appear to be physically abused. The only indication of what he'd suffered was the traumatized expression in his eyes.

"That's okay, we can save the rest for later," she said, bundling up the leftovers.

They reached the hotel parking lot where they'd left Nick's car, and there was a heated debate between Jonah and Nick about what to do next.

"Go home to your pregnant wife, Jonah," Nick said stubbornly. "If I need anything more, I'll let you know."

"I'm not leaving when you're wounded," Jonah argued. "Besides, where are you going to go?"

"My mother's uncle has a cabin in Wisconsin," Nick said. "I thought we'd go there for a while. I still have my laptop and we can maybe do some searching while we're there. Hopefully, we'll hear some good news from my boss soon."

"A cabin?" Joey echoed, his eyes wide with enthusiasm. "Can we go to the cabin, Mom? Can we?"

She couldn't bear to deny Joey anything. At least not now. Of course, they'd have to go back home, eventually, to figure out their next steps, now that she didn't have her company anymore. "If that's what Nick thinks is best," she murmured.

"I don't have enough cash to keep going to motels," he said, his tone apologetic. "Besides, Morales is going to report back to whoever hired him that you weren't there alone. I'm worried they might be able to spot my car if we stick around here. I think the cabin is the safest place for us to be right now."

Jonah didn't look convinced. "I still don't like leaving you alone," he grumbled. "But Mallory's due date is next week so I should head home. Promise you'll call if you need me?"

"Yes. And I'll give you the address to my uncle's cabin, too." Nick rattled off the address as Jonah punched it into his phone.

Soon, they were back on the road. Nick had managed to wrap gauze around his arm, which helped stop the bleeding. Jonah insisted on leaving the first-aid kit with them, and Rachel accepted it gratefully, knowing that as soon as they'd reached the cabin, she'd need to do a better job of cleaning up Nick's wound.

She stayed in the backseat with Joey, unwilling to leave him there alone. As Nick's car ate up the miles, crossing over the Illinois/Wisconsin state line, she closed her eyes and clutched her son's hand, wondering if their life would ever be normal again.

Nick glanced in the rearview mirror as he drove, noticing that Rachel had fallen asleep. He was glad she was getting some rest, but Joey, however, was still wide-awake. Dusk was already darkening the sky, and Nick's goal was to make it to the cabin well before nightfall.

"Are you doing okay back there?" he asked softly, trying not to disturb Rachel.

Joey nodded, although his gaze seemed troubled. "The bad man isn't going to come after me again, is he?"

Nick's heart lurched at the panic in Joey's young voice. No matter what happened, the poor kid was going to have nightmares about the kidnapping for a long time to come. He made a mental note to discuss with Rachel the need for Joey to get counseling.

He didn't want to lie to the boy, but he didn't want the child to live in fear, either. He chose his words carefully. "The reason I'm taking you and your mom to the cabin is to keep you safe from the bad man," he said finally. "I've already called my boss and asked him to put out an arrest warrant for the bad man, too. Once he's in jail he won't be able to hurt you or your mom any more."

Joey nodded and seemed to relax at that explanation. "I'm glad you're a police detective," he said.

Nick caught the boy's gaze in the rearview mirror and flashed him a warm smile. "Me, too." He paused, before asking, "Joey, you mentioned you were in a basement room with a mattress, a toilet and a locked door. Do you remember anything else? Anything that might help the police track down the bad man?"

Joey's lower lip trembled as if he might burst out sobbing. And as if she instinctively knew her son was upset, Rachel woke up. "Joey? What's wrong?"

"I c-can't remember anything else," he stuttered. "I couldn't see because the bad man put a black hood over my head!"

Nick winced when Rachel glared at him. "You don't have to remember anything, sweetie," she said gently, daring Nick to disagree. "I don't want you to worry about the bad man anymore. All that matters is that you're safe here with me. We're going to make sure nothing happens to you, okay?"

"Okay," Joey mumbled.

He sighed and dropped the touchy subject. He didn't want to upset Joey, but at the same time, they needed to know what, if anything, the boy remembered.

Maybe once they reached the cabin, Joey would relax enough to open up about his ordeal. Refusing to discuss what happened wasn't going to help Rachel's son get over what happened.

But talking through the events just might.

He didn't voice his opinion though. Instead, he concentrated on trying to remember the route to his uncle's cabin. The farther north he drove, the more the temperature dropped. There was evidence of a recent light snow, although nothing deep enough to worry about. He hadn't been to Uncle Wally's cabin in the past year, since his uncle had passed away, leaving the cabin to his mother. And since Nick's parents had chosen to retire in Florida last year, he doubted anyone had been up there since he and Wally had been there the summer before his uncle's passing.

Nick's wife and daughter had enjoyed spending time up there, too. He smiled remembering how Sophie had laughed as she played in the fallen leaves. For the first time, remembering his family didn't cause his heart to ache. He'd treasure every moment they had together.

He forced his attention on his surroundings. Twice he had to backtrack, because the area looked so different from what he remembered. But then he caught sight of the red fire sign with the numbers 472 and knew he'd found it. The gravel driveway was barely visible between towering evergreen trees, and so completely overgrown with brush and weeds that he only went far enough to make sure the car was out of sight from the road, before shutting off the engine.

"Sorry, but we'll have to walk in from here," he said, grabbing the bag of clothes in one hand while keeping his weapon ready with the other. Just in case. "I'm afraid we'll get stuck if we drive in any farther."

"That's okay," Rachel replied, opening her door and pushing it against the brush. Joey climbed out right behind her as if eager to be out of the car. He saw Rachel reach for Joey's hand, but when her son eagerly strode through the tall brown grass without so much as glancing at her, she let her hand drop back to her side.

"Be careful," he called to Joey as he came over to walk beside Rachel, their feet crunching against the half-frozen brush.

"I hope there aren't poisonous snakes around here," she said nervously, as she followed her son's progress down the driveway.

"December is too cold for snakes," he assured her.

He wanted to reach for her hand but sensed she was still angry with him. "I'm sorry, Rachel. I didn't mean to upset you or Joey."

"Then stop asking him questions about what happened," she said wearily. "Don't you think he's been through enough?"

"I think you've both been through more than enough," Nick said in a low voice. "But we can't afford to relax now. For one thing, Morales knows we saw him and that you didn't come to the barn alone."

"He has the money, what more could he want?" she asked.

"I don't know, but I'm pretty sure he planned to kill you both," he rasped out.

Before Rachel could respond, Joey shouted, "There's the cabin!"

Sure enough, Nick could make out the familiar log cabin through the bare tree branches. The place looked smaller than he remembered, but as long as the wood-burning stove worked, he thought they'd be fine.

"We'll need to discuss this more, later," he said quietly to Rachel. "For now, let's get settled, okay?"

When she nodded, he lengthened his stride to catch up to Joey. Rachel didn't want to believe she and Joey were still in danger, but he knew they were. And he vowed to do whatever it took to keep them safe.

Rachel explored the small kitchen area inside the cabin, relieved to note that there were plenty of canned goods, soups and stew for them to eat. Everything was coated in a thick layer of dust, but nothing was outdated or spoiled. She frowned, knowing that the place needed to be cleaned but that it would be impossible without water.

"First we'll build a fire to make it warm in here," Nick was telling Joey. "Then we're going to prime the pump outside."

"What does that mean?" Joey asked, hovering near Nick as he stacked wood in the large wood-burning stove in the center of the room. There were dried leaves and twigs, too, and soon he had a roaring fire going.

"The well has to be closed up in the winter, or else the pipes will freeze," Nick explained. "We'll prime the pump to get the water running again. I'll show you how it's done."

Rachel watched Joey and Nick interact with a distinct male camaraderie. She knew her son longed for a male role model, which was one of the reasons she'd gotten him involved in sports like basketball. At least his coach was a decent role model for her son.

But to see Joey bond with Nick like this was worrisome. What would happen once this nightmare was over? When Nick went back to his job, leaving her and Joey to make a new life for themselves? She and her son might even have to move in order for her to find work.

The last thing she wanted was for Joey to be hurt again. He'd already suffered so much. The image of the way he'd reacted when Morales ripped the hood off his head was seared into her memory.

Granted, Nick wasn't going to hurt her son on purpose, not the way Morales had. But she knew, with deep certainty, that her son would eventually be hurt just the same.

This was exactly why she hadn't dated or tried to form any relationships with men. And even though she knew most men weren't connected with the Mafia, she wasn't sure she was ready to think about a relationship of any sort. Friendship, yes. But she'd stayed alone because she knew Joey was at a vulnerable and impressionable age. Avoiding relationships was easier than allowing Joey to get close to someone, only to be hurt if the relationship didn't work out. When Nick and Joey went back outside to work on the pump, she grabbed several cans of stew and set them on the counter.

Nick wanted to talk later, and that was just fine with her. Because she wanted to talk to him, too. He had to understand that he needed to keep his distance from Joey.

For her son's sake.

The interior of the cabin warmed up to the point she could take off the bulky jacket and the dark sweatshirt, wearing just the long-sleeved crew neck T-shirt. She stripped off the sheets draping the furniture, sneezing as the dust ticked her nose.

When Nick and Joey returned a few minutes later, they were both grinning from ear to ear. "We did it, Mom!" Joey exclaimed as he and Nick stamped their feet on the mat inside the doorway. "We primed the pump and now we have water."

"Great," she said, forcing a smile when her son looked up at her. "I'm going to clean the place up a bit, and then I thought we'd have the canned beef stew for dinner." Lowering her voice, she slanted a quick glance Nick's way. "Don't forget, we need to change the bandage on your arm, too."

"Plenty of time for that… Let's eat first," Nick said. "We're lucky to have electricity. Apparently my parents are still paying the bills."

"The cabin belongs to your parents?" she asked, curious in spite of herself.

"To my mother," Nick corrected. "I'm going to hike back to the car to get my laptop."

"Can I come, too?" Joey asked.

She opened her mouth to protest but was interrupted by the sound of Nick's phone ringing. He scowled at the display and then walked down the hall, obviously seeking privacy as he answered. "Yeah?"

She couldn't hear much of the conversation and was still trying to figure out a way to prevent Joey from following Nick around like a lost puppy, when Nick came back to the main room, his expression grim.

She tensed, fearing more bad news. "What's wrong?"

"They found the Jeep and, Morales, uh, is no longer a threat," he said carefully, glancing at Joey in a way that told her the man who'd kidnapped her son was dead. "But I'm afraid there's no sign of the duffel bag or the cash."

Her heart squeezed painfully in her chest and she couldn't think of anything to say.

"Unfortunately," Nick continued, "whoever hired Morales appears to have gotten away with it."

TEN

Nick mentally kicked himself as Rachel's expression froze at the news. He felt helpless knowing that Morales had been killed and all of Rachel's money was gone. The chance of finding out who had set up the kidnapping was slim to none at this point, now that their best lead—Morales—had just become, literally, a dead end.

After a long moment, Rachel let out a sigh and shrugged, avoiding his direct gaze. He knew she had to be upset at losing her company like this, but if that was the case, she didn't let on. "I'm glad Morales won't be able to hurt anyone else ever again," she murmured. "Maybe it's wrong, but I can't help thinking he ended up getting exactly what he deserved."

It was on the tip of his tongue to explain how God expected them to forgive those who trespassed against them, but there was a tiny part of him that tended to agree with her. He could forgive Morales and even the guy who'd hired him, but he also knew that those who sinned often paid the price.

If they were alone, he'd go into more detail about the crime scene, but since Joey was listening, he chose his words carefully. "The man behind all this is a professional, but we can't give up. We'll figure out who it is sooner or later."

"I know," she agreed, although her expression didn't exactly radiate confidence.

"Do you want to come for a walk with us to the car?" he offered. Oddly enough, he didn't want to leave her here in the cabin alone, especially after giving her such depressing news. "Shouldn't take us more than fifteen minutes or so."

She hesitated but then nodded. She put both her sweat-shirt and the jacket back on and crossed over to join them. He held the door as they trooped outside, and he sniffed, appreciating the woodsy scent intermingled with fire-place smoke that lingered in the air, bringing back fond memories of the good times he'd spent up here with Uncle Wally and with his family.

Joey grabbed a small branch that had fallen from one of the trees and swatted the brush as they walked. Rachel stayed next to Nick, and his hand accidently brushed hers, making him wonder what she would say if he took her hand in his. She'd never said a word about the kiss, although he hadn't mentioned it, either.

But he'd certainly thought about it. Too much. He wanted to kiss her again. But this wasn't the time or the place.

"Are you okay?" he asked under his breath when Joey had gotten far enough ahead of them that he couldn't hear them.

"Fine," she said, kicking a rock with the toe of her athletic shoe. "I knew the risk, right from the start. As I told you before, getting Joey back safe and sound was worth every penny."

Nick couldn't help playing the what-if game. What if

he'd insisted on getting the FBI involved? Would they have gotten Joey back and still have Rachel's cash, too? Would they have caught the guy who'd killed Morales? Would Rachel and Joey be safe at home where they belonged?

As much as he wanted Rachel and Joey to be okay, it bothered him to think about the fact that once this was over, he wouldn't be seeing either of them again. Immediately, he felt guilty for even considering replacing Becky and Sophie with Rachel and Joey.

No, he couldn't do it. As much as he cared about Rachel and her son, he and Rachel would be much better off if they simply remained friends once this was over. Maybe he could be sort of a big brother to Joey. Do things like taking him to ball games or just playing catch. Surely, Rachel wouldn't mind having some downtime—being a single mother couldn't be easy.

The more he thought about the possibility of staying in touch with Joey, the more he liked it.

But, first, he had to keep Rachel and Joey safe, while figuring out a way to get her company back.

"I'm going to need your help in order to keep investigating all the possibilities," he murmured.

"I'm not sure how much help I'll be," she protested wearily. "And what's the point of getting your computer? I can't imagine there's any internet available up here."

"The last time I came up with Uncle Wally, I was able to get a signal from someone else's internet tower as they didn't have it secured with a password." He caught her surprised gaze and shrugged. "Figured it was worth a shot to see if the signal is still available."

"There's the car," Joey shouted, running forward as if they were in a race. "Open the trunk, Nick!"

He caught a glimpse of annoyance in Rachel's gaze and tried to figure out what he'd done to upset her as he pushed the button on his key fob, making the truck spring open. Joey grabbed his computer case and proudly brought it over to him. "Here you go," he announced.

"Thanks, Joey," he said, looping the strap over his shoulder. Before he could say anything more, the boy ran back to shut the trunk for him, too. Nick grabbed the first-aid kit from the front seat and then locked the car.

"We need to talk later," Rachel whispered as Joey made his way back over to where they waited.

"Okay," he agreed, even though deep down he could tell by her tone that, whatever she wanted to talk about, it wasn't going to be good.

Rachel knew she was overreacting to Joey's eagerness to assist Nick, but she couldn't seem to help herself. As they made their way back to the cabin, she quickened her pace to keep up with her son rather than lagging behind with Nick.

"Hey, stop here a minute and look up at the stars," she said to Joey. "Aren't they beautiful?"

"Wow, there's so many," Joey whispered in awe.

"Out here in the country it's easier to see them," she explained. "Back home, the lights from the city tend to get in the way."

Nick came up to stand beside them, tipping his head back to enjoy the view, as well. For a moment, she could almost pretend they were a family, rather than hiding up here fearing for their lives.

This was what Anthony had stolen from her all those years ago. And she hadn't even really understood how much she'd missed what she'd never had, until now.

A loud noise, like a tree branch snapping in two, made her jump, and she instinctively reached out to grab Joey's hand. "Stay with me," she whispered, drawing him close.

"Rachel, take Joey and this stuff back to the cabin," Nick said in a low voice.

A shiver snaked down her spine and she glanced around warily. They were surrounded by trees, which wasn't reassuring, since she couldn't see much in the darkness. She took the computer case from him and slung it over her shoulder. She held the first-aid kit tight to her chest. Despite being irked with Nick earlier, she was loath to leave him now. "Come with us," she urged softly.

"Could be nothing more than a deer or some other animal," he assured her. "Go inside and lock the door. I'm going to take a look around."

Nick was armed and could probably take care of himself, yet it was still difficult to leave him alone. But now that she had her son back, she wasn't about to risk losing him again, so she gave a jerky nod.

"Come on, Joey," she whispered, shielding him as best as she could as they quickly ran in the direction of the cabin. Even after getting safely inside, she couldn't relax. She secured the dead bolt lock into place, set down the laptop and the first-aid kit on the rough-hewn kitchen table and then doused the lights. She hoped the darkness would shield them from anyone watching from outside, although there wasn't much she could do about the yellow glow of the fire.

"I thought the bad man was gone?" Joey asked fearfully.

"He is gone," she said, trying to smile. "You heard what Nick said—I'm sure the noise was probably from a deer. Nick is being extra careful because he's a police detective and that's what policemen do. Come sit on the sofa in front of the fire with me."

Joey went over to the sofa and she desperately searched for something to use as a weapon. A kitchen knife would only work if the thug came in close, so she bypassed that option. Her gaze fell on the trio of fireplace instruments Nick had used earlier to help start the fire. The poker was long, made of cast iron and was pointy on the end. Since the poker gave her the best chance to protect herself and Joey, she carried the stand of fireplace instruments to the right side of the sofa and set the poker so that it was well within reach, before she snuggled in next to her son.

"I'm scared," Joey whimpered beside her.

Her heart squeezed in her chest. "I'm not going to let anything happen to you, sweetie, and neither will Nick," she said. "You're not alone anymore. We're safe here inside the cabin with Nick protecting us."

He responded by burying his face against her arm, clinging tight. She hugged him close, a wave of helpless despair washing over her. How much more could the poor kid take? He'd already been through so much. More than any child should have to bear.

She'd thought that getting Joey back would solve all her problems, but she was wrong. Because they were here, cowering in the darkness of the cabin, fearing the worst.

Nick was right—they needed to keep investigating in order to find the person who'd set up the kidnapping. Because they wouldn't be safe until they knew the truth.

Tense with fear and worry, she stared at the front door of the cabin, hoping and praying Nick would return soon.

Nick melted into the trees, moving slowly and carefully, the way Uncle Wally had taught him all those years ago. He hadn't liked hunting deer the way Uncle Wally had, but he'd learned enough from his uncle to move quietly through the woods. He held his gun ready, in case he stumbled across a man or wild beast.

White-tailed deer tended to feed in the early morning or early evening, so there was a good possibility that a buck or a doe moving through the woods had made the noise. There weren't bears in the area, at least not that he knew about. The snapped branch had seemed too loud for a small animal like a raccoon or a skunk, although possums could grow to a fairly good size. Maybe one had fallen out of a tree?

Nick was sure he hadn't been followed on the ride up to the cabin, so he found it hard to believe the kidnapper could have found them. Even if the kidnapper had the brains and the means to track him here, it would take a lot of expert digging to connect the cabin to him.

He made a slow, wide circle around the cabin. He didn't see anything out of the ordinary, no signs of anyone lurking around. He came across a deer bed about twenty yards behind the cabin, which made him relax. Deer were close by, so it was likely that's what they'd heard.

There was a small structure back there, too, and he moved forward cautiously. When he got closer, he wrinkled his nose at the smell, realizing this was the old outhouse that Uncle Wally had used before installing the well and the small but functional bathroom. He opened the door and flashed his small penlight inside, to make sure it was indeed empty. Then he made his way back around to the front of the cabin.

The lights were off inside, although he could see the flickering flames from the fireplace. He stood on the porch for another few minutes, straining to listen. When he didn't hear anything, he tapped lightly on the door. "Rachel? Open up, it's me, Nick."

After a few minutes, he heard her disengage the lock and open the door. "Did you find anything?" she asked.

"Just a deer bed in back of the cabin," he said cheerfully. He closed the door and relocked it. "Not only does that prove that deer are close by, but also that they've felt safe enough to make a bed here."

Rachel's smile was strained as she nodded and glanced over at her son, who was burrowed into a corner of the sofa. "Did you hear that, Joey? There's a deer bed behind the cabin."

"What kind of bed?" Joey asked, a puzzled frown furrowing his brow.

"Deer like to sleep in tall grass. Not only is the grass soft, but it also keeps the deer hidden during the day. In the early-evening hours they get up and move through the trees, looking for something to eat."

"What do they eat?" Joey asked.

"Speaking of eating, how about I heat up our supper?" Rachel suggested, heading over to the kitchen area.

He crossed over to sit beside Joey. "White-tailed deer are vegetarian, meaning they eat grass, leaves and berries. In the winter, when there aren't as many leaves, they eat the bark off the trees." He remembered his uncle Wally explaining that culling the herd of deer by hunting them in season was better than letting them starve to death. Logically he agreed, but that didn't make it any easier to kill the beautiful, graceful animals.

Joey continued to ask questions and he patiently answered them, figuring that the more they talked, the more the child would be able to relax and feel safe.

"Dinner's ready," Rachel called a few minutes later.

Joey crawled out from his spot on the sofa to cross over to the kitchen table. Nick threw another log on the fire and then joined them.

He clasped his hands together and bowed his head. "Heavenly Father, we thank You for providing us food and shelter tonight, and we ask that You continue to watch over us, keeping us safe from harm. Amen."

"Amen," Rachel echoed.

After a brief moment, Joey, too, said, "Amen."

Nick lifted his head and smiled at them both. "Thanks for praying with me. And this looks great, Rachel, I appreciate you cooking dinner."

"All I did was heat up the beef stew in a pot on the electric burner," she protested. "I don't think that counts as cooking."

"It does in my book," he said. The hearty beef stew hit the spot and Rachel and Joey must have been hungry too, because between the three of them, they finished every bite.

"I'll clean up," he said, carrying his and Joey's empty bowls over to the sink.

Rachel looked as if she might protest but then must have decided to take the opportunity to spend time with her son. He heard them exploring the cabin, although since it wasn't very big, it didn't take them long. Rachel brought a quilt with her from the back bedroom and covered them with it as they sat on the sofa, staring into the fire.

Seeing Rachel snuggled up next to Joey filled him with bittersweet longing. If he were alone, he'd probably think about Becky, but right now, he found himself captivated by the way the light from the fire flickered over Rachel's hair.

Washing the dishes didn't take long, and when he finished he pulled out the computer and tried to find the wireless signal that he'd used the last time he was here. Sure enough, the signal was weak but available, as it still wasn't password protected.

He searched for information on Dr. Karl Errol since he still thought that Josie Gardner's suicide wasn't just a coincidence. He soon discovered that Dr. Karl Errol had attended Johns Hopkins to earn his doctorate and had worked for a large international pharmaceutical company before coming to work for Rachel.

Sitting back in the chair, he tried to figure out why a highly respected research scientist from Johns Hopkins had left a large pharmaceutical corporation to work for Simon Inc.

"Joey's asleep," Rachel said, interrupting his thoughts. She came over to the table, pulled up a chair next to him and sat down. "You should let me take a look at your arm."

Nick grimaced and then nodded reluctantly. He worked his arm out of the sweatshirt sleeve while she jumped up and heated up water on the two-burner stove.

The angle was too awkward for him to see the extent of the injury and he was glad it didn't throb as much as it had at first. Rachel came over with the first-aid kit they'd brought in from the car, along with a small pan of hot water.

"This might hurt," she warned as she picked up a soft cloth and began cleaning the wound.

He didn't say anything, too distracted by her nearness as she fussed over him. He couldn't help remembering the kiss they'd shared and wondered if she'd let him kiss her again. Soon.

"Almost finished," she murmured, and he blinked,

realizing she was putting antibiotic ointment over the flesh wound before wrapping it with gauze.

"Thanks," he murmured huskily. When she turned away to take the water back over to the sink, he carefully put his arm back into the sleeve of his sweatshirt.

Once she'd finished cleaning everything up, she came back to the table. It took all his willpower to turn his attention to the investigation at hand. "Tell me about Dr. Karl Errol. How long has he worked for you?"

Rachel frowned. "He's been working for me for about three years now," she said slowly.

"How did you come to hire him? Did he apply for a job? Or did you purposefully recruit him away from his other company?"

"Neither. Josie Gardner is actually the one who recommended him for the job. She apparently met him at a research convention and talked about some of the work we were doing. He was very interested and Josie convinced me to make him an offer. To be honest, I was surprised when he actually accepted it."

"Why do you think he did? Accept the job, I mean?"

Rachel shrugged. "During our interview, he mentioned that he liked the way I put so much time and effort into research and development for new medications. He claimed that his old company had gone stagnant and that he was looking for change."

Nick hesitated, knowing that she wasn't going to like his next question. "Could it be that he was searching for a place where no one was constantly looking over his shoulder? Because maybe he liked to cut corners? What if the problem with your new diabetes medication happened in the first place because he hid something important?"

"No way... Josie would have been all over that," she said.

"Maybe that's why she committed suicide."

She stared at him for a long moment. "It's possible, but why would Karl do something like that in the first place? Why bring forward a medication that has life-threatening side effects?" She blew out a breath. "Don't you see? There's no logical reason why anyone, especially a well-respected researcher, would risk ruining their reputation and their career by doing something so crazy."

He hated to admit she had a point. What could the motivation be? He shifted several scenarios through his mind. "What if he's doing it on purpose to sabotage your company?" he mused.

Rachel closed her eyes and rubbed them. "Again, Nick, for what purpose? What's the link between this and Joey's kidnapping? I keep telling you that none of this makes any sense. The only logical explanation is that someone within the Mafia needed cash and orchestrated Joey's kidnapping to get it." She sighed impatiently. "Sabotaging the company would only make it more difficult to come up with the money. Whatever is going on within the company probably isn't connected."

He understood why she chose to believe the Mafia was behind the kidnapping. For one thing, the threatening letters did seem to point to the crime syndicate. But what if someone inside her company had sent them, pretending to be with the Mafia? He thought she had blinders on when it came to thinking anything bad about the people who worked for her.

"Rachel, hear me out for a minute, okay?" he said, leaning in toward her. "You said the lawsuit was filed last year and that you have already offered a generous settlement, right?"

"Yes, that's correct."

"Was your settlement accepted?"

She flushed and shook her head. "Not yet."

Interesting. "What if that was essentially the start of this mess? What if all of this—the failed medication, the lawsuit and now the kidnapping were just ways to put you out of business?"

"Who would want to put me out of business?"

"You tell me," he countered. "Which company is your biggest competition?"

"Global Pharmaceuticals," she answered automatically.

Global Pharmaceuticals. The same company where Karl Errol used to work. "That's it! The link we've been looking for. Don't you think it's possible that Karl Errol, who used to work for Global Pharmaceuticals, is actually doing corporate espionage for them? That he's sabotaging your company on purpose?"

The dawning horror in her eyes made him feel bad for shattering her trust, but, at the same time, he firmly believed they were finally onto something.

Now, all he needed was a way to prove it.

ELEVEN

Rachel didn't want to believe Nick's theory, but she couldn't deny that his idea had merit. "Seems odd that Global would go to such drastic lengths to put me under," she said softly. "But, okay, let's say they did convince Karl to sabotage my company. And that the failed diabetes medication was part of the master plan. How does kidnapping Joey fit into the picture? Removing me as the CEO isn't going to put the company under. Gerry Ashton has been working for the company over the past seventeen years and he's perfectly capable of running the company without me."

"Isn't there anything about your management styles that could make the difference between success and failure?" Nick pressed.

Rachel clenched her teeth in frustration. She didn't understand why he remained so focused on someone working against her from inside the company rather than the Mafia link.

Although now that Morales was dead, she was forced to admit they might never know for sure who was behind the kidnapping.

"The only difference between Gerry and me is that I

take more risks in research and development," she said. "Gerry tends to be more conservative."

"That's all? Nothing else?" Nick appeared disappointed by her response.

"The only other thing we disagreed about was settling the lawsuit," she admitted. She still remembered the heated argument they'd had. Gerry had pushed so hard she had been forced to take the issue to the board of directors. "He wanted to continue to fight, but I managed to convince the board that settling right away would be better for us in the long run. And there's still hope that the lawsuit will be settled soon."

"How long has Ashton worked for you?" he probed.

"I've only been in charge as the CEO for the past three years, since my father died. Gerry was a VP colleague during the years my father was in charge." Before he could ask another question, she quickly changed the subject. "I need to talk to you about Joey."

Nick's eyebrows lifted. "What about him?"

She took a deep breath and released it slowly, trying to figure out a way to articulate her concern without hurting his feelings. "Joey is at a vulnerable age, and I think it's clear he's looking for a father figure. I've noticed he's been following you around, and I'd appreciate it if you didn't encourage him. Please try to keep your distance."

He stared at her for a long moment. "I haven't encouraged him on purpose," he finally said. "Besides, I'm not sure I understand what your problem is. Showing your son how to build a fire and how to prime a well isn't a big deal."

"Maybe not, but can't you see that I don't want him to rely on you too much? Once this is over…" She trailed off, unable or maybe unwilling to put her deepest fears into words. "I just don't want him hurt," she repeated lamely.

"I'm sorry you feel that way, Rachel," Nick said with a frown. "I was hoping that Joey and I could hang out once in a while, even after this is over."

Her jaw dropped in surprise. It had never occurred to her that Nick would want to continue to see her son. And, for some reason, she found the idea disconcerting. "Well, uh, I guess I'll think about it," she said, unable to come up with a good reason for refusing him outright.

Nick's intense gaze bored into hers and she squirmed in her seat, feeling as if he was seeing right through her. She couldn't explain why the two of them forging a relationship after this was over bothered her so much, but it did. She glanced at her sleeping son and rose to her feet. "I'm going to take Joey to the back bedroom."

"Good idea," Nick agreed readily. "I'll stay out here, since I'll need to keep feeding wood into the fireplace, anyway."

She nodded, relieved to have an excuse to avoid Nick for the rest of the night. The way she'd warned Nick to stay away from her son was just as important for her to remember, as well. In all honesty, she was becoming far too dependent on Nick. She crossed over to lift her sleeping son into her arms. At nine years old, he was too big to carry, but she managed, staggering under his weight yet unwilling to ask Nick for help.

The bedroom was cool, being farther away from the fire. She set Joey on the bed and, amazingly, he didn't wake up. She shivered and searched for more blankets. Luckily, she'd found earlier a huge hope chest filled with handmade quilts. She retrieved several of them to use as covers and then stretched out on the bed next to Joey.

After everything they'd been through, she was physically exhausted. But her mind raced, replaying every moment of the past twenty-four hours. No matter what she tried, her mind wouldn't settle and it was only after she recited the Lord's Prayer, the only prayer she remembered from her childhood, that she finally managed to fall asleep.

Nick dozed, waking himself up every few hours to put more wood on the fire and to make sure everything was all right outside. He hadn't gotten much sleep the night before, when they'd spent the night in the car, so he had to depend on the deeply ingrained training his four years in the Marine Corps had given him in order to keep watch, despite his bone-deep exhaustion.

He tried to formulate a plan for the following day, but every time he closed his eyes, he fell asleep. When he dragged himself off the sofa at six in the morning, dawn had lightened the darkness and the fire had dwindled.

It didn't take long to bring the glowing embers back to life. Since it was too late to go back to sleep, he washed up in the small bathroom. He opened the medicine cabinet, thankful to find a somewhat rusty razor along with some ancient shaving cream. There were other items his uncle had left up there, too, but he limited himself to using the razor.

When he came out of the bathroom, he heard movement from the back bedroom. He wasn't surprised when Joey's head peeked out from behind the door. "Hi, Nick," he whispered.

"Good morning, Joey," he whispered back. Rachel must still be sleeping or he was sure she'd have already put an end to the brief conversation. At some point during the wee hours of the morning, he'd figured out that the main reason Rachel didn't want him spending time with her son was that she thought he might get too attached to Joey, after the way he'd lost his own child.

Still, he couldn't ignore the kid gazing at him with wide green eyes, so he gestured for Joey to come out of the bedroom. "Are you hungry?" he asked.

Joey nodded eagerly and slipped through the narrow opening, quietly closing the door behind him. The boy was wearing the same clothes as the day before, not that he seemed to mind. "What's for breakfast?"

Good question. "I don't know. Let's take a look, okay?" He put a hand behind Joey's back, urging him down the short hall to the main room. Rachel couldn't be too upset with him for not waking her up, he rationalized, since she obviously needed the rest. "I think I saw some oatmeal," he said to Joey. "Do you like oatmeal?"

"With brown sugar," the boy said excitedly.

"I'm not sure we have any brown sugar," he said cautiously. "But I think there's some regular sugar, which should work just as well."

Joey stopped in front of the fire, holding his hands toward the flames as if he were cold. "Did you keep the fire going all night, Nick?"

"Yep. It's our main source of heat for the cabin." He found a box of oatmeal, but it wasn't the instant kind, so he followed the cooking directions on the label.

Joey kept up a constant stream of chatter, and Nick couldn't help admiring the boy's quick mind. Rachel's son was interested in everything, from camping to sports. To help pass the time until breakfast was ready, he showed Joey how to carve small animals in pieces of wood with his penknife.

As they talked, he realized he couldn't have kept his distance from the boy if his life depended on it.

When the oatmeal was ready, he poured the steaming breakfast into two medium-size bowls. His uncle actually did have some brown sugar stored in an airtight container, so he liberally sprinkled their breakfast before taking Joey's hand in his.

"We have to pray before we eat," he said.

"Why?" Joey asked, his gaze curious.

Nick sensed he was heading down a path Rachel might not approve, but he wanted Joey to be given the option of believing in God. "Because we need to thank God for the food we're about to eat."

Joey pursed his lips. "Is God in heaven?" he asked.

"Yes, and He's always there for us, whenever we need Him."

Joey frowned for a moment. "You think God was with me when I was in the dark, stinky room?" he asked.

Nick's heart clenched and he nodded. "Yes, Joey, I do. Your mom and I were praying for God to watch over you the whole time you were gone."

"Really?" Joey brightened at the news. "I wish I would have known that," he confessed. "Maybe I wouldn't have been so scared."

Nick wished the same thing, but no sense in going back, trying to change the past. In his opinion, it was never too late to believe in the Lord.

He closed his eyes and bowed his head. "Heavenly Father, we thank You for the food and shelter You've provided for us, and we ask You again, to keep us safe from harm. Amen."

"Amen," Joey echoed.

Nick lifted his head and opened his eyes to find Rachel standing behind Joey's chair. She'd approached so quietly he hadn't heard her. He tensed, expecting an argument, but she simply added "Amen" to his prayer.

He immediately pushed back from the table. "Here, take my bowl of oatmeal, I'll get more."

She hesitated for a moment but then accepted his hot cereal and took a seat next to her son. He was touched at how they both waited until he returned before eating.

They were too busy eating to talk much. He watched with amusement as Joey quickly emptied his bowl. "Can I have seconds?" he asked anxiously.

"Of course," Nick responded, exchanging a knowing look with Rachel. Joey hadn't eaten much yesterday, but it appeared his appetite had returned.

"So what's the plan for today?" Rachel asked.

"I'm not sure yet," he answered honestly. "I should check in with my boss again, see if he can give us anything further to go on."

She darted a glance at Joey and nodded. He sensed there was more she wanted to say but didn't feel she could talk freely in front of Joey.

When they were finished with breakfast, Rachel insisted on doing the dishes, so he took the opportunity to do a quick perimeter check. The only problem was that Joey wanted to come with him.

He glanced helplessly over at Rachel, silently pleading with her to help. As much as he liked spending time with the boy, he needed to make sure the area around the cabin was secure. And he didn't want Joey to come outside with him until he was convinced they were safe.

"Joey, I need you to dry the dishes for me, okay? There will be time later for you to play outside."

"That's women's work," Joey mumbled, lightly kicking at the chair.

"No, it's not," Nick corrected. "I did the dishes last night, so it's only fair you take your turn."

Joey's disgruntled expression faded as he considered Nick's words. "All right," he finally agreed, going over to pick up the dish towel.

Rachel ruefully rolled her eyes and he quickly ducked outside before he broke into a wide smile. Sometimes, it paid to be able to double-team kids.

The thought caused him to pause before heading soundlessly into the dense wood. As a single mother, Rachel didn't have anyone to count on when it came to raising Joey. She had to play the role of both parents.

Was it any wonder she was so protective?

He focused on the task at hand, moving slowly and methodically so he didn't miss any signs now that it was daylight. The day was overcast, denying him the sunlight he would have preferred. He stood in the clearing, imagining that the log cabin was the center of a large clock with the south side, straight ahead from the door, at the twelve-o'clock position. He began to make his way around the circle.

In the three-o'clock area, he found a tuft of brown fabric stuck to the tip of a branch that was roughly shoulder height. He stared at it for a long minute, trying to estimate how long it had been there.

He could check the internet for how long it had been since the last snowfall, but he figured, from the dusting on the ground, that it had been within the past day or two. But if the snowfall had been light, the tuft of fabric might have survived intact.

By December the gun deer-hunting season was over,

but bow-hunting season lasted until January. Was it possible that someone dressed in camouflage-colored clothing had been through here recently, bow hunting? Uncle Wally's land was posted, but considering no one had been up here lately, he figured the No Trespassing signs didn't mean much.

He wanted to believe there was a hunter in the woods rather than some other random person. Because if it wasn't a hunter, then he was forced to consider the fact that this cabin might not be as safe as he'd thought.

Rachel finished the dishes and then went over to straighten up the quilts on the bed. Near the end table, she found an old Bible. Opening the flap, she was surprised to discover it belonged to Nick's mother.

She carried the Bible back to the main living area, wondering if Nick's mother had left it here or if it belonged to Nick, himself? The book was clearly old and well used. The edges of the paper were gold and there were small cutouts for each of the Bible sections. In the center there was a place for family names and she discovered it had been filled in with neat handwriting stating the names of Nick and his two sisters.

She hadn't known about Nick's sisters. And she realized there were probably a lot of things she didn't know about Nick.

Curious, she opened the book and scanned the various chapters. It wasn't easy to decipher the meaning of the writing since, according to the title page, it was written in the Authorized King James Version.

"What are you reading?" Joey asked, coming over to sit next to her on the sofa.

She glanced down at her son, remembering the conversation he'd had with Nick before breakfast. It had nearly broken her heart to hear Joey describe how alone he'd felt in the dark room where Morales had kept him. She realized now that she'd done her son a disservice by not teaching him religion. "This is a Bible, which is a collection of God's words," she explained, hoping she was describing it right.

"Are there stories in there?" he queried, leaning over to see for himself.

"Yes, there are," she replied, although she wasn't sure exactly where they were. She vaguely remembered some Bible stories from her childhood, but how to find them in this huge book?

She opened the Bible to the New Testament, and the pages opened to the Gospel according to Saint John. "'In the beginning was the Word and the Word was with God and the Word was God,'" she read out loud. Joey leaned against her, seemingly content so she continued, "'The same was in the beginning with God. All things were made by him and without him was not any thing made that was made. In him was life; and the life was the light of men.'"

Soon, she got into the rhythm of the words, and the lyrical quality of the text helped her to relax. So intent was she on reading that she didn't hear Nick return.

When she glanced up, she saw him watching her, a gentle smile on his face. She stumbled over the next sentence and then stopped.

"You sound like you've been reading the Bible your entire life," he murmured, admiration reflected in his gaze.

She felt herself blush. "I hope it's okay that I'm reading your mother's Bible," she said. "I found it on the bed-side table in our room."

"She'd be thrilled," he assured her. "John's Gospel is one of my favorites. Although you also might try the book of Psalms—those are where I go when I need to reconnect with God. Or we might want to review the Gospel surrounding the birth of Jesus, as that's what Christmas is all about."

"All right," she agreed, thinking that this was the first time in her entire life that she'd had a conversation about the Bible with a man.

Actually, with anyone. Yet she found it wasn't the least bit awkward, at least with Nick.

Joey scrambled off the sofa and ran over to Nick. "Did you find any deer in the deer bed?" he asked, the Bible stories forgotten.

"Nope, didn't see any deer there today," he said with a wry smile.

She frowned and set the Bible aside. "What did you find?" she asked, sensing there was something bothering him.

He shrugged. "Could be nothing, but I think I'll call Jonah, just in case."

She did not like the sound of that. "Just in case what?"

He hesitated. "Just in case the bit of fabric I found outside doesn't belong to a hunter poaching on my uncle's land."

Nick tried Jonah several times before he connected with his friend. "I might need some backup," he said bluntly.

"What happened?" Jonah asked.

In the background he could hear Mallory's voice but

not exactly what she was saying. "I found some fabric stuck to a tree branch about fifty feet from the cabin. Can't be sure it's a random hunter or someone who could have followed us."

There was a moment of silence. "I want to help you, Nick, but Mallory has been having contractions. She says it's probably false labor, since she's not due until next week, but I'm not willing to take the chance."

"Hey, no problem," he hastened to assure his friend. "Stay with Mallory, I'm sure we'll be fine."

"Maybe you should call for backup? Or, find another place to stay," Jonah suggested.

"Yeah, maybe." Neither option thrilled him. He trusted his boss but didn't want to bring in anyone new. And if they left, he'd have to use his credit card, since he was almost out of cash. If the Mafia was involved, they likely had the ability to track them that way. Not to mention, he rather liked the coziness of the cabin. "Take care of Mallory, and call me if I'm going to be an honorary uncle."

"Nick, wait," Jonah said, before he could hang up. "I did find something interesting. I know you weren't keen on the Mafia angle, but guess who's back in Chicago?"

Nick rubbed his hand along the back of his neck. "Tell me you didn't find Frankie Caruso."

"Bing, bing, bing—you win the grand prize," Jonah joked.

Nick could barely drudge up a smile. "Where was he spotted?"

"That's what was so interesting. He was at a fundraiser put together by the mayor to raise money for diabetes research."

Diabetes research? "Are you sure?"

"I'm sure, but check it out online if you need more information."

Another coincidence. "Why does the Chicago mayor care about diabetes?"

"Because his wife was recently diagnosed with diabetes, and he thinks there should be more research into finding a cure."

"Okay, thanks for the heads-up," Nick said. After ending the call, he crossed over to the table and booted up the laptop.

He quickly pulled up a search engine and put in Caruso's name along with the word *fund-raiser*. Sure enough, there he was standing next to the mayor and his wife.

As he stared at the elder Caruso, he couldn't help thinking that Rachel may have been right all along. Caruso might have been the mastermind behind Joey's kidnapping. Seeing as he was such good friends with the mayor, it could be that Caruso wasn't happy about Rachel's failed diabetes medication. Could be that the mayor had a bone to pick with Rachel's company, too.

What better revenge than to kidnap her son, forcing her to sell off her shares of the company? And the added bonus? Making himself rich in the process.

TWELVE

Rachel could tell something was bothering Nick, but with Joey sitting right there, she was hesitant to ask too many questions about the investigation.

"Mom, can I work on my deer carving?" Joey asked from his favorite spot on the sofa.

"Deer carving?" she echoed with a raised brow. Nick's sheepish expression gave him away. "You taught him to do that?" she asked.

"Um, yeah. Hope you don't mind."

She should mind, but oddly she was touched that he'd taken the time. "Are you sure it's safe?"

"My uncle taught me how to carve when I was about his age, and I stressed the importance of being careful with the knife."

"All right, go ahead, Joey." At least carving would help keep her son occupied. She crossed the room to glance over Nick's shoulder at the computer screen. Only to be distracted by the scent of his shaving cream. It was strangely comforting and she had to fight not to put her arms around him.

Nick seemed impervious to her quandary. "Do you recognize anyone in the photograph?" he asked.

Forcing herself to concentrate, she narrowed her gaze on the photo. Suddenly, her stomach clenched with recognition. She pointed at the screen. "Frankie Caruso."

"Yeah, with the Chicago mayor and his wife," Nick murmured. "The mayor's wife was recently diagnosed with diabetes, and this was a fund-raiser to support research for a cure."

Another link to diabetes. "I'm sure Frankie is the one who hired Morales," she said. "It's the only thing that makes sense."

"Maybe." Nick jammed his fingers through his hair. "I need to go through the entire timeline from start to finish. There has to be something we're missing."

"I'll help," she offered. Her phone rang and she pulled it out of her sweatshirt pocket, surprised to see there was still one bar of battery left. Wincing, she saw the caller was Edith. It seemed like days since she'd spoken to her assistant. "Hi, Edith, how are you?"

"I'm putting in my notice," the woman said in a crisp tone. "You should have told me that you intended to sell off your shares of the company, Rachel. If I'd have known, I would have looked for somewhere else to work."

The reproach in the older woman's tone only sharpened her guilt. "I'm sorry, Edith, you're right—I should have told you. But why are you leaving? I'm sure Gerry could use all the support he can get."

"Gerry Ashton is not you, Rachel. Nor is he your father. I've been loyal to the both of you, but now that you're both gone, I see no need to stay on."

She was flabbergasted with Edith's decision. "Maybe you should take some time to reconsider," she said. "Gerry has been with the company for seventeen years— I'm sure everything will be fine."

"I've made my decision." Edith's tone held an underlying note of steel. "And I'm telling you because you're the one I was working for."

Rachel sensed there was nothing she could say to talk her senior assistant out of resigning. "I'll make sure you get all your vacation pay, Edith," she said, even though technically she didn't own the company anymore. Surely the payroll staff would still listen to her. "And if you change your mind—"

"I won't. Goodbye, Rachel."

Rachel disconnected from the call just as her phone battery gave out.

"Edith resigned?" Nick asked with a dark frown.

"Apparently." She sank into the seat next to Nick, trying to grapple with the news. "I feel terrible about this. Edith has been with the company for thirty years."

"It's not as if you sold off your shares on purpose," Nick reminded her gently. "This isn't your fault."

Yes, it was her fault, but she couldn't deny that she'd do it all again in a heartbeat if it meant getting Joey back safely. Up until now, she'd convinced herself that her life was the only one impacted by her decision.

She took a deep breath and met Nick's sympathetic gaze. There was nothing she could do now but move forward. "Let's work on that timeline…."

Nick wanted nothing more than to reach over and pull Rachel close, to comfort her. She looked as if she'd lost her best friend, and maybe she had. He suspected Edith had been her rock, especially after her father passed away.

There wasn't anything he could say to her to make her feel better, so he took her cue and agreed to work on the timeline.

"I need paper," he muttered. He'd prefer a large white-board or bulletin board, but paper would do in a pinch, far better than the computer.

"I think there was some in the bedroom, I'll be right back." Rachel returned a few minutes later with a tattered notebook. "Sorry, but this is all I could find," she said.

"Perfect," he said, taking the notebook from her hands. Their fingers brushed and he tried to ignore the tingling that radiated up his arm. This wasn't the time or the place to think about kissing Rachel again. He tore several sheets of paper out and set them side by side.

"We should probably start with the failed diabetes medication," Rachel said.

He nodded in agreement. "Do you remember the dates and times of the letters and phone calls?"

She reached over and took the pencil from his hand to write in the information. Her nearness was disconcerting. "And here's the date I called you," she added.

"And the same day, you took Joey to his basketball game," he said.

"Yes, that's the part that has bothered me." She scowled at the timeline. "I don't think I was followed, for sure not by the black truck."

Nick had to concur, since he'd followed her and had made sure no one had followed him. "It seemed the kidnappers were one step ahead of us for the first twenty-four hours—until we exchanged your cell phone."

"You thought they were tracking the GPS in my phone, right?"

"Was it a company phone?" he asked, slanting a sideways glance at her. "Or your personal phone?"

"It was a company phone, which also served my personal needs. I saw no reason to have two phones, and it's handy to have ready access to my work email at all times."

"Okay, so who would have access to the serial number for your company phone?" he asked.

Rachel shrugged. "Lots of people. Edith, for sure, and probably some of the staff in billing."

"Do you have an informatics department? Who takes care of interfacing your work email to your phone?"

"We contract with a small company, called Tech Support Inc., and they come in once a month for a day or two to update the computers, scan for problems, that kind of thing."

He'd never heard of Tech Support Inc. but a quick internet search didn't reveal anything alarming. "How long have you had a contract with them?"

"For several years," Rachel responded. "I hardly think they would give out private information like that."

"They might to someone within your company," Nick countered. "Say for instance, Karl Errol?"

"Maybe, but I doubt it. Karl is a researcher—wouldn't they see that as suspicious?"

"Not if he gave them a good reason. Or if he had someone else call, pretending to be you or Edith." He stared at the timeline for a moment. "I think it's clear that whoever tracked your cell phone was someone from inside your company, Rachel," he said slowly. "Not Frankie Caruso."

Rachel's emotions rolled up and down like a yo-yo, and Nick wasn't helping matters. First Frankie was involved, and then he wasn't. The kidnapping was related to her failed diabetes medication, and then it wasn't.

Her head ached and she pressed her fingertips to her

temples, trying to ease the pressure. "I'm not sure what to think," she said finally. "Maybe we should go back to Chicago, see if we can talk to Karl."

Nick was still entering dates and times into their makeshift chart. "Josie's suicide is bothering me," he muttered half to himself. "Would make more sense if it was actually murder staged to look like a suicide."

That caught her attention. "Why?"

"Because suicide indicates she felt guilty about something," he explained. "If she was part of the cover-up related to the failed diabetes medication, then okay, I could buy that idea. But if she stumbled onto the truth and intended to come talk to you about it, then I'm more inclined to believe it was murder."

A chill snaked down Rachel's spine. "The meeting I was supposed to have with Karl and Josie the day I received the threatening letter and called you—it was set up by Josie. She told me that she had something important to discuss with me and insisted that Karl be there, too."

"That fits with my homicide theory," he said. "Do you think Edith knows anything more about what Josie wanted to discuss with you?"

"I doubt it. Edith was more concerned with fitting all the necessary meetings into my schedule. She wouldn't ask Josie why she wanted to talk to me. If Josie said it was important, then she'd find the time to make it happen."

Nick grimaced and then turned his attention back to the timeline. She found it hard to concentrate, though, too preoccupied by the idea of her employee possibly being murdered.

How Nick worked homicide cases on a regular basis

was beyond her comprehension. She admired his strength and his dedication, more than she should.

She glanced over to the sofa and frowned when she didn't see her son sitting there. For a moment panic set in. "Where's Joey?"

Nick glanced up in surprise. "He was there a few minutes ago."

She jumped up from her seat next to Nick. "Joey?" she called, her tone sharper than she intended.

Joey didn't answer but suddenly there was a loud crash from the direction of the bathroom. Without hesitation, she rushed over. "Joey?" She knocked on the bathroom door. "Are you okay in there?"

"The smell," she heard Joey whimper. Concerned, she opened the door, grateful there was no lock.

Joey was huddled on the floor, silent tears streaming down his cheeks. The medicine cabinet door was open and it took a minute for the harsh scent of aftershave to register, because she was focused on the smears of blood on the sink. "Joey, what happened?"

"Don't tell Nick," he whimpered.

She tried to figure out what happened. "Don't tell Nick what?"

"I cut myself with the knife," Joey managed to blurt out between sobs. "I didn't want to tell you because I didn't want Nick to be disappointed in me."

Her heart wrenched in her chest, and she knelt beside Joey and pulled him into her arms. "Nick won't be disappointed in you, sweetie. Let me see the cut."

He held out his hand, and she could see the slim cut along the pad of his thumb. There was a small bit of blood and she needed to examine the cut to make sure it wasn't so deep it needed stitches.

"Let's get that cleaned up, okay?" she suggested calmly.

"I don't like the smell," Joey said again.

She frowned and turned on the faucet, sticking his thumb beneath the gently running water. The broken bottle of stinky aftershave was lying on the floor, the liquid seeping into the wooden floor. "What happened, Joey?"

"I was looking for a Band-Aid," he said, sniffling back his tears. "And I accidently knocked it over."

"Is everything okay?" Nick asked from the doorway.

Joey's big green eyes once again filled with tears. "I'm sorry, Nick."

"Hey now, don't cry." Nick sent her a pleading look. "I don't care about that bottle of aftershave, it was old anyway."

But Joey shook his head. "No, I'm sorry about the knife," he said. "I was being careful like you said, but it slipped and I didn't want you to know I cut myself."

"I'm not mad at you, Joey, so don't worry about it, okay?" Nick flashed her son a reassuring smile.

Rachel was glad to see that the cut wasn't that deep, and she held Joey's hand under the warm water as she rummaged in the open medicine cabinet. "Do you have any tape and gauze I can use to keep it clean and dry?" she asked.

"We still have Jonah's first-aid kit in the kitchen," Nick assured her. She relaxed and nodded, remembering how she'd used it to change the dressing on Nick's wound.

"All right, let me put a towel or something around his thumb," she muttered. "Keep your hand in the water, okay?"

Joey nodded and did as she asked, while she searched for something to use. She found an old but clean hand towel in dark brown and figured the bloodstains wouldn't be too noticeable. "Okay, here, let's wrap this around your hand."

Joey sniffled again but allowed her to wrap the towel around his thumb. He turned toward the door, but his foot slipped in the slight puddle on the floor, making him wrinkle his nose in disgust.

She led the way into the kitchen, getting Joey settled in one of the kitchen chairs on the opposite side from where they'd been working on the timeline, while Nick brought over the first-aid kit.

"There's some triple antibiotic cream in here, too," he said, handing over the supplies.

"Good thing." She put a dollop of ointment over the cut and then carefully wrapped it in gauze and tapped it securely in place. "There, how's that?" she asked when she was finished.

Joey nodded. "Can you make the smell go away?" he asked.

She didn't quite understand why he was so upset about the smelly aftershave. It actually wasn't awful, the brand was well-known and obviously had remained popular over the years. She exchanged a perplexed glance at Nick. "Ah, sure, I'll clean up the bathroom floor, okay?"

"Are you hungry?" she heard Nick ask, as she walked down the hall to clean up the mess in the bathroom. "I can heat up some soup."

She filled the sink with soapy water and took yet another hand towel and did her best to clean up the spilled aftershave. But even after she finished, the scent still lingered.

There wasn't much she could do other than try to cut through the scent with a stronger cleaning agent.

She went back into the kitchen and found Nick heating up some chicken noodle soup for Joey. "Do you have any bleach or vinegar?" she asked in a low tone.

He grimaced. "I doubt it, but check in the pantry."

Calling the rough wooden open shelves a pantry was a bit of a misnomer, and she examined the contents but couldn't find anything she could use to help eliminate the odor.

"Don't worry," Nick said reassuringly. "I'm sure it will fade over time."

"No!" Joey shouted. "I don't like the smell! Make it go away!"

She rushed to Joey's side, wrapping her arms around her son. "Shh, sweetie, it's okay."

"Wait," Nick said, coming over to put a hand on her shoulder. "Does the smell remind you of something, Joey?" he asked.

Realization dawned slowly, and she pulled away just enough to look down at her son's face. Joey gazed up at her and then looked over at Nick. He didn't speak, but he slowly nodded his head yes.

Her heart clenched in her chest as the implication sank deep.

"What does the smell remind you of, Joey?" Nick asked gently. "Can you tell me?"

There was a long silence before Joey answered. "The bad man," he whispered.

"The bad man who put a hood over your head and carried you away after the crash?" Nick asked.

This time, her son shook his head no. "The other bad man. I didn't see him, but he spoke in a mean voice and he smelled bad. Like the bottle I accidently spilled in the bathroom."

The second bad man? For a moment Rachel couldn't move. Could barely comprehend what Joey meant.

Then she raised her head and locked gazes with Nick. And read the truth reflected in his eyes.

Forcing her to acknowledge that Joey had been somewhere near the man who'd arranged the kidnapping. Thinking back, she realized that their initial theory must have been correct. Morales had dumped the black truck shortly after the crash, catching a ride with someone else. The man who'd ordered the kidnapping in the first place.

Which meant her son might be able to recognize the voice of the man who'd masterminded the entire operation.

Once they found him.

THIRTEEN

Nick tore his gaze from Rachel's when he heard the soup boiling. He rushed to the stove to remove the saucepan from the electric burner. "Soup's ready," he said.

Rachel shook her head, as if there was no way she'd be able to eat, but he knew they had to try to keep things normal, for Joey's sake. He filled several bowls with the steaming soup and carried them over to the table in two trips.

"Try to eat something, Joey," he urged. "You don't have to think about the bad man anymore."

"But I can still smell him," Joey whined.

"Try the soup, and I'll clean the floor again," Rachel murmured.

"After you eat something," Nick said, gesturing to the empty seat. She put a hand over her stomach but sat next to her son. He gave Rachel credit for trying, when she leaned over her bowl. "Hmm, smells good."

Joey leaned over his own soup and took a tentative sniff. The aroma of chicken soup seemed to appease him enough to take a sip. "Tastes good," he admitted.

Rachel took a sip, too. "Yes, it does."

They hadn't prayed, so Nick said a quick, silent prayer

of thanks before taking a spoonful of his soup. The three of them sat in companionable silence as they enjoyed the simple meal. When Joey had finished, Rachel pushed away and carried her bowl to the sink. As soon as she'd rinsed her dishes, she returned to the bathroom.

Nick scrubbed a hand along the back of his neck, knowing that no matter how many times Rachel scrubbed the wooden floor, the scent of Wally's aftershave would linger.

In Joey's mind more so than in reality.

He quickly washed the dishes, while Joey went back to sit in front of the fire. The sad expression on the child's face made his heart ache. Sophie's life had been cut short by the car crash, but she'd always been a happy child. Loved school and had lots of friends. Both he and Becky had doted on their daughter. The thought of Sophie suffering the way Joey had made his chest hurt.

No matter how important this timeline was, he simply couldn't ignore Joey. Rachel returned to the room, looking dejected as she dropped onto the sofa beside her son.

"Hey, Joey, how would you like me to read the story of Christmas to you from the Bible?" he asked.

"The Bible has the story of Christmas in it?" Joey asked, his eyes wide with curiosity.

Rachel winced and he understood she was feeling guilty that Joey didn't know the real meaning of Christmas. "Yep, it sure does."

"Okay."

Nick picked up the Bible and settled onto the recliner. He opened his mother's Bible to the Gospel of Luke, Chapter 2 verse 7. "'And she brought forth her firstborn son and wrapped him in swaddling clothes and laid him in a manger; because there was no room for them in the inn.

"'And there were in the same country shepherds abiding in the field keeping watch over their flock by night. And, lo, the angel of the Lord came upon them and the glory of the Lord shone round about them; and they were sore afraid. And the angel said unto them, Fear not: for, behold, I bring you good tidings of great joy, which shall be to all people. For unto you is born this day in the city of David a Saviour, which is Christ the Lord.'"

He continued through verse twenty and when he finished reading, he was humbled to realize that both Joey and Rachel were staring at him, as if hanging on every word.

"And that is the true meaning of Christmas," he murmured, encouraged that this would be another step for both of them in their journey to believe.

Rachel loved listening to Nick read from the Bible, but she also felt bad that she hadn't taught Joey about God and the story of Jesus before now.

"That was a nice story," Joey said with a wide yawn.

She kissed the top of his head. "It was a wonderful story, wasn't it? I want you to think about God whenever you feel afraid, okay?"

"I will," Joey's voice was soft and sleepy.

Nick set the Bible aside and returned to the kitchen table to continue working on the timeline.

She needed to help Nick, but she didn't want to leave her son. It wasn't until Joey's head tipped to the side, indicating he'd fallen asleep, that she eased away and went to sit beside Nick.

"I suppose you think I'm a terrible mother," she said softly.

He glanced at her in surprise. "Why would I think that?"

The shame was almost too much to bear, but she forced herself to get this out in the open. "Because I didn't teach Joey about God. Because I didn't raise him to believe."

"It's never too late to start, Rachel," Nick murmured. He reached up and tucked a strand of her hair behind her ear. "And no, I don't think you're a terrible mother at all. If you weren't raised to believe in God, then it's no wonder you raised your son the same way."

She was silent for a long moment, wishing she dared to ask him to hold her. She thought back to her childhood. "I think my parents believed in God—at least, I remember going to church when I was young. But by the time I was Joey's age, we suddenly stopped going to church… and I pretty much forgot most of what I learned."

"Do you know why your parents stopped attending church?" he asked. The way he took her hand and interlaced his fingers with hers gave her the strength she needed.

"My mother lost her parents when I was nine, and they died about six months apart. And then when I was in high school, she was diagnosed with breast cancer. She passed away my freshman year in college." The pain of losing her mother had been terrible, but she and her father had clung together to get through it. Easy to look back now and piece together what had happened. The deaths of her grandparents had hit her mother hard, and maybe for some reason she'd pulled away from God. Her father, too, especially after losing her mother.

"I've seen that happen sometimes, where a sudden death causes a loss of faith," Nick said, giving her hand a gentle squeeze. "But to be honest, Rachel, those are the times when you should lean on God the most. I know it's hard—I struggled to keep my faith after my Becky and Sophie died."

"I can't imagine how difficult that must have been for you."

He was quiet for a moment. "Becky and I were high-school sweethearts so when I lost her, I felt like I lost my best friend. But now, after all these months, sometimes I have trouble remembering exactly what she looked like."

"Oh, Nick," she murmured. No one had ever loved her the way Nick had loved his wife.

He forced a smile. "I guess that might be God's way of making me realize I have a different path to follow. I know it's not easy, but if you open your heart to the Lord, you will be rewarded."

Maybe he was right. Certainly she'd felt some sense of peace when she'd prayed for Joey's safety. She stared down at their entwined fingers for a moment, feeling connected to Nick in a way she'd never experienced with Anthony.

The thought scared her. She didn't want to have feelings for Nick. Didn't want to open herself up to the possibility of rejection. She trusted Nick to keep her and Joey safe, but to trust him with her heart? That was asking too much.

The expression in his eyes when he spoke of his wife made her realize that he might not be ready for a relationship, either.

She took a deep breath and forced a smile. "So, let's get back to that timeline, huh?" she suggested, releasing his hand and turning toward the notebook paper he'd left on the table. "Where did we leave off?"

There was a troubled look in his eyes as he stared at her for a long moment before he sighed and turned toward the timeline. "We left off at the time of Josie Gardner's suicide or possible murder," he said.

She nodded. Was she wrong about what Nick wanted? Maybe, but, somehow, it was easier to talk about who might have kidnapped her son than her tangled feelings toward Nick.

The rest of the day passed by quicker than she would have imagined. Dark clouds rolled in, bringing the threat of a storm, but while the wind kicked up a bit, no snowflakes fell.

Nick walked around outside again, and she was reassured by his diligence. He continued to work on the timeline long after they'd taken a break for dinner.

She bowed her head while Nick thanked God once again for providing the hot meal and shelter. There weren't many options for dinner, so they had to eat more of the canned beef stew again but no one complained.

"Are we going to be home in time for Christmas?" Joey asked.

"Christmas is three days away, I'm sure we'll be home by then," she assured him.

Nick looked as if he didn't necessarily agree. "We can celebrate Christmas here, too, if we have to," he pointed out.

She knew he was right. "If we have to, we will," she agreed. "But hopefully things will get back to normal soon."

After dinner, Nick continued to work on the timeline.

She found a game of checkers on the pantry shelf and played a few games with Joey to help keep him occupied. Soon Nick came over and asked if he could play the winner, and she was truly disappointed when Joey beat her.

As she watched Nick and Joey play, she was struck by how easy it was to feel they were a family. Had she been wrong to warn Nick to keep his distance? He was everything a role model should be: kind and considerate…strong yet gentle. What a wonderful husband and father he must have been. So different from her ex.

Joey won again, and he let out a whoop. She had to make sure her yearning for a family of her own wasn't visible on her face when she gave Joey a high five.

Several games later, after Joey had yawned for the fifth time in a row, she deemed it time for bed. "Say good-night to Nick," she reminded her son.

"Good night, Nick, you're the best dad ever," Joey said.

Her breath froze in her chest and she stared at her son in horror. Why had he said that? It was as if she'd somehow projected her secret wishes into her son.

"You're welcome, Joey," Nick said thickly. "Get some sleep, now, okay?"

"Come on, Joey," she mumbled, completely mortified by the turn of events. "Good night, Nick."

"Good night." Nick gave her a searching look, which she avoided meeting head-on—too afraid he'd see the same sentiment in her eyes. He picked up the Bible and as much as she was tempted to stay and listen while he read some more she had no choice but to go with her son, who was still afraid of the dark. Besides, she couldn't imagine trying to explain why Joey had called him the best dad ever.

She'd never been more acutely aware of how her son had been impacted by growing up without a father. Had he been looking for a surrogate father this whole time?

Was it any wonder he'd latched on to Nick?

She and Joey took turns in the bathroom, the scent of the aftershave far less obvious now, though still lingering in the air. Joey wrinkled his nose but otherwise seemed fine as he crawled under the pile of quilts on the bed.

Joey immediately fell asleep but, just like the night before, her mind refused to settle. She tried to remember some of the Bible phrases Nick had read but could only recall a line or two.

She kept replaying the moment that Joey had called Nick the best dad ever. She hoped Nick didn't put too much importance on what her son had said. The way she already had.

At some point she must have dozed, because a noise startled her awake. Another wild animal moving through the woods? She stayed perfectly still, straining to listen.

After several moments, she crawled from beneath the quilts and moved silently over to the window overlooking the back side of the cabin. There weren't any stars out as they were well hidden behind a blanket of clouds.

She heard it again, the same thunk that had woken her. Did animals make that kind of sound? Somehow she doubted it. She stuffed her feet into her athletic shoes and cautiously made her way down the hall to find Nick.

Nick shot upright when he felt a hand on his arm. "What?" he asked harshly, blinking the sleep from his eyes as he gazed up at Rachel.

"Get up, I think I heard something outside," she whispered.

His pulse kicked into triple digits and he swung around to put his feet on the floor. "Are you sure?" he asked in a low, raspy voice as he quickly slid his feet into his shoes and tied the laces.

"I don't think it was an animal," she said, her eyes wide with fear. "It was a thunking noise and I heard it twice."

Nick wrestled with guilt, knowing that he should have taken Jonah's advice and found a new place to stay. But it was too late for self-recriminations. He needed to get Rachel and Joey safely out of the cabin. "Wake up Joey and make sure he's wearing his winter jacket and his shoes, okay?"

"Okay." To her credit, Rachel didn't panic and went to do exactly as she was told.

He used the poker to break up the remains of the fire, and closed the iron doors on the fireplace, to help douse the flames and eliminate even that small bit of light. The room was plunged into darkness and it took him a minute for his eyes to adjust. He tucked his weapon in his shoulder harness and then went over to peer out the large picture window.

He couldn't see much, but that was okay, since it helped keep them hidden, as well. When Rachel and Joey returned, he crossed over to them. "Be as quiet as possible, okay? Follow me...we're going outside."

Rachel snagged his arm. "Aren't we safer in here?"

"No, we're boxed in. Try to trust me on this, Rachel."

He could barely see her in the darkness. "I do trust you, Nick."

Whether or not he deserved her trust remained to be seen. But they had to move, so he simply led the way over to the front door. As quietly as possible, he eased back the dead bolt, although the click was louder than he liked. Without wasting time, he opened the door and cast a quick glance around the clearing.

Joey and Rachel crowded behind him, waiting silently for his direction. He took a moment to pray for their safety, before guiding them out onto the front porch, keeping as close to the cabin as possible.

Rachel sent Joey first, and then followed from behind. He didn't have to tell her to make sure the door didn't slam shut as she softly closed it before making her way over to where they stood. The night was so cold they could see their breath in the air, and the frozen leaves and brush would make it far more difficult to move silently through the woods.

First, he needed to figure out which was the best direction to go. He waited for a long moment, listening to the sounds of the night. It was too cold for any insects, but at least the wind had died down.

As much as he wanted to use the car to escape, he couldn't deny the possibility that the intruder had already found it and disabled it. At least, that's what he would have done.

No, their best bet was to stay hidden in the woods for as long as possible. He didn't dare use his cell phone yet, as the light from the screen would only broadcast their position to whoever was out there.

The closest grouping of evergreen trees was to the left in the nine-o'clock position, so he bent down to whisper in Rachel's ear. "Follow me to the evergreens."

He could feel her head nod, her hair brushing his face. Satisfied, he inched across the porch, praying the boards wouldn't creak.

The trek to the group of evergreens seemed to take

forever, but the moment they reached them, he felt himself relax. Thank goodness they were all wearing dark clothing, and, without the moon, he hoped their pale faces wouldn't attract too much attention.

"Stay here, I'm going to take a look around," he whispered again, right next to Rachel's ear.

"No, wait," she grabbed his arm in a tense grip. "I smell smoke."

He paused and tried to estimate how long the scent of smoke would linger in the air after he'd put out the fire inside the cabin.

"There!" Rachel whispered urgently, pointing to an area behind the cabin.

He saw what had captured her attention. Orange flames flickering in the darkness.

Fire!

FOURTEEN

Rachel stared at the small flickering flames in horror. The kidnapper must have found them. Who else would do such a thing? She knew Nick thought Morales had been ordered to kill her and Joey, but they'd managed to get away. The kidnapper must have come back to finish the job. And what if she hadn't woken up from the thunking noise? Would they have died inside the cabin? Had that been the kidnappers' plan all along?

Cold fear slid down her spine.

Thank You, Lord, for saving us!

"I think the outhouse might be on fire," Nick whispered. "And if that's the case, I'm afraid the fire will spread to the cabin." He paused, looking out over the trees. "Looks like the wind is blowing north. We'll need to head south so that we're heading in the opposite direction."

"Okay." She wasn't about to argue. Joey's hand was trembling inside of hers, from the cold or fear or both. She tightened her grip reassuringly, knowing she'd do whatever was necessary to keep him safe. "Lead the way."

Nick stayed between the trees, moving slowly and

silently away from the cabin. She did her best to follow in his footsteps, but it seemed like twigs snapped loudly beneath her feet and her clothing brushed and snagged against the tree branches with every step. The cold night air blew sharp against her face, but she knew the fire was the bigger threat compared to the stinging cold.

Although both could be deadly.

They hadn't made it very far when a loud crack echoed through the night.

"Get down," Nick urged.

Someone was shooting at them! She instinctively dropped low, ducking behind a tree while covering Joey's body with hers, protecting him the best she could.

They waited motionless for what seemed like an hour but was likely only a few minutes. There was no further gunfire and she wasn't sure if that was good news or bad.

Was the kidnapper tracking them through the woods right now?

"We need to split up," Nick whispered, his mouth close to her ear.

"No! We need to stick together!" she whispered back.

"Listen to me." Nick's tone was harsh. "We need to get help. You and Joey are going to take my phone and head southeast. When you're far enough away, call 911."

"I don't even know where we are," she murmured anxiously.

"The address here is 472 and Highway MM."

She silently repeated it to herself, committing the address to memory.

"I'm going to draw the gunman away from you and Joey. So you need to get moving, now."

"I still think you should come with us," she whispered again. She couldn't help remembering the last time she'd tried to save her son by sending him out of the mangled wreck of their car only to watch him be captured and kidnapped. What if the same thing happened to Nick?

"Go!" he said, and he turned and fired in the direction from which the gunshot had originated. "I'll hold him off long enough for help to arrive."

She hesitated, torn between two impossible choices. She desperately wanted to get Joey to safety, but she also didn't want to leave Nick, unable to bear the thought of anything happening to him. Yet she knew her son was depending on her so she did as Nick asked, staying low and easing back into the cover of the trees, keeping Joey close to her side.

Joey must have understood the acute need for silence since he didn't say a word as they made their way through a particularly thick grove. When they'd gone about twenty yards, she crouched behind a large tree and took out Nick's phone. She unzipped her coat, using the edges of her jacket to help hide the unmistakable glow of the phone screen as she called 911. The operator seemed to take forever to answer, and when she finally did, she hoped she remembered everything correctly.

"Please send help," Rachel said urgently. "Someone is shooting at us and he's also started a fire. The address is 472 and Highway MM."

"Are you hurt?" the dispatcher asked.

"Not yet, but please hurry!" There was another loud crack followed by a cry of pain and she instinctively clutched Joey close, using her body as a shield to cover her son's.

Even though she'd dropped the phone, she could still hear the dispatcher's voice talking. She frantically searched the ground with her fingertips. The snow was cold, making her fingers numb, but she eventually found the phone and powered it off.

"Are you all right?" she asked Joey softly, fearing that the kidnapper had seen them despite her efforts to keep the screen hidden from view. "He didn't hit you, did he?"

"No, I'm not hurt," Joey whispered. "I'm scared."

Her heart ached for him. "I know, but remember what Nick taught us? God is watching over us. God will keep us safe."

Joey nodded solemnly. "I'm going to keep praying."

Tears pricked her eyes. "Me, too." She gave her son a quick hug and then glanced back over her shoulder searching for Nick. Panic swelled in the back of her throat when she couldn't see him. What if he'd been hit? The orange glow from the fire was brighter, indicating that it was beginning to spread.

Dear Lord, please keep Nick safe! Please keep us all safe!

"I smell the bad man," Joey whimpered.

Since all she could smell was smoke, she didn't necessarily believe him. But at that moment, a bright spotlight illuminated the woods, blinding her. The light was only forty feet away! She shoved Joey behind her and tried to edge closer behind an evergreen tree.

"Stay right where you are, Rachel!" a voice shouted. "If you move, I'll keep shooting."

She froze at the familiar voice. *Gerry?* Abruptly, all the puzzle pieces clicked into place. Gerry Ashton always wore strong aftershave, very similar to the kind Joey had spilled in the cabin. And now she clearly recognized his voice.

Her mind wrestled helplessly with the truth. The man she'd trusted more than anyone else in the company had been the one who'd hired Morales to kidnap Joey. Had Gerry also kept her son locked up in his basement? The thought made her furious. To think she'd played right into his hands by begging him to buy her shares of the company. Had he sent the letters, too, pretending to be part of the Mafia?

Gerry was one of the few who'd known about how her father had helped her escape Anthony. Maybe he'd used the Mafia link on purpose to scare her. She wasn't sure if he'd killed Josie Gardner, too, or if the researcher had really committed suicide, but it was clear he intended to kill her and Joey, right here, right now.

Everything suddenly made sense in a sick, horrible way.

How could she have been so blind? So stupid? How could she not have known? Edith must have suspected something wasn't right with Gerry, which was why she'd quit.

She should have asked her assistant for more information. But it was too late now. She forced herself to keep facing Gerry even as she whispered to her son. "Stay hidden behind the tree."

Joey soundlessly moved deeper into the branches. She lifted her arm to shield her eyes against the glare. "Don't shoot!" she shouted. "I'm not armed."

"No, but your boyfriend was." She tried not to react to Gerry's use of the past tense in reference to Nick. "You and Joey need to come back to the cabin, Rachel. Right now," Gerry demanded.

The cabin? Was he crazy? No way was she doing that. What was Gerry thinking to suggest she take her son anywhere near a burning building? If the cabin wasn't on fire yet, it soon would be. She'd rather take her chances getting lost in the woods. But how long could she hold him off? Gerry must know that she'd already called for help, especially if he caught a glimpse of the glow from Nick's cell phone.

And where was Nick?

"Why?" she asked, stalling for time. "Give me one good reason why I should make it easy for you to kill us?"

Another crack shattered the night and she gasped and ducked, half expecting to feel the searing pain from being hit by a bullet.

"That was just a warning shot," Gerry snarled. "Next time, I'll make that kid of yours an orphan."

She sucked in a harsh breath, feeling trapped. If they tried to run, Gerry could easily follow them with the light. She had no idea where Nick was, and she prayed he wasn't lying in the woods, bleeding to death. As the seconds stretched into a full minute, she wondered why Gerry didn't just shoot her and get it over with. What did he hope to gain in this weird cat-and-mouse game?

The glow of the fire burned bright behind Gerry, and suddenly it dawned on her that Gerry wanted them to burn inside the cabin. Maybe he thought that would make their deaths look like a tragic accident. Bullet wounds would be too obvious.

Grimly, she realized he had no intention of letting any of them live through this.

"Why are you doing this, Gerry? You have the money! And the company!" She thought it was best to keep him talking.

"Your father promised the company to me! That idiot Morales was supposed to kill you both. You're too smart for your own good, Rachel. I knew you'd figure out that I was the one behind this sooner or later."

She wasn't about to admit she hadn't realized that until right now. "Why did you decide to take over the company now? Why not back when my dad died?"

"Because Nancy was threatening to divorce me," Gerry said in a vicious tone. "I signed a prenup so I get nothing. I needed that company. And you were going to give all that money to settle the lawsuit!" He released a ragged breath. "You didn't deserve to keep it. But just taking over the company wasn't enough. Everyone kept asking about what it would take to bring you back. Leaving me no choice but to get rid of you both once and for all."

He was crazy, no doubt about it. How were they going to get away?

Another gunshot echoed, and this time she saw the spotlight waver, as if Gerry had ducked.

Nick! Nick was alive!

The next gunshot hit the spotlight dead on, shattering the bulb. But even with the spotlight off, there was too much light from the roaring fire that quickly engulfed the dry timber of the log cabin.

Rachel took the opportunity to move from their current location, urging Joey to stay shielded behind her as they darted around more trees. But then she froze when another crack of gunfire shattered the night.

She whipped around and, from the glow of the fire behind her, Rachel watched Gerry's dark shadow stagger and then finally go down.

She hesitated, torn by indecision. Was Gerry dead? Or at least hurt badly enough that he couldn't keep shooting?

And where was Nick?

She crouched beside her son for long, agonizing moments. She didn't want to risk Joey's life by taking him over to find Nick, but at the same time, she didn't want to leave him here, alone.

"Rachel?" Nick's voice was weak. "Are you and Joey all right?"

Her head shot over to the right, her eyes trying to pierce the darkness. "Yes, we're fine," she called back. "But where are you?"

"Over here." Nick's voice was definitely lacking strength—she could barely hear him over the roaring of the fire. "I've been hit."

Nick kept his eyes glued to where Gerry Ashton's body lay sprawled on the ground. If the man so much as twitched he'd shoot him again.

His eyes blurred and he blinked in an effort to bring the world back into focus. The smoke was getting thicker and he knew he couldn't stay too long. His left arm felt like it was on fire, and the loss of blood was making him dizzy. Figured he'd got hit in the same area as when they'd saved Joey during the money exchange.

Only this time, the injury was much worse. Propped against the tree, he tugged on the string from the hooded sweatshirt he wore, until it came free. Using the string like a tourniquet, he awkwardly wrapped it around his arm and used his teeth to tie it tight. He wanted to drag himself over to make sure Gerry was really dead, but on the off chance that the guy was only pretending in an effort to draw his prey closer, Nick decided it was safer to stay far away.

Where were the cops and the firefighters? He'd heard Rachel calling 911, so he knew reinforcements had to be on the way. Wally's cabin wasn't going to survive the fire, but he was more concerned about the fire spreading through the woods. Drought conditions had hit hard the previous summer, and despite the thin layer of snow covering the ground, he thought the trees were burning too fast.

As if on cue, a large pine tree to the right of the outhouse went up in flames, the tiny needles glowing red as they burned. Knowing they didn't have a lot of time left to get somewhere safe, he forced himself upright, using the tree for support.

"Nick!" He was caught off guard when Joey came running toward him. He opened his mouth to yell at the boy to stay down, when he realized that Gerry hadn't moved, not even an inch despite the fire growing closer.

Joey's second bad guy was finally dead.

"Hey, it's okay," he managed when Joey flung his arms around his waist, burying his face in his stomach. "I'm okay."

"I thought you were dead," the child sobbed.

Rachel looked upset at Joey's statement. "Where are you hit?" she asked.

"My left arm same as before, but never mind that, now. We need to get as far away from the fire as we can. It's been so dry up here that the fire will soon burn out of control."

"Lean on me," Rachel offered, slipping her shoulder beneath his injured arm and sliding her other hand around his waist.

He didn't like the fact that he was so weak that he had little choice but to allow her to help him. Surprisingly, Joey went around on the other side of him, and together they moved as quickly as possible away from the fire.

"Joey, can you find the gravel driveway?" he asked, since his vision was blurry again.

"I think so," Joey said. "This way!"

The three of them stumbled toward the direction of the driveway with a deep sense of urgency. Nick refused to look back over his shoulder, too afraid he'd see the fire nipping hotly at their heels.

There was another loud whooshing sound, and he knew another tree had gone up in flames. They had to get out of here, and fast!

When the gravel crunched beneath his feet, he let out a sigh of relief. Joey's sense of direction had been perfect. They continued moving as fast as they could, putting more distance between them and the raging fire. The smoke was still hanging thick between the trees.

He coughed and a spear of pain shot down his arm. He ignored it, more concerned when he heard Rachel and Joey coughing, too. How much time did they have before they succumbed to smoke inhalation?

Dear Lord, show us the way to safety.

"Come on, Nick, don't give up now!" Rachel urged in a raspy voice. Obviously the smoke was getting to her, too. And what about Joey? He was so young that Nick was afraid it wouldn't take long for the smoke to damage the boy's lungs.

He hadn't realized his steps were lagging behind, and he forced himself to move faster for both Rachel and Joey's sake. They deserved a chance to get out of here, alive.

Within five minutes, Nick practically fell over the hood of the car, and he slumped against the metal frame gratefully. For the first time in hours, he allowed himself a flash of hope. "Maybe we can drive out of here," he proposed, fumbling in his pockets for the keys. He found them and tugged them free. "Think you're up to it?"

"I'll try," Rachel said, jumping eagerly at his suggestion. She stepped forward to take the keys, and she opened the driver's door. But before she could slide inside, a man appeared out of the woods, holding a rifle.

"Don't move," he barked loudly.

"Karl!" Rachel exclaimed. Then, in a move that was so subtle Nick almost missed it, she pushed Joey behind her, probably intending for him to climb into the safety of the car. "What are you doing? Why do you have a gun?"

Karl? Nick stared in shocked surprise as he realized that the stranger was Dr. Karl Errol, the researcher he'd suspected was secretly working for Global Pharmaceuticals. His instincts must have been right on. The researcher must have purposefully set up Rachel's company to fail. But seeing him here, as if he'd teamed up with Gerry Ashton, didn't make much sense. Why would the researcher who'd tried to destroy Rachel's company work alongside Ashton, who clearly wanted to take over the company himself?

He didn't know for sure, but obviously Errol wasn't messing around. The way he held the rifle in his hands told Nick he wouldn't hesitate to kill them.

FIFTEEN

Nick gritted his teeth as Rachel tried to reason with Karl Errol. "Gerry is dead, Karl. You don't have to do this. Just let us go."

"I'm not working for Gerry," Errol said finally. "And my boss isn't going to accept failure."

Nick tried to think of a way out of this mess. But he couldn't come up with a safe option. Granted, he still had his weapon, but he didn't dare try to take Errol out while the guy held the rifle pointed directly at Rachel. Maybe if he was at full strength he could rush the guy, catching him off guard.

But he'd lost too much blood to risk it. He was far more likely to fall flat on his face before he reached Errol. He seriously felt as if a strong breeze would blow him over.

"Who's your boss, Karl? Why are you doing this?" Rachel asked, taking a step toward him. It was all Nick could do not to shout at her to stay back. "Have you really been working for Global Pharmaceuticals this whole time? Why? Why did you hate me so much you wanted to put me out of business?"

Errol shook his head, as if waging an inner war with

himself. "I didn't have a choice. I followed Ashton here and waited, hoping he'd take care of things for me. But he botched the job. Leaving me no choice."

Nick tried to take heart in knowing the guy hadn't shot them yet, even though he'd had time. Maybe there was a way to get through to him.

But how?

"There's no point in trying to reason with him, Rachel. He doesn't care about anyone but himself. I told you he killed Josie Gardener," Nick told her in a scathing tone. "She stumbled upon the truth and was going to let you know what she'd found out. So he killed her and set the whole thing up to look like a suicide."

"No!" Errol shouted. "I loved Josie! I would never hurt her. But she didn't love me."

A cold chill snaked down his spine. Now they were getting somewhere. "Who did she love, Karl?" he asked mildly.

"Ashton." Errol's tone reeked of loathing. "But that jerk didn't deserve her love. He had an affair with her even though he had no intention of leaving his rich wife."

"Ashton is dead. He won't hurt anyone ever again, Karl." Rachel's tone was soothing. She took another small step forward, holding her hand out. "Just put down the gun and we'll work this through, okay?"

"Stop!" he screamed. "You can't fix this. Don't you understand? I did it for Josie! I secretly worked for Global to make enough money to compete with Ashton. I told her I could afford to buy her nice things, and take her to fancy places. But she didn't care! She wanted to live in sin as Ashton's mistress rather than to give me the chance to make her happy."

Slowly the picture became clear. "Are you saying that Ashton killed Josie?" Rachel asked incredulously.

"Yes, because she was pressuring him to leave his wife. Maybe he was afraid she'd tell his wife about the affair. And if he divorced his wife he'd lose all the big bucks he'd gotten accustomed to spending. But none of that matters anymore." He blew out an angry breath. "I'm glad Ashton's dead. You saved me the trouble of killing him. But, unfortunately, I have no choice but to kill you, too." Errol tightened his grip on the gun.

"Wait! You do have a choice. What if I promise not to press charges against you?" Rachel asked in a desperate tone. "Then will you put the gun down? I promise I won't turn you in to the authorities. All I want is to go home with my son."

For a moment Nick thought she may have convinced Errol with her heartfelt plea. But then Karl slowly brought the rifle up to shoulder height and bent his head forward as if to take aim.

"No!" Joey came charging out from the back end of the car carrying a thick tree branch. His shout startled Karl enough that he jerked around toward Joey's direction, shooting wildly.

"Joey," Rachel shrieked.

The boy didn't stop. He must not have been hit by the wild shot, because he swung the tree branch with all his might, aiming at Karl's knees.

Nick made a split-second decision, gathering every ounce of his strength to propel himself across the small clearing toward Errol. As the guy fell down, howling in agony, Nick kicked the rifle up and out of the way and threw himself on top of the researcher.

Within moments, Rachel had the rifle safely in her hands. "Get out of the way," she shouted.

Nick rolled off Errol and she quickly brought the heavy stock down on Errol's head, knocking him unconscious.

The sound of sirens, hopefully from both ambulances and fire trucks, echoed through the night. Finally, there was hope that help was soon to arrive. He didn't have the strength to move, so he stayed right where he was.

"Joey, are you all right?" Rachel asked.

"Yes. I was afraid he was going to shoot you." Nick heard the boy's footsteps creeping forward. "Nick? Are you okay?"

He tried to crack a smile. "Fine, buddy. Just tired. I'm going to rest for a minute, okay?"

Rachel dropped to her knees beside him. "Come on, Nick," she pleaded. "You can't stay here—you need to get up! Karl isn't dead and we can't be here when he wakes up."

The panic in her tone pierced his soul, so he pushed himself upright with his good arm, biting back a groan of pain. He was still dizzy and knew he'd already lost too much blood. The artery in his arm must be nicked.

Somehow, with Rachel and Joey's help, he managed to get back on his feet. The three of them staggered toward the car and he leaned against the frame gratefully. There was no telling how long Errol would remain unconscious, so he knew they had to get out of there, and quickly. "Rachel, do you still have the car keys? Let's see if we can drive out of here."

"Good idea." Rachel slid behind the wheel and jammed the key into the ignition. He closed his eyes in despair when he heard a *click-click* as she attempted to start the car.

"I'm sorry, Nick," Rachel lamented, and got out of the car. "Either Karl or Gerry must have done something to the engine."

He opened his eyes and nodded wearily. "I shouldn't be surprised. Guess we'll have to try and make it to the highway by walking."

"Nick, you're bleeding!" Joey exclaimed.

He glanced down and winced when he saw the dark stain of blood smeared across the palm of Joey's hand. "Yeah, but it's just a scratch," he said, downplaying his injury. "I'll be fine as soon as the ambulance gets here."

Joey still looked horrified, and he hated knowing he was causing the child to be afraid again. Hadn't the poor kid been through enough? He'd never forget the way Joey went charging after Errol with the tree branch. The kid was a true hero. "Listen, Joey, can you hear the sirens? The police will be here soon. Everything's going to be all right."

"Let's go, Nick." Rachel slid her arm around his waist, putting her shoulder under his arm to help support him. He silently prayed for strength as they made their way down the rest of the gravel driveway. The hazy smoke made it difficult to see and to breathe. The three of them coughed as they walked. He could barely see a few feet in front of his face, so he had no way of knowing if they were anywhere close to the highway.

After about ten minutes, he could feel his strength waning, even with Rachel trying to take most of his weight. He stumbled on a large rock and knew he was going to fall. Instantly, he let go of both Rachel and Joey so he wouldn't take them down with him. He groaned loudly when he hit the ground, hard. For a moment everything went black and he stopped fighting, stopped struggling, welcoming the darkness.

"Nick! Are you all right?" From far away, he could feel someone shaking him and calling his name. Rachel? He didn't have the strength to reassure her.

Once he'd prayed for the Lord to take him so he could be with his wife and daughter again. But it hadn't been his time. Was God going to take him now? Just when he'd found Rachel? He didn't want to leave Rachel and Joey, but he didn't have the strength to fight anymore.

"Take me home, Lord," he whispered. "I'm ready to come home."

"Nick!" Rachel tried not to panic as she stripped away his coat so she could look at his arm. Not that she would be able to see much in the darkness.

"Is Nick going to die?" Joey asked, his voice trembling with fear.

"Not if I can help it," she muttered. Nick's jacket wouldn't come off and she soon realized he'd tied a string around the upper part of his left arm in an attempt to stop the bleeding.

"No, God wants me home...." he muttered, weakly pushing her hands away.

Rachel couldn't believe Nick was just going to give up. She remembered him mentioning his wife and daughter were up in heaven. Was he willing to give up his life in order to be with them again? Didn't she and Joey mean anything to him?

Maybe not, but that was too bad. She wasn't ready to let him go. She untied the string and yanked the jacket sleeve off. His blood-soaked sweatshirt confirmed her worst fears.

He was hit badly, far worse than he'd let on.

Working quickly, she felt for the worst part of the injury, trying not to wince when her fingers sank into the open wound. Once she'd found it, she retied the string around his arm above the injured area. What else could she use to stop the bleeding? She shrugged out of her coat, took off her sweatshirt and then put her coat back on. Using the sleeve of her sweatshirt, figuring it was cleaner than the hood, she balled it up and pressed it against the gouged area across Nick's biceps.

"Come on, Nick. Help me out here," she urged as she leaned all her weight against him, hoping to slow the blood loss. But Nick didn't move, didn't so much as flutter an eyelash.

"Wake up, Nick," Joey said, shaking Nick's other arm. "You have to wake up!"

The sounds of sirens grew louder. "Hang in there, Nick. The ambulance is almost here!"

Still, Nick didn't respond, not even when the ambulance and the firefighters arrived. Two paramedics came over to help Nick while the rest of the firefighters headed in with a huge water truck to the wooded area to douse the fire.

"He's lost a lot of blood," Rachel cautioned, when the two paramedics nudged her aside.

"Let's get an IV in, stat!" the female paramedic said curtly.

"I've got it," the younger man replied. "Fluids wide open until we can get the O neg blood flowing."

"His blood pressure is low—I'll get the packed red blood cells out of the ambulance," the woman continued.

She darted away and returned with a small cooler less than two minutes later. She quickly opened the cooler and took out what looked like packages of blood.

Rachel kept Joey close to her side as they watched the two paramedics work on Nick. Once they had the blood infusing into his veins, they brought over a gurney and began to strap him securely onto it.

"Could we go with you? Please?" Rachel asked, stepping forward. "Our car has been tampered with and we don't have a ride out of here. There's also a man who tried to kill us still back in the woods."

The two paramedics grimaced. "I'm sorry, but that's against the rules," the younger man said.

"Besides, the police will want to talk to you, especially if there's still a threat here in the area," the female paramedic added kindly. "We're taking him to Madison General Hospital and I'm sure one of the officers will give you a ride."

Her heart sank, but she also knew they were right. She had little choice but to stand there with her arm around Joey and watch as they bundled Nick into the ambulance.

"Do you think God will listen if we pray for Nick?" Joey asked, after the paramedic jumped into the driver's seat, started the engine and pulled out onto the highway.

She gathered him close and nodded. "Absolutely, Joey," she responded. "Dear Lord, we ask You to please keep Nick safe in Your care. Amen."

"Amen," Joey echoed.

Tears burned her eyes as she realized that no matter what happened moving forward, her son was going to be hurt by Nick's leaving. Because he already cared about Nick, already saw him as some sort of surrogate father.

And she couldn't blame him, because if she were honest with herself, she'd admit she was falling for Nick, too. Maybe he didn't feel the same way, but she couldn't imagine a life without him.

Please, Lord, let him live!

"What do you mean you can't find Karl?" Rachel asked, her tone rising incredulously. With the smoke growing thicker in the woods despite the firefighters' attempt to douse the raging flames, the police officer had stashed her and Joey in the squad car while they went searching for the scientist. "He was lying on the ground about twenty feet away from the car. You found the car, right?"

"Yes, ma'am, we found the vehicle. And we looked all over but didn't find any sign of the research doctor or the weapon." The tall, dark-haired police officer had introduced himself as Sean McCarthy.

Rachel shivered and hugged Joey. The thought of Karl Errol being out on the loose in the woods with his rifle wasn't at all reassuring. She wished now that she had taken the gun with her. She glanced through the passenger-side window, hoping that Karl had taken the opportunity to escape rather than to seek revenge.

She could still barely comprehend that Gerry Ashton had decided to kill her and Joey as retaliation for her father giving her the company. And because he thought she was onto him. She felt sick to her stomach, thinking about how she'd been duped by the man she'd trusted.

Once again, her instincts had led her wrong.

"You say you believe Karl Errol was secretly working for Global Pharmaceuticals?" Officer McCarthy asked.

"That's what he admitted to. I'm still having trouble

understanding how two people hated me enough to try and kill me."

"Can't say that I have much experience with corporate espionage," McCarthy admitted.

"Me, either," she murmured. She didn't want to think about greed and corruption anymore. Right now, she wanted to see Nick. To make sure he was all right.

"Officer McCarthy, will you please take us to Madison General Hospital?" she asked, willing to beg if necessary. It seemed as if hours had passed since the ambulance had driven away with Nick. She wanted nothing more than to get far away from this place where Nick had almost died and where she and Joey had feared for their lives, too. "We've given you our statements. It's not like we can't discuss this in more detail later, right?"

Officer McCarthy hesitated but then nodded. "All right. We'll head over to the hospital. If Detective Butler is awake, I'll get his statement, as well."

Her shoulders slumped with relief. She didn't bother telling the officer that the likelihood of Nick answering any questions was slim to none. She wouldn't be at all surprised to find that Nick was already in surgery, having the injury to his arm repaired. If he survived long enough to get to surgery.

No, she refused to believe the worst. God was surely watching over Nick. He'd been a good Christian his entire life.

She didn't even want to consider the alternative. That God would take Nick home to be with his wife and daughter.

The ride to the hospital didn't take too long, although Joey was half asleep by the time they arrived. With Officer McCarthy as their escort, they made their way to the waiting area and were given a quick update about Nick's condition.

"Detective Butler is still in surgery," the woman behind the desk informed them. "But he should be out soon. Now tell me what relation are you to the patient?"

Rachel swallowed hard. "I— We're good friends. He, uh, has sisters, but I don't know how to get in touch with them." She knew he had parents, although she wasn't sure how to contact them, either. How was it that she was more familiar with the names of his dead wife and daughter than his living family members?

Maybe calling herself a friend was stretching the truth. She was just a woman who'd needed Nick's protection and his expertise. Nothing more, nothing less.

The kiss they'd shared didn't mean anything. And she'd be stupid to think it had.

She and Joey went to sit down, and soon Joey was snuggled against her, falling asleep. She tucked Officer McCarthy's business card in her pocket and let her head drop back against the wall.

As soon as they found Karl Errol, this nightmare would really be over. She and Joey could go back home to their normal lives. Granted there would still be some red tape before the money was returned her, but she was convinced it would all work out.

She wondered how long Nick would have to stay off duty as a result of his gunshot wound and hoped it wouldn't be too long. Grimly, she realized there was no way she'd ever be able to repay him for everything he'd done for her and for Joey.

He'd put his life and his career on the line for them. More than once. Without Nick's help she wouldn't have managed to get Joey back.

Not only had he kept them both safe, but he'd also taught them to believe in God.

Yet all she could offer in return was to pray for him to recover with the full use of his arm.

"Ms. Simon?" A hand shook her awake and she blinked, momentarily confused as to where she was. Then she recognized the unmistakable antiseptic smell of a hospital.

"What?" She winced when her neck muscles tightened painfully as she turned toward the hospital employee. "Nick? Is he out of surgery?"

"Yes. The doctor is on his way down to talk to you."

Joey was still asleep beside her and she tried not to wake him as she eased away. She rubbed her hands over her gritty eyes and was surprised to find that the sky outside was beginning to lighten.

A harried surgeon wearing green scrubs came into the room. "Ms. Simon? I'm Dr. Wagner. Detective Butler's surgery went well. We were able to save his arm, although it was touch and go for a while as his brachial artery was injured. He's just about finished in the recovery area and then will be sent to the ICU where they can watch him more closely." He smiled compassionately. "You'll be able to visit him in about forty-five minutes or so."

Her mind was spinning with all the information he'd told her. Although she was certainly relieved that Nick had made it through the surgery, she still couldn't help worrying. "Is there any way he could still lose his arm?" she asked.

For a moment hesitation shadowed the doctor's eyes. "We're going to keep a close eye on his circulation. If there's any change, we'll take him back to surgery. We'll know more after twenty-four hours or so."

Rachel nodded to indicate she understood. "Thank you," she whispered.

The doctor flashed a brief smile before he turned and left. Joey woke up, complaining that he was hungry. Unfortunately, Rachel didn't have any money on her, not even an ID. They'd left everything they had in the cabin, which was likely burned beyond repair by now.

"Here, these are meal passes for the cafeteria," the woman behind the desk said, offering up two small plastic cards. "They're worth about five dollars each."

"Thank you so much," Rachel murmured, taking them gratefully. Getting something to eat would help pass the time until she and Joey could visit Nick in the ICU.

It was closer to an hour later before the ICU called down for them. She held tightly on to Joey's hand as they went into the critical-care area. Nick's room was the second door on the left, so they cautiously approached.

"He looks bad, Mom," Joey choked out, his eyes filling with tears. "He looks like he's going to die."

"Joey, listen to me. The doctor said Nick is stable. He wouldn't lie to us. It's just that Nick is connected to lots of machines right now." She did her best to soothe her son, although she felt just as awful seeing Nick like this.

Rachel stepped forward and took Nick's uninjured hand in hers. "Nick, it's me, Rachel. Joey is here, too. The doctor said you're going to be fine. Do you hear me? You're going to be just fine."

Nick's eyelids fluttered for a moment and he looked directly at her. She smiled. "They said your arm should heal. I don't want you to worry about anything, okay?"

"Where am I?" he asked, his eyes full of confusion.

She tried not to let her fear show. "You're at the hospital in Madison. You just had surgery on your arm."

"But I—can't feel my arm," he whispered in agony.

"Your arm is right here." She patted the heavily bandaged limb gently. "The doctor said there's a good chance you'll make a full recovery." She made sure her tone was encouraging.

"I can't—" Nick stopped, closed his eyes, and turned his head away as if shutting her out.

Rejection seared her soul and she stepped back, keeping her expression neutral for Joey's sake. She didn't want to leave, but he'd made his feelings clear. Did he really think he was going to lose his arm? Where was his faith in God?

She didn't want to think that Nick preferred to be alone through this difficult time, but really, how much did she truly know about him? Maybe he only wanted his family here. Like his parents or his sisters.

She was just a woman he'd gone out of his way to help. Obviously, there was nothing more for her to do here.

She took a deep breath, trying to ease her heartache. This was why she'd avoided becoming emotionally involved. Only this time, she wasn't the only one who would be hurt.

Joey's heart would be broken, as well.

SIXTEEN

Nick fought the rising sense of despair. The doctor had told him that they'd saved his arm, but what was the point if he couldn't use it? His entire career would be over.

He shifted and groaned, and pain slashed through his left arm, robbing him of his breath. Was it a good thing to know he could feel pain? He forced his eyes open and stared at the heavily bandaged limb. His fingers were hugely swollen and no matter how much he tried, he couldn't move them. He concentrated on feeling them move, but no luck.

Nothing. He felt nothing.

With a disgusted sigh, he closed his eyes again, feeling guilty for the way he'd treated Rachel and Joey. They hadn't deserved his anger. He should be thanking God for saving his life, but instead he was focusing on the fact that his arm might never work right again.

Shame burned the back of his throat. He'd taught Rachel and Joey about having faith but couldn't manage to keep his own. Obviously, he owed them an apology.

But where had they gone? Now that he was awake, the pain in his arm throbbed in conjunction with the beat of his heart. His throat was still sore, no doubt from the smoke he'd inhaled out in the woods.

Abruptly, he wondered how Rachel and Joey were doing. After all, they'd inhaled a fair amount of smoke, too. Had they been checked out by a doctor? He shifted in the bed again, and a loud series of beeping noises brought a nurse running into his room.

"Relax, Mr. Butler, you need to calm down."

He almost corrected her—he was a detective, not a mister—but didn't want to waste his energy. "I need to know if Rachel and Joey Simon are both patients here, too," he croaked.

The nurse frowned down at him, as if she were worried about him. "They were here visiting you about twenty minutes ago, don't you remember?"

Twenty minutes? For some reason he thought it had been just a few minutes ago. "Are they still here?"

"I'll check for you, but you have to stay calm," the nurse said firmly. "The doctors spent a lot of time reconstructing the brachial artery in your arm. I can guarantee they won't appreciate having you damage their hard work by trying to get out of bed."

"Just find Rachel and Joey for me," he managed, not bothering to explain that he couldn't move his left arm if he tried.

The nurse left the room and it seemed like a long time before she came back carrying a small IV bag. "I have your antibiotic here," she said as she logged into the computer. "Just give me a few minutes here, okay?"

He did his best to give her the time she needed to scan his wristband and the medication, before she hung it on the IV pump. Only when she finished did he ask. "Rachel and Joey?"

"I'm sorry, but apparently they went home," she said, her tone full of sympathy.

Home? How? As far as he knew Rachel didn't have any money or a vehicle. Had she hitched a ride with someone? Borrowed money? What?

He stared at the four walls surrounding him, feeling totally helpless. He was in no condition to follow Rachel, to make sure she and Joey were still safe. Had the police arrested Errol? He certainly hoped so. No doubt they'd be here soon to get his statement about the events that had transpired outside of Uncle Wally's cabin.

Still, he couldn't believe Rachel and Joey had left without saying goodbye.

Exhaustion weighed heavily on Rachel's shoulders as she and her son made their way back down to the hospital waiting room. She needed to figure out a way to get home, no easy feat since Chicago was about three hours from Madison. A taxi was probably out of the question, which left a bus or a train.

When she asked the woman at the front desk about a train, she shook her head. "Sorry, there's bus service to Chicago, but no train."

Of course there wasn't a train. Why would anything be easy? She was about to ask about borrowing a phone, when the police officer who'd brought her and Joey to the hospital arrived. "Ms. Simon? Could we talk for a few minutes?"

Did she really have a choice? She forced a smile, knowing that her bad mood wasn't Officer McCarthy's fault. "Sure."

"Let's talk in the chapel across the hall," the policeman suggested. "There's more privacy."

She nodded and drew Joey along with her as they crossed over to the chapel. She sank into a wooden pew and gazed at the simple yet beautifully crafted stained glass cross over the mantel. She imagined this room was used by many family members praying for their loved ones to get better.

Unfortunately, Nick didn't want her anywhere near him while he was recovering. He'd rather face his unknown future on his own.

She forced herself to push away her painful thoughts. "What can I do for you?"

"I just want to go through the events one more time," Officer McCarthy explained. "We found the dead body of Gerald Ashton, as you mentioned before. But we still haven't found the man you referred to as Dr. Karl Errol. And I have to tell you, the vehicle that was parked there is gone, too."

She shivered, hoping Karl had taken the car to parts unknown. Although certainly they could trace the car's license plates? Officer McCarthy assured her they were looking for the vehicle. So she took a deep breath and began describing the events of the night before. Midway through, Sean McCarthy interrupted, asking her to start at the beginning.

With a sigh, she went back to the night Joey was kidnapped, explaining what they'd done. The officer's expression was grim by the time she finished. "I'm not sure if that cop of yours deserves a medal or a demotion," he said. "You're lucky things didn't turn out worse."

She thought Nick definitely deserved a medal, but she didn't say anything. "Look, Officer McCarthy, Joey and I need to figure out a way to get back to Chicago."

"I can give you a ride to the bus station, if that helps," he offered.

She smiled wanly and nodded. As much as it went against the grain to ask for handouts, they'd need money for bus tickets. "Would you loan me the money for tickets? I promise I'll pay you back."

There was the slightest hesitation before he nodded. "Sure, no problem."

Relief at having one problem solved was overwhelming. "Thank you so much," she whispered.

Officer McCarthy looked uncomfortable but gave a brief nod. "Okay, let's go then. I'll come back later to get Butler's statement. He's not going anywhere soon, and I'll probably get a more coherent story once he's feeling a little better."

Thinking of Nick made her sad all over again, but she tried to hide her feelings from Joey. They followed Officer McCarthy to where he'd left his car, parked right in front of the hospital in a clear no-parking zone. The traffic around Madison was crazy busy and the ride to the bus station seemed interminable. Staring out the window to calm her frayed nerves, the Christmas decorations reminded her that the holiday was only two days away.

Inside the bus station, Officer McCarthy used his credit card to pay for their tickets, and then he handed them some cash. "Get something for you and the boy to eat," he said roughly. "And I hope you have a merry Christmas."

Tears pricked her eyes at his kindness and she'd already made a note of how much money she owed him. "Thanks again, for everything," she said softly. "And I hope you have a merry Christmas with your family, as well."

He gave both of them a nod before making his way back outside. She sank into one of the hard plastic chairs inside the bus station since the next bus didn't leave until twelve-thirty in the afternoon. Thankfully, just a few hours more and they'd be on their way home.

Waiting was the worst, but finally they boarded the bus and settled into their seats. The bus was busy with what looked like college kids heading home to their families. The ride to Chicago took much longer than she'd anticipated, partially because of the frequent stops and then because of the heavy traffic the closer they came to the city.

While they were stuck in a snarling traffic jam, Rachel realized that she didn't have her house keys. She hadn't been home since the night of Joey's kidnapping. She'd left her mangled car with the keys in it at the scene of the crash as every ounce of energy had been focused on finding her son.

With a groan, she rested her forehead on the cold glass window and realized she'd have to take a taxi to her office to pick up her spare set of keys. Yet another delay before she and Joey would finally get home.

She could hardly wait.

Nick stared at Officer McCarthy in horror. "What do you mean you didn't find Errol? And now my car is missing? Are you telling me he's still out there on the loose?" The monitor above his head sounded an alarm and he took a deep breath, trying to calm his racing heart.

"Yes. That's exactly what I'm telling you. The only body we found was Gerald Ashton's. He died of a gunshot wound to his chest."

Nick momentarily closed his eyes, feeling bad that

he'd taken a life. He'd been protecting Rachel and Joey after being wounded himself. But that didn't really make him feel better.

"Where's Rachel? And Joey? We need to keep them safe in case Errol decides to come after them."

"I took them to the bus station, bought them tickets to get home and gave them a little extra cash so they could get something to eat."

"You *what?*" Nick shouted, and this time, he didn't care about the beeping alarms. He tried to throw off the covers and make his way to the side of the bed, but it wasn't easy when his left arm was wrapped up tighter than a mummy. The doctors had explained the numbness was due to some sort of pain block they'd put in, which made him feel even more like an idiot for the way he'd acted toward Rachel.

But nothing was going to stop him from doing the right thing—now.

"Mr. Butler!" his nurse cried as she came running into the room. "What are you doing?"

"It's Detective Butler," he ground out between clenched teeth, trying to ignore the sweat that beaded on his brow. "And I'm getting out of here."

"You can't leave!" The nurse looked appalled and she crossed the room to push him back into bed even as she called out for help.

Frustrated to discover he didn't have the strength of a gnat, he threw a desperate glance at McCarthy. "Help me out, here. Don't you understand? Rachel and Joey are in danger as long as Karl Errol is still on the loose! The guy is working for Global Pharmaceuticals."

"I'm calling your doctor," the nurse threatened, acting as if she hadn't heard a word he said. Or maybe she just didn't care.

"Yeah, you do that," Nick said with a disgusted sigh. "Because I'm pretty sure I have the right to leave against medical advice."

"Only if you can make it out of here without passing out cold," the nurse said tersely, holding his gaze with bold determination.

"Now, just hold on a minute," McCarthy said, holding up his hand and trying to wedge himself between Nick and the nurse. "If you really think Ms. Simon and her son are in danger, I'll help you. No need to act like a lunatic."

Nick couldn't help feeling like a lunatic. He couldn't explain the bad feeling he had about the way Rachel and Joey had left him. Without saying goodbye. Without having Karl Errol in custody. That creep actually had his car!

"Fine," he bit out, knowing that he didn't have the strength to stay seated on the side of his bed for much longer. "What's the plan?"

"How about if I send some backup out to meet Ms. Simon and her son at the Chicago bus depot," McCarthy offered. "They can drive her home, stick around a bit to make sure everything's all right."

It was a start, but not good enough. "We need to get to Chicago, ASAP. I need you to help me get out of here," he said to McCarthy. "I'll need help since I can barely keep myself upright. We need to get to Rachel before Errol does."

"I don't know if that's a good idea," McCarthy hedged.

"I do. Trust me—I'll take full responsibility for my decision." Last year, Jonah had been in a similar situation, leaving the hospital against doctor's orders. And he'd been fine.

Nick had to believe everything would work out fine this time, too.

Dear Lord, please give me the strength I need to keep Rachel and Joey safe.

Rachel held on to Joey's hand tightly as they navigated the crowds at the bus depot. Without luggage, it was easy to push her way through the swarming mass of people to the door, and before long they found their way to the taxi stand. Now that they were back in Chicago, she couldn't wait to get home. But first a quick trip to her office building.

Her desperation must have shown as a taxi came barreling to a stop right in front of her. She thought she heard someone call her name but then figured she was imagining things. She urged Joey in first and climbed in after him.

"Where to?" the cabbie asked in a thick Middle Eastern accent.

"Simon Incorporated," she told him, rattling off the address. He nodded and pulled out into traffic, earning a loud protest from the guy behind him.

She almost closed her eyes, because the taxi drivers in Chicago were maniacs behind the wheel, and she always expected to get in a crash. But somehow, miraculously, they always managed to get to their destinations unscathed.

"Are we home yet?" Joey asked plaintively. She knew he was exhausted, and he'd truly taken everything in stride better than she could have expected.

"Almost. We're going to stop by my office first, so I can pay the taxi driver and get our house keys," she said in a hushed voice, hoping the driver didn't understand

English very well. She didn't think he'd have agreed to take her anywhere knowing that she didn't have anything more than ten dollars in her pocket, courtesy of Officer McCarthy's donation. She intended to get a check in the mail to him first thing in the morning, thanking him again for helping her out.

Joey sighed heavily but didn't whine or complain.

The traffic worked against them again, and she kept a wary eye on the time, hoping they'd get there before the office building shut down for the day. It was almost five o'clock in the evening and already pitch-black outside, except for the brightly lit buildings and the various Christmas decorations, of course.

She chewed her lower lip nervously. Hopefully, even if everyone was gone, the security guards would let her upstairs. Maybe Gerry hadn't had time to completely take over her company. Just the thought of explaining how Gerry had died was enough to overwhelm her.

It was five-fifteen when the taxi driver pulled up in front of her building. "Keep the meter running... I'll be right back."

"No! You pay first!" he protested.

"Look, I promise you I'll be back. We need to get home. I don't have a car."

He stared at her with eyes black as midnight but then he nodded. "If you not back soon, I come after you."

She breathed a tiny sigh of relief. "I will, I promise." Sliding out from the backseat, she waited for Joey to join her and headed inside.

Carrie, the perky receptionist, left promptly at five, but there was a security guard seated in her spot. Being inside the office building after being gone for so long seemed a little strange yet, at the same time, blessedly familiar. "George, how are you? How are the kids?"

"Great, Ms. Simon, just great. What are you doing here so late?"

"I forgot something up in my office. Would you mind letting me use the master key?" She hoped and prayed that Gerry hadn't told everyone to keep her out of the building.

"Sure, no problem." George held out a key. "Just bring it back when you leave."

"I will." She didn't hesitate, but went straight over to the bank of elevators. The doors opened immediately, taking them all the way to the tenth floor without a single stop.

She unlocked the door, noting that the entire office area was completely dark, as if everyone had gone home early. And considering it was nearly Christmas, she understood why. She flipped on lights as she walked down the hall to her office.

Her door stood open, which she thought was a little odd. Edith always kept the door closed and locked when Rachel wasn't there. Then again, the woman had given her notice. For all she knew, Edith hadn't even shown up for work today.

Hovering in the doorway, she reached inside to flip on the lights. She blinked for a moment so that her eyes could adjust before crossing the room to her desk and rummaging for cash and her keys. Joey plopped into her desk chair, spinning from side to side.

She was relieved to find her secret stash of bills was right where she'd left it. She grabbed the money and the spare set of keys.

"I've been waiting for you, Rachel."

The voice came from the hallway, and she swallowed a scream when she jerked her head up to see Karl Errol standing in the shadows. Her heart dropped to her stomach when she realized he'd traded the rifle for a small handgun, which he pointed directly at her. From this distance it would be hard for him to miss.

"Karl!" She faced him in the doorway, making sure to keep Joey behind her, hoping her son would figure out a way to slide down behind the desk. All the while, she kept her eyes locked on the research scientist. She couldn't believe Karl was here. How did he know that she'd stop by on her way home? Or had he planned to wait for her all night, surprising her in the morning? She swallowed hard, wishing she'd asked George to come up with her.

How long did she have to stall here before the cabbie came looking for his money? Or would he simply give up and drive away? She tried not to think the worst. "I'm so glad you're all right. We looked everywhere for you!"

"Yeah, right. You left me there to die, Rachel," he sneered with obvious reproach. "Good thing I still had the distributor cap for the car, hmm?"

"What do you want, Karl?" she asked, fed up with pandering to his ego. "What more could you possibly want from me?"

"I need to finish what I started," he said enigmatically. "I always finish the job."

"Why?" she asked helplessly, tired of the games. "Haven't you caused enough damage? You've ruined my company's reputation, and for what? Love? You don't have the faintest idea what true love is. Josie never would have accepted your love if she knew what you've done."

She couldn't help thinking of Nick. How she'd left

him in the hospital without even giving him a chance to explain what he'd gone through. Maybe he had shut her out, believing the worst about the damage to his arm, but sooner or later, he would have come around. If she'd learned anything about faith, it was that leaning on God's strength could help you through the darkest days. She was suddenly ashamed of her actions. She should have stayed. She should have given him a second chance.

Should have told him how she felt.

Now she could only hope and pray she wasn't too late.

"Do you honestly think that Detective Butler won't figure out that you're the one who killed me?" she continued, since Karl hadn't responded. "He's not stupid, Karl. I promise Nick won't rest until he finds you and makes sure that you spend the rest of your life behind bars."

"I have protection. My boss will protect me."

"Protection? From your boss? William Hanson, the CEO of Global? Or the Mafia?"

The way Karl reacted to William Hanson's name let her know she'd nailed it correctly. For once she didn't mind being wrong about the Mafia connection.

"You think William Hanson cares about you? I'm betting that as soon as you kill me, he'll do whatever it takes to get rid of you."

Karl scowled. "He won't kill me—I helped him out. He's already beaten you to market with a new diabetes drug. One that doesn't cause blood clots."

The thought of Karl purposefully ruining the new medication she'd put out to market made her seethe with anger. Not just because of her company's reputation, but because of the innocent people he'd hurt.

"So why kill me if Global has the new medication out?"

"My boss doesn't like loose ends. And since Ashton

couldn't manage to do my dirty work for me, I have no choice but to finish this on my own."

Her heart leaped into her throat when he lifted the gun. "No matter what you do to me, Nick won't stop searching for you. I've already told the police about you, too. You'll never be safe, Karl."

Karl didn't answer; instead, he simply stared at her as if he hadn't heard a word she'd said. She had no way of knowing if she'd even gotten through to him.

She tried not to panic. Facing a crazy man with a gun was much harder when she didn't have Nick's reassuring presence nearby. But she'd left Nick back at the hospital in Madison.

She and Joey were on their own.

SEVENTEEN

Nick dozed during the long ride back to Chicago. Even with Sean McCarthy using flashing red lights and sirens, the trip took longer than he wanted. The doctor back in Madison had been really angry about him leaving, but he couldn't worry about his arm.

Rachel and Joey were far more important.

They swung by Rachel's house, which thankfully wasn't that far from her office building, but the place was locked up tight with no sign of anyone having been there. He told Sean to head over to the office building next, figuring that Rachel probably needed her keys.

When they reached the office complex, Sean parked behind a taxi with the "in service" light on. Nick managed to get out of the passenger seat under his own power, holding his left arm protectively against his body to minimize the pain as much as possible. Now that the numbing agent had worn off, he could feel his arm, but mostly all he felt was pain.

When they walked into the building there was a foreign taxi driver yelling at the security guard behind the desk. Nick couldn't understand half of what the guy was saying, but it became apparent that the taxi driver had brought Rachel and Joey here and wanted his money.

"Pay the man," he told Sean, before turning his attention back to the security guard who wore a name tag with the name George. He didn't know if that was a first name or a last name. "Are Rachel and Joey Simon upstairs in her office?" he asked.

"Yes, they went up about five minutes ago," the security guard said.

"Did anyone else go up either before or after her?" Sean asked, after paying the taxi driver.

"I've only been here about twenty minutes, but no one else went up while I was here." George cast a curious glance between Sean and Nick. "Is something wrong?"

"We don't know for sure," Nick said. "But we're heading up right now to make sure she's all right. If we don't come back down within ten minutes, call the police."

"Maybe I should go with you?" George offered.

"No, you need to stay here," Nick told him. "Make sure no one else goes up, do you understand?"

George nodded. "Got it."

Sean had already made his way over to the one of the six banks of elevators, and he was holding the door, waiting for Nick. He fought a wave of dizziness as he hurried in.

The ride to the tenth floor was quick and when the doors opened, the ding of the elevator seemed exceptionally loud. He hoped no one had overheard it.

"Stay back," Sean warned in a whisper, as he made his way into Rachel's office suite.

Nick had his weapon tucked into the waistband of his jeans but was hampered by the need to hold his left arm still, so he nodded, knowing that he would only be a liability if he didn't give Sean the room he needed.

The moment they opened the glass doors to the office area, Nick heard talking. And from the way Rachel was pleading with someone, he suspected Karl was there.

He couldn't see much with Sean in front of him, but the hint of desperation in her tone wrenched his heart. It was his fault she was here with Joey. If he'd responded differently in the hospital she probably would have stayed.

Especially if he'd had asked her to stay.

Please, Lord, keep Rachel and Joey safe!

Rachel saw something move behind Karl's right shoulder, but she did her best to keep her gaze trained on his so that he wouldn't figure it out.

"Karl, please. Give me the gun. I can tell you're not a cold-blooded killer," she said, stalling for time. She couldn't tell who was creeping up behind Karl, but just knowing she and Joey weren't alone was enough to give her hope and strength.

Besides, she was getting mighty tired of people pointing guns at her.

"Stay back or I'll shoot," Karl threatened, although the gun in his hand wavered just a bit.

"You want money, Karl?" she asked. "Because if that's the case then I'll double their fee if you'll put the gun down. I'll give you enough to change your name and leave town. Think about it—you'll get a fresh start."

Surprisingly, he seemed to consider her offer. But just as he was about to speak, an arm came around from behind and snatched the gun from his grasp.

"What the—" Karl's sentence was cut off when he was slammed up against the wall, Sean McCarthy's arm planted firmly across his neck.

Rachel sagged against the edge of her desk in relief. She'd never been so happy to see a cop in her life. She didn't know how Sean had gotten here from Madison so fast, but she was thankful just the same.

"Karl Errol, you're under arrest for attempted murder and corporate espionage, and anything else that you've done that I haven't figured out yet," Sean McCarthy said, pulling out his handcuffs and clasping them firmly over Errol's wrists. The way the research scientist sagged against the door convinced her that he'd finally given up.

Thank You, Lord.

"Rachel? Are you and Joey all right?"

She straightened and looked past Sean into the hallway, tempted to pinch herself in the arm to make sure that she wasn't imagining Nick standing there. "Nick? Is that really you?"

After making sure Joey was okay, she found herself staring at Nick, unable to look away. He was propped against the wall, holding his left arm against him, his mouth bracketed with pain.

"Yeah. I had to make sure you and Joey were all right," he said.

She was so glad to see him, even though it was obvious he shouldn't be here. "What were you thinking?" she scolded as she rushed forward to meet him. "You should have stayed in the hospital. What if you lose the circulation in your arm?"

"It's nothing compared to the thought of losing you," he murmured, holding her gaze with his. "I'm sorry I hurt you, Rachel. I didn't mean to. I never should have allowed my faith to waver."

Her heart melted at his words, and she would have engulfed him in a huge hug if not for the fact that Nick looked as if he was hanging on by a thread. His brow was damp with sweat and his face was pale, two indications that he absolutely should not have left the hospital.

"Nick!" Joey cried as he ran forward, putting his arms around Nick's waist and hugging him hard. She caught the wince on Nick's features, but he didn't protest. "You're here!"

"Yeah, I'm here, buddy."

"Are you all better now?" Joey asked, tipping his head back to look up at Nick.

"Not exactly..." Nick said drily.

"Not at all," Rachel interjected with a deep frown. "You need to get back to Madison, Nick. The surgeon told me that the first twenty-four hours are critical. It's barely been twelve hours since surgery and a good portion of that had to be traveling here."

"Maybe you're right," he said, and the fact that he didn't try to argue with her was worrisome.

Before she could say anything more, he let go of Joey and slid down the wall to the floor.

"I told him to stay behind, but did he listen? No, he didn't." Sean's tone held disgust. "I guess we'd better call 911, the only way he's getting out of here is in an ambulance."

"I've already called 911," George said, coming down the hall toward them. "You made me nervous, and when you didn't come down right away, I decided to make the call. Good thing I did. The cops should be here any minute."

"Make sure there's an ambulance, too, would you, George?" she asked. She'd sat down on the floor beside Nick, holding his head in her lap, unwilling to let him go, even for a minute.

"That surgeon is going to say 'I told you so,'" Sean joked, as he stared down at Nick's prone figure.

"Was worth it," Nick murmured in a voice so soft Rachel was sure she was the only one who could hear him.

"Rest now, Nick," she said, smoothing her fingers down his rough, bristly cheek. "We're safe now...."

There was a lot of commotion when the police arrived and soon after an ambulance crew showed up carrying a gurney.

She thought Nick was out cold, but suddenly his eyes opened and he reached for her hand. "Come with me to the hospital," he said hoarsely.

"I'll meet you there," she promised. "Just do what the doctor says this time, okay?"

Grimacing, he nodded his head. Then she slid out of the way, allowing the paramedics to lift Nick onto the gurney.

And for the second time in less than twenty-four hours, she stood with her arm around Joey, watching as the paramedics wheeled away the man she loved.

After Sean had handed Karl over to the Chicago authorities and she'd once again given her statement to the police, she convinced Sean to take her and Joey home.

Once there, she gave him the money she owed him, even though he kept trying to wave it away.

"Please take the money," she begged. "You've already done so much for me and my son. Please?"

Sean reluctantly took the cash. "Do you want me to drive you to the hospital before I head home?" he asked gruffly.

She hesitated but then shook her head. "No, we can take a cab or the subway. Getting around Chicago is much easier than trying to get around in Madison," she teased.

"Hey, I live out in the boondocks, so this is all new to me," the officer said with a wry grin. "We don't get this kind of big-city crime where I come from."

Her smile faded. "Be glad, Sean. Be very glad."

He slung his arm across her shoulder in a friendly hug. "Don't worry, this was enough excitement to last me quite a while."

After he left, she decided to take a shower before heading back to the hospital. She urged Joey to take one, too.

Freshly scrubbed and wearing clean clothing made her feel like a new person, although it was clear her son was still exhausted. She was tired, too, but she wanted to see Nick in the hospital, one more time, before they came home to sleep.

And even though she knew she could call a babysitter to stay home with Joey, she preferred to keep him with her, despite being certain the danger was finally over.

Besides, she figured Joey would feel better, knowing firsthand that Nick was going to be all right.

When they arrived at Chicago North Hospital, they found Nick was a patient in a regular room rather than being back in the ICU. They walked into his room just as a voice announced through the overhead speaker that visiting hours would be over in fifteen minutes.

"Hey, how are you feeling?" she asked, crossing over to Nick's bed. Joey stood at the foot of Nick's bed, regarding him thoughtfully.

"My ears are blistered from having the doctors yell at me for fifteen minutes straight, but otherwise I'm good." His expression was more relaxed, and the brackets around his mouth had vanished, which she assumed meant he'd been given some pain medication.

"You look much better," she murmured. "And you deserve to have your ears blistered after that stunt you pulled."

"They wanted to transport me back to Madison General, but I guess the doctor there wasn't too interested in having me back." A hint of a smile played along the corner of his mouth. "Can't say that I blame him."

"How's the circulation in your arm?" she asked, glancing at the limb that was currently propped up on two pillows.

He moved his fingers and shrugged his right shoulder. "Pretty good, I guess. I can move my hand a bit more. No harm done, at least according to the surgeon here. I think that's one of the reasons he didn't push the issue of sending me back. Apparently, surgeons don't like to pick up other surgeon's leftovers."

She laughed, extremely relieved to hear that Nick wasn't any worse for wear.

"How long will you have to stay in the hospital, Nick?" Joey asked anxiously.

"Shouldn't be more than a day or two," Nick responded.

Joey's expression clouded. "But that means you'll be in here over Christmas."

"That's okay," Nick said quickly. "I don't mind."

There was another overhead announcement instructing all visitors to leave the building, so Rachel reached over and took Nick's good hand in hers, squeezing gently. "We'd better get home. I promised Joey that he would be able to sleep in his own bed tonight."

"All right." Nick's eyes were at half-mast and she suspected that he'd be asleep before they made it out the front door.

"See you tomorrow," she promised, releasing his hand. "Come on, Joey. Let's go home."

"Bye, Nick." Joey flashed a grin before following her out of the room.

As they left the hospital to flag down a cab, she decided that since Nick was going to be in the hospital for Christmas, they would need to bring Christmas to him.

Nick hated being stuck in the hospital. The only bright spot in his day was that his arm seemed to be doing better. The doctors had taken down the bulky dressing to examine the incision and hadn't put it back on, making him feel ten pounds lighter.

"Looks better than it should," the surgeon told him grudgingly. "Considering you went several hours without your blood-thinning medicine, you're extremely lucky."

"I'm blessed," Nick corrected with a grin. "Truly blessed." He'd slept on and off during the night, waking up between pain medication doses, but he'd had plenty of time to think about what had happened up at the cabin. How much he'd wanted to live, when he'd managed to convince himself that he'd be happy for God to call him home. After missing his wife and daughter for so long, he realized that God meant for him to move on with his life. He wasn't sure what he'd done to deserve a second chance, but he couldn't deny the way Rachel and Joey had wiggled their way into his heart.

Now, if he could only find a way to convince Rachel to take a chance on him.

Outside his window, he noticed snow was beginning to fall. He wondered if that change in the weather was part of the reason that Rachel and Joey hadn't come in to visit him yet.

He couldn't bear to think that maybe they wouldn't show at all. Rachel had said she'd see him tomorrow. Surely she wouldn't have said that if she hadn't meant it.

But when the lunch hour came and went he began to lose hope. He exercised his fingers the way he was supposed to and wondered if he could convince Jonah or someone from the precinct to bust him out of here again.

If she didn't show up soon, he'd have no choice but to go to her.

"Knock-knock," a voice said from the doorway. Relief flooded him when he realized that Rachel and Joey had arrived.

"Come in," he called, struggling to sit farther up in his bed. He was tired of looking and feeling like an invalid.

The first thing he saw was a small pine tree about three feet tall covering most of Joey's face. His smile widened when he saw Rachel coming in behind the boy, lugging a large bag.

"Merry Christmas," she said as Joey set the small pine tree on the bedside table.

"Merry Christmas," he responded, unable to suppress his broad grin. It was after all, Christmas Eve.

"Close your eyes," she said, as she plunked the bag down on the guest chair. "We'll tell you when you can open them again."

He'd rather have gazed at Rachel all day but did as she requested. He could hear Joey giggling amidst the sounds of paper rustling. With his eyes closed, he could smell the refreshing scent of pine from the small tree.

It seemed like forever, but finally the rustling and the giggling stopped. "You can open your eyes now, Nick," Joey said excitedly.

He opened his eyes and gasped in surprise at the way they'd transformed his room. Not only was the tiny tree decorated with miniature lights, but there was a small nativity scene set out on display along with several strands of garland strung festively around the whiteboard on the wall.

"Beautiful," he murmured, and he wasn't talking about the Christmas decorations.

Rachel looked lovely, no doubt in part because she'd finally gotten a decent night's sleep. Her smile was shy and it took him a minute to realize she had what looked to be a brand-new Bible in her hands.

"I hope you don't mind, but I thought we could read the Christmas story again tonight," she said. "Or we could read the Psalms since I know you mentioned they're your favorite. I read Psalm 23 this morning and I can certainly understand why you like them so much. I feel blessed to have found God. And I owe it all to you."

His throat was tight with pent up emotion and he had to clear it before he could speak. "I'd like that," he managed, keeping his gaze centered on her. "Very much."

"I, um, didn't know how to get in touch with your family, so they don't know that you've been injured...."

"Rachel, come here," he said, holding out his good hand.

She approached him and put her hand in his. He was conscious of Joey watching them curiously so he couldn't say exactly what he wanted, but she needed to know the truth. "I'm happy just having you and Joey here, and I don't need anyone else."

Her gaze was uncertain. "Are you sure? Christmas is a time for families."

"I'm sure." He lifted her hand and kissed it, wishing that Joey wasn't there so he could kiss her properly. "You and Joey are all the family I need."

She blushed but didn't pull her hand away. "I'm glad," she murmured.

And it wasn't until much later, when Joey had fallen

asleep in the chair, that he was able to tell Rachel how he felt.

"I'm falling in love with you, Rachel," he said softly.

She sucked in a quick breath. "How can you be so sure?"

He tried to think of a way to put his feelings into words. "I thought I was happy, living my life alone, doing my best to put the bad guys behind bars. But when you and Joey came into my life, I realized that I never felt as alive as I did with the both of you."

Her eyes glistened with tears. "I've been so afraid to get involved with anyone after Anthony. I told myself that I was protecting Joey, but I think in reality, I was protecting myself."

He took her hand and drew her closer. "Rachel, give me a chance to show you how much I love you. There's no rush, you can take all the time you need, if you'll just give me a chance."

"All right," she whispered.

"Is that a yes?" Nick asked, needing to hear her say the words.

She smiled and leaned over to kiss him, which was perfect since he wasn't able to get up and cross over to her thanks to the IV pumps keeping him tied to the bed. "That's a big yes, Nick. Because I've fallen in love with you, too."

He grinned, wishing she'd kiss him again, hardly able to believe his good fortune. Or rather, maybe he could.

For God had known the path he should take, all along.

EPILOGUE

Three months later...

Nick paused outside Rachel's doorway, patting the pocket that held the ring he'd purchased for her as he tried to quell his nerves.

He'd gone back to work last week, although he was still on desk duty thanks to his arm injury. He was grateful that each week his arm strength seemed to get a little better, so he didn't complain. Turns out there really wasn't any Mafia connection to Global Pharmaceuticals. Just a greedy CEO who'd hated Rachel's father. When Karl had implicated him in the espionage related to the defective diabetes drug, he'd crumpled like a house of cards.

Rachel and Joey's nightmare was truly over.

As glad as Nick was to know they were safe, getting back into the normal routine of doing investigations had cut into the time he'd been able to spend with Rachel and Joey.

Especially Rachel.

Last night, he'd picked up Joey after his last basketball game and had asked the boy's permission to marry his mom. Joey had been thrilled and Nick could only hope that the youngster had managed to keep his secret.

He pushed the doorbell, listening to the chimes echo through the house. He was pleasantly surprised when Rachel opened the door. "Hi, Nick."

"Hi, Rachel." He drew her in for a long kiss. "I've missed you," he murmured, gazing down at her upturned face.

"I missed you, too," she said with a smile. "Are you ready to go?"

"Sure. Is, uh, Joey around?"

"Yes, he's decided to have a friend sleep over tonight. Suzy, the babysitter, doesn't seem to mind."

Nick grinned. "Just give me a minute to say hello."

"All right," she agreed, standing back so he could come inside. The boys were sprawled in front of the television in the living room, playing some sort of basketball video game. Suzy was sitting with earbuds in place, listening to music.

"Hey, Joey, how are you?" Nick greeted him.

"Pause the game," Joey said to his friend, as he jumped off the sofa. "Hi, Nick!"

Nick bent his head down to Joey's. "Did you keep our secret?" he asked.

Joey's eyes gleamed as he nodded. "Yep."

"Good." He relaxed a bit. "Thanks, buddy. Now try not to interrupt us at dinner, okay?"

Joey rolled his eyes. "Why would I? Suzy is here. Besides, me and Ben are going to be busy playing our game, anyway."

"All right, see you later, then."

"Suzy, text me if you need anything," Rachel called out as he returned to her.

"Don't worry, we'll be fine," Suzy responded.

Nick drove Rachel to the small Italian restaurant where he'd reserved a private table in the corner. "How was work today?" he asked.

"The lawsuit has been settled and the new researchers seem to be doing all right so far." Rachel's smile dimmed. "The company will be on shaky financial ground for a while, but we'll make it."

"I know you will," Nick replied, admiring her determination. He pulled into the parking lot and handed his keys to the valet service before escorting Rachel inside.

"My favorite restaurant." Rachel beamed as they were seated. "I already know what I'm having."

"You should, since you have the menu memorized." He waited until the server had taken their order before reaching across the table to take her hand. "Rachel, these past few months with you have been wonderful."

She smiled and squeezed his hand. "For me, too, Nick."

The timing seemed right, so he took a deep breath and rose to his feet. Two steps brought him to Rachel's side and when he went down on one knee, her eyes rounded and her mouth formed a small O.

"Nick?" she whispered, looking a bit like she was in shock.

He smiled gently as he pulled the ring box out of his pocket and opened it. "Rachel, Joey has already given me his blessing. He told me he'd be thrilled to have me as his dad. So now it's up to you."

Her eyes filled with tears and for a moment he almost panicked, until he saw the tremulous smile bloom across her face. "I love you, Rachel. Will you please marry me?"

She barely looked at the ring, instead holding his gaze

with hers. "Yes, Nick. I'd love nothing more than to be your wife. And to have you be Joey's father. Of course, I'll marry you."

Yes! He did a mental fist pump but managed to draw her to her feet so that he could kiss her. He held her tight, wishing he never had to let her go.

The entire restaurant erupted into a round of applause.

He had to chuckle as he pulled away. "I love you, Rachel. And I promise to make you happy," he vowed.

She tilted her head to the side, her gaze solemn. "I love you, Nick, and I promise to make you happy, too."

He didn't doubt the sincerity in her tone for a moment and knew that he was doubly blessed to have found true love for the second time.

* * * * *

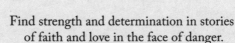

"Do you think I've been followed?"

Tanner hesitated, then decided he couldn't lie to Sidney. "Yes, I think so."

She shuddered. "I'm surprised Santiago's men didn't take a shot at me when I was standing outside Camella's doorway."

Yeah, that had been troubling him, too. Although it was clear that while Sidney was a target, the goal was to have her influence the outcome of the trial.

Something she couldn't do if she was dead.

Considering the amount of time it would take to bring another judge up to speed, he felt certain Santiago wouldn't want another postponement.

But then why kill Camella? Just to prove to Sidney how vulnerable she was?

Maybe, but in his mind, murdering the nanny didn't make any sense. Not if Santiago's men wanted to sway the outcome of the trial.

He shook his head and told himself that mystery wasn't his to solve. His sole responsibility was to keep Sidney and her daughter, Lilly, safe.

And he wouldn't mind some help. Using the hands-free functionality of his SUV, he called his boss, James Crane.

"Things are heating up in Cheyenne," Tanner informed him. "I could use some help."

"I can send Colt Nelson to assist," Crane offered. "Fill me in on what's going on."

Tanner quickly explained about the murder of Camella Monte and how he currently had Judge Logan and her young daughter with him. "We're heading to Fort Collins. Could you ask Colt to meet me there?"

"Yes. Keep me updated," Crane said.

Tanner disconnected the call when the crack of gunfire echoed around them.

"Get down!" he shouted at Sidney while he frantically searched for where the gunman was shooting from.

"Lilly!" she cried hoarsely.

"I know." Tanner was thankful the SUV hadn't been hit. At least, not yet. He wrenched the steering wheel and went cross-country, rocking and rolling over the rough terrain, toward the small town of Wellington, Colorado.

He was desperate to find a safe place.

Don't miss
Rocky Mountain Standoff *by Laura Scott,*
available January 2022 wherever
Love Inspired Suspense books and ebooks are sold.

LoveInspired.com